MW00628451

le of Sand

right © 2020 by Barbara Kloss

ghts reserved.

is a work of fiction. Names, characters, organizations, places, events, media,
ncidents are either products of the author's imagination, or are used
ously. No part of this book may be reproduced in any form or by any
ronic or mechanical means, including information storage and retrieval
ms, without written permission from the author, except for the use of brief
ations in a book review.

ed by Melissa Frain
er Design by Damonza

BOOK TWO IN THE GODS OF ME

TEMP
OF
SANI

BARBARA KLO

Tem
Cop
All

Thi
and
fict
ele
sys
qu

Ed
Co

For Brighton,
who is the cute little reason this book is one year late.

PRONUNCIATION GUIDE

Alma: ALL-muh
Anja: AHN-yuh
Avék: uh-VECK
Bahdra: BAH-druh
Chakran: CHAH-krun
E'Centro: EE CHEN-tro
Felheim: FELL-hime
Fyri: FEER-ee
Gamla Khan: GAHM-luh KAHN
Il Tonté: ill tahn-TAY
Imari: ih-MAH-ree
Istraa: ih-STRAY-uh
Jadarr: yuh-DAHR
Jarl: yahrl
Jenya: JEN-yuh
Kahar: kuh-HAHR
Kai: k-eye
Kazak: kah-ZAHK
Kjürda: kyerda
Kourana Vidéa: koor-AH-nuh vee-DAY-uh

Kunari: koo-NAH-ree
Leje: leh-zheh
Liagé: lee-AH-zhay
Majutén: mah-zhoo-TIN
Mo'Ruk: muh-ROOK
Nazzat: nuh-ZAHT
Niá: NEE-uh
Oza: O-zuh
Qazzat: kuh-ZAHT
Ricón: ree-CON
Roi/Roiess: roy/roy-ESS
Sar Branón: sahr bruh-NON
Saredd: suh-RED
Saza: SAH-zuh
Sebharan: seb-uh-run
Sieta: see-ET-uh
Sol Velor: soul veh-LORE
Su'Vi: soo-VEE
Sulaziér: soo-lah-zee-AIR
Surina: sur-EE-nuh
Survak: SHUR-vack
Tallyn: TA-linn
Taran: TAIR-in
Tarq: tark
Trier: tree-AIR
Tyrcorat: TEER-core-at
Vondar: vahn-DAHR
Ziyan: z-eye-ANN
Zussa: ZOO-suh

THE WILDS

the Five Provinces

Túl Bahn

Skanden   Craven

White   Riverwood
Rock
THE CROSSING

THE RIM

THE FINGERS

DAVROS

Stovichshold

Sanvik   CORINTH

Skyhold

GRAY'S
TEETH

Rodinshold   BLACKWOOD

BREVERA

ISTRAA

Trier

SOLVELD

THE DIVINE TALENTS

SHIVA
Pronunciation: SHE-vuh
Common Name: Restoration
Manipulation of bodily healing through life's blood.
Specific talents relating to *Shiva*: healing, necromancy.

VOLORÉ
Pronunciation: vuh-LORE-ay
Common Name: Enchantment
Permutation of the physical with metaphysical through Asorai's word.
Specific talents relating to *Voloré*: wards, tallas

ZIAT
Pronunciation: TSEE-at
Common Name: Sight
Manipulation of sight and illusion
Specific talents relating to *Ziat*: perception, sight (past, present, future)

SAREDII
Pronunciation: sah-RED-ee-eye
Common Name: Guardianship
Manipulation of Shah energy upon the physical
Specific talents relating to *Saredii*: enhancement of physical
strength, manipulation of natural environment

PROLOGUE

S *ix Months Prior...*

I F I T W E R E N ' T for the heat, Gamla never would have found the bodies.

He'd traveled this path countless times, this vague thread of sand and rock that tied the Baragas' small mountain villages to the rest of Istraa. Where those who did not care for societal decrees dwelled, instead surviving off of the desert on their own terms.

Where life was so much simpler.

Still, sickness did not discriminate, and being that Gamla was Istraa's alma—healer—he checked in on them from time to time. Through the years, their relationship had grown symbiotic: he would give them news of the world, and they would give him a much-needed respite from it.

Today, however, he found no rest.

An unforgiving sun boiled in the desert sky and the air shimmered with heat, warped like steam. Gamla found it increasingly difficult to breathe.

He stopped his camel along the path, dismounted, and leaned back against a rock as he gazed across the wondrous expanse of the Majutén. His loose linens clung to his sweaty skin, and when he wiped his face with the tails of his headdress, salt residue rained from his mustache and beard.

Saints, the desert was ruthless today.

His camel snorted and dug an impatient hoof into the sand. Even he did not like this heat.

Gamla took a sip from his water skin, and he was just about to push off the rock and climb back into the saddle when he caught a whiff of something foul baked into the air. The stench of rot and disease.

He knew the odor well.

For the desert was always hungry, always taking, watering its barren soil with the blood of the unprepared.

Gamla might have let it go, but he remembered the pig farmer. For months now, Junat had been complaining that something was stealing his pigs. However, his only evidence was that today he had six when yesterday he had seven. Junat blamed a wild cat; there were plenty in these mountains.

But Gamla had his suspicions. He'd had them for weeks.

Gamla pushed himself from the rock and adjusted his headdress. "I'll be right back," he said to his camel, and then followed the scent. Into the red rocks, and the narrow spine between the Baragas' broad shoulders.

He navigated the uneven terrain, his keen nose directing his steps while the relentless sun beat upon his back. He descended onto a sort of natural landing, rounded a clump of red rocks, and stopped in his tracks.

Before him lay a pile of mutilated carcasses. Flies swarmed, maggots writhed, and vultures tore at fresh pig entrails. The stench was so strong, even Gamla almost gagged. Junat had been right. Someone was stealing pigs, but not just from Junat.

And not for eating.

A heavy sense of foreboding weighed upon Gamla's shoulders, and he cautiously scanned his surroundings. A small path stretched beyond the gruesome mound, leading to a crack in the red rock wall ahead.

A cave.

The air shifted behind him, and Gamla turned. A few paces away stood a man wrapped in black cloth, watching Gamla with dark, Sol Velorian eyes. Swirling, inked glyphs painted his dark skin, his earlobes stretched long around silver loops, and red smeared his mouth, pooled in the creases. Dripped down his inked chin.

Gamla's blood turned to ice.

He'd guessed rightly, but oh, how he'd wanted to be wrong.

"Gamla Khan." The voice grated.

Gamla took an involuntary step back. "Who are you?" He didn't ask *what*. He already knew the answer to that.

The Liagé smiled with bloodstained teeth. He waved a bloodied, inked hand and spoke a word. The spell pulsed from his palm, and Gamla collapsed.

1

R icón held up two fingers.

Hold.

Hold.

Imari crouched, her thighs burning as she watched the sand. Waiting.

Waiting.

There.

She met Ricón's gaze; he'd seen it too. Still, he held up his fingers, holding her off. Making her wait. This was his hunt, he had said. Let him lead.

Imari might have been offended, but she'd suspected Ricón's command had less to do with *her* and more to do with his need to make up for the past—all those years he hadn't been there as he should have been. While she appreciated his attention, she wished he'd show a little more faith in her abilities. She'd survived The Wilds; she could handle a snake. Still, she didn't feel like fighting him, so she kept quiet and let Ricón lead.

Ricón pulled his scim free. It glinted in the dawn, catching the sky's fire. He glanced over at Imari, jerked his chin, and Imari tossed the locust she'd caught this morning. It plunked in the sand a few feet before the pale rocks, unmoving but not dead. Not yet.

More waiting.

And then...

A shape emerged. First the head, bobbing and searching, hesitant. Its tongue flickered as it tasted the air, and then slowly it slithered over the sand, toward the locust. Sideways.

Sivetan. Sidewinder.

It was a little one, about the length of Imari's forearm. Hardly enough for the five of them to share. Imari was keen to let this one go, but Ricón took another step and the toe of his boot grazed the rock's edge.

But Imari was no longer looking at the sivetan. She'd gone rigid, her attention narrowed at Ricón's feet. Ricón hadn't noticed —she barely had—and there was no time to warn him. She grabbed the nearest rock and lunged. The sidewinder scuttled off in fright as Imari slammed her rock down with a sickening crunch.

Ricón glanced down. His eyes widened as Imari stood, both of them gazing upon the crushed skull of the enormous horned viper lying dead at Ricón's feet.

The silence stretched.

"*That* should feed all five of us," Imari said, now meeting Ricón's dark gaze.

His lips pressed into a thin line.

"Sorry about the sivetan."

Ricón stood quiet, then grabbed the viper by the tail. Imari was lucky to have spotted it. Its thick, armored scales blended perfectly with the rocks.

"Tama," Ricón said, quiet. Thank you.

She nodded once, then started across the sand, toward the other three in their small convoy.

Imari spotted Jenya first, standing with the horses while shaking last night's sand from their blankets. The woman's black eyes slid down the length of the viper swinging from Ricón's grip.

"He's big," Jenya said simply.

"He almost took a bite out of my heel, but..." Ricón gestured at Imari.

Jenya's attention jumped from the crushed skull to Imari. Jenya was a saredd—one of Trier's most esteemed warriors—but she was also the first *female* saredd Istraa had ever known. And every time Jenya looked at her, Imari couldn't help feeling that Jenya was adding to some list, categorizing her threat. Marking her.

All of them did, in their own way.

"They might be *my* saredd, but they are saredd first," Ricón had said one evening, when Imari had voiced her concern. "Never forget that."

And their fealty is to Istraa, he had not said. He had not needed to.

According to Ricón, tensions were high throughout Istraa. These last few months, groups of Sol Velorian labor had gone missing, many of their owners hacked to pieces, and a handful of Istraan temples had been burnt to the ground with the kahar—priests—still trapped inside. The Sol Velorians had a leader, apparently, though no one knew his or her identity.

It sounded so similar to what Corinth had recently endured.

Needless to say, now was not the best time for Sar Branón's bastard Liagé—a Sol Velorian born with Shah power—to miraculously reappear.

As if Imari's mysterious Liagé half weren't enough to make Ricón's saredd suspicious, ten years in The Wilds had seasoned her marrow with new things—things they didn't understand. She felt it every time she caught them watching her. She might have an Istraan papa, and she might have been raised in Istraa, but she was not one of them. The years had turned her wild, like The Wilds that had kept her. She was...different.

Avék—the most insouciant of the three—approached them, his karambits dangling from his waist like silver claws. The wind inflated his loose pants, and without his headwrap, his long black hair flowed freely. He grabbed the viper from Ricón and spared Imari a cursory glance as he took the snake to Tarq, who was the largest of them and entirely without humor. Imari had wondered at her brother's rationale for bringing him, until she witnessed Tarq throw a knife fifty yards and strike a coyote square in the skull.

It had been the best dinner they'd had since leaving Skyhold.

Tarq sat sharpening his knives beside a small fire, his dark eyes fixed on Imari as they often were. Always watching, never trusting.

She tried not to take offense—they didn't know her, not yet—but sometimes it was hard.

Scrape. Scrape. Scraaaape.

Avék tossed the viper, and it landed at Tarq's feet.

Scrape.

"Tarq," Avék said flatly.

Tarq allowed one more scrape before setting his knives down. He grabbed the viper by the neck, observed the crushed skull, and glared at Imari. "You smashed the glands."

"I didn't have time to be particular," Imari said.

Tarq frowned.

Imari approached and held out her hand. "I'll do it, if it's too much trouble."

He eyed her. "You ever skinned a snake before, *cala*?"

Girl.

Not surina. Not Imari. Just *girl*.

She supposed it was better than some of the other names she'd been called.

Imari flashed her teeth. "You might be surprised by what I've skinned."

Tarq's gaze sharpened. The others stopped and glanced over too.

She probably shouldn't have said it, but she'd grown tired of being overly polite to assuage their suspicion, and to little effect. Finally, Tarq walked over and dropped the viper at her feet.

"May I borrow your knife?" Imari asked.

He only looked at her.

It was Ricón who finally produced a small blade, which Imari took. Ricón exchanged a heated glance with Tarq, who resumed sharpening his knives, while Imari crossed their camp, sat down, and got to work.

Wards, it niggled at her. How they all watched her and whispered at night when they thought she slept. It was also why she hadn't touched her bone flute since leaving Skyhold two weeks ago.

She'd wrapped it in linen and tucked it deep within her saddlebags, out of mind and sight. Sometimes, while they rode, when the golden sands of the Majutén stretched endlessly before them and the wind lamented its desolation—those times, her soul ached for the flute. To hold it in her hands, to run her fingers over the smooth bone, to feel its warmth against her palms. She resisted, imagining the saredd's reaction when the flute's glyphs flared with moonlight at her touch.

But she could not stop the music.

That night in Skyhold had unleashed something inside of her, and the world had become a symphony of sound. It was in the earth, thundering beneath them as they rode, the wind as it howled across the dunes. Sometimes the music pulled her in so deeply that she did not realize she'd begun to sing in harmony— not until Ricón would stop her, touch her arm and say her name. Bring her back. Once, she'd almost slipped from their shared saddle, and would have, had Ricón not caught her waist.

Those times, she understood the saredd's fear. Because she felt it too.

She wished there were someone she could speak to about her power—someone who could teach her how to use it, control it. There were three she could think of, but Tolya was dead, Tallyn might be dead, and Rasmin could not be trusted.

Imari still didn't understand Rasmin's role in all of this. He had been Corinth's Head Inquisitor—built his life interrogating and torturing Liagé. He'd discovered her in The Wilds, convinced Prince Hagan to bring her to Skyhold under the guise of healing his father, King Tommad. Of course, Prince Hagan's real intent had been to use her power to control his enemies. She'd assumed this had been the Head Inquisitor's purpose as well, but as it turned out, the Head Inquisitor was Liagé.

He was also part owl.

Imari focused on the task at hand, carefully carving off the viper's head, making sure to avoid the crushed venomous glands. Once she'd severed the head completely, she tossed it at Tarq's feet.

The scraping stopped.

She didn't glance over to see his face, though she imagined it well enough. Avék crouched beside her, but not too close. Never too close. They always kept a distance.

"You're quick," Avék said. It sounded like an accusation.

Imari cut a slit down the middle, peeled the skin from the meat, and set the skin aside, her hands slick with blood. "I've had a lot of practice."

Avék studied her. Imari felt Tarq's attention too. She ignored them both, pulled out the guts, and, by the end of it, she had one long piece of snake meat.

"May I?" Avék asked, gesturing to the snake skin.

"Go ahead," Imari said, wiping Ricón's blade clean.

Avék picked up the skin and took a seat near Tarq as Ricón walked over and observed her handiwork. He looked as though he wanted to ask, but didn't know where to start. It was how he'd looked at her for much of their journey south.

"Tolya taught me," Imari explained. She wrapped the meat around a stick, stabbed the ends to pin it in place, and set it atop the embers. Flames licked, meat sizzled. She settled back and watched it cook, remembering the woman who had kept her alive. Tolya, with her wild gray curls and weathered face and ageless determination.

"You miss her," Ricón said.

Imari wrapped her arms around bent knees. "She was all I had for ten years."

The silence stretched as the years crowded uncomfortably between them.

"You have us now, mi a'fiamé," Ricón said quietly. "And I will do *everything* in my power to keep you safe."

Safe.

Would she ever truly be safe, being what she was?

Sar Branón, Istraa's king and their papa, had no idea Imari was on her way home. Ricón had lied about his destination, fearing discovery for this delicate and dangerous mission, but for all Ricón's promising that their papa would be happy to see her, neither of them could really know how he would react. After all, he'd proclaimed his bastard daughter dead to all the world ten years ago.

It was not lost on Imari that Sar Branón could lose his life for this betrayal.

But Ricón had meant his words as a comfort, and even though they weren't completely true, she loved him for trying. She loved him for believing he could make them true.

She handed his blade back, hilt first.

He looked at the blade, at her. Wrapped his hand around hers. "You keep it." He squeezed her hand, let go and stood.

And Tarq began playing his oud.

Tarq hadn't touched the little instrument once along their journey, though Imari had spotted it bouncing from his horse's flank. In fact, she'd begun doubting it was his. She certainly hadn't expected this abrasive and hulking saredd to spare any sensitivity for music, and it surprised her even more that he had a delicate touch.

He plucked the strings, the oud a tiny and fragile thing in his enormous hands. Rhythm pulsed as his palm slapped the surface like a steadily beating heart. Notes teased for resolve, dancing quickly over tight intervals. It was a familiar piece, one she hadn't heard in a very long time, because it was about Istraa's persistence in a war that had almost destroyed them.

Imari could easily guess why Tarq had chosen it.

Still, it was beautiful, and Imari closed her eyes, letting the notes steal her away. Letting them throw her into a mesmerizing story of triumph. She saw Vondar—the palace in Trier, Istraa's capital—or her memory of it. Gleaming towers stood strong and defiant while Azir's war railed against the pristine white walls.

The image flickered—distorted.

The scene vanished, replaced by an ocean of sand. It rolled in all directions, sweeping and desolate beneath a dark and violent sky. A lone figure stood upon the horizon. Imari could not see a face from this distance, but she felt the figure's sharp attention.

Fear carved into Imari's soul. Like an off key to Imari's major, a note warped and bending out of tune.

A flash.

A tree, black and bare, its branches gnarled and twisted and rotten. Its trunk bent like a stubborn old man, its roots clawed into a rocky floor as it clung defiantly to the world. The branches began to grow, stretching and coiling like vines. Black tendrils reached and searched.

You are mine, sulaziér...

The voice rumbled from the bowels of the earth, more vibration than tone, and it rattled every string inside of her.

Those branches lashed out like whips; the tree's great, fleshy tentacles wrapped around her arms and legs. Imari screamed, and a branch stabbed *through* her mouth. She choked, gurgling on diseased bark and blood. More branches speared her arms and legs. They ripped through skin and tissue like grappling hooks, anchored to her bones, and jerked her forward. Imari would have cried out, had she voice to cry with, and the wooden spears pulled her *into* the tree.

Her world turned dark, hopeless and cold—so cold. Colder, even, than a winter night in The Wilds. This was an absolute absence of heat and light. An infinite abyss of nothing.

And yet, she wasn't alone.

She felt a rage that wasn't her own—a maddening, chaotic fury that infused the nothing—and that horrible voice screamed, ripping apart the last vestiges of her consciousness. Heat flared deep within as her power ignited. Fire shot through her veins, scorching her arms and legs, burning up the rage and wooden spears. And there was light, white and blinding. The horrible scream faded and stopped. *All* of it stopped—the tree, the darkness, the rage. The world fell quiet.

Still.

Until the only light left was the sun burning red through the backs of her eyelids.

"*Imari.*"

It was Ricón, and she didn't think this was the first time he'd said her name.

Imari's eyes snapped open as she gasped for breath, heart pounding, her body slick with sweat.

"Imari, what is it? What's wrong?" Ricón demanded, eyes wide with concern.

Imari realized she was on the ground, curled on her side. Her body ached in a dozen places, where the branches had stabbed through her skin. Panicked, Imari glanced down at herself, over her arms, but there were no punctures. No branches, no blood. Nothing.

It was just a dream.

But it had felt so real.

Beside her, Ricón knelt in the sand. A brilliant sun illuminated him from behind, and Tarq, Avék, and Jenya stood over him, watching her. Tarq was not holding his oud anymore.

Ricón's callused hand felt cold against her forehead. "Tell me what you need."

Imari unfurled her body and rolled, painfully, onto her back. "I... " Her throat felt scorched, and the taste of blood and bark lingered on her tongue. "Water. Please."

Avék produced a small water skin, which she took and drank. Cool water flooded the fire in her throat, quenching the flames in her body. She took another sip, handed the skin back to Avék, and then she climbed to her feet while Ricón steadied her with his hand. Questions filled his eyes, but she did not answer them. Not here, not now. Not in front of them.

And also...

What would she say?

Imari started for the horses with uneven steps, and Ricón followed.

"It's your power, isn't it?" he whispered once they were away from the others.

Unlike his saredd, he didn't completely mistrust this part of her. The Liagé part. But right then, Imari wondered if he should.

You are mine.

Astrid had spoken those words, that night in Skyhold's hall. But this had come from something else. Not in all her life had Imari felt such raw, unbridled power.

Or evil.

Imari pushed the rising fear out of her mind and checked her saddle's straps. "I'll wait here."

Ricón didn't move.

She hoped he'd let this go.

"You should eat," he said.

"I'm not hungry."

He stood there waiting—wanting explanations Imari could not give. Explanations Imari was too afraid to explore just then.

"Ricón, please," Imari whispered, meeting his gaze.

She saw the battle in his eyes, but at last he turned and walked back to the others. Imari sighed and rest her forehead against her horse's flank.

No, she thought. There was no place safe for her. Not in all the Five Provinces.

Survak leaned against *The Lady*'s rail, eyeing the dark and empty docks of Sahl's Bay. He never liked setting anchor. Too many eyes, too many questions. But they'd needed provisions, and this small port along The Wilds' southeastern edge supplied them, while the water also provided natural protection against any wandering shades. Most of his crew had opted to spend the night ashore, for it was a rare opportunity to find warmth, be it hearth or shared bed. For most, both.

He exhaled, his pipe smoke silver beneath the full moon. Survak didn't like full moons. They reminded him of wolves.

He dumped the ash from his pipe into the placid seawater, and he'd just started for his quarters when he spotted a cloaked figure on the docks, standing in the amber halo of a lamppost.

Not a member of his crew.

Survak tucked his pipe into his furs and strode forward, stopping at the ramp where he kept a crossbow strapped against the hull.

"Can I help you?" Survak called out.

The figure stood with unsettling calm.

And then collapsed.

Survak whistled for his remaining crew and hurried down to the dock, where lamplight spilled over midnight robes and a hideously scarred face. Survak cursed and sprinted the rest of the way, boots slamming on the dock's wooden planks.

"Tallyn…" Survak dropped to his knees and shoved a motionless Tallyn onto his back. Tallyn still breathed, but barely, and a nasty cut deformed the good side of his face—so deep, Tallyn's cheekbone shone white beneath. Survak had never grown accustomed to Tallyn's scars, and Maker's Mercy if the old Liagé didn't look like a demon just then.

Paz and Rikk arrived. Rikk sucked air through his teeth.

"The hells happened to him?" Paz asked.

"Help me carry him," Survak said.

Paz and Rikk exchanged an apprehensive glance.

"Hurry," Survak urged. "Before someone sees."

Survak, Paz, and Rikk hoisted Tallyn between them, half dragging and half carrying him onto *The Lady*.

"In there." Survak nodded toward his captain's quarters. They crossed the deck, Survak kicked the door open, and together, they lay Tallyn upon Survak's small cot.

The moment Tallyn's head touched the pillow, he bolted upright. Paz jumped, startled, and hit his head against the hanging lantern. The lantern slipped from its hook, hit the ground with a splintering crash, and the flame sputtered out, plunging them into darkness.

Suddenly, a strange white-blue light appeared. It burned like a miniature sun, hovering above Tallyn's curled palm, while he sat rigid, eye pure black and teeth bared.

All three of them froze.

Survak held up placating hands. "Tallyn…it's me…"

Tallyn did not seem to hear him.

"*Tallyn.*"

Tallyn blinked. His gaze settled on Survak, focused a second later, and then his attention drifted to the others. He pushed the light into the lantern upon Survak's nightstand, blue morphed into quiet orange flame, and then he sagged back, closed his eye, and loosed a slow exhale.

Survak exchanged a glance with his men. "Water," he whispered to Paz. "And probably some akavit."

He always kept akavit on hand. It was a dangerous habit, but one Survak found difficult to break.

The cabin door creaked as Paz left.

"Keep an eye on the docks," Survak said to Rikk, who ducked out after Paz.

Survak swept the shattered glass into a neat pile, and then stood over the bed, eyeing Tallyn. "I thought you were dead."

He hadn't heard a single word from Tallyn after he'd transported the Istraan and her wolf prince across the Hiddensee over a month ago. He had, however, heard about Tallyn's fight with Ventus and the silent at Riverwood, but in the silence that'd followed, Survak assumed Tallyn had died. Clearly he had not, but the wound on his face was recent.

Tallyn's chest rose and fell with labored breath. "Tül Bahn..."

Survak frowned.

"I tried to..." Tallyn strained, his teeth clenched in pain. "Two got away."

Survak stilled. Tallyn had tried to kill the rest of the silent, now that Ventus was dead. "The hell were you thinking?" Survak hissed.

Tallyn only winced in response.

Survak cursed and raked a hand through his cropped hair. Those two remaining silent would come looking for Tallyn. "Tallyn, I'm sorry, but I can't keep you. I won't risk my crew—"

"We have to go back."

Tallyn was not talking about The Wilds anymore.

Survak went very still. He sensed it—a storm brooding upon the horizon, eating up the sea as it drew nearer. That storm had never left, but always waited just beyond his sight.

Now it was here. The inevitable winds and rain and thunder of the past, coming back to claim him and drag him under.

Tallyn's good eye opened, and the pale blue fixed on Survak. "It is time to go home."

Old fire burned in Survak's heart. "You know I'd never make it into Felheim's harbor."

"I can help with that." A pause. "I think you'll find this Angevin quite...different than his father."

Survak didn't agree. All Angevins were the same: cunning, greedy, vicious.

Still, that pale eye stared.

"Find another rutting ship." Survak started for the door.

"You knew this day would come," Tallyn said at his back. "You sensed it the moment I brought you his wolf."

Survak stopped, eyelids squeezed tight, and his chest constricted with old pain—pain still so near to the surface, even after all these years.

"He needs you," Tallyn said, softly but firmly. "It is time to go home, Captain Vestibor."

Survak's hand curled into a fist. "I don't have a home anymore." Survak exited the cabin and slammed the door shut behind him.

IMARI LAY ON HER SIDE, wide awake. It was their last night in the Majutén desert. Tomorrow, they would reach Trier, Istraa's capital. Tomorrow, she would return home for the first time in ten years and face all of the uncertainties and fears that had kept her awake these past two weeks.

But that wasn't what kept her awake tonight.

It was the nightmare. Whenever her consciousness would drift, she'd be rudely awoken by the pain of branches tearing into her flesh, and the hopelessness and rage of that dark abyss. That terrible voice rumbling through her, more vibration than sound: *You are mine.*

Imari rolled onto her back and gazed at the big Majutén sky, where thousands of stars dusted the infinite black. In them, she traced the shapes of Nián, goddess of fate, and Sareddi, Istraa's warrior god. Similar to Corinth, Istraa worshipped many gods, but Istraans also worshipped the sieta—sainted men and women who had existed in the flesh, who had done such good during their time in this world, they'd ascended to godhood.

Sieta Estara had always been a particular favorite of Sura Anja, Imari's step mama. Sieta Estara had died a martyr, protecting her children from a "wicked" Liagé enchantress who meant to enslave them, and that act of love had rebounded and destroyed the enchantress. Sura Anja had insisted that Vana, little Imari's kunari, tell Imari the story at least once a week.

Little Imari had never liked Vana's stories very much.

Imari had not seen these constellations in years; The Wilds' massive pines and surrounding mountains had always blocked them from view. She found other shapes too as she slowly oriented herself in a sky that had once been so familiar, and then her gaze slid farther south until—without meaning to—it rested upon Asiam's star-flecked hand.

To Istraa, Asiam was simply the head of their many gods, but to the people of Sol Velor, he was *everything.* The Sol Velor worshipped only one—a god they called Asorai.

The Maker, who cradled all of creation in his generous palm.

Imari gazed at that cluster of stars in his hand. Asiam. Asorai. She'd never spared the semantics much thought before. As far as she'd been concerned, all gods were the same—ideas fabricated by mankind and used to control weaker men. Tools to justify others' suffering while taking privilege for themselves and their few chosen. Imari had hated them all, and what they had represented. But now...

She did not know what to believe.

She couldn't deny a higher power, for there *had been* another presence that night in Skyhold—one who had spoken to her directly and lent her supernatural strength to overcome the impossible. And when she closed her eyes, when the world was quiet, like now, she felt him near. A presence that persisted in the stillness, a constant that followed her every step like some silent champion.

"There are always extremes, Sable," Tallyn had said to her months ago. "Since the beginning, mankind has put his own twist on the Maker's will, as Ventus did and does still. It's what men do. We are masters at manipulating truth to suit our desires. But don't condemn the Maker for the sins of man."

If there were a Maker, and if Tallyn were correct in that men like Ventus had twisted the Maker's will to suit his own selfish design, then...who was the Maker, really? And, moreover, what did he truly require of his people?

She remembered the voice that'd spoken to her during a moment of darkest despair. Contrasting the raging voice of her nightmares, and the legion that'd spoken through Astrid, this voice had been pure and good: *Do not fear, I am with you... You are my chosen, and through you, I will make a great nation. If only you have the courage.*

Imari had no idea what that meant, or what to do with it.

A cool breeze swept across the sands and Imari shivered, pulling her Corinthian-blue cloak tight.

Jos.

No—Jeric.

King Jeric Oberyn Sal Angevin.

It was still difficult thinking of him as Corinth's king. He'd given her this cloak as a parting gift. It'd belonged to his mother, and she'd been thankful for it every day. Winter was pleasant in the desert, but its nights still burned with cold, and his cloak had kept out the chill.

Also, she liked having a piece of him with her.

Leaving Jeric had been difficult. Far more difficult than she'd expected, and she wondered if it had been difficult for him too. She wondered if he thought of her as much as she kept thinking of him.

The sky brightened with the promise of dawn, and Imari glanced around. Ricón and his saredd slept soundly, scattered on the sand, and the horses munched on tufts of grass nearby. Tired of laying hostage to her tangled thoughts, Imari crept to her feet and padded across the sand. Ricón's gelding lifted his head as she approached, and she rubbed his broad nose. "Sh," she whispered, holding one finger to her lips. She walked on, and he went back to his breakfast.

It felt good to move—to stretch her stiff limbs—and the early morning solitude breathed life into her weary soul. She'd spent the last ten years living on the fringes of society, and after being the object of everyone's scrutiny these past two weeks, Imari was exhausted.

This was only the beginning, she knew.

She eventually stopped at a trough between two small dunes and gazed at the glittering stars above. *Who are you?* she wondered at the heavens. How did one talk to a god? She'd never been one for prayer, and she refused to emulate those gaudy platitudes spewed by sanctimonious priests.

"I have no idea what to do with this power you've given me," she whispered to the stars—to Asorai's hand cradling them. "How do I navigate my way in a world that hates what I am? And how do I help the Sol Velor?" For they are *my* people too, she thought.

Of course, there was no answer, not that Imari had expected one. Still, she felt a prick of disappointment.

"What are you doing?"

Tarq's voice shattered the quiet. Imari tensed and looked back. Tarq stood a few paces away, at the bottom of the dune, his black eyes glinting like shards of nightglass. It bothered her that she hadn't heard him approach. It also bothered her that she couldn't see their camp from her low vantage point.

"I couldn't sleep," she answered simply. "Time to go?"

Tarq regarded her a long moment, and then pointed his scim toward camp. Imari took a deep breath and walked forward, but as she started up the dune, Tarq took two steps and blocked her path with his scim.

She glanced up, met his gaze.

Imari was no stranger to contempt. She had seen it plenty, taking many forms over the years, such as the way Tarq looked at her then. His mere posture was a threat as he searched for a deception he clearly felt so certain were there, if only he looked hard enough. His black eyes flickered over her Corinthian cape, roving with contempt over the rich blue wool. Jeric's cape had been a constant point of contention. Ricón had asked her not to wear it, but she couldn't bring herself to put it away.

And so Imari stared defiantly back at Tarq, though her pulse quickened. Tarq was no force to ignore, but to look away—to cower—was to admit guilt. And she was done carrying the guilt placed on her shoulders by other people's fears.

"Don't wander, *beram*," he said at last. Bastard.

Tarq wouldn't dare call her that in front of Ricón.

As if summoned by the insult, Ricón appeared over the crest of the dune. "Is there a problem?" he called out.

Tarq lowered his scim and took a quick step away from Imari.

"There's no problem," Imari said lightly. "Tarq was just making sure I was all right." She smiled at Tarq, and his expression darkened.

"Time to go?" she asked Ricón.

"Sei," Ricón said at last, peeling his gaze from Tarq, who'd already started climbing the dune. "Horses are ready."

. . .

WITHIN THE HOUR, they were riding across the Majutén's dunes, the winter sun huge and warm and bright. Tarq didn't say another word—didn't even glance in Imari's general direction, though Ricón's gaze kept drifting toward his largest saredd. Tarq's behavior obviously concerned him. And it should. It sat like an ill portent of what was to come.

The sun had just touched the Baragas' broad backs when they reached the edge of the Majutén.

"Go on. We'll catch up," Ricón said to the others.

Jenya gave him a lingering glance, but followed Avék and Tarq down the steep yet well-traveled thread that carved into a wide and sweeping valley.

Trier.

It was a city that should not exist—a pride of life, in this land of sand and rock. It defied nature with its palms and pools and white stucco, a treasure of pearls gleaming beneath a cerulean sky. And at its heart, framed by six enormous white towers that stood like sentinels around their sar, was the magnificent golden dome. Vondar. The palace.

Her home.

And there it was. Real and tangible, and waiting for her as though she'd never left.

The palace blurred and her eyes burned.

"We'll go when you're ready," Ricón said quietly.

She would never be ready for this. "I am ready," she whispered.

At last, he clucked his tongue and urged their horse after the others. They navigated Trier's outer farms, made possible by a network of canals, and Imari inhaled deep, breathing in the scent of dried grasses and dust and woodsmoke—a smell her heart remembered, even after all these years. A few curious goats ambled to the fence to investigate, and beyond, she spotted field workers replenishing empty troughs with grain and water.

Sol Velorian field workers.

Of course they were Sol Velorians. Istraans never toiled like this, so they employed Sol Velorians for hard labor. They were paid, though minimally. Not quite slaves, but far too poor to buy freedom, and thus Istraa kept them subjugated.

Which compounded yet another issue that had increasingly nagged at Imari ever since leaving Skyhold: Jeric had promised to free Corinth's Sol Velorian slaves, and Imari had promised to help. But after spending almost two weeks with Ricón's saredd, with no obvious improvements in their attitude toward her, how could she possibly expect the rest of Istraa to give heed to her plea? If she started demanding Istraans release their Sol Velorian labor, or at the very least offer competitive wages, Istraa would think *she* was this elusive Liagé leader.

These thoughts plagued her as they left the fields and entered the trade district, where incense and fire and sweat made the air thick, where stucco facades squashed together, and the world became a symphony of life and color and dust. Lanterns festooned across the narrow streets like garlands strung with stars. Merchants guarded stands overcrowded with baskets of spices and fruits, while Sol Velorians bartered for their masters, and a maze of textiles swayed in the evening breeze. Notes from a mizmar wove through the din, giving melody to the percussive staccato of chatter. The musician was also Sol Velorian, and a few coins glittered in a woven basket at his feet.

"Get back, damned scab," Tarq snapped.

Imari glanced over to see Tarq kick back a Sol Velorian woman who had ambled close. The woman—who'd been holding a basket of figs—cried out and stumbled back, and tripped over a textile stand. The basket flew from her hands, and figs rolled everywhere as she scrambled to gather them up. No one offered to help.

Tarq met Imari's gaze.

That is what you deserve, his expression seemed to say.

Imari squared her jaw and looked decidedly ahead, her hands

flexed. Tarq's sentiment toward the Sol Velor was nothing new, nor was it surprising. Istraa might not be as cruel to the Sol Velor as Corinth had been, but they still viewed the Sol Velor as *less*. Less important. Less valuable.

Less human.

And Imari felt shame—shame that little Imari had not spared it a thought before.

Imari's shame and frustration simmered as Ricón urged their mount away from the crowds and into the quiet side streets. Perhaps he wanted to spare them the extra attention. Already, people looked over, curious and straining to get a better view. Plain clothes did little to hide a prince in his home—especially a prince traveling with three famous saredd.

Or, perhaps, Ricón had seen what Tarq had done, sensed the subsequent shift in Imari's mood, and wanted to spare more kindling from feeding the slow fire of her anger.

Whatever his reasons, they drew steadily closer to Vondar, and the buildings crowded tighter and taller as the wealthiest huddled around their crown. Where her papa waited, completely unaware that Imari was coming home.

That she was already *here*.

Ricón rested a warm and reassuring hand upon her arm. "Try to relax," he said over his shoulder.

Imari realized she was squeezing his waist, and relaxed her grip.

Too soon, they reached Vondar's high walls, which ran a perimeter around the palace, abbreviated by a handful of heavily guarded archways. Towers crowned every crest—the largest situated above the main gate—and city guards stood watch. She spotted a few saredd amidst the guards, distinguishable by their black cloth and the harness of weaponry strapped to their torsos. Black scarves veiled their faces, leaving only eyes visible—eyes that fixed on their group as they approached.

Jenya stopped and spoke with one such saredd who stood near the gate.

"Do not speak," Ricón warned Imari, though he did not need to. Imari had left her voice somewhere on the edge of the Majutén.

"Mi sur," said an approaching guard. He was not saredd, but a basic city guard, dressed in loose brown pants and a red tunic accented by an embroidered waistcoat. Two sheathed scims dangled from his waist.

Ricón dismounted and helped Imari down.

"I'll take him." Jenya gestured to Ricón's gelding.

Ricón and Jenya exchanged a glance. Ricón nodded and turned his attention to Imari. "Ready?"

Never in a hundred years. "Yes."

Together, they walked past the curious city guards and watchful saredd, who now stood over the gate to get a better view of Ricón's mysterious guest. Imari proceeded through the thick archway and out the other side, pausing to gaze upon Vondar's wide stair.

Maker's Mercy, she'd never thought she would see those steps again. They were shorter than she remembered. Narrower, too.

"It'll be fine," Ricón whispered beside her.

Imari hoped he was right. She ascended with unsteady legs while her insides tied in knots. More city guards waited on the landing above, and the massive bronze doors hung open, giving a glimpse of the grand atrium beyond.

Of the past.

Her gaze trailed the gilded columns to their dizzying arches. The mosaic floor glittered in the brazier light, like the flecked patterns of a kaleidoscope, and a fountain of Nián stood at its center, her marble hands pouring water into the glittering pool at her feet. During the day, Istraa's wealthier citizens occupied this space, seeking council with their sar, or to conduct business with

one another. The atrium was mostly empty now, save two kahar
—temple priests—talking quietly off to the side.

"Sable."

Ricón waited ahead. For Imari's safety, they had agreed to use
her Wilds name until they'd spoken with their papa.

Papa...

The mere thought was like a beacon, luring her steadily
forward, through the broad archway in back. The public wasn't
permitted beyond the atrium without escort, and to emphasize
this, two saredd guarded the entrance. They bowed to their sur,
looked curiously at his charge, but she and Ricón were through
the archway before their attention could linger.

And they stepped into Vondar's private halls.

Over the years, Imari's memories had faded and blurred, and
she'd wondered—no, *feared* she'd forgotten Vondar. Its beauty,
the way it welcomed the desert but kept out the fire. But as she
followed Ricón through those wide and airy halls, past the
painted pots and desert blooms and waving palms, her heart
remembered what her mind had not. The lingering scent of
jasmine, the heat radiating from the stucco, always keeping the
palace warm. The breeze was like a constant and welcome guest,
weaving through the open windows and wide colonnades, and
when Ricón turned up a stair, Imari knew immediately where he
was taking her.

"We're going to your room?" Imari whispered.

"For now," he said, glancing about conspiratorially. "I need to
find him first."

They reached Ricón's door. He pushed it open, and Imari
stepped inside.

By the wards.

She remembered every inch of this room. The plush cushions
in the corner where she'd read, when she'd wanted to avoid Vana.
The animal-skin rug still lay before the wide hearth, compliments of a wildcat that had almost killed Ricón first. And then

she spotted that hideous tarantula, now dead and on display in a glass case upon the stone mantel.

Ricón had found the tarantula on a hunt and kept it as a pet for years, much to Imari's chagrin. And in exchange for keeping her hiding spots secret, Imari had begrudgingly helped him catch poor and unsuspecting beetles for that tarantula to eat.

Ricón followed her gaze and smirked. "He didn't last long after you left. I think he missed you."

"Or he starved." She smirked. Even for a tarantula, it was big. She touched the glass. She'd hated spiders as a little girl, but they didn't seem so terrible now.

"I'll be back as soon as I can," Ricón said, then added, "Please don't climb out the window while I'm gone."

"Don't worry. I can't reach the roof from your balcony."

Ricón eyed her. "You're a lot taller now."

"True. On second thought, you had better hurry."

Ricón's smile mirrored her own, but then the future hovered uncertainly over them both, stealing their levity.

Ricón stopped before her and touched her cheek. "It will be all right, mi a'fiamé. Trust me."

3

P urpose drove Ricón's steps down the wide corridors. Servants and guards bowed, though he hardly noticed, his thoughts fixed on the task ahead.

Ricón found his papa dining in the hall with Ismael and Bayek—two members of his papa's private council, and also two of Trier's wealthiest. Ricón couldn't say that they were friends, only that they were friendly. Time, shared experiences, and common interest tended to shape its own sort of bond, no matter how many scars it created in the process. Kai, Ricón's younger brother, sat with them as well, lounging with thinly veiled disinterest while cradling his glass of ruby red nazzat. Always present, rarely engaged.

Sar Branón was just lifting a dumpling to his mouth when he spotted Ricón standing in the archway. The dumpling stilled at his lips. A tense beat passed, and then he set the dumpling down and sat up straight. "Ricón."

The chatter ceased; the others glanced over. Kai startled upright so suddenly, his nazzat sloshed onto his lap. He cursed and set the drink down, distractedly wiping at his pants.

"A word, mi sar," Ricón said shortly.

The sar gazed upon his oldest son with relief, and anger. Mostly anger.

"Excuse us," the sar said to the others, though he looked only at Ricón.

Ismael and Bayek stood, somewhat awkwardly, bowing to Ricón as they departed. Kai lingered, eyeing his older brother, because Ricón had never told Kai where he was going. He'd never told Kai *that* he was going. And not even Kai—master of social graces—could hide this bitter grievance completely.

How that grievance would amplify once Kai discovered why.

"Kai," Sar Branón said, tone clipped.

Kai's gaze flickered to their papa and a muscle worked in his jaw. Finally, he dipped his head and stood, pausing before Ricón.

The silence strained, shadowed by their growing differences. Or, rather, by Kai's growing *in*difference.

"It is good to see you, mi a'dor." Kai clasped Ricón on the shoulder.

"You as well."

Ricón wished it were true.

Kai crossed to the door with easy steps, though Ricón noticed the stiff set of his shoulders, and the door clicked softly behind him.

Ricón looked back at his papa—the sar of Istraa, who was a cauldron frothing at the rim.

"You lied to me," Sar Branón snapped.

Ricón had expected it. *Welcomed* it. Which was why he'd left Imari in his room.

"Yes. I lied," Ricón replied just as sharply. "I am sorry for that, but—"

"*Sorry?*" Sar Branón cut him off. Spittle flew. "You told me you were going to Andai. Instead, you left it undefended."

"I did not leave it undefended," Ricón pushed back. "I sent a dozen guards—"

Sar Branón slammed his fist on the table, rattling the glassware. "Dashá, Ricón! You took three of my very best saredd. They are not yours to dispense! We need them now more than ever, with this heretic running loose, and you *never* abandon your people when they have need of you."

Ricón took a step, his body tensed. "Your own dama has needed you for the past ten years. Where were you then?"

It was as though all the air had suddenly been sucked out of the room, and Sar Branón fell impossibly still.

"Surprised?" Ricón continued. "Yes, well imagine *my* surprise when I received a letter from the Wolf of Corinth stating that Imari was in Skyhold."

Ricón watched the color drain from Sar Branón's face.

Sar Branón stood very slowly, gripping the table's edge for support. "The Wolf knows."

Ricón gave him a disparaging smile. "Ironically, the Wolf is the only reason she *isn't* dead."

Sar Branón's gaze sharpened on Ricón. "What do you mean?"

Ricón explained everything Imari had shared along their journey home, and when he reached the part about her imprisonment in Corinth, Sar Branón abruptly turned and walked to the window. Ricón finished, and Sar Branón stood quiet for a very long time.

"Why did you send her away?" Ricón asked, taking a step toward his papa. It was an old argument that had left a stain upon their relationship all these years. No one else knew the truth about Imari. Not even Sura Anja—Sar Branón's wife, and Ricón's mama. How Ricón had come to know the truth was purely accidental, and Ricón had sworn on his life not to breathe a word of it. And he hadn't. He hadn't dared jeopardize Imari's safety.

But in the end, that promise had mattered little. She'd been discovered anyway.

"You had to have known she couldn't hide that power forever," Ricón continued, taking another step. "You've seen what happens to the Liagé. Surely we could have kept her here and—"

"No."

The word was quiet, but decisive and firm. As it had always been.

"How can you still believe that?" Ricón argued. "After everything I've just told you—"

"Where is she?"

Ricón looked at his papa. "If you send her away, I will go," Ricón said, and he meant it. "I will not make Imari face this alone. Not anymore."

Sar Branón turned to face his son then, and the expression there stopped Ricón. It was the face of a broken man, his shoulders slumped slightly in defeat, and when he finally spoke, his voice was just as rattled and weary. "I can't send her away. She is known. There is nowhere safe for her now."

Ricón frowned, wondering what his papa meant, but before he could ask, Sar Branón stood tall, and his shoulders expanded with sudden resolve as he said, "Take me to her."

IMARI PACED before Ricón's dark windows while nerves churned in her stomach.

"Maker's Mercy. I cannot do this..."

Perhaps she'd been too hasty. Perhaps she should've used Jeric's one thousand crowns to make her own life, away from all of this. Away from the memories and pain. Away from the family she did not deserve—not after what she'd done. What if...

What if her papa hated the very sight of her?

She didn't know if she could bear it, if he did. A confirmation that she was as horrible as she'd feared, as monstrous as they'd claimed.

Imari wrung her hands, pacing faster. She could sneak away. Ricón's rooftops weren't really that high, and she had the means to survive. Jeric had seen to that, and even if she miraculously ran out of his money, she could find work as a healer. Of course, she'd have to change her name again, and she'd have to be very careful not to build too much of a reputation, because then others would come looking for her and...

She stopped and pressed trembling palms to her temples. She was going to be sick.

And then a knock sounded on the door.

Imari glanced over as the door opened, but it was not Ricón who stepped through.

It was her papa.

Not a mirage. Not a memory.

Not this time.

A chill swept over her, head to toe.

She'd wondered if she would know him. If he would look the same, or if the years would make him a stranger. And they *had* changed him—aged him like fine nazzat, amplifying all of his best seasonings. But he was still her papa. She would've known him in a Belfast crowd under the darkness of night. Wards, she even knew the shape of him as he stood there, filling the doorway and staring at her.

His beard was longer and threaded with silver, and the wrinkles at his eyes had deepened. They were more numerous too, and shadowed, weary. His fine white linens hugged his frame a little tighter, especially at his midsection, where a golden belt pulled everything close, but the added weight did not steal his bearing. Authority seeped from his pores as it had always done—this sole force that held a nation of volatile egos together.

Sar Branón Masai.

Her papa.

How her heart ached just then.

So many words crowded behind Imari's lips, but emotion choked and strangled every one. Her eyes burned, and his figure blurred.

He took a distracted step forward, the motion unsteady. "Imari." Her name fell out of his lips at a whisper.

For years, she had yearned to hear his voice, and the sound of it now nearly overwhelmed her.

"Papa." Imari's voice cracked, and she covered her mouth with her fingers.

Sar Branón reached her in three strides and wrapped her fiercely in his arms.

And Imari's tears spilled over.

By. The. Wards.

She had not expected the flood of emotion. She had not expected it to *hurt*.

For so long Imari had believed that the life she had made was enough. That she had grown past the pain and loneliness, and finally tucked her family away in a box of discarded things—things she did not need.

Lies.

All of them, lies she had told herself so that she could endure each day. So that she could live with herself and the horrible thing she had done. But standing there, wrapped in his arms, it was as if he'd grabbed hold of that box, plucked it from beneath her strong facade, and ripped open the lid, dumping her horror and pain and regret all over the floor.

Imari sobbed, clutching her papa's tunic for dear life. For all the tears she had not shed, for the guilt she always carried, for the grief she had been unable to share because she had been sent away and forced to hide the truth: that she had killed her little sister. That she had killed Sar Branón's littlest daughter. He *should* hate her, but he only squeezed her tighter.

Somehow, his forgiveness was harder to accept than the hatred she deserved.

And then Ricón's arms were encircling them both, his chest shuddering against her shoulder. The three of them stood there like that, wound together in regret, and time stood still. The moment expanded.

"Papa... I am so sorry..." Imari managed, but words weren't enough. Words would never be enough for what she had done.

Sar Branón pulled back just enough to look at her, his eyes wet with tears. Ricón took a small step back too, giving them space.

"No, Imari." Sar Branón placed one palm to her cheek and wiped a tear. "I am sorry. I..." His gaze moved over her face. "I never blamed you. Not once."

His words were a salve upon raw wounds. Imari pressed her trembling lips together, unable to stop her tears.

"I..." Her papa stiffened and glanced back.

Imari followed his gaze to where Sura Anja—his wife, and Ricón's mama—stood like granite.

The sura's thick braid draped over one shoulder, and her silk shawl fell at an angle as if she'd thrown it on in haste and sprinted here. Judging by her expression, Sar Branón had not told her the truth about Imari.

"Mama..." Ricón started placatingly, but Anja's gaze cut like a knife.

Ricón closed his lips.

Anja turned a hostile gaze upon Sar Branón. "You lied to me." Her words were fire. Torture.

Loathing.

"I did," he said. There was no shame in his voice, no regret.

Anja's lips twitched and she stepped into the room. Ricón took a small, protective step before Imari, but Imari wished he hadn't because Anja's expression only darkened.

Anja stopped before her husband. And slapped him across the face.

The sound cracked, splintering the silence, and Imari flinched.

"Mama!" Ricón hissed.

But Sar Branón snatched Anja's retreating hand and held it firmly between them. Her slender wrist looked so tiny in his wide fist.

"How *dare* you..." Anja seethed.

Sar Branón leaned close, matching her fire with his own. "Never strike me again."

"Sorai is dead because of her!" Anja screamed. "Does that mean nothing to you?"

"Our daughter is dead *because of me*," Sar Branón said fiercely. "And I will not reject the one still living."

Tense seconds labored as a decade of bitterness burned between them. Finally, Anja turned her gaze upon Imari. The sura might be furious with her husband, but for Imari, she held something much, much deeper.

Anja jerked free of the sar's grasp. She glared at Ricón, who—to his credit—did not flinch, but stood protectively before Imari. Anja gave the slightest shake of her head and stormed out of the room. Right past another figure, who Imari hadn't seen standing in the doorway, watching them.

Her other brother, Kai.

His dark eyes focused on Imari, and his entire being went suddenly and completely still. "Saints above..."

4

"Found him early this morning," Klaus said, then added grimly, "This is the fourth attack this week."

Jeric surveyed the carnage, the vicious mutilation. The scout's blood soaked the soggy earth and painted the pines with death. Jeric knew what had done this. Truth be told, he'd suspected the moment Grag Beryn, the hunter, had found a wolf's remains two weeks ago.

Which was Jeric's first problem.

A shade in these parts shouldn't have been possible. Shades were nightmares from The Wilds' perilous woods, constrained by old powers and a violent gorge. His sister, Astrid, had managed to defy those constraints, manufacturing her own shades deep within the Gray's Teeth Mountains, but those had leapt to their deaths the night she'd attempted—and failed—her coup.

Apparently, she'd made more, and Jeric could not locate them.

Which was Jeric's second problem.

"You searched the area?" Jeric asked.

"Yes, Your Grace. Didn't find a single print. It's like...it knows how to hide its tracks."

"Where did you find the other three victims?" Commander Anaton asked. He'd been roped into this too, since it was his scout who'd gone missing two nights ago.

"The first was along the Muir, the second due west of here, about two miles," Grag said, nodding in that direction. "The third, we found in the Gray's foothills."

Nowhere near one another.

"Are we sure there's just one?"

The commander's question hovered in the air.

"No," Grag said at last, meeting the commander's gaze. "We're not."

The commander pressed his lips together.

Braddok crouched beside Jeric, picked up a scrap of Corinthian-blue fabric, and held it up. "The hells was she thinking bringing those things here?"

"Perhaps His Majesty should ask her."

The comment had come from Commander Anaton, full of barbs and accusations.

Which, as it turned out, was becoming Jeric's third problem.

Braddok stood to full height, like a bear. "You watch your tone, Commander."

Jeric also stood, but more to hold Braddok off. "I intend to," Jeric said, eyes locked on his commander.

The commander's face flushed, but he moved on, redirecting his fury to the scene, while Braddok followed the commander with his eyes.

Jeric did not fault the commander for his anger. He was afraid. They all were, after what Astrid had done. They sought retribution, but Jeric had not given it to them. Not in the way they wanted.

"Has every attack been this...thorough?" the commander asked.

"Aye. We're still not certain the last victim was a wolf," Fyrok replied.

"We found part of a jaw," Grag explained. "It wasn't much, but it looked canine."

When Grag had found the first wolf, Jeric had hoped it merely the perverted antics of a disgruntled jarl trying to sabotage Jeric's new reign. Gods, he had plenty of those. But once Grag had found the second wolf, Jeric's hopes had burned like akavit. In hindsight, he should've prioritized finding the shade right then, but his time had been swiftly monopolized, palliating truth to mollify his herd of rabid jarls.

And now one of Corinth's scouts was dead.

Jeric walked on. He stepped around the scene, making his perimeter wider and wider as he walked farther from the group. There had to be something—some clue they'd all missed. Life always left evidence.

After some time, Jeric heard Fyrok call out, "Should we head back?"

Everyone looked toward Jeric, but Jeric did not notice. His attention was fixed on the ground.

"What is it, Wolf?" Braddok called out. He jogged toward Jeric, leaves crunching beneath his heavy tread. "Found something?"

Jeric crouched, pushing dead leaves and pine needles aside, and he picked up a second Corinthian-blue fiber. He followed the trajectory with his gaze, to where a murder of crows perched with unnatural quiet over a dense cluster of manzanita.

Downwind.

Jeric drew Lorath from his belt and started for the manzanita. Branches snapped and clawed at him as he forced his way through, and he soon spied more threads of Corinthian blue caught on the brambles. Old blood stained some of the leaves— old blood, and new.

The three scars at Jeric's side ached—scars he'd earned from a shade two months ago. Jeric adjusted his grip, ears pinned on the forest, but the trees would not speak. Even the crows seemed content to watch the hunt unfold.

Never a good sign.

Suddenly, the tangle of manzanita broke into a natural clearing, completely tucked away from the outside world, and at its center sat a bloodied pile of bones and intestines, and a human foot. Flies buzzed, and the stench of rot and decay hit Jeric so hard he almost vomited.

"Gods, that's ripe." Braddok coughed behind him.

"Find it?" the commander called out.

Klaus reached Braddok, paled, and started gagging.

"Well, we know where the bastard's been hiding," Braddok answered.

This shade had found a perfect burrow, and it bothered Jeric that it had considered the wind's direction. While it was true that shades had once been men, in Jeric's experience, once Changed, there was no trace of the man left.

He thought of Gerald.

"Then where is it now?" the commander asked sharply.

A tense silence settled over their group.

Jeric glanced up. The treetops swayed, and waning daylight flickered through their high, creaking boughs while the crows watched.

"Let's head back," Jeric said. "It's getting dark."

No one argued.

If only his godsdamn jarls were this agreeable.

They exited the manzanita in much the same way they'd entered: with brute force and a lot of cursing. Pieces of manzanita stubbornly clung to them as they made their way back to the horses. Klaus still looked pale, and also a little embarrassed. They'd been searching for a week, and it had taken Jeric less than one hour.

Braddok noticed. "Don't be too hard on yourself. He's the best there is. Best to just have a pint and accept your mediocrity.

Works for me every time." Braddok smacked Klaus on the shoulder, but it did little to dislodge the heaviness that had settled there.

Within the hour, the six of them had crossed into the Valley of Kings and approached the enormous skal-black wall that embraced the city of Skyhold, Corinth's capital. Twilight gleamed upon the enormous skal statues of their most revered gods, Aryn and Lorath, who stood sentinel on either side of the main gate. Scaffolding partly obscured their figures because they'd been left unfinished. Their construction had begun under the reign of Jeric's grandfather, labored by the hands of Sol Velorian slaves, and it would have completed end of this year had Jeric not freed the statue workers five days ago.

Now, the scaffolding stood like the dark skeleton of an abandoned dream, but Jeric had made a promise. And he intended to keep that promise, though his jarls resisted him at every turn. Notably when he'd demanded Jarl Stovich release the slaves working Corinth's skal mines.

"The mines are the only thing keeping Corinth's treasury full," Jarl Stovich had said, during one very heated council. "Find me three hundred men willing to work the mines *without* coin, and perhaps I'll consider."

Godfrey, master of coin and questionable things, had confirmed Corinth's dire financial situation, no thanks to Jeric's profligate father. Unfortunately for the council, Jeric viewed the word "no" as a direct challenge, and he'd immediately released all the slaves at the gate.

Which, as it turned out, only hurt Jeric's cause, because the slaves had no place to go, and no one would take them in. Some abandoned Corinth altogether, but most stayed, knowing no other way of life. They now crowded Skyhold's lower quarters, where the poorest of them lived, and the empty scaffolding stood like a warning to all: *See what would happen if we released the skal workers? The pandemonium that would ensue?*

Once inside the city gates, Grag, his hunters, and Commander Anaton departed ways, though Jeric instructed both leaders to keep their men out of the Blackwood until they caught the shade. He would not have more blood on his hands.

He had plenty of that already.

Jeric and Braddok rode a slower pace through the city, where lamplighters worked quickly to bring light to the descending dark. The wind grew teeth and snow began to fall, dusting the city in a fine layer of white. So far, their winter had been mild, and Jeric was glad for it.

"Whadya say to the Barrel?" Braddok asked. His breath rose in a cloud, and snow flecked his ruddy beard.

Jeric flexed cold fingers and glanced in the direction of the Barrel. It was tempting. *Very* tempting.

Tomorrow was to be Jeric's official coronation. In all the chaos surrounding the death of his father and brother, there hadn't been a moment to spare for a crowning ceremony. Godfrey had finally arranged for it, and mostly behind Jeric's back.

"One last drink before you're officially thrown to the vultures?" Braddok winked.

"You just don't want to pay."

"That's not the *only* reason."

Jeric chuckled. "You go on."

Braddok realized Jeric was serious. "Oh, come on, Wolf! It's your last night! You could use a drink and a good bed."

But Jeric had made up his mind. He smiled, and Braddok grumbled things Jeric chose to ignore.

"Have a pint for me," Jeric said, turning his horse away.

"You'll regret this tomorrow!" Braddok said after him.

"Probably," Jeric agreed, then tossed a small coin pouch over his shoulder.

Braddok snatched it from the air, the coins inside jangling. "Bastard."

Jeric urged his horse onward, away from Braddok, away from

the main streets and commotion and light. The snow fell harder, turning the world quiet, almost peaceful, and he thought of Sable.

No, Imari.

Surina Imari Masai.

He still found it difficult to think of her by her true name. To him, she was still Sable. The healer from Skanden, who had saved his life multiple times, though she'd had every reason to let him die. She probably would have let him die had she known who he truly was. As it turned out, he hadn't known the truth about her either: that she was the surina of Istraa, Sar Branón's illegitimate daughter, long thought dead. The one who had accidentally killed her sister with music—with magic. One of the Sol Velor's Liagé.

The very ones he, the Wolf of Corinth, had spent his life hunting.

And he had kissed her.

He'd almost done it again, right in front of her brother, their saredd, and all of Jeric's closest advisors. The only thing that'd stopped him was the added danger it would cause Imari. Jeric held no delusions that the long-standing rift between Istraa and Corinth would be mended over one rescue mission, and that sort of unsanctioned attention from a Wolf King would only increase Istraa's mistrust of their newly-returned surina. Jeric's advisors wouldn't have approved either, but they could all go to hells.

He stopped his horse at the edge of Aryn's Temple, or what remained of it. It had collapsed the night Astrid had attacked two weeks ago. Witnesses claimed the ground had shaken and great cracks had splintered the marble walls before the dome had come crashing down, crushing everything—and everyone— beneath. All of the inquisitors were dead, buried deep in Aryn's ruins.

All except for one: Rasmin, Corinth's Head Inquisitor. Rasmin had flown away that night, and no one had seen him since.

That godsdamned lying piece of scat.

Jeric dismounted. The snow muffled his footsteps as he approached the temple remains. He stopped beside a massive skal face, broken in half down the center. Lorath, the god of justice. The god for whom Jeric had named his sword. The god for whom Jeric had built his life.

A life Jeric was no longer certain of.

Jeric stared at the broken face, at the cold and vacant eye. At the mouth that never spoke.

What have you become, my darling Jos? Jeric heard his mother's words instead.

Jeric gazed upon the ruin of his religion. The gods had always been his mirror, the reflection by which he'd shaped his decisions. But by Imari, that mirror had shattered—broken, like the temple before him, and now he felt suddenly...lost.

Lost, and about to be crowned Corinth's king.

Jeric shut his eyes and breathed in deep. The cold burned his nose, filled his lungs. For a moment, he simply stood there like a fixture in a graveyard, but he found no answers. Only more questions.

At last, he opened his eyes. There was still one problem he *could* solve, and it needed solving tonight.

The snow was falling hard by the time he'd handed his horse to the groomsman and stepped inside Skyhold's great fortress, where warm and cheerful air engulfed him. The hall was busier than usual, as late-arriving guests dined and drank and thawed themselves by the many blazing hearths. Jeric ducked through a doorway before anyone could stop him, though the corridors weren't any emptier. Servants tended to needy masters, and at one point, Jeric stopped to redirect a lady from Rodinshold, who'd emerged from the wood closet in her night robes looking adrift. Eventually, traffic thinned and disappeared completely, and Jeric reached the door to the old dungeon.

This dungeon had been retired for storage decades ago, until

Hagan had found Imari. It was here, in the belly of the fortress, that his brother had kept her. Where no one would know what he'd taken.

Jeric would never forgive himself for that.

Now, this dungeon kept his sister, Astrid. *She* was the source of the commander's anger—the entire council's anger. Astrid was a traitor and a murderer. A demon in the flesh. Her death should be their retribution for the horror she had wrought. But Jeric could not bring himself to do it.

She was the only family he had left.

He pushed through the door and into the guardroom. A handful of guards glanced up, their game of Spades spread on the table between them.

One guard stood. "Sire."

"Any improvement?" Jeric asked.

"No, sire," the guard replied.

A second guard stood, grabbed a lantern from the wall, and opened the door. Jeric ducked through, and the two guards followed behind with the lantern.

At the turn of Astrid's corridor, Jeric stopped and held up a hand. "Wait here."

"But Your Grace—"

"If she gets through that door, a few paces will be the least of your concerns."

Uneasy quiet.

"Yes, Your Grace," one guard replied, and they both stayed put.

Jeric walked on and stopped before the door to Astrid's prison. Her cell was pitch black and silent, and the air reeked of urine and feces. Jeric glanced back at the guards, who waited faithfully down the hall, and he took a step closer.

Torchlight danced upon the door's shining skal-black surface, giving shadow to the ancient etchings. Jeric wondered at a world where Corinth's skal smiths had worked harmoniously with Sol

Velorian enchanters, though he doubted those enchanters had anticipated just how this door would later be used. Jeric's men had extracted this relic from the temple remains. It had been enough to hold the inquisitor's Liagé prisoners; Jeric hoped it would be enough for Astrid. So far, it had been.

He grabbed the torch from the wall and held it closer, straining to see Astrid through the small square of bars in the door. "Astrid?" he called out.

No answer.

"Astrid... Talk to me. *Please*." He studied the shadows, listening for the slightest shift in the air.

Nothing.

Perhaps she was dead already.

It would make this easier, he thought grimly.

Jeric's fingertips hovered over the door's surface, as if he could reach out and touch her, bring her back. As if he could take away her suffering, and all of the horrible things she'd endured at the hands of their brother, Hagan. All of the horrible things Jeric had not realized, because he had been too busy hating and hunting the very power that protected them now.

With a sigh, he dropped his hand.

"Jeric...?"

The voice was so frail—so thin, he almost did not hear it.

"Astrid...?" He leaned closer, hopeful, and held the torch high. Still, he could not see her. "Astrid, I'm here. Talk to me."

"Jeric, I'm scared." Her voice trembled like that of a frightened child.

It pained him. "I know, and I am—"

"It's everywhere..." she continued.

A beat. "What's everywhere?"

"The darkness. Jeric, I am so cold..."

Jeric gripped one of the bars with his free hand. "Listen to me, Astrid. I am going to help you. I swear on my life. We will fight this together—"

Suddenly, black fingernails sank into his hand, breaking skin. Jeric hissed and dropped the torch. It rolled, shadows slithering on the walls.

"Your Grace!" the guards shouted behind him.

Her fingernails dug deep, drawing blood. Jeric fought to pull away as Astrid's startlingly gaunt face appeared behind the bars. Her pupils were too dilated, her eyes too pale and pillowed by cavernous shadows, while her lips cracked and bled, stretched too far over bared gray teeth. Her hair, which had once been a shimmering blushed gold, was now dull as straw, matted and tangled with chunks missing from her scalp, as though she'd ripped it out.

Jeric pried his hand free of her iron grip and stumbled back into a guard.

And there was laughter. A dark, malignant sound that gurgled from the depths of the five hells.

"He means to save us," she said in that voice of many, of one. A voice that would haunt him forever.

The legion.

"Let her go," Jeric snarled.

"Let us free, and we might consider."

"I don't bargain with demons."

Astrid merely stared at him with those too-pale eyes, and then she cocked her head to the side like a bird. "Tell us... How did you find your scout?"

Jeric went rigid. Behind him, the guards exchanged a glance.

Astrid's tongue slid over her dark teeth, relishing. "He wants to know how we know. Should we tell him?" Astrid licked her lips. "No, we think not. We like watching the pretty wolf dance."

Jeric gazed upon this creature that had once been his beautiful sister, and in that moment, his answer became painfully clear. "You will die tomorrow."

"You cannot kill us."

"You were cast out of this world once. It will be done again."

She gnashed her teeth, startling Jeric back one step, and she curled long and bloodied fingers around the bars. But the moment her fingers touched skal, the etchings flared white. A brilliant, unfiltered white. Astrid shrieked and let go, whimpering like an injured pup. She cradled her hands and hunched away from the door, then sat in the middle of the floor, in the lines of torchlight. There, she swayed back and forth, back and forth, moaning lowly with her head bowed.

Jeric stood there a moment as regret settled heavily upon his chest, and then he left his sister's cell for what he knew would be the very last time.

5

You are mine.

Imari bolted upright to a dark room. *Her* room, she swiftly recalled, and it took her a moment more to convince herself that she wasn't still dreaming. The wood stove glowed innocently in the corner, and the night lay quiet. Calm. Imari inhaled deep. Just a dream. It was just a dream.

But *wards*.

That voice still rattled in her mind, and points of pain throbbed all over her body, where those fleshy branches had speared her skin.

Imari absently rubbed at her arms and glanced at the low table, at the three bottles of nazzat—all empty, thanks to Ricón and Kai, who had visited with her late into the night. Perhaps she shouldn't have helped them empty those bottles. In Imari's experience, alcohol was the worst of friends. It lied and it flattered, and then stole your integrity in the morning.

Which was why she *usually* used it strictly as an antiseptic.

But being with her brothers last night, after all these years, she'd lost herself to the moment. Where there were no shades and no fear of darkness, and no need for wards to protect them.

The nazzat had helped dull the awkwardness those lonely years had created, and then they had laughed and joked and exchanged countless stories. Imari had joined in wholeheartedly, eager to make new memories. Ones that weren't full of pain and horror and loneliness. She had plenty of those.

The draperies over the wood screen wall swelled like sails, and Imari went rigid.

Ricón had closed those screen doors last night. She remembered, because he'd checked the lock three times, and she had teased him for being ridiculous.

Curious, and more than a little wary, Imari climbed out of her blankets and padded toward the large screen, the travertine floor cold upon her bare feet. Even *if* someone had scaled the high wall of this tower, there was no way they would they have gotten past the guards...

Imari stopped cold.

Her bone flute lay beside the emptied nazzat. And beneath it lay a square piece of paper.

Imari moved the flute aside—the etchings flared at her touch —and she lifted the crisp parchment, opened the single, stiff crease to find a black feather within.

An *owl* feather.

Her gaze shot through the open door, to the starless sky beyond her veranda. *He* had been here. He had followed her all the way from Skyhold, and snuck into her room while she'd been asleep. The thought of him slinking around this space while she slept made Imari shudder.

She glanced down at the paper, picked up the feather, and read the inked words beneath, scrawled in elegant script.

You must practice.
Something moves in the shadows that I cannot See, but when it comes to light, and it will very soon, you must be ready.

No signature. Not that it needed one.

She read the note again. Rasmin and his rutting cryptic words —vague, like his attempts at explaining the Shah. She'd thought his understanding had come from years of torturing information from those who'd possessed it. She hadn't realized his understanding had come from personal experience.

Imari strode to the wood stove and threw open the grate. Metal screamed and sleepy embers blushed within.

"Here's what I think of your advice, *Inquisitor*." She touched paper to ember. The paper ignited and flame curled the edges like ribbon, eating them up and staining them black. She tossed the paper into the stove, and the feather with it. "May you burn in the deepest hell, you rutting monster."

Imari snatched the fire poker and stabbed at the coals, throwing sparks. She thought of all the Sol Velorians and their Liagé that Rasmin had tortured, and the Sol Velorian slaves Hagan had murdered in front of her every day she had not played.

Every day she had not given them the power they had sought.

Another thought struck her then: would it be so different here in Istraa? Once the people moved beyond the shock of her existence and learned what she could do—and they would learn, eventually. What then? With rumors of this Liagé leader rampant across Istraa, would her papa's rois and roiesses—those who governed Istraa's various districts—choose instead to use Imari in the same way Hagan had intended?

Regardless, one thing was certain: Rasmin was not giving up on her so easily.

Imari dropped the poker and crossed the room, passed through the screen door, and stepped onto her veranda. Cold air shocked her skin through her thin nightdress; the velvety black sky had brightened to a woolen gray with the oncoming dawn.

"You're right," she said, searching the clouds for him. "I *will* practice. So that if you—or anyone else—tries to use me again, I will be ready. And I will fight back."

And she would. Somehow.

A knock sounded upon her door, which surprised her, considering the early hour.

"One moment." Imari stepped out of the cold and shut the veranda doors. She shoved her flute into a drawer, threw on a silk shawl, and said, "Come in."

The door opened and her papa stepped through.

Wards, she didn't think she'd ever grow used to seeing him again.

He was fully dressed this morning, his long hair tied neatly back in contrast to his unruly beard, but the weariness in his eyes betrayed him. "I thought you might be awake."

She gave him a slight smile. Her papa had always been an early riser, but looking at him, at the fatigue in his face, she couldn't tell if he'd risen early or simply never slept.

His gaze snagged on her unused four-poster bed, plush with silk sheets and a mountain of fluffy pillows. He then spotted the blankets heaped upon the floor beside it.

Imari couldn't tell him that it had been too much. She didn't want to explain how she'd felt like a foreigner in her old room, with its luxury and soft textures and warmth. She couldn't explain how the cold had become familiar. Surviving had become familiar. And she couldn't really explain how struggle had fortified her bones, and that she didn't want comfort to make her frail again.

Her papa looked at her then, and she suspected he saw it all anyway.

"I'm sorry I didn't get the opportunity to visit last night," he said, breaking the awkward quiet. Weariness stole the bass from his tone. "But I imagine you and your brothers probably enjoyed some conversation *without* a father's input." He gave a small, knowing grin, which Imari returned.

Sar Branón had said he'd join Imari and her brothers later, after he spoke to his wife, but then later had become early morning, and he'd never arrived. Out of all the inevitable reunions, Anja had been the one Imari had dreaded most. For both herself, and her papa.

"We did," Imari answered, then, "How...is Anja?"

"As good as can be expected, I suppose." His gaze slid to the door she had just closed, as if he could see the city beyond. "She went to Jadarr first thing this morning to fast and pray."

Jadarr was the largest of Istraa's temples, located at the city's center.

"I'm sorry, Papa," Imari said quietly.

His gaze settled back on her. "Do not apologize for my mistakes, Imari."

He was speaking about so much more than his wife.

His mustache twitched, and then he turned abruptly, and said, "You three were up late." He gestured at the nazzat as he rounded the divan and sat.

Eager to change the subject.

Truthfully, Imari was too. Anja was never an easy one to discuss.

"Well, we had a lot to talk about," Imari replied, joining him on the divan.

She looked at him, and he looked at her, and the quiet expanded, all tangled with the past. The years had altered them both, and not just on the outside. Time and experience had set them on different trajectories. Or, rather, it had set Imari on a completely different trajectory. She was Istraan, but The Wilds now flowed in her veins, and her papa gazed at her as if she'd been seasoned with a new herb he couldn't quite place.

And then, suddenly, he smiled. "I still can't believe you're here."

The quiet might have been awkward, but his smile was real, and in that moment, Imari felt that everything might just be all right. That no matter what happened—no matter what obstacles lay ahead—at least she wasn't alone. She had a family who loved her, and no one could take that precious gift away.

Imari sighed and sagged back upon the divan. "I still can't believe it either," she admitted, glancing about her room. It still felt like a dream, being back in this once-so-familiar place.

"Tell me how you were found," Sar Branón asked. "Ricón told me a little, but I'd like to hear your perspective."

So Imari explained while her papa listened. She held nothing back, and he asked questions here and there for clarification, but remained otherwise quiet while his posture grew heavier and heavier as if each of her confessions were another stone hefted upon his shoulders. He seemed particularly interested in Jeric, as Ricón had been, and there she *did* hold back. It struck her that the moments that mattered most to her were the very ones she could not share, not comfortably anyhow—not yet—and so she tucked those deep and locked them away for her sole enjoyment.

When she finished, Sar Branón sighed and leaned back, one finger tapping absently upon his knee. "Saints, I'd hoped he'd been exaggerating." And then he sat forward, looked at her, his expression full of regret. "I'm so sorry I sent you away, Imari. That you endured all of that on your own."

She held his gaze, searched his face. "Then why did you?" Of course, she'd drawn her own conclusions; she'd had ten years to think about it, and the reasons she'd constructed spanned a wide spectrum from *because he hated her* to *he believed The Wilds her best chance at survival.*

But like he'd asked of her, she wanted to hear his perspective.

Her papa rested both elbows upon his knees, threading his fingers together. He still wore the engraved gold ring on his index finger—his sar's ring—and the wide band upon his thumb, but she did not see the ring Anja had given him.

"Because we could not know how or when your power would manifest," her papa answered at last. His brow furrowed. "Ten years. One day. And who could we ask for help without giving you away? Had you been unable to hide your power, my rois and roiesses would've demanded your execution. Kourana Vidéa would not have hesitated. She was already asking for trial—Saád's crimes were still too recent, you remember, and his followers had just gone into hiding. If we hadn't given you a trial, we would have faced the wrath of the Five Provinces. King Tommad was already breathing fire down my neck."

Imari studied her papa, because in everything he had said, her thoughts snagged on one word. "You said *we.*"

She wondered if he'd meant mama. Her *real* mama.

Sar Branón tapped his thumbs together. "It was Gamla's idea."

Imari sat forward, surprised. "*Uki...?*" Her uncle? And then another thought struck her. "Stars... Uki knew Tolya, didn't he?"

Her papa's expression was answer enough.

Of course her uncle would've known Tolya. Why hadn't she considered this before? Healers knew other healers. Especially someone like her uki, renowned throughout the Five Provinces for his unparalleled healing abilities.

"Gamla orchestrated your death, and your transport," her papa continued. "He made the tonic that put you to sleep. He swore Tolya would be enough to keep you safe, and I trusted him implicitly." On this point, her papa's voice took an edge.

"She did keep me safe," Imari replied, feeling defensive for Tolya. "Uki couldn't have foreseen everything."

Her papa pressed his lips together. "No, he could not."

"Ricón said Uki is missing."

Her papa's gaze met hers, though his posture closed a little as he nodded once, slowly.

"Ricón also said he left six months ago," Imari pressed. "On his usual rounds to the Baragas, and that he never returned. He said you never even found his camel."

That was all Ricón had known—he'd sworn to the saints—but the circumstances and the timing had deeply bothered Imari.

Six months ago was also when King Tommad had fallen ill. When Corinth's Sol Velorian slaves had begun disappearing, and when Astrid had become...legion.

And Imari did not believe in coincidences.

"Papa, what happened to him?"

Sar Branón inhaled so deeply his nostrils flared a little. "I don't know."

"But you have suspicions."

"I truly don't know, Imari," he said. "I visited those villages myself, but I found nothing. Sebharan's best trackers found nothing. I've done everything I can to find him, but it's like he...vanished."

Imari studied him. "Do you think he's gone?"

"That is the general consensus among my council."

"And what do *you* believe?"

He sighed, and a deep crease formed between his bushy brows. "I don't believe for a moment that Gamla suffered an accident. He knows those roads better than the people who live there."

Imari agreed. Gamla did. "So you think he was taken then?"

"Yes." A pause. "Though why, I can't say. The fact that he's *my* brother should be reason enough, however, no one has come forward with ransom."

"Maybe someone needs him for his healing abilities."

"That would be the other reasonable explanation, and *if* this person were willing to risk my wrath for it, they must have believed they couldn't contact Gamla directly. Though I still can't figure why anyone would believe that. Gamla never denied any Sol Velorian who called upon his services—"

"What if they don't want to be known?" Imari asked, sitting forward. "You've considered it might be related to this...Liagé leader?"

"Of course I've considered it, but even if this *leader* exists, certainly the Sol Velor have Liagé Restorers at their disposal." At

Imari's look of surprise, Sar Branón added, "I'm no fool, Imari, and neither was Tommad. I know there are still Liagé hiding within Istraa's borders, though I don't know how many, nor where they are. We never came down as hard on them as your Wolf and his family did. They've left us alone and stayed hidden, and so I turned my head, though now I wonder if I should have..." His voice trailed, that crease forming between his brows again. "If this leader does exist, I imagine he will—"

"Or *she*," Imari interrupted.

Her papa tipped his head. "*Or she* will have Restorers at their disposal, and would therefore have no need of Gamla's more... primitive methods of healing."

Imari sat quiet, thinking on all her papa had said. Knowing Liagé still dwelled within Istraa gave her a flare of hope, because she *had* wondered. Her papa was right in that Istraa had never been as hard on the Sol Velor as the other provinces—to the growing resentment of those other provinces—but hearing her papa voice it aloud made it more real. And maybe...

Maybe Imari could find one such Liagé in hiding and convince them to teach her how to use her power.

But in the meantime: Gamla.

What in all the stars would someone want with Gamla?

Imari rested her chin upon her hand, tapped her cheek. She thought of Tolya, and her time in The Wilds. Of her own meager attempts at using and understanding Shah power.

"They want his knowledge." Imari spoke the thought aloud even as it entered her mind.

Her papa frowned. "What do you mean?"

"Papa." Imari dropped her hand. "Gamla understands the workings of the human body better than anyone I've ever met. Including Tolya."

"Yes, but with Restorers at their disposal—"

"Shah power isn't so simple as that, Papa," Imari interrupted him. "You don't just...tell it to do something, and it's done." Imari batted a hand. "It's a *process*. When I fought Astrid—well, the legion—I had to actively direct that power at her, and even then, I didn't defeat the demon. All I managed to do was hold it until they could slap Liagé bindings around her wrists, and even that left me unconscious for two full weeks. I imagine Gamla's knowledge as a healer would be very useful to anyone, regardless of what method of healing a person uses. That's assuming he's been taken."

Her papa studied her a long moment. "Well, that definitely gives me something else to consider." And then he turned to face her.

Imari knew at once that he had something heavy to say, and that she probably wasn't going to like it.

"Since we're on the subject of your power," he started. "There is...another matter I need to discuss with you."

Imari regarded him, wary.

"In two hours' time, I will be meeting privately with my small council to discuss your return and...how best to proceed with the rois and roiesses." A beat, uncertain. He looked at her; his fingers stopped tapping. "You will be present."

She saw it in his eyes then, the fear and apprehension. He wanted her there because he wanted his small council to see her. He wanted them to know she was flesh and blood, and not just an arbitrary list of horrors, so that they would support him as he faced all the men and women who helped him manage Istraa.

So that they would not think Imari was this Liagé leader and demand her execution on sight.

"I understand, Papa," she said quietly, very aware of the drawer where her flute lay hidden.

"I have given this some thought," he continued, "and while I don't have all the answers, and I certainly can't predict their reaction to you, they *are* people of practicality. We have a foe we cannot find, and truthfully, I'm not sure we could overpower them, should we actually succeed in finding them." Here he paused and looked straight into her eyes. "But you...you have something we do not, Imari. The flute."

The flute.

Not *her*.

As if *it* held the power.

And this was the point that had kept her brothers arguing with her late into the night. Ricón and Kai had encouraged her to blame the flute—at least until the people were comfortable knowing that their surina was not dead. Best not to add another complication, Kai had said, and Ricón had agreed. And it wasn't completely a lie. For a very long time, Imari *had* believed the flute to blame for what she'd done.

It seemed her papa was happy to perpetuate this lie too—maybe even convince himself that it was true.

"I believe the gods chose this moment to bring you home for a reason," her papa continued steadily, as if bracing himself for an objection he couldn't quite predict. The Wilds had changed her, after all. "Convince the council why we need your flute, Imari, and we might all come out of this alive."

Irritation pricked her. "You know it's not the flute, Papa."

He gazed steadily back. "They do not need to know that."

That irritation dug deeper, wormed beneath her skin. "Papa, I've been hiding the truth for ten years, and look how that turned out—"

"It's not forever, Imari," he said, with an edge of impatience. "Just until things settle."

"Is that what you told yourself when you shipped me off to The Wilds ten years ago?"

Imari hadn't meant to say it, but there it was. Twisting and ugly and bitter.

Sar Branón closed his eyes and exhaled long. "Imari." He sounded so weary. And when he opened his eyes again, pain pulled them tight. "I know you're tired. So am I. And while I can't change the past, I *can* protect your future, and forgive me, but I do not want to lose you again."

The pain and conviction in his voice—his expression. Imari lost her fight, and she clenched her teeth and looked away.

He placed a hand over hers. It covered hers completely. *"For now—"* he continued, softer this time "—it will go easier if my advisors believe the flute is to blame."

Imari looked sharply at her papa. "Easier isn't always right."

He didn't look away. "No. It's not." His lips parted, as if to say more, but he stood abruptly instead. "I'm sorry to leave like this, but Sebharan is waiting for me in the hall. Another temple was burnt down just yesterday."

Imari looked up at him. "With the kahars inside?"

He nodded a fraction, his expression grim.

"Where this time?" she asked.

"Rozzi."

Rozzi was a village situated along the Baragas' southern edge, where mountain runoff made a small patch of soil viable for wheat.

Before Imari could ask, her papa added, "The fields were burnt to the ground, their owners nailed to stakes, and their labor nowhere to be found."

Imari's gaze dropped to the floor.

He touched her chin, lifting it as he gazed down into her face. "I don't mean to frighten you, but you need to understand what we're up against."

"I know, Papa," she said, and she did know.

He moved his hand from his chin to her cheek. "I love you, Imari. Do not believe for a moment that I am asking you to hide out of condemnation. I'm asking you because I lied to the world, and we might pay for that lie with our lives. I don't want to lose you again, and I'm doing my best to find the safest path forward for all of us. Please trust me in this."

Imari's chest squeezed as she said, quietly, "All right."

Her papa gazed at her a moment more, and then he leaned forward and kissed her cheek. "Your attire should arrive within the hour," he said, standing. "Jenya has agreed to attend you."

Hardly why Jenya had endured saredd training, Imari was sure.

Her papa started for the door.

"Who was she?" Imari asked.

Sar Branón stopped in his tracks.

Imari wasn't sure what made her ask just then—perhaps all this talk of the past and the Shah—but there it was, as if the question were so tired of waiting, it had pushed its way right out of her.

"Please, Papa. I just want to know who she—"

"Not now." His voice rang unsteady, his back to her still.

Little Imari would not have pushed, but she was not little Imari anymore. It was partially his fault.

"Then when?" Imari persisted. "Papa, it might help if I knew who—"

"I said *not now.*" He turned to her then. Anger colored his cheeks, and the quiet fury simmering in his eyes chased her insistence away.

Imari closed her lips.

And then he left, closing the door firmly behind him.

She did not see him stop at the end of the hall. She did not see him close his eyes and breathe in deep, battling a memory only he possessed.

For the one who shared it was gone.

"I am trying," Sar Branón whispered. "But saints above, she is too much like you."

6

J eric shut the door to his private chambers and closed his eyes. Astrid had known about the scout.

*Gods*damnit.

He dragged a hand over his face and opened his eyes. Little half-moon shaped cuts marred his hands where Astrid had sunk her nails into him. Jeric cursed again and rubbed his hand as he looked around. The servants had readied his room. A fire blazed in the hearth, his bedsheets had been pulled back, and a platter of breads and nuts rested upon the table beside a full bottle of akavit—a Corinthian staple. Which Jeric hated.

Perhaps that was why they kept bringing it.

This was Jeric's last night here, in this room. After tomorrow, he would take the king's chambers. Where his father had slept. And Hagan, for six nights.

Jeric crossed the room, and tossed his weapons and cloak onto the bed. He had just sat down upon his favorite leather chair when a hand rested upon his shoulder.

On instinct, Jeric dropped, swung his arm wide to grab his assailant's wrist, and twisted—hard. His assailant cried out in pain—a woman, Jeric realized, and when he finally looked at her, he cursed and let go, standing. *"Kyrinne...?"*

Lady Kyrinne Brion, Jarl Stovich's daughter, and she currently hunched before Jeric, cradling her delicate wrist, her eyes startled wide with confusion and panic.

"What are you doing?" he hissed.

Her lips pursed, her cheeks flushed. "I wanted to see you, and I thought..." Her voice trailed off as Jeric pushed his palms to his temples and turned away from her.

"Jeric, I am so sorry," she said quietly. "I didn't mean to frighten you."

Jeric laughed darkly. Lady Kyrinne...frighten *him*. No wonder the jarls had lost faith. Gods, he was losing faith in himself.

He should've taken Brad up on that offer.

Jeric dropped his hands and turned back around. Lady Kyrinne studied him, looking awkward and embarrassed. It was the first time he'd seen her composure crack.

"How did you get in?" he asked. His voice came out harsher than he'd intended.

Her confidence faltered. "Bastion."

Of course. "Ah."

Quiet.

The embers crackled in the hearth.

"It is your last night..." Lady Kyrinne started, her expression beseeching. "I thought I could help you...pass the time."

Yes, she had always been good at that, and he'd usually welcomed it. But tonight, he wanted to pass his time alone.

Kyrinne stepped toward him slowly. Her heavy Corinthian-blue robe complemented her eyes, and long honey-blonde hair cascaded over her shoulders to her waist, highlighting her curves. She *was* beautiful.

Curiosity flecked her eyes. "What is the matter, my love?"

The endearment irked him. It had never irked him before, but it did now. They had shared plenty, but it wasn't love.

"Just tired," Jeric said tightly.

Kyrinne stopped before him and pressed a palm to his cheek. Her strong perfume accosted his senses. "Then let me help you relax."

She didn't wait for a response; she didn't need to. They both knew this dance. Instead, she leaned forward and kissed him with a hot and eager mouth.

Jeric was not in the mood.

He pulled away and took a decisive step back from her. "Not tonight," he said, then added quietly, "You should go."

Lady Kyrinne looked at him. A challenge lit her eyes, and then she let her robe fall to the floor. There was nothing underneath. Firelight danced upon her skin and sumptuous curves, daring him to resist. A lure that'd reeled him back time and time again.

Jeric didn't move, his mind a battlefield. He did not want this, but his body had wants of its own.

She took a small step, closing the gap between them. The heat of her bare breasts warmed through his tunic, and he felt himself losing a very important battle. Quickly.

"There you are, my handsome Wolf," she whispered upon his lips, then slid her hand into his hair and pulled his mouth down to hers.

This time, Jeric kissed her back. He couldn't help himself. His hands moved over her body, over her soft and familiar shape.

Soft, because she had never wanted. Never suffered.

She moaned against his mouth, tearing desperately at his tunic, and then her hands slid lower, unclasping his belt with practiced ease.

No, a voice inside of him growled.

He grabbed her hands and stopped them at his belt.

She nipped his lip, thinking it a game, and tried pushing his waistline lower.

Jeric held firm and pulled back, looking straight at her. "Kyrinne."

A long beat passed, and Kyrinne let go.

"You must truly be exhausted," she said coyly, though Jeric caught the edge.

He gave no apology, no excuse. He wasn't sure he could give one, had he tried. Instead, he buckled his belt, gathered her robe, and held it out to her. Kyrinne hesitated as a deep blush crept up her neck, and finally, she took the robe.

Jeric did not offer to help her dress. She slipped behind the privacy screen, though Jeric couldn't fathom why she cared for modesty now.

Still, he was grateful.

He was pouring himself a glass of akavit when she reemerged —dressed, thank the gods. She looked at the glass, at him.

"You hate akavit," she said.

"I do." He took a drink, savoring the fire as it burned down his throat.

Silence.

"Have you chosen your first for tomorrow's ceremony?" she asked, eyeing him.

Jeric sucked akavit residue through his teeth. "I haven't actually thought about it."

She wanted to know whom he'd dance with, because his first choice would make a political statement—one Jarl Stovich had craved since the day Kyrinne had been born. Even more now that Jeric occupied the throne.

He felt Kyrinne watching him. He should say something— something easy and unaffected and charmed. Hagan would have. Hagan had always been a master at crafting words.

Hagan also would not be sending her away.

Jeric took another sip, swallowed the fire, and glanced over at Lady Kyrinne. "Good evening, Lady Kyrinne," he said instead.

Lady Kryinne's lips tightened, and she dipped into a low and elegant curtsy. "I apologize for interrupting your solitude, Your Grace. May the gods grant you a restful sleep and bestow their favor upon your long reign."

Jeric watched her leave and softly close the door behind her. He poured himself another glass of akavit and downed it in one long gulp. His thoughts anchored on Istraa, specifically upon a certain woman now residing there, and it was a very long time before he fell asleep.

Jeric awoke with a start. His room was dark, save the one candle struggling in a pool of wax, and he glanced at the window. The snow had stopped. A full moon shone in the clear night sky, and the world slept.

And yet.

Jeric sensed a wrongness he could not explain.

He sat up and winced. A nasty headache throbbed behind his eyes, and Jeric cursed at himself. He had known better.

He slid off of his bed, though he couldn't recall falling on top of it. His tunic lay heaped on the floor where Kyrinne had left it, and his boots sat on the floor before his leather armchair. At least he'd had the sense to take those off.

Gods, Kyrinne.

Jeric dragged a hand over his face and then strode to the table, where an insightful servant had left a pitcher of water beside the empty bottle of akavit. He poured himself a glass, downed it, and poured himself another. As if he could wash Kyrinne away with the akavit.

The foreboding persisted, nagging with each pounding ache.

He crossed to the window and gazed upon the city of Skyhold, blanketed in white. From here, he could see the main gate and the guards standing at the ramparts, their silhouettes illuminated by silvery moonlight. His gaze slid farther beyond, where the Blackwood stretched. Where a shade hunted.

And Astrid had known.

Thinking on Astrid, he looked to the very base of Skyhold's northern tower, where lantern light...

Should have been visible through the guardroom's small window.

Jeric tensed, eyes fixed on the dark window, and the warning inside of him blared.

Astrid.

He slammed down his glass, water forgotten, threw on his tunic and boots, and strode for the door. There, he paused, backtracking to grab his sword, and then threw open the door, startling Bastion.

"Your Grace...?" Bastion called after him, but Jeric jogged on, raising one hand to warn him off.

Thankfully, Bastion did not follow.

Skyhold's drafty halls lay dark and quiet, and with each step, Jeric's foreboding intensified. He glanced down every turn, checking for signs of his sister. Lanterns burned innocently, the halls sat empty, but the normalcy did little to assuage him. The guard station wasn't the only way into those dungeons.

Jeric reached the hall to the guardroom and cursed. The guard who'd been stationed before the door was nowhere in sight. Jeric sprinted for the door and kicked it open.

The smell of death greeted him.

The guardroom was dark, but a body lay just within, dusted with light from the outer corridor. It was the guard who had been stationed outside the door. His neck twisted unnaturally, and his eyes stared, vacant.

Jeric's attention narrowed on the archway within, the one leading to the dungeons—black as pitch.

Astrid was gone.

He knew it in his core, sensing that horrible truth with his heart more than his nose. He grabbed a lantern from the hall and stepped back into the guardroom. Another guard lay near the dungeon entrance, impaled by his own sword. The game of Spades sat abandoned, cards drowning in blood.

Jeric crept forward, his ears pinned on the quiet. He found two more guards lying in the corridor, dead like the others, and the stench of burning soured the air, like cauterized flesh. The smell intensified as he reached the mouth of Astrid's dark corridor, and he held up his lantern.

He spotted the guards first, sprawled upon the floor. Their faces were frozen in a twist of horror, skin ashen and webbed with black veins, their eyes missing. Someone else had killed the guards near the entrance, but these, Astrid had taken for herself.

Beyond them lay Astrid's door.

It smoldered upon the floor like the dying embers in Jeric's hearth. The Liagé etchings curled like burnt paper, charred and blackened, and the thick skal lay folded in half like a discarded book. Broken stone littered the ground as if the door had been ripped from the wall by sheer force.

And the cell beyond was empty.

Gods*damnit.*

"We have classified the Shah into four talents, each named after Asorai's four Divines, from whom the talents originated. Shiva: the art of using life's blood to manipulate Shah energy for healing. Voloré: the ability to enchant the physical with metaphysical properties, through application of Asorai's Word. Ziat: the ability to See what has been, and is, and is to come. And Saredii: the ability to manipulate Shah energy within the physical world."

~ The Shah,
*A collection of teachings
according to Moltoné,
Liagé Second High Sceptor.*

7

I mari stood before the double doors to Vondar's great hall, with Ricón beside her.

"Try not to look so angry," he whispered.

"That's just how I look when I'm terrified."

Ricón raised a brotherly brow. "You faced much worse in The Wilds."

She stared at those doors, at the two saredd standing on either side, spears crossed and guarding her fate. "Debatable."

Ricón gave her a small smile and tipped his head closer. "Well, this time you won't be facing them alone. I will be with you." He gave her arm a gentle and encouraging squeeze.

The morning had passed much too quickly. Immediately after her papa had left, two servants—one of which was Sol Velorian, though she resisted all Imari's attempts at conversation—had arrived, promptly shoved Imari into the washbasin, and scrubbed her skin raw. Her arms still burned from the scented oils they'd rubbed into them, and her scalp ached where they'd ravaged her tangles with an unforgiving comb. They'd painted her face and then dressed her in a gown her papa had chosen. Simple, yet elegant, long and flowing and sleeveless, the ivory silk a complement to her bronze complexion. Nothing to suggest outright that she was a surina, but rather someone worthy of distinction.

When she had finally gazed at her reflection, she'd hardly recognized herself. A highborn Istraan had stared back, which was undoubtedly her papa's intention.

But it had not made Imari proud.

For this was Sorai's birthright, and Imari could not look at herself, dressed as she was, without remembering what she'd stolen.

I am the worst of thieves, Imari had thought then—thought still.

One of the massive doors cracked open, and Ricón squeezed her arm.

It was time.

The saredd uncrossed their spears and pushed the doors open.

Imari took a deep breath, and Ricón led her forward. The saredd did not turn, but their eyes followed her every step through those doors and into Vondar's magnificent hall.

This hall was Istraa's pride, a tribute to the gods and celestial in design. The duoma—dome—crowned all, its small oculus giving the gods and saints a glimpse of their insignificant little world. Colorful mosaics swirled upon the floor and white columns stood like trees, branching into the high arches above. Muted light poured through the open windows, and palms danced upon the portico beyond, their wide fronds waving in the gentle morning breeze. Scattered throughout the hall were a dozen shallow copper basins filled with burning coals to dull the morning's brisk edge.

But they could not dull Imari's painful memories.

Her gaze drifted to the spot where the table had been that night, where her papa's guests had fallen asleep to her music. And then her gaze settled on the small door beyond, where another little girl had waited in secret, listening. Imari swallowed and fixed her eyes decidedly ahead.

Where her papa and his personal advisors waited.

There were seven in total, including her papa and Sura Anja, who sat atop the dais. The others occupied chairs at the base of the dais, four on one side, and Kai on the other, situated beside an empty chair that was probably intended for Ricón. Kai looked tired this morning. Shadows framed his eyes and dehydration had stolen some of his color, but he still managed a small and conspiratorial smile when she met his gaze.

Imari recognized the others, though it had been years since she'd seen them. Nearest her papa sat Kourana Vidéa, Istraa's High Priestess and the grand overseer of Jadarr—Istraa's largest temple. She wore crimson robes embroidered in gold, and her long black hair fell like a sheet down her rigid back. Rigid as the laws and statutes she upheld and enforced with the aide of her many kahar—Istraa's priests.

Beside her sat Bayek, one of her papa's oldest friends and closest advisors: Istraa's master of secrets. Bayek had always been a shrewd man, his demeanor as mysterious as his network of spies. Interminably a skeptic, he gazed at the world as if every-thing in it conspired against him—including Imari, as she slowly approached.

Sebharan—a trim, middle-aged man and master of the Qazzat, where both saredd and guards trained—sat on Bayek's other side, leaving Jeol, master of coin and pretension, on the end.

These were her papa's personal advisors. The people her papa needed to convince—that *she* needed to convince—because he would need their support completely in the uncertain days to come.

Ricón led her steadily forward, their footsteps loud in the oppressive silence. Avék stood off to one side, though Imari hadn't recognized him initially. Like the saredd guarding the door, Avék wore the traditional black saredd cloth and headwrap, but his silver karambits finally gave him away. Tarq and Jenya, who were similarly dressed, kept watch upon the portico.

Her papa was not testing fate this morning.

The small council looked on, uncertain glances flickering between Imari, Ricón, and Sar Branón. Trying and struggling to piece their curiosity into a clear and proper picture.

Ricón stopped before the dais, and Imari stopped beside him. Up close, Anja looked dreadful. The thick kohl around her eyes failed to hide the heavy bags beneath them, splotches of anger blushed her cheeks, and she was dressed in the melancholy black of mourning.

This doesn't bode well, Imari thought, and suddenly wished Anja had stayed at Jadarr this morning.

"Mi sar," Ricón said.

Sar Branón acknowledged Ricón with a look, and gave Imari a slight, approving nod.

"What is this about?" Jeol demanded. Jeol had always been a demanding sort of person. Miserly too. Which was, consequently, how he'd become master of coin. He was never miserly with his accoutrements, however: many rings pinched his stubby fingers, and a thick gold chain graced his neck.

Bayék's shrewd gaze slid from Anja to Imari, and there it focused. Like a lens contracting sunlight onto a sheet of parchment, burning a hole.

Imari's heart pumped faster.

Sebharan, who had no margin for suspense, sat forward and asked, "Well? Is *she* why you left, Sur Ricón?"

"Yes," Ricón said simply.

"And who is she?" Bayek asked.

A beat.

Imari's palms began to sweat as she waited for those fateful words to fall.

"My daughter."

Sar Branón's words dropped at a whisper, but they filled every space, every nook and high corner, reverberating in the hall long after he had spoken them.

The council stared, bewildered and perplexed, and Imari's heart drummed so loudly she was certain all could hear it.

"But Sorai is—" Bayek started.

"Not Sorai."

Bayek's lips hung open in a rare moment of obfuscation, and a silence followed such as Imari had never heard in this place. Every pair of eyes fixed on her in utter disbelief while the truth stood tall and breathed. Even Tarq and Jenya peered over from the portico, curious how this would play out.

Imari forced herself to keep from fidgeting. To not wither beneath their stares and scrutiny. Instead, she gazed steadily at her papa while drawing strength from Ricón's solid presence beside her.

It was the Kourana who finally shattered that brittle silence. "I watched my kahar lay her in the vault. I prayed over her dead body myself." Her shrewd gaze landed on Sar Branón like a swift gavel of judgment.

"It was an herb," Sar Branón said without remorse. "A tincture Gamla made. For me."

These words settled in, dropping more pieces into their puzzle, giving clearer shape to the truth.

"You...*lied* to us," Jeol said.

"I did," Sar Branón admitted. "And I am sorry."

"Sorry?" the Kourana said sharply. "Mi sar, your daughter committed an egregious sin against the gods, and you *hid* her. *Without* atonement."

Imari wanted to mention that she had spent the last *ten years* atoning for her sin, but Ricón seemed to sense this and squeezed her arm a little harder.

"Is it any wonder Istraa suffers now?" the Kourana continued with rising enmity, glancing about the council for support, before looking back at Sar Branón. "You hid this transgression rather than offering restitution, as required by the gods—"

"It wasn't a transgression; it was an accident," Sar Branón countered fiercely. "A *terrible* accident. I lost one of my daughters, Kourana Vidéa. Surely, you cannot fault me for not wanting to lose both."

But the Kourana was unmoved.

"You have sinned against the gods, and now all of Istraa is suffering for it." The Kourana leaned forward, one rigid finger raised. "*This* is why the gods have not answered our prayers."

"How relieved you must be to finally have a scapegoat for your failing kahars," Ricón said lowly.

The outburst surprised Imari—it surprised Kai and her papa too, judging by their startled expressions—and then Imari thought maybe Ricón hadn't squeezed her arm to keep *her* quiet.

And his words were like a bolt of lightning upon dry grass.

The hall suddenly ignited with shouts and accusations, while Sura Anja looked on with righteous satisfaction.

"You spit on the gods—" the Kourana snarled.

"—betrayed us all!" Bayek shouted.

"—deserves death—" Jeol added.

Imari couldn't take anymore. "Please stop!" she shouted over the din.

Only Sebharan and Bayek heard her.

Imari growled in frustration and broke free of Ricón's hold, which got his attention too. "All of you—stop! *Please!*"

The Kourana stopped yelling at Sar Branón, if only out of irritation at being interrupted, but now Imari had all of their attention.

She took another step, as if to take hold of the floor, the hall. "Sar Branón speaks the truth. What happened was an accident, *I swear*. I never meant to hurt Sorai, and—"

"You are nothing but poison to this family, and I curse the day I chose not to leave you on Vondar's front steps to die."

The words had come from Sura Anja, and the contempt in her voice made Imari forget whatever else she'd been about to say.

"Anja." Sar Branón glared at his wife.

But Anja stood abruptly, facing her husband. Then the council. "I've had enough."

"Anja, sit down and—" Sar Branón started.

"*No*. I will not sit here while you insult our daughter's memory by claiming that Liagé bastard as your own." Her gaze cut to Imari, searing like a branding iron.

"*Mama*." It was Ricón this time.

But Sura Anja descended the dais's steps, black skirts billowing in her dark storm. The sura stopped before Imari and gazed at her with such loathing it stole Imari's breath.

"Mi sura, I am *sorry*," Imari said, knowing the words would never undo what she had done, but she didn't know what else she could say, and she wanted so desperately for Sura Anja to stop hating her so completely.

But Anja's expression only twisted. Imari thought the sura might strike her, but Ricón took a step, shielding Imari from his mama, and Anja turned that scalding gaze upon her oldest son.

"Mama, *please*," Ricón said through clenched teeth.

Anja's expression tightened painfully, and she walked on in her storm of fabric and electric rage, footsteps clicking furiously down the hall, until she shoved through the doors.

Gone.

Imari flexed and opened her hands, clenching her teeth to hold her composure, but all she wanted to do was run—run right back through those doors, and far away from all of this.

"Tell them why you're here now," Sar Branón said.

Sar Branón's words broke through her grim and spiraling thoughts, and she caught his gaze, the meaning in them clear.

Remember what we talked about, his expression said.

Imari breathed deep, gathered herself, and tried to focus. "I was discovered by Corinth's Head Inquisitor," she said at last, addressing the council.

This wasn't the place her papa had wanted her to start, but it was the place she needed to. She'd had some time to consider her papa's words after he'd left, while the servants had been scrubbing her skin raw.

Sar Branón frowned.

"Corinth knows you're alive?" Bayek snapped, watching her. The entire council watched her, and new tension settled in the quiet.

Because Imari's very existence sat in defiance of Provincial law. It inherently pitted Corinth against them, thus creating enmity with the remaining Provinces—which was the very last thing any of them needed or wanted.

It was also *exactly* why Imari had started with this, specifically: she could not have her papa's council believing Jeric—or Hagan, for that matter—had been holding her ransom, because that would be considered an act of war. Which meant more problems for Jeric, and the very last thing Imari wanted was to widen the chasm between their nations.

"Yes," Imari answered. "But King Jeric is not a problem—"

"Corinth is always a problem," Jeol murmured, and the Kourana sneered with agreement.

"I assure you that—"

"*How* did Corinth discover you?" Bayek interrupted.

Imari exhaled, her nostrils flared. "That, I don't know exactly, but the Head Inquisitor is gone. King Jeric has deemed him a traitor, and he's been exceedingly generous due to any damages caused. I assure you that we have no enemy in Corinth."

"Then why risk holding you at all?" Bayek asked. "He kept you a secret from the other provinces, which leads me to conclude that Tommad had personal reasons for holding you ransom—"

"Tommad didn't—" Imari started, but Jeol cut her off.

"Well, we all know King Tommad grossly overspent Corinth's resources." Jeol absently turned a ring on his finger as he looked to Bayek. "Perhaps he wanted us to repay his debts. He's got plenty of them, particularly with Brevera, and from what I've heard, Brevera is starting to collect on that debt."

Bayek nodded in confirmation. "The Angevins have always been guided by gold, and Hagan was even worse. It's probably best he's gone, though I don't like the idea of a Wolf ruling—"

"They were not holding me ransom," Imari cut in, frustration leaking into her voice. "King Jeric wants to work *with* Istraa. It's why he released me as soon as it was safe to do so."

"You seem to be…intimately aware of the Wolf's motivations," the Kourana said. Her tone baited, but Imari did not bite, though she felt her papa watching her also.

"I am," Imari answered, staring straight back at the Kourana. "I'm the surina of Istraa, and it would have been extremely shortsighted of Corinth's new king to not thoroughly absolve himself of guilt in a matter that would put his people in danger of war."

The Kourana tilted her nose to the heavens, her lips pursed.

"You're Liagé."

Bayek's words struck so suddenly, and so unexpectedly, given the path the conversation had taken, that it took Imari by surprise. Judging by the rigid postures of her brothers and papa, it had taken them by surprise too.

Undoubtedly why Bayek had cast that hooked line.

"It was never about the flute, was it? It was *her*." Bayek jabbed a damning finger at Imari. "It was *always* her."

"*No*," Ricón said, when Imari didn't deny it. "It was the flute that—"

"Is it true?" the Kourana asked sharply, her gaze shifting between Imari and Sar Branón.

"This is—" Sar Branón started.

"I want to hear it from her," Bayek said, eyes still fixed on

Imari. "You lied to us about the very existence of your daughter. I want to hear *her* answer. I *think* you owe us that much."

A silent exchange passed between Bayek and Sar Branón, and Sar Branón finally looked to his daughter in silent fury.

"Imari?" He didn't bother hiding the fury from his voice, either.

All eyes fixed on her then. The Kourana sat forward, gazing at Imari down her straight and narrow nose.

"I..." Imari stopped, clenched her teeth. She looked at her papa, at Ricón and Kai, who expected her to say exactly what they had asked her to say, but...

She was so tired of lying—of being who everyone else needed her to be. And if she'd learned anything during her time in The Wilds, truth was always discovered, and Bayek would ferret out hers eventually. He was master of secrets for a reason, and she had been the greatest secret of all.

And she did not want to start a life here based on lies.

"I thought it was the flute," she continued, feeling Ricón's attention burn in her periphery. "We all did. Sar Branón did not lie about that. But I have recently discovered that the power lies within *me*."

Sar Branón's face turned crimson and he closed his eyes.

Kai pressed his lips together and glanced away.

Beside her, Ricón only stared.

"I knew it," the Kourana hissed with satisfaction.

Jeol tapped his ringed fingers.

Sebharan, alone, looked intrigued.

Bayek stared at Imari, and a crease formed between his brows. It was clear that he had not expected Imari's honesty. He looked straight at Sar Branón and then sat back in his chair. "I am sorry, mi sar, but I stand with Sura Anja. If Imari were anyone else, her life would already be forfeit."

"It was an accident, Bayek," Sar Branón said through his teeth. "Imari is not a danger to—"

"I agree with Bayek," the Kourana interrupted, sitting up straight in her high-backed chair. "The saints are quite clear on the point of the Liagé. Harboring her, within Vondar's walls, after you've already turned the gods against us with your lies—"

"I am not the reason your kahar are being burned alive in your temples," Imari cut in, and the Kourana blinked. "I am not the reason your labor is vanishing"—here, she looked at Jeol —"and I am certainly not the one orchestrating it." On this point, she looked at Bayek. "So don't pin your failure to protect Istraa on me."

This time, Kai bent his head forward and rubbed his temples.

Ricón, however, looked away, and Imari thought it was probably to hide a grin.

The Kourana sat forward, seething. "You're not in a position to—"

"With all due respect, Kourana, I am the surina of Istraa. Last I understood, that position stood above yours."

The hall fell silent.

Yes, Ricón was definitely hiding a grin.

"Istraa is already divided," Imari continued, addressing the full council. "I understand that the timing of my arrival is inconvenient for everyone, but here we are. Do not divide Istraa more by turning us against each other. I am not your enemy; neither is Corinth. The fact of the matter is that we *do* have an enemy currently hiding within our borders, that no one seems able to find, and I have a skill that might allow me to help." Imari paused, looked into each of their faces. "*Let me help*. I know I can. Let me help you find this leader before more Istraans die."

Imari's words were met with quiet. A charged and uncertain kind of quiet. The Kourana sat back in her chair, still seething. Jeol turned his rings. Bayek watched her, frowning in the way people did when they were mildly impressed against their will.

Thankfully, her papa did not look so angry anymore. In fact, he almost looked pleased.

Sebharan sat forward. "If you truly are Liagé, and the Head Inquisitor found out about it, what did Corinth want with your power?"

The leader of the saredd and all the guard studied Imari with open curiosity, no malice to his voice. No emotion at all, really. He simply wanted the facts—untainted and unbiased—so that he could make his best judgment. For that alone, Imari could have kissed him.

She didn't, of course.

Her papa nodded encouragingly. "Go on, Imari. Tell them what you told me."

Imari explained everything, much as she had to her papa this morning, and once she finished the part about Astrid, with particular emphasis on her own role in subduing the legion, a heavy silence descended over the great hall. Glances flitted between the council, Bayek settled back with unease.

It was better than contempt, Imari mused.

Ricón glanced over at her and nodded once, fractionally. *Well done*, his eyes seemed to say.

"Could it be related to what's happening here?" Jeol said to Bayek, who was staring absently at Imari while rubbing his chin.

"I believe so," Ricón answered this time. "I had a fruitful conversation with King Jeric before my return, which led us both to believe that Corinth and Istraa are suffering at the hands of some common enemy. Who that is, neither of us could determine, but Imari is correct: the Wolf King wants to work *with* us, to get to the bottom of this. Particularly to find out what happened to his sister. With Imari's help, of course." Ricón glanced sideways at Imari, and Imari gave him a small smile in return.

"Well, dashá," Jeol said at last, heaving a sigh.

Then, quiet.

"I agree," Sebharan said suddenly, and everyone looked to the Qazzat master. Sebharan, however, looked only at Imari. "We need your help, surina."

Imari detected no subversive machinations in his words, just fact. A man of black and white, concerned only with which pieces to place on a battlefield and how best to deploy them.

"Sebharan," the Kourana said, her tone dripping with righteous condescension. "We cannot let desperation drive us to employ methods that the gods have strictly forbidden—"

"The power Corinth has faced is beyond any of us," Sebharan replied, still matter-of-fact. "The gods have entrusted us with Istraa's protection, and the fact remains that Skyhold would have fallen to a demon had it not been for Imari's power." Here, he gestured at Imari. "Our own surina. And being that the enemy has not been subdued or eradicated, it would be wise to consider asking Imari to stand beside us. Unless you enjoy watching your kahar burn."

The Kourana bristled, her lips forming a firm line.

"Still, the timing..." Bayek's gaze narrowed, considering. His hand dangled over the arm of his chair, his fingers dancing. Tickling various ideas. "The rois and roiesses might think it's a trick. That *she's* the heretic leader, using *this* throne as means to liberate their Sol Velorian labor. And if Naleed suspects...your throne is lost."

Imari hated that Bayek had referred to the anonymous Liagé leader as a heretic. As if the power alone made the person evil.

"There's also the question of how the other Provinces will react once they discover your lie," the Kourana added sharply, her anger straining on its leash. "Granting a Liagé this position of power, despite her birthright, is a direct violation of Provincial law."

Jeol frowned with a nod.

"King Jeric already knows the truth about me," Imari said, reminding them. "And he has not moved against us."

"*Yet*," the Kourana snapped. "How do we know the Wolf isn't allying the other Provinces against us as we speak?"

Imari felt a swift and defensive rush of anger. "If Jeric meant to attack us, he wouldn't have asked Ricón to bring me home."

Bayek's eyes narrowed on her, and Imari silently cursed herself for using Jeric's familiar name.

"Perhaps it was a trap," Jeol suggested.

"For what benefit? He had every reason to keep me, based on those laws Kourana Vidéa just mentioned, but *he did not*. He did everything in his power to see that I was brought home safely." She left out the part where he'd given her a thousand crowns, so that she'd have options—options she was still entertaining.

Bayek's gaze probed deep. "You put far too much trust in that *corazzi*."

She trusted "that corazzi" far more than she trusted any of them, but she stopped herself before the words toppled out of her mouth.

"However." Bayek looked at the Kourana. "I have not caught wind of any collaborations against Istraa."

"You also had no notion of Surina Imari's existence, so forgive me if I don't place all of my faith in your abilities," the Kourana said.

"Perhaps if my words came with coin, you'd place more faith in them—"

"Bayek," Sar Branón interrupted, giving him a sharp look.

Bayek bristled, but quieted.

"The point remains," Sar Branón continued, "that we need to figure out how to explain Imari without it resulting in the rois and roiesses usurping my throne."

Sar Branón's words had the intended effect, and everyone looked to Imari as if she were a difficult knot to untangle. Their decision about Imari affected each of them directly, because Sar Branón had appointed them to their positions, and if Sar Branón were overthrown, their positions were also forfeit.

"We don't," Kai said suddenly, drawing all eyes.

Kai glanced at Imari, at the others. "We don't say a word about Imari until we catch the heretic."

That word again.

Both of Bayek's brows climbed his forehead. "You think we can hide a *surina*? I'm flattered by your faith in my abilities, mi sur, but even I'm not *that* good."

"No, you misunderstand me. I'm not saying we don't mention her at all. I'm suggesting we don't mention her *as Imari*."

Kai's words were met with interest.

Imari frowned. They had not discussed this last night.

"Then who would she be?" the Kourana asked with condescension.

Kai looked at her. "Sable, our new healer. A student of Gamla Khan himself."

Imari stared at her brother.

"Ah, yes." Jeol brightened, catching on, and waving one of those ringed fingers around. "She's had years of practice; she said it herself. And we do need another healer, now that Gamla is gone."

In Imari's periphery, Avék flitted two fingers in agreement.

"So your answer is...to keep lying," Imari said flatly.

"Only until we catch the heretic," Kai replied.

Imari flinched. "And then what happens?" she snapped. "Continuing to lie to the people will only make the truth harder to—"

"I think it wise," Bayek cut in. He'd stopped tapping his fingers and sat up straight in his chair. "Let the people get to know her first. Let *us* get to know her. She may serve and care for Istraa—prove her loyalty and devotion to our people. And then, perhaps, there will be no need for trial. I can help there, spreading word about our new healer and all the good she is doing for Trier."

This received a nod from Jeol and a slight tip of the head from Kourana Vidéa.

"It's a good idea," Sebharan said.

Imari, however, felt increasingly hostile. "The only thing you're going to prove is that I'm a liar, and I deserve to be feared."

"They won't fear you when you bring the heretic to justice," Bayek said, now fully on board. "They'll understand why we lied, and they will revere you for it."

"I don't care about heroics—" Imari started.

"*Just* consider it, Imari." Her papa interrupted this time, sitting forward upon his throne. "Bayek is right. Rumors are spiraling about what happened in Corinth, and announcing you right now, after what happened with Astrid..."

He didn't need to finish for Imari to understand.

"But this..." Kai continued eagerly. "*This* is our opportunity to show the people that you are on *our* side. Not theirs."

Our side. Their side. She was neither, and she was both, but before Imari could object, the council voiced their unanimous agreement. Ricón alone remained quiet.

"Well? What do you say, Imari?" her papa asked, looking hopeful for the first time since she'd walked through those doors. "Could you be Sable just a little longer?"

8

Jeric sprinted through Skyhold's dark and empty halls.

Scat.

Scat. Scat. *Scat.*

He turned a corner, took the stairs two at a time, and spotted Galast ahead, keeping watch over the courtyard.

Upon hearing Jeric, Galast turned and stood at attention. "Your Grace...?"

"Find Hersir," Jeric commanded.

Galast did not hesitate, did not ask. He bowed to his king and jogged in the opposite direction, heading for Corinth's Lead Stryker. Finally, Jeric reached the door to the Head Inquisitor's old office, kicked it in, and ducked inside.

Gods, it still smelled like the man. Musty, old, and irritating.

Jeric didn't need a lantern; bright moonlight shone through the tall and narrow windows, illuminating this coveted trove of appropriated Liagé artifacts. It was, as his father had called it, a veritable torture chamber. The jarls had recently demanded Jeric dismantle it once and for all, but he hadn't had the time.

Fortuitous, it seemed to him now.

Jeric rummaged through the shelves, shoving aside jars and

scrolls and books. He crossed to the table, threw open the drawers, and rifled through them.

"Where are you..." he growled. He slammed the drawers shut and moved to the trunk, smashed the lock with Lorath's hilt, and shoved the lid open as he set Lorath aside, then tore through the trunk's contents: maps and Liagé texts and Sol Velorian silk.

One pair of Liagé manacles, enchanted to suppress Shah power.

Jeric set those beside Lorath.

More trinkets, more books. Intercepted correspondences.

Two nightglass blades, compliments of Jeric's last raid.

He set the nightglass beside the manacles.

Jeric frowned at the now-empty trunk. "I know you're here somewhere..." He reached inside and pressed his palms against the trunk's panels, feeling and searching.

There.

Jeric skimmed the panel's seam with his fingers, found the depression, and pushed. The panel clicked and slid away, revealing the small hollow within.

Where a small bundle of cloth lay neatly hidden.

Jeric grabbed the bundle. It weighed exactly what he would have expected, which furthered his hope as he unfolded the cloth wrapping. He lifted the last fold to find the pendant resting within—a small, smooth, and black skal stone engraved with Liagé markings, suspended by a thin leather cord.

The necklace had passed through Jeric's ancestors—a wardstone, gifted by a Liagé enchantress long ago, during a time when Corinth had lived peacefully with the Sol Velor. This wardstone had saved the life of King Tommad the First—Jeric's many-great grandfather, for whom his own late father had been named. The enchanted pendant had shielded him during the war against Azir Mubarék and the infamous Mo'Ruk—Azir's four powerful Liagé generals. Or so Jeric had always been told.

Jeric trailed his fingertips over the etched grooves and held the stone nearer the window. Moonlight reflected off the polished skal, though the etchings remained dark, seeming to absorb the moon's pale glow.

For one hundred years, this pendant had been on display beneath Tommad the First's portrait in Skyhold's great hall. But immediately after the Sol Velorian uprising twenty years ago, led by Azir's descendant, Saád Mubarék, Jeric's father had taken that pendant—and all Liagé artifacts—and had them destroyed.

"We will erase them from this world, starting with the work wrought by their infernal hands."

The Head Inquisitor had insisted they keep a few items, like the Liagé manacles, and his father, seeing their value, had agreed. But King Tommad would not be swayed on account of the heirloom, and thus ordered it destroyed.

It had been Tommad's legacy. He was a torch to the pyre of Liagé heritage, and Jeric had helped him feed the flames, for Jeric had taken all of his findings from his hunts and given them to the inquisitors to erase.

People included.

But Jeric had always suspected Rasmin of keeping more than he'd led on. Jeric could never prove this, of course, nor had it been a priority. This pendant had been of particular interest to the Head Inquisitor, so Jeric had always wondered.

Jeric slipped the pendant over his head and tucked the stone beneath his tunic. The stone warmed at his sternum, soft as a breath—one that did not fade. Just two months ago, Jeric wouldn't have hesitated to imprison a person for owning such an artifact. The irony now was not lost on him.

He wondered, briefly, how things would have been different if he'd worn this pendant into The Wilds. If Hagan had worn it during his coronation.

What a shortsighted father he'd had.

What a shortsighted man Jeric had been.

Jeric gathered the nightglass and the manacles, shoved them

both into a satchel he'd found on a shelf, and left Rasmin's office for Braddok's chambers. When Jeric finally reached Braddok's door, he made a fist and pounded.

No answer.

"*Brad*," Jeric hissed, pounding again, and then he remembered: Braddok had gone to the Barrel. Jeric cursed, and was just starting back down the hall when Braddok's door creaked open.

A haggard Braddok peered through, eyes blinking with delirium. Braddok took one look at Jeric, spotted the satchel slung over Jeric's shoulder, and then slammed the door shut.

Jeric stood there a bewildered second, and then leaned close, palm pressed to Braddok's door. "*Brad. Get dressed. Astrid escaped.*"

The latch clicked, and Jeric lowered his hand as the door slowly cracked open again. Braddok stood there, gaping at Jeric, all traces of somnolence gone, and then he dragged a hand over his face with a groan, as if Jeric were a bad dream he could wipe away. "*Scat.*"

"Would you let me—" Jeric started, but Braddok leaned behind the door to speak to someone within.

Ah.

Braddok hadn't returned from the Barrel empty handed.

Braddok turned back to Jeric, gave him a warning look, and then opened the door completely. Jeric spotted Bria inside, her long brown hair in disarray as she hastened into an overcoat. Jeric hadn't seen her since Braddok's black eye six months ago.

Jeric had never asked. It was an unspoken rule between them.

Braddok whispered something into Bria's ear and kissed her once, quick. She hurried on, ducked through the door, but paused before Jeric.

"Your Grace." She bowed and hurried off down the hall.

Jeric looked at Braddok.

"Don't." Braddok's expression dared as he opened his door wide.

Jeric held up a surrendering hand and strode right in, and Braddok closed the door behind him. "So? What happened?"

Jeric told him what he'd found, how he suspected Astrid had help.

"Who in the five hells would help...*that*?" Braddok asked.

"I don't know, but we need to hurry."

Braddok's gaze sharpened on him. "Wolf. Your coronation is *tomorrow*. Send Hersir—"

"To do what?" Jeric took a step toward his friend. "Hersir can't stop her. You know that."

"Neither can you! Did you forget what she did to you during Hagan's coronation?"

Jeric slid the pendant from beneath his tunic and let it dangle between them. Braddok's eyes narrowed on the pendant, on Jeric. Braddok knew what it was. Anyone raised in the fortress would have known.

But Braddok only looked more resolute. "You don't have a rutting clue how that works. *If* it works..."

"It worked against Azir—"

"We don't know if that's true! Gods, Jeric!" Braddok threw his meaty hands into the air. "Astrid broke through a warded skal door, and you think a godsdamned stone is gonna save you?"

"Why in the hells do you think I'm here right now?"

Braddok stared at Jeric one long, hard moment, and then he closed his eyes, as if closing them would make it all go away.

"Godsdamnit," Braddok relented with a heavy sigh. "How many do you want?"

Jeric looked at Braddok. "The whole pack."

By the time Jeric reached the stables, Braddok was saddled and waiting with the rest of Jeric's pack.

"You gonna tell us what this is about, Wolf?" Chez asked, as Jeric strode for Eide, his stallion.

"No." Jeric checked the straps and secured his satchel.

"Not even a hint?" Aksel pressed.

"Not till we're out of the city."

Aksel and Chez exchanged a glance, and Stanis's brow furrowed.

Jeric's relationship with Stanis had strained since Imari. He hoped bringing Stanis now hadn't been a poor decision on his part, but Jeric needed all the help he could get.

"I'll have you know, I was in the middle of winning a Spades tourney when this lout marched in and interrupted me and all my glory." Chez tipped his chin at Braddok, who scoffed, and said, "You lost three rounds in a row. I saved your sorry ass from a fourth."

"All part of my strategy. I was making a comeback," Chez defended, and Braddok rolled his eyes. "Could at least give me something to soothe my losses."

"I will," Jeric said with a smirk as he climbed onto Eide's saddle. "Once we're out of the city. I don't need more ears." He gestured toward a little door, where the groomsman slept.

Chez grumbled his acquiescence, and some insults Jeric chose to ignore while he took quick inventory of his men, their arms. Satisfied, he guided Eide around and started for the stable doors.

"You told Hersir?" Braddok whispered to Jeric as he brought his mare alongside Eide.

"I did."

"And...?"

"If this doesn't kill me, Hersir might."

Braddok smirked, all big teeth in his wild red beard. "Tell him to get in line."

Jeric chuckled, then gave Eide a swift kick.

The five of them exploded through the stables and galloped down Skyhold's empty and moonlit streets. Once they reached the main gates, Jeric stopped and whistled sharp, gave a quick command to the guard, and the portcullis groaned open. He exchanged a quick look with Braddok, then took the lead. They tore across the open lawn, made silver beneath a full moon, and toward the imposing wall of Blackwood.

There, just outside the dense treeline, Jeric slowed Eide to a halt. The others stopped their mounts behind him.

"Ah, so we *are* going on a little midnight shade hunt," Chez said to Aksel, as he held out his palm.

Aksel groaned and dug into his pocket for what—Jeric imagined—could only be coin.

Jeric dismounted. "Not quite."

Chez frowned, confused, while Aksel said triumphantly, "Ah ha!" and slid the coin back into his pockets.

Jeric dug into his satchel and handed over the two nightglass blades—one to Braddok, the other to Stanis. "I don't have enough for all of us."

Stanis held up the blade and eyed Jeric with confusion.

"I thought you just said we're *not* hunting shades?" Chez asked, clearly still set on his bet.

"We're not," Jeric replied. "We're hunting Astrid. These are preventive maintenance."

A beat.

And then Aksel started laughing.

"Well, scat," Stanis said.

Chez groaned.

"How the hells did she get out?" Stanis asked, and Jeric relayed the story he'd given Braddok.

"And you think *we* can stop her," Chez said dubiously. Braddok gave Jeric an emphatic look.

Which Jeric returned. "No idea," Jeric replied. "But we're going to try."

Chez sat forward in his saddle. "You know, Wolf. These little errands are becoming deadlier by the day. I'm starting to wonder if the risk is even worth the rutting reward..."

"You scared, Chezter?" Braddok taunted.

Chez raised a brow. "Of a demon? Yeah. I am."

"Good. You should be," Jeric said. "We'll probably die."

Aksel laughed and shook his head. "Always so optimistic."

Jeric flashed his teeth. "*But*—" He eyed his men, all serious-ness. "—if we do survive this, I swear you won't want for anything for the rest of your greedy little lives."

"Hm. You sure about that?" Chez said. "Because I'm picturing a hold of my own. Maybe that parcel south of The Fingers, right along the coast—"

"Estwich's?" Aksel asked.

"That's the one. I want his castle. You know, the one that looks over the cliffs..."

Jeric rolled his eyes to the moon, climbed back in the saddle, and gently urged Eide forward.

"Whadya say, Wolf?" Chez said as they all followed Jeric into the edge of the Blackwood. "Think you can afford me? A demon for a hold. Sounds like a fair trade. I get a hold. You get me on your council. Win-win."

Jeric grunted. "Absolutely no seat on my council. I'm not *that* desperate."

Chez chuckled. "Deal. Ah...I can almost smell the sea..."

"That's probably just your own body odor," Stanis mused.

"Since we're bartering..." Braddok chimed in.

"Oh gods, here we go..." Aksel murmured.

"I want the Barrel."

Jeric eyed his friend. "Gods, I already feel bad for Björn."

"I don't. Bastard's cheated me out of enough coin."

Behind him, Stanis snorted. "Chezter asks for a castle, and you want a rutting *tavern*?"

"You pissin' on my dreams, Stan?" Braddok called over his shoulder.

"I just think you could dream bigger."

"All right," Braddok conceded. "Then I'll also hang a huge

sign above the door that says, 'All welcome. Except for Pissin' Stan'."

Chez and Aksel laughed. Even Jeric grinned.

"Shut it," Stanis said, but in good humor.

"You've gotta admit, it's got a nice ring to it..." Aksel added.

"Say it again, and you'll find me pissin' on your head next time you're sleeping."

Jeric's men quieted as they moved deeper into the forest. Shafts of moonlight pierced the thick canopy, illuminating patches of snowy ground below, though a thin fog had settled between snow and bough, shifting like ghosts. Jeric flexed his fingers over Eide's reins and stopped to listen. His men stopped too, just behind him, awaiting his command. They had long since learned to trust their wolf's senses.

Eide shifted beneath him, and his black ears flickered.

"I know, boy," Jeric whispered, rubbing Eide gently between the ears.

Jeric sensed it too.

Though he saw no discernible tracks, something had passed through this place. He felt it in his bones. But whatever it was had gone.

Jeric clucked his tongue, and urged Eide onward.

Eventually, they reached the place where the land sloped down to the Muir's broad banks. There, Jeric stopped Eide, his men fanned out behind him, and the five of them gazed upon the Muir, which snaked through the snowy forest like a river of ink. Suddenly, the wardstone upon Jeric's chest pulsed with warmth.

"What is it?" Braddok asked.

Jeric frowned. "I don't know." He scanned the trees, the river-bank, then gave his men a quick signal and dismounted. They followed suit, weapons ready.

Jeric gave Eide a reassuring pat, then took three steps down the wide embankment, and froze.

Before him, about thirty paces away and situated upon the

Muir's shallow banks, sat the infamous Kissing Rocks—the pair of lone boulders that leaned against each other like lovers, which marked the sewers' exit. But now that Jeric's vantage had shifted, what he'd originally taken for part of those rocks had separated into a figure standing in two inches of water.

The wardstone at his chest burned hotter.

Braddok stopped beside him, following Jeric's gaze with his own.

"She's still here," Braddok whispered. Jeric heard the unease in his voice, though he tried to hide it.

"Wait here," Jeric whispered.

"Like hells—" Braddok started.

Jeric grabbed his arm. "I want to talk to her first. Alone."

"You've already tried—"

"That's an order, Brad."

Jeric rarely used his rank over Braddok, and he hated doing it now, but he needed to do this. He needed to be sure.

Braddok fumed, his furious gaze darting from Jeric to Astrid.

"Fine," Chez replied for them all, slotting poisoned darts onto his weaponized vambrace. "But if she even looks at you wrong, I fire."

"Fine."

Braddok relented. Satisfied, Jeric released Braddok's arm, and then started for Astrid.

With every step, the wardstone at Jeric's chest grew warmer and warmer, though Astrid didn't show any signs that she heard his approach. Wind tore at her tangled mess of hair and her threadbare clothing. Sewage stained her calves, though the river had washed her feet clean.

And the wardstone grew hotter.

Jeric was a dozen paces away from her when she said, without turning, "I knew you'd come."

It was Astrid's voice—full and strong and edged with a malice he'd never heard from his sister, but it was *her* voice.

Jeric stopped with his hand on Lorath's wolf-shaped hilt. "What are you doing—"

"Why her?"

Jeric frowned, not understanding, while the wardstone pulsed steady warmth into his body.

"You risked *everything* for that scab, and yet *I* suffered for years and you did *nothing*."

Jeric's chest constricted, his fingers clenching the ice-cold wolf hilt. "Astrid, I'm sorry. I had no idea—"

"Liar," she snarled. Pale and bloodied hands flexed at her side. "You're *the Wolf*. You did not see it because you did not *want* to."

He hated that she was right.

"I can't fix the past. I know that." He took another step. "But let me help you now. I swear to the gods—"

"Piss on your gods," she hissed. Her last word warped, divided, and she turned around.

Dread and revulsion knotted inside of him.

Astrid's eyes were pure black, her skin ghastly white in the moonlight. Dark gashes scarred her face, and open wounds bled freely. She was all contrast, made of the darkest blacks and the palest whites. Shadows slid beneath her skin and shapes pushed from within, morphing and perverting her once-beautiful features. She was a thing of nightmares and horror. A demon, dressed in skin.

Suddenly, the wardstone burned white-hot and light blazed through his cloak. Jeric gasped in pain, clutching at the pendant through the layers of clothing, and Astrid laughed in mockery. The heat seared like a hot ember against his bare skin, and Jeric grabbed the leather strap and ripped the wardstone from his neck. The light flashed—blinding. So bright Jeric looked away, and when the light finally vanished and his eyes adjusted, the wardstone was gone. It had burned right through the leather strap, leaving charred ends dangling in the breeze as little bits of ash floated to the ground.

"What a hypocrite he is." Astrid's voice was gone; the legion spoke to him now. "Wearing the artifacts of the very ones he hunted..." The legion made a tsk-tsk-tsk sound.

Jeric dropped the leather strap and glared at the thing occupying his sister. "Let her go, demon."

The legion smiled wickedly with Astrid's chapped and bloodied lips, and an otherworldly glow lit her black eyes. "Come and take her."

Shadows moved in Jeric's periphery, and a hooded form passed through the thin fog, beneath a shaft of moonlight.

A silent.

Jeric couldn't fathom why one of Ventus's silent were here, but there was no time to consider. Jeric's scars suddenly flared, and a slinking creature appeared behind Aksel and Stanis.

"Shade!" Jeric yelled at his men.

Another shade leapt from the trees, for Braddok.

Jeric sprinted, drawing Lorath and abandoning Astrid, but he'd only made it four paces before the silent landed in front of him, blocking his path.

The silent hissed, teeth bared, and rushed him so fast, Jeric barely managed to deflect.

Gods, he'd forgotten how fast they were.

"Watch out, Stanis! Their claws are poison!" Jeric heard Braddok yell.

Braddok tried to get to Jeric, to help him fight the silent, but a third shade appeared, cutting him off.

The silent whirled, driving Jeric back, farther and farther, strike after powerful strike. Jeric searched for an opening, but the silent was too quick, too—*everywhere*. It was all Jeric could do to hold it off. And then—finally—Jeric found his opening. He feinted right, forcing the silent left.

Directly into Jeric's well-positioned dagger.

The silent arched with a wail, but before Jeric could pull his dagger free, the silent wrapped long, powerful fingers around Jeric's wrist, holding him firm, and plunged its own dagger into Jeric's side.

"Wolf!" Braddok screamed from the trees.

Pain exploded in Jeric's side. He yelled through his teeth and staggered back, Lorath in one hand while his other pressed to the hole in his side. Blood soaked his tunic. The silent licked the blood from its dagger and smiled viciously, teeth stained with blood, and then it lunged again.

But Jeric anticipated it.

He took one calculated step, arched Lorath overhead, and severed the silent's head from its body. The body collapsed in a heap, while the head bounced and rolled to a halt at Astrid's bare feet.

Jeric heard quick steps behind him, followed by a sharp *thwick* and a canine whimper as the last shade skidded to a fatal end with a nightglass blade protruding from its skull.

"Impressive," said the legion, those black eyes observing the carnage without emotion.

Jeric leaned a little, struggling to stay standing as he gazed down the flat of his blade, at Astrid. "I'll ask you once more." He heaved a breath. "Let her go."

The legion vanished in a cloud of darkness that reappeared—impossibly—*right* in front of him. "Silly wolf. You should have stayed in your cage."

Jeric didn't have time to react. Astrid's palm struck his chest where the wardstone had seared his skin. Something cracked, and Jeric was flying. He collided with the ground, breath punched from his lungs as pain shot through his ribs. His men yelled and ran for him, but the legion raised a palm, spoke a word. Energy pulsed in a burst of air. It struck his men in one concussive blast, and they went flying backward.

Jeric was pushing himself up when Astrid dug a knee into his spine and shoved him to the ground.

Pain lanced his ribs again, and Jeric gritted his teeth. "You won't...win."

Astrid grabbed a fistful of Jeric's hair and jerked his head back, leaned close. Her breath stunk of rot and decay. "We already have."

Jeric writhed, struggling to break free of her grip, but her fingers would not yield.

And then Astrid opened her mouth wide and vomited nightmare.

Inky darkness leaked out of her lips and poured onto the soil around him, frothing and hungry and cold, lapping at his body. Tendrils coiled around his arms and legs like vines, and began snaking toward his mouth. Jeric fought—in vain—as dots swam in his eyes.

The darkness touched his lips, burned like ice.

Just then, a bolt of brilliant white-blue light flashed from deeper in the trees. Astrid screamed, a horrible, dissonant wailing sound. Air exploded above him, the pressure surrounding him vanished, and Astrid landed ten feet away on her back. She flipped onto all fours, teeth bared like a wild animal, and with a furious snarl, she bounded off into the hazy trees.

Jeric rolled onto his back, straining to breathe as his vision swam. She'd broken one of his ribs. Possibly two. And he was losing too much blood.

"Brad...?" Jeric called out, though he couldn't get a full breath. "Stanis?"

He staggered to his feet just as a dark shape melted from the shadows.

Godsdamnit. It was another silent.

9

Gamla leaned against the unforgiving bars of his cage as blood dripped into a nearby basin with a constant and tinny *plink*.

Plink.

Plink.

Gamla did not know how long he had been there. Weeks. Months. Without the sun, time bled together, distilling into moments of usefulness or uselessness. Gamla tried to find sleep during the latter.

When the necromancer did not have need of him.

But it was also this need that had saved Gamla's life, because Gamla's singular understanding of the human body had proven useful—very useful, indeed.

Candles flared to life like little orange blooms atop skinny black stems, and Gamla winced, blinking fast as the necromancer reentered the cave. The necromancer did not spare Gamla a glance as he carried a body over his shoulder.

This body looked to be in far better condition than the previous four.

Unease tingled at the back of Gamla's neck. It wouldn't be long now.

The necromancer slid the corpse from his shoulders and lay it upon the hard cavern floor. He arranged the corpse's rotted arms out and legs apart, and then he walked to the hanging pig carcass, with its blood dripping into the shallow basin.

Plink.

Plink.

Plink-plink.

The necromancer dipped two fingers into the basin, held them to his mouth, and licked them clean with his studded tongue. His eyes rolled back, his body shuddered, and when he opened his eyes again, a milky white shone within. The light faded and he smiled deliciously, then gathered the basin, set it down beside the corpse, and proceeded to paint a perfect circle around the body—in blood.

Gamla watched the necromancer with equal parts fascination and horror. Gamla had been versed in many ways of healing—even the forbidden kind. But these spells called to another, darker plane.

The necromancer bent over the body and painted symbols upon the corpse, not a care for the maggots writhing in its skin, or the oozing, necrotic tissue. Finally, the necromancer finished, wiped bloodied hands upon his robes, and stood, admiring his work.

And then he turned to Gamla.

Gamla tensed with new habit.

"It is time," the necromancer said. He raised a bloodied palm, spoke a word. Energy pulsed, and Gamla's cage hinged open with a rusty creak.

Gamla limped out of his cage, muscles tight and cramped as the blood flowed back into them.

"Give him the heart." The necromancer pointed a sharp and bloodied fingernail at the corpse.

Gamla hesitated, then grabbed the last human heart he'd suspended in a cylinder of preservative. He'd preserved five in total, though the necromancer had already used four, all stolen from the Sol Velorians' recent dead. Gamla brought this last to the corpse. Up close, Gamla gazed at the face, where maggots wormed in empty eye sockets and the jawbone lay completely exposed. He wondered who it had been. How long it had been dead and where the necromancer had found it.

"The heart," the necromancer repeated, sharply.

Gamla set the cylinder down, returned to the table where his scalpel and forceps lay, and brought those back to the rotten corpse.

And he began to cut.

The stench made him heave, and he would have vomited if he'd had any food left in his stomach. Very carefully, he made incisions over the corpse's chest and used forceps to peel back the old skin. He retrieved the heart from its suspension, pried open the sternum, and then placed the heart into the new hole, preservative dripping everywhere and smearing some of the necromancer's painted symbols.

The air shifted and he felt the necromancer standing over him.

Needle and thread appeared. "Sew him up."

Gamla hesitated, grabbed the needle and thread from the necromancer's bloodied fingers, and began to sew. His nose scrunched from the stench, and he gagged a few more times as beetles scuttled out of the chest cavity. Finally, Gamla finished and staggered back with a cough, eager to get away.

The necromancer bent over the corpse and checked Gamla's work.

"Back to your cage," the necromancer said.

Gamla did not hesitate, and his cage door slammed shut behind him.

The necromancer repainted the symbols Gamla had smeared,

then stood just outside of the painted circle and shut his eyes. More inked symbols decorated the backs of his eyelids.

A breath.

And then...

The necromancer began to chant. Low and constant, a steady percussive beat. As he spoke, he wiped the blood from his fingers onto one cheek, then the other. His forehead, his lips. Until blood smeared his face completely.

His chanting quickened, commanding.

Something about this spell struck Gamla as different than the previous four times.

An unnatural gust of wind ripped through their cave, and all the candles flickered out. But the wind did not stop. It roared in their small space, wild and angry, and the air turned ice cold.

Yes, this was very different.

Gamla hunkered back in his cage, against the bars, trying and failing to see what was happening, as the necromancer's chanting grew louder.

And louder.

Rock groaned, straining against the necromancer's demands. Resisting the urge to spit forth the soul the necromancer wanted.

The ground quaked. Bits of rock broke from the ceiling and Gamla ducked as the pieces fell, slicing his arms.

And then it stopped. All of it stopped.

The candles ignited once more, their flames innocent and calm. Gamla's gaze whirled, resting on the dark heap upon the floor, where the necromancer had collapsed.

For a split second, Gamla's hopes surged. Perhaps the necromancer had finally exhausted his power. Gamla understood enough about Shah power to know that to pull a single chakran from the spirit plane was to test fate.

And this was the necromancer's fifth.

But then, to Gamla's crashing hopes, the necromancer rose,

staggering to his feet as his eyes shone with that milky light. Gamla looked to the circle, where the corpse had been.

Where a naked, and perfectly healthy male body now lay. And though he lacked hair, though his skin was too pale and his features overly pronounced, the man reminded Gamla so much of another.

The man breathed; his back arched with one long and wheezing inhale, as though he'd been underwater for a century. Finally, he sagged back to the floor, his breath slow and even.

And he opened his eyes.

10

Sar Branón turned the key to Gamla's door, pushed it in, and Imari stepped into the waiting darkness.

She'd known her uki was gone, but the complete emptiness of this room pained her. Even when Gamla traveled his usual circuits, there'd always been residual signs of life in this space. Lingering warmth. The bite of incense. But only ghosts greeted her now.

"I should have brought a lantern..." her papa said.

Imari's gaze skirted the shadows and snagged on one: a small lantern, composed of two squashed metal boxes stacked on top of one another, with a jagged appendage rising from the back like a chimney—or a tail, rather. Imari grinned. Her uki had kept that old chimp-shaped lantern, even after all these years.

"Hang on," Imari said, and carefully, so as not to trip over this precious maze of artifacts, she made her way toward the lantern —a lantern Gamla had made in little Imari's honor. Her finger-tips grazed the smooth metal surface, and those tiny metal protrusions that Gamla had fashioned to look like hands. To her delight, the fire-striker still lay in the chimp's metal clutches. She picked kindling out of the jar beside it, dropped it atop the lantern's dark coals, and clicked the fire-striker. Sparks flew; little flames bloomed. Imari cupped her hands and breathed life into those flames until the coals caught fire, and the chimp-shaped lantern glowed with warm, amber light. Its eyes gleamed mischievously as Imari placed the fire-striker back in its hands.

"You were always his favorite," her papa said, closing the door, then added conspiratorially, "Don't tell your brothers."

She grinned. "I wouldn't dare."

Sar Branón's attention turned to the disaster surrounding them. Or, at least, it looked like a disaster to everyone else, but Gamla had always known every item in this place.

"How can I possibly find anything if I put it away?" Gamla would always say.

Imari had tried that line on Tolya once. It hadn't worked.

Books and rolled parchments and glass jars lay everywhere, heaped in piles and shoved on shelves that bowed from the weight of it all. Many of those jars housed poisonous and venomous insects—the source of many antidotes. Dried flowers and herbs dangled from the ceiling's old wooden beams, casting long shadows upon the walls, and Imari could hardly see the tabletops for all the books. A thick wooden screen composed the far wall, but that screen was currently veiled by heavy draperies. Gamla always pulled those draperies closed when he would leave, to keep out the world. Oftentimes, he had closed them when he was here, too.

He'd always preferred plants to people.

Beyond the screen and draperies, though Imari couldn't see it now, stood a wide veranda, where Gamla kept a jungle of potted plants. Where, Imari remembered, a giant ceramic pot sat in one corner, below a particular rod of ironwork that protruded from the wall, which had made reaching Gamla's rooftops possible.

"I never did figure out how he could find anything in here," her papa said suddenly. His attention settled on the small door that led to Gamla's private chambers. A small cot lay within, which her uki had rarely used. "Will you be all right staying in here for the time being?"

Imari gazed upon this achingly familiar space, with its tangled mess of herbs and antidotes and healing books thick as mudbricks. It was like being surrounded by old friends. "Yes, Papa. It's perfect."

And Imari wondered if being Trier's new healer wasn't such a terrible thing after all.

Soon after her papa had left, the servants who'd helped her bathe arrived with attire deemed suitable for Trier's new healer. Imari quickly changed out of the silk and into a long, embroidered tunic with fitted pants—both shaded the rich turmeric of Majutén sand. Imari picked up the complementary winterberry-red sash, but paused.

Wards, she hadn't seen colors this rich since...well, ten years ago. Istraa was renowned throughout the Provinces for its vibrant dyes, which little Imari had adored. But now, Imari could not look at this color without remembering where it'd come from: the color vats in the Ajadd district, tended by Sol Velorians, who were not adequately compensated for their labor.

Imari breathed in deep, trailed her fingers over the soft silk. Jeric had promised to free Corinth's slaves. How in the stars was she going to find equity for Istraa's? After the council meeting, that task seemed impossible. Or at least very far away.

She neatly folded the sash and set it upon her pillow like a problem to be solved later, then strode back into Gamla's office and got to work. Though her uki was not there, she took great care with his inventory. She didn't try to organize it—he'd be furious, if he returned. So instead she simply made note of each item, the location, and quantity, tucking certain elements into a satchel she'd found. It was almost like being in Gamla's company.

She picked up a little jar of clipped aloe. "Oh, Uki..." She sighed. "Where are you?"

Imari had just finished packing the satchel when Sebharan finally arrived. After the council's unanimous decision to hide her in plain sight, as Sable, Sebharan had requested her assistance at the Qazzat, where Istraa's guard and saredd lived and trained.

Avék had accompanied Sebharan, undoubtedly at Ricón's request, since Ricón had other business in the city. Imari had told Ricón she'd be fine, but apparently he had ten years of being an older brother to make up for.

"I'm ready," Imari said, joining them in the hall.

"Good," Sebharan said simply. Always a man of efficiency.

She pulled her turmeric shawl over her head, slung her satchel over her shoulder, and followed Sebharan and Avék out of Vondar and into Trier's dry and dusty streets.

Puffy clouds blocked the midday sun, and a stiff breeze shoved through the crowded buildings, threatening colder weather. But no matter how badly winter struck the desert, it was nothing compared to a winter in The Wilds, and for the first time in years, Imari found herself actually looking forward to it. Still, she hugged her shawl close, already missing the warmth of Jeric's cloak—really, just missing *him*—but she didn't dare wear his gift now.

They eventually reached the Qazzat. Unlike the rest of this city, with its color and chaos and life, the Qazzat was a discipline of black and white. Right and wrong. No excess or waste. Not even with its architecture. The main building was rectangular in shape, rising straight and tall and proud. A rigid row of cathedral-cut windows had been carved right out of the pristine white stucco, and within each arch stood a saredd, pure black against the white. An enormous statue of Sareddi—the Istraan warrior god, for whom their saredd had been named—stood in the courtyard at its feet. His chiseled face was hard and severe, and he observed the world through crossed marble scims, as if forever defending his righteous stronghold from evil.

It struck her that Sareddi was Istraa's equivalent for Lorath— the Corinthian god Jeric had served above all others. Both gods stood for justice, leaving no room for mercy. Only what was right according to their law, and death for those who defied it. Jeric's god had demanded Imari's life, but Jeric had not given it. In fact, he'd given her something else entirely: friendship.

And...maybe something more.

They reached the Qazzat's main doors, and Sebharan exchanged a quick word with the saredd standing guard. The guard pushed the doors in, Sebharan stepped through, and he motioned for Imari and Avék to follow.

Imari had never been inside the Qazzat. She wasn't sure what she'd expected, but it wasn't this. The room within was almost as large as Vondar's great hall, but instead of travertine and palms, it housed a training yard. Saredd paired off and sparred while a dozen spectators looked on and took note. Imari found herself watching too, because the saredd form was an art. A religion. Their technique was as beautiful as it was deadly, like the night-shade she'd grown in The Wilds. Admire from afar but handle with care, or it meant swift and sudden death.

Above the arena, a black banner fell like a ribbon, and embroidered across its face were the words: Hazzet Fiatá.

Always faithful.

Always faithful to Sareddi, god of war. A god that despised Liagé.

Sebharan motioned for Imari and Avék to wait while he approached a severe-looking saredd with a long black and silver ponytail that fell to the red sash at his waist. Imari thought of the sash she'd left on her bedside, made by Sol Velorian hands. The man with the red sash looked at Imari, his dark eyes appraising her while Sebharan continued speaking, and then both men approached.

"Alma Sable," the severe-looking man said, tilting his head with respect. Alma—healer. "I am Fenuk, the head instructor here. Thank you for coming."

"Of course," Imari replied swiftly, feeling the point of Avék and Sebharan's attention like a scim at her throat. "I am happy to be of service. Where are you keeping your ill?"

"In the barra. I'll take you there now."

Fenuk led them through a small door in back, which led to a private courtyard filled with targets and weapon racks and guards. Fenuk took a path to the side that hugged the wall of an adjacent building, well out of harm's way. Imari started to follow, but then she spotted a Sol Velorian boy on the opposite side of the courtyard.

The boy looked about ten, wearing scraps too large for his skinny frame, and his head had been shaved. The boy carried a shoulder yoke bigger than he was, with two full water pails dangling from each end. The load bent his back and bowed his shoulders, and it would eventually deform him, making him useless in the eyes of his masters. Imari had seen it before.

And for the Sol Velor, uselessness was condemnation.

Imari watched the boy bear that impossible load, adjusting his balance with an iron will as he approached his destination: a trough at the courtyard's edge, so the guards could drink.

The little boy met Imari's gaze.

Imari had the strangest sensation that she'd seen him before, but that couldn't be right. He wouldn't have been alive when she'd been a little surina, but there was something undeniably familiar about those dark eyes, and the power in her belly stirred.

The boy's eyes opened wider, his lips parted, and then he lost his balance.

Imari watched in slow horror as the boy pitched forward and the pails flew, dumping water all over the stones. The guards stopped and looked over. Fenuk, however, stormed right over to the boy, grabbed him by the collar, and jerked him to his knees.

"Sorry, I—" the boy started.

Fenuk struck the boy across the face so hard it sent the boy sprawling to the ground.

Imari's heart lurched. *No.*

"Pick it up, you damned scab." Fenuk ripped a whip from his belt and snapped it across the boy's back.

The air cracked; the boy cried out.

It happened so fast that for a blink, Imari could not process what was happening. Blood began soaking the boy's tunic, and Fenuk raised the whip again.

"No...*stop it!* Leave him alone!"

Fenuk stopped, whip raised, and everyone looked to the one who had dared interrupt. Sebharan, who had been waiting at the end of the path, started back toward Imari, while Avék glared at her with warning.

Fenuk stood at full height, his dark gaze fixed on Imari. "Who in Shael do you think you are?"

"Calm down, Fenuk," Sebharan cut in sharply. "Our new alma has come from a small village in the Baragas, and she's still learning the rules around here." He looked at Imari, as if he'd said it for *her* benefit, and not Fenuk's.

"It's my fault the boy fell," Imari said, fighting the urge to grab that leather cord and whip Fenuk with it. "I distracted him, and I didn't think he should be punished—"

"That is not for you to decide," Fenuk snapped. "This is my field. Stick to yours."

Imari's hand flexed around her satchel's strap. Avék's eyes held warning, and the courtyard watched. In her periphery, the boy gathered his yoke and pails, and hurried off.

"Sable," Sebharan said suddenly. His gaze darted from Fenuk to Imari, and Imari could see that he already regretted his decision to bring her here.

Imari tipped her chin at Fenuk. "My apologies." She looked at

Sebharan then, and only at Sebharan, before she lost all self-control.

Sebharan gestured for Imari to go on, as if he didn't trust her to follow. Imari turned her face from the place where the boy—now gone—had fallen, and walked on while the courtyard resumed sparring. Avék kept pace beside her, and Imari's anger festered and burned.

Istraa had employed Sol Velorian labor for as long as she could remember, but little Imari had never seen...this. She'd suspected it happened, yes. From the murmurings and attitudes of some toward the Sol Velorians, like Tarq. Little Imari had not given these things a second thought, and right then, she hated herself for that. That she'd never questioned, that she'd never cared.

Not until she'd realized she was one of them.

And here she'd always believed the Wolf the monster.

These thoughts nicked at her as she followed Fenuk down a narrow stair and to a structure that wasn't as well tended as the rest of the Qazzat. Its stucco cracked and crumbled, and many of the roof tiles were broken. Fenuk opened the wooden door, and Imari was immediately struck with the stink of disease and... chamber pots.

Maker's Mercy.

Behind her, Avék cleared his sinuses.

Imari held her shawl over her nose, though it did little to dull the stench as she ducked through the door and into a small, dark room. There were two windows, but their shutters were closed, and she counted nine pallets of straw on the ground. All but one of them were occupied.

"Why are the windows shut?" Imari asked tersely.

"I was trying to keep the illness confined," Fenuk replied.

"If you confine it, it'll never leave." Imari strode around the pallets, careful not to step on anyone, and threw open the shutters to let in light and fresh air. Someone moaned at her feet, and

Imari glanced down. It was a man about her age. His cheeks were sunken and sallow, and judging by the particularly fetid stench coming from his chamber pot, she deduced how he'd lost his mass.

Again, she saw Fenuk strike that little boy.

Wards, she should let them all rot.

"Where can I dump these?" Imari gestured at the pots, thankful for a task to channel her growing rage.

Fenuk showed her the hole where they dumped human waste, and then he and Sebharan left her to it—thank the wards. She could hardly stand to be in Fenuk's presence a second more.

Avék stood near the door, watching her closely while she worked. He didn't offer help; she wouldn't have let him if he'd tried. She needed this time alone, to work through her anger.

Imari tested each man's temperature and color, and she spoke briefly with the conscious ones. Two suffered nasty infections from knife wounds, and aside from the man suffering an intestinal issue, the rest had fallen ill with a respiratory disease. She moved beds around to reduce further contamination, trimmed necrotic tissue, and once she'd finished all she could for the day, she left the bottle of Rosaca—an astringent—and jar of soprese fibers on a stool, and joined Avék outside. There she stopped and closed her eyes, breathed in deep. Trying to clear her lungs, her head.

Trying—and failing—to shake this gnawing rage.

"You're very good," Avék said quietly, but his compliment only fueled her anger.

Imari's eyes snapped open, but she did not meet his gaze as she said, tightly, "Shall we head back?"

IT WAS late afternoon by the time Imari returned to Vondar. She immediately set to work making tonics and remedies for the next day, while Avék resumed his post outside of her door. She was busy tying together herb blends when Ricón came to check on her. He'd spent the day with Kai in Trier, making political rounds, and he'd brought encouraging reports from Sebharan. Specifically that "Trier's new healer" had "already eased the pain of Istraa's elect."

Imari had cringed at those words, and took it out on the string in her hands, which snapped as she tied a knot.

Ricón hadn't noticed.

In addition to this news, he'd also brought a tagine of spiced lamb, chickpeas, and carrots. Normally, the smell alone would have made her salivate, but right then, her stomach turned. She could not shake the memory of that boy. His wide eyes when he'd spotted her. So strangely familiar. And then she saw Fenuk, whipping his little back.

Ricón talked on while Imari absently dipped her flatbread in sauce, occasionally nodding her head so he wouldn't suspect her dark mood and distractedness.

"You did well today," Ricón said suddenly.

Imari's bread stilled in her hands.

You did well.

Again, she saw the whip.

"Keep it up, and you might find yourself even more popular than I am." Ricón winked and picked up his glass of nazzat.

Imari dropped her flatbread into the tagine, stood, and walked over to the counter.

"All right, what's wrong?" Ricón set down his glass of nazzat. "You've been quiet ever since—"

"I saw a Sol Velorian boy today."

Ricón stopped at her words and eyed her steadily. As if sensing—and dreading—the direction of this conversation.

"He spilled water, and Fenuk whipped him for it."

Ricón regarded her, hearing everything she did not say, and then he inhaled deeply. "This is nothing new, Imari." He did not say it because he agreed, but to assuage her. "And I daresay that boy lives a better life here than he would anywhere else."

"You think we're *better* because we *only* whip them?"

"That's not what I said."

"It's what you meant."

"No, it isn't." He looked hard at her. "*What I meant* is that at least here, in Istraa, they can earn wages."

"Those aren't wages. They're *crumbs*."

"It's enough for them to buy food and water, and a roof over their heads—"

"How generous of us."

Ricón's eyes flashed. "It's more than *your* Wolf ever gave them."

He meant for the insinuation to rankle her, but she was far too angry for that now. "Funny you should mention *my* Wolf, because last I heard, *he* was setting Corinth's slaves free."

"He'd like you to think so."

"What's that supposed to mean?" Imari shot back.

"Imari." Ricón sat forward and folded his hands with a heavy sigh. "There's no way in Shael that Corinth will free the Sol Velor, and you know it. Their economy depends on those workers. *As does ours.*"

"So you're saying he lied?"

"I'm *saying* that you put far too much faith in him." His eyes searched her face, beseeching. "He is still a wolf, mi a'fiamé. You'd do well to remember that."

"Yes, apparently I have a talent for putting too much faith in people. Especially my own brother."

Ricón looked at her. A muscle worked in his jaw. "That's not fair."

Imari sighed, then leaned against the counter, and folded her arms. "Look." She hesitated. "I don't want to argue, I just..." She stopped, looked at him. Wished she could make him understand. "They're *people*, Ricón. Just like you, and me, but we—"

"They are *not* like you and me," Ricón said, standing now.

"You want to believe that, and I understand why—I do—but we *are not* the same, Imari... Saints! I don't need to tell you this! You saw it with your own eyes! You know what their Liagé can do. Istraa does not have the ability to fight that kind of power."

Imari stared hard at her oldest brother. "So what you're really saying is that you're afraid."

"Of course I'm afraid!" Ricón threw his hands up. "It terrifies me, and it should terrify you too, but instead you're..."

He realized what he had said, and he shut his mouth. "Imari, I..."

She turned her head away and glared at the counter.

"I'm sorry," he whispered. "I didn't mean it like that."

But he did. He loved her in his own way, but at the end of it, he didn't trust the power flowing in her veins. He saw her how he wanted to see her: as little Imari. The one he had known before, the one who had not challenged his sense of right and wrong.

Ricón saw her in halves. He loved her *despite*. But Imari wanted him to love her *whole*.

"Listen," Ricón said at last. His tone deflated. "I know I can't possibly understand all you're feeling right now, but...I just got you back." He looked deeply into her eyes. "And I'll be damned before I lose you again. Can you just...set this aside for now? Until things quiet down? Be Sable? Take up Gamla's scepter and be our healer. Let the people see that they can trust you. And then we can talk about this." A beat. "Please, mi a'fiamé."

She met his gaze, though a wildfire raged inside of her. "Fine."

His gaze moved over her face, and his lips parted and closed. He seemed to sense that things were not fine. Not at all. That something very important had just happened. But he did not attempt to unpack it just then.

Perhaps he did not want to see what lay within.

Whatever his reason, he seemed eager to move past this and glanced about the room before asking, "Will you come for tea tonight?"

"I can't," she lied.

"Mama won't be there."

Imari shook her head. "I have too much to prepare for tomorrow."

She didn't think he believed her.

But he didn't pry for truth. Instead, he nodded once and started for the door. "If you change your mind, we'll be on the terrace."

She wouldn't.

Ricón stopped at the door and glanced back. Suddenly, the years were like a monster, clawing at the fabric of what had been Imari's most treasured relationship.

Despite.

And then, quietly, he left.

She stood there staring at the door, listening to his footsteps as they retreated. She waited until the sky turned lavender, and the glow of lanterns filled the city, and then she cracked open her door.

Avék glanced over.

"I am going to bed early this evening," she said.

Avék tipped his head, unsuspecting.

Imari closed the door. She exchanged her shawl for a coal-colored one, grabbed a little jar of salve, which she shoved into her pocket, and then she tiptoed to the wooden screen in back and opened the doors. Cold snapped her clothing, and a black night greeted her.

I'm sorry, Ricón, she thought. *But I need to understand the whole.*

Imari climbed onto the large pot and reached for the iron-work, as little Imari had done a hundred times before. And then she was gone.

11

The silent passed through a shaft of moonlight, and Jeric spied a familiar face, disfigured by thick, silvery scars.

"*Tallyn…?*" Jeric clutched his wounded side, hardly believing his eyes.

Braddok, however, had not yet recognized their newcomer, and rushed Tallyn like a battering ram.

"Brad, *wait.*" Jeric strained, staggering forward.

Braddok skidded to a halt, and his eyes widened with recognition. "The hells did *you* come from?"

"I was on my way to find you," Tallyn replied, walking cautiously toward them. "Fortuitous, it would seem."

Aksel limped over, favoring his right leg, and Stanis approached, clutching his bleeding left arm.

"You know this man?" Chez stood a few paces away, aiming a dart at Tallyn's face.

"Yes. From…The Wilds." Jeric's world tilted, and he swayed on his feet.

It did not pass unnoticed.

Braddok took three steps and yanked Jeric's hand away.

Braddok cursed. "Aks. Grab a bandage from my saddle."

"My feet aren't broken, godsdamnit. I can walk." Jeric shrugged Braddok off. The motion threw his balance, and he took a quick step to steady himself.

"Like hells you can," Braddok hissed, then to Aksel he said, "Left side. Hurry."

Aksel started jogging, but stopped abruptly. "So...the horses are gone."

They all glanced over to where their horses had been. Only a patch of trampled snow remained.

Chez groaned.

"So we find them." Jeric took a step, but this time, his knees gave and he dropped.

Braddok caught him. "You aren't going anywhere, your Wolfiness."

Jeric didn't have the strength to argue. He didn't have the strength to say *anything* as darkness crowded his vision.

"He's lost too much blood," Tallyn said.

"Yeah, I see that," Braddok snapped. "Chez, how bout your vambrace?"

"He needs more than a strip of leather."

"No scat, but right now, I'm more concerned with making sure he doesn't bleed out on the way back."

"I might know a trick."

Tallyn's words were met with uneasy quiet.

"With your permission, of course," Tallyn added carefully.

Stanis took a step. "Touch him with your godsdamned sorcery, and—"

"Do it," Jeric managed, wincing.

All his men looked at him, at the blood soaking his tunic, and Stanis didn't utter another word. Jeric's men stepped back to give Tallyn space—except for Braddok, who held the tip of his sword at Tallyn's chest.

"I won't hesitate," Braddok warned.

"I know."

Braddok lowered his sword, but gripped Jeric's arm with his other hand to hold him steady as Tallyn stepped closer. Tallyn lifted the edge of Jeric's shirt and examined the incision without expression, while Jeric fought for consciousness.

"So? Can you fix it?" Aksel asked, straining to see.

"Yes." Tallyn met Jeric's gaze with his one good eye. "But it will hurt."

"Can't be worse than rutting shade poison." Jeric laughed darkly, then winced.

Tallyn looked marginally argumentative, then reached out and pressed two ice-cold fingers to Jeric's wound. Jeric flinched from the contact, watching as Tallyn painted symbols—in Jeric's blood—on both sides of the wound. One above, one below. Tallyn pulled his hand away just a little, letting his bloodied fingertips hover above the wound. He closed his eye and spoke three small words—Liagé words.

Words of power.

Warm air burst from Tallyn's palm and the symbols flared with light, and heat. Those symbols grew brighter—hotter, as their shapes unraveled. Like a knot, untangling before his eyes. The ends reached for each other, the two untangled symbols now threading together into a new, combined pattern. The new symbol formed right over his wound and *melted* the edges of his skin together.

Jeric hissed through his teeth, his body swayed, but Braddok held him firmly on his feet. A strange tingling moved from the wound and into his chest, dulling the ache in his ribs, and when that heat grew almost unbearable, when he thought his molars might crack from clenching, Tallyn dropped his hand and stepped away.

The light vanished, taking the heat and tingling with it, and Jeric felt shockingly...fine. No pain, no exhaustion, no dizziness.

As if he hadn't been injured at all.

Jeric glanced down at himself. Blood still stained his

abdomen, but the wound had sealed shut with a thin seam of congealed blood, and the pain in his ribs was gone completely. He inhaled a full, painless breath.

A trick, Tallyn had said.

That was more than a rutting trick.

"You'll still need to be easy on it," Tallyn said, a little breathless, and his shoulders sagged with fatigue. "It'll need a good washing too. I'm...sorry I couldn't get here sooner."

Jeric looked sharply at Tallyn. "You knew that silent was on its way here."

Tallyn took a moment to catch his breath. "Yes...it was... answering her command."

Jeric's eyes narrowed. He remembered the dead scout, and how Astrid had already known about it. If what Tallyn had said were true, it meant Astrid had reached *beyond* the wards and contacted a silent.

"How does he know that?" Stanis asked.

"Because of his connection to the silent," Jeric answered, and Tallyn did not deny it.

It was the reason Jeric still did not trust Tallyn completely. This alta-Liagé. The nature of magic used to create Tallyn, and the other silent, had bound them to one another. Tallyn's scars disfigured most of the inked symbols that linked him to the others, which was how he'd evaded Ventus in The Wilds all those years, but it had not severed his tie completely.

"Then you also know what she's after," Jeric said.

Tallyn looked straight at Jeric, and a great pit settled in Jeric's stomach.

"She's after Imari."

Jeric's pulse roared in his ears, and he shut his eyes tight.

Gods*DAMNIT*.

This was his fault. All of this was his fault, and now Imari was in danger...

Jeric's eyes snapped open. "Do you have a horse?" he asked Tallyn.

"I came by boat."

Of course. "Is it still in Felheim?"

"Yes, but—"

"And you trust the captain?"

"Wolf...?" Braddok started, sensing where this was going, and moving in direct position to stop it.

"Absolutely," Tallyn replied. "But he leaves at dawn, so you'd better—"

But Jeric was already walking.

"Wolf!" Braddok called after him, jogging to catch up. "Gods-damnit, would you hold on a second?"

"I don't have a second." Jeric kept walking. Felheim was only an hour on foot. If he hurried, he could...

Braddok grabbed Jeric's arm, and Jeric whirled on him in a fury.

Braddok ducked, hands raised. "Would you just listen to me for a godsdamned second—"

"Imari is in danger *because of me.*" Jeric leaned in Braddok's face. His fear was a living, breathing thing. Wild and consuming. "I *have* to warn her—"

"Then send a godsdamned letter! You're Corinth's *king.* You can't just hightail your ass all the way to Trier—"

"I've just unleashed a demon, Brad," Jeric said through his teeth. "Sar Branón will see this as a direct attack. A letter is not enough."

"It's gonna have to be enough, because Corinth needs *you*—"

Just then, Stanis collapsed.

Chez caught him, but barely, and the unexpected weight pushed him into Aksel, who just managed to support all three of them. Stanis's arms now hung limp and exposed, revealing the gash along his left forearm—a gash stained with black.

Jeric cursed and jogged back to his men, while Braddok groaned and followed.

"Is that...shade poison?" Chez asked.

"Aye," Braddok said heavily.

"Do you have it with you?" Jeric asked Tallyn.

Tallyn shook his head. "I used my last of it on you."

"Last of what?" Aksel asked.

"Can you make more?" Jeric asked sharply.

"No. The little I had was given to me. I *can* buy us time by slowing the spread, since it's fresh. But I don't have the power to cure this." Here Tallyn paused. "Imari does."

Braddok glowered, but then Stanis screamed and convulsed, and Braddok cursed. "Imari can fix *this*?"

"With her power, yes," Tallyn replied. "But I must hurry, if he's to have a chance."

"Go ahead," Jeric said without hesitation, stepping back to give Tallyn space.

"Lay him down," Tallyn said to Chez and Aksel, and—with Jeric's help—they lowered Stanis to the ground.

Too well, Jeric remembered the pain. That bitter cold and infinite darkness, and the blood. The taint had never quite left his tongue. Even now, his scars tingled as if responding to their like. If Stanis survived, this would change him forever.

Tallyn crouched beside Stanis and unfastened his tunic, exposing his chest. Jeric's men watched in silence as Tallyn dipped his finger in Stanis's black blood and painted a Liagé symbol over Stanis's heart. He finished, sat back on his heels with his head bowed and eyes closed, and spoke a word. Energy burst —a shock of cold air—and the symbol upon Stanis's heart shone with that strange, white-blue wardlight, and then pulsed like a heartbeat.

A very quick, very frantic heartbeat.

Tallyn began to chant. He spoke the same few words, over and over again, and gradually, the pulsing glyph slowed.

Slower.

And slower.

Until Stanis slackened with unconsciousness.

Tallyn sagged forward and his inhale wheezed. "I will have to...monitor his heart." Tallyn breathed heavily. "How long I can keep it slow depends on him, but...it should be enough to get him to Trier."

Jeric looked at Braddok. "Help me carry him?"

This time, Braddok didn't argue.

THEY REACHED Gilder Sound within the hour. Felheim's harbor was a contrast of silhouettes, made silver by the moon, and a special blend of salt, smoke, and dead fish brewed in the air. From their vantage point, Jeric could see the lights of Gilder Keep —the watchtower carved into the enormous rock jutting from the center of the Sound, adjoined to the world by an impressively high bridge. The Sunguard lived there, keeping watch over all that drifted in from the Yellow Sea.

At one time, these waters had been rife with life. Ships from all over the world—even beyond the Provinces—traded here. That had all ended with Jeric's father, as the Provinces had learned to fear Corinth too. Only locals inhabited the Sound now. Sometimes Davros sailors docked to abbreviate lengthier voyages, but for the most part, Gilder was left to Corinthians.

Tonight, those docks lay empty, save one small canoe bobbing upon the glittering black water.

Jeric looked at Tallyn, who did not appear concerned in the slightest. "Look's like your captain already left."

"No, it's just there." Tallyn gestured at the docks.

Braddok stopped beside Jeric, and wiped his brow. Stanis dangled over his shoulder like a sack of flour. "I don't see a rutting ship."

"Good," Tallyn said simply, and walked on.

Braddok and Jeric exchanged an uncertain glance, and Jeric continued after Tallyn. Thin black wisps of cloud feathered across the brilliant moon, and the wind pushed harder by the water's edge, cutting through Jeric like a cold knife.

"Best wait here," Tallyn said, once they reached the docks. "I need to warn him at least."

"Warn who?" Jeric asked, but Tallyn walked on, leaving Jeric alone with the rest of his words.

"You sure we can trust this..." Braddok started, but his words died as Tallyn stepped off of the dock and onto a boat ramp that hadn't been there a second ago. One moment there was nothing, and then there was a boat ramp.

Suddenly, Tallyn's ability to hide in The Wilds took on an entirely new meaning.

Jeric's lips curled into a grin. *Tallyn, you clever son of a bitch.*

"*The actual hells...?*" Braddok said.

"Please don't drop Stanis," Jeric cautioned.

Braddok, realizing Stanis was, in fact, sliding off of his shoulder, adjusted his position, and both men stared as Tallyn stepped onto a ship that also had not been there a second ago.

"Is that...*The Lady*?" Braddok asked.

"It appears so."

It was the ship that had smuggled Jeric, Braddok, and Imari from The Wilds, across the Hiddensee and to the Black Cliffs of Voiar.

Survak's ship.

Of course Tallyn had taken this ship, but Jeric could not fathom what might propel the old marauder to transport a wolf and his pack all the way to Istraa. Survak hadn't been thrilled about transporting Jeric the first time.

"Bastard's been holding out on us," Aksel mused.

"Careful with your choice of words..." Chez smirked at Jeric.

At the top of *The Lady*'s ramp, two figures stepped into view. Jeric vaguely recognized their faces, but didn't know their names.

Not that it mattered. None of them had liked him very much, though they'd all been quite taken with Imari.

Jeric couldn't blame them.

Seconds labored into minutes, and finally, just as Jeric was about to climb *The Lady*'s ramp regardless of Tallyn's warning, Tallyn appeared with Survak right behind him.

Survak did not look happy.

Wind pushed through the harbor, creating white caps and rattling fishing nets like an angry spirit. Beside him, Stanis twitched on Braddok's shoulder with a moan.

"Survak," Jeric said, as Survak and Tallyn joined them on shore.

"Wolf," Survak replied brusquely. His gaze settled on Stanis, and he fell very still.

Survak had undoubtedly seen shade poison before.

"Tallyn explained the situation?" Jeric asked, glancing briefly at the alta-Liagé.

Survak dragged his gaze back to Jeric. "Aye."

"Two thousand crowns when we return."

It was a nothing short of a fortune, and behind him, Chez sucked air through his teeth.

But Survak stood unimpressed. "I don't want your blood money, Wolf."

Jeric's eyes narrowed. "Then what are your terms, *Captain*?"

Survak looked at Stanis, and a muscle worked in his neck. "I will take you to Zappor. Get him to the healer, and do everything you can for him." Survak's gaze cut back to Jeric. "And then I never want to see you again."

Jeric studied the sea-weathered captain, suspicion creeping into the back of his mind, but before he could say another word, Survak turned and started back up the ramp.

Jeric caught Tallyn's gaze, but Tallyn only gestured for Jeric to go ahead.

"You're sure about this?" Jeric asked.

"He'll be all right." Tallyn nodded after the retreating captain.

The Lady's crew gathered on deck as Jeric and his pack stepped on deck. Survak might have given Jeric permission to board, but he was not welcome, and judging by the crew's various hostile expressions, Jeric's true identity was secret no longer.

It was going to be a long journey.

Survak waited at his private quarters, where Imari had slept all those weeks ago. "Bring him here." He pushed the door in and golden light spilled on deck.

The crew eyed Jeric and his men as they followed the captain. Jeric spotted two more crew members perched on the rigging above, watching them, as Braddok carried an unconscious Stanis into Survak's cabin. It was cramped quarters with all of them inside, and the memory of Imari tightened Jeric's chest unexpectedly.

Gods, he hoped they reached her in time. Both for Stanis's sake, and to warn her before Astrid arrived.

Survak stood by the door, his features unreadable as he watched Braddok lay Stanis upon the cot.

"You really believe the Istraan can heal him?" Survak asked Tallyn.

"I know she can," Tallyn replied.

Survak's jaw clenched, his gaze drifted back to Stanis. There was deep emotion in the captain's eyes that Jeric could not place, but he did not ask. He would not press his luck.

Instead, Jeric said, "Thank you, Survak."

The sea captain's expression tightened. "Just stay out of my way," he said, then stormed out of the cabin and slammed the door.

12

Gamla's rooftop was much closer than Imari remembered. She didn't need all of the divots in the stucco that little Imari had needed, and with a few well-timed pulls, she clambered easily onto the tiles.

A sharp wind snapped her loose clothing as she gazed upon Trier, aglow with buttery lantern light. It looked like a treasure at night, all glittering and gold. How different this was than her nights sneaking around Skanden, where darkness festered and the bitter cold burned. Where fear was a constant companion, and monsters trapped the world behind warded walls.

Even from these lofty heights, the dancing melody of a mizmar touched her ears, and for a moment, Imari simply stood there, taking it in. Reveling in Trier's beauty—a beauty little Imari had taken for granted. Trier was breathtaking, especially at night, but then she suddenly remembered the reason it was all possible.

The reason she had snuck out of Gamla's chambers in the first place.

Imari adjusted her shawl and kept walking, tiptoeing across familiar paths. She knew them by heart, even after all these years.

Which tiles were broken, which ones were loose. Which ones might startle those in the rooms beneath.

Like Ricón's.

Imari vaulted from rooftop to rooftop like a little chimp, quick on her feet. She was forced to hide twice, as the saredd standing guard upon those higher, exposed walkways changed shifts, but then she was on her way again, navigating the tiles to the place where a lattice had been.

It was not there now.

Imari scanned the shadows for another way down to the small courtyard below. She could jump, but not without breaking an ankle. And then she spotted a crimson banner hanging from a rod that protruded from the wall, about four feet beneath the roof's edge.

That would work.

Imari gripped the edge of the roof, slid her legs over the edge, and slowly lowered herself

down...

            down...

                        down.

She paused, gave herself a quick pep talk, and then let go. She dropped like a stone, but just managed to catch hold of the iron rod as a guard stopped at the courtyard's edge.

Imari cursed and propped her feet against the wall, trying to make herself as small as possible so that the banner would hide her completely, but the silk wrapped around the iron rod made it difficult to grip, and her hands began to slip.

One finger.

Two.

The guard was still there, scanning the courtyard.

Please, go away, Imari pleaded in her mind.

A third finger slipped. One more, and she'd drop.

Finally, just as the guard moved on, her last finger slipped. She landed in a crouch that jarred her shins, but nothing twisted or broke, thank the wards.

Still, Imari waited, just to be sure the guard hadn't heard her fall, but the archway remained empty, quiet. Imari inhaled deep.

Maker's Mercy. She would have to find a better place to climb down next time.

Imari stood, wiped her sweaty hands on her tunic, then checked the little jar in her pocket, and hurried on. Through the archway opposite and down a narrow colonnade, using columns and shadows and palms to hide. Somewhere, laughter lilted on the breeze—a staccato accent to the mizmar's drifting melody. She finally reached Vondar's main doors and spotted Tarq standing guard.

Well, dashá.

Imari ducked into an alcove, behind a statue of Beléna, goddess of beauty. Directly behind that statue, a narrow window had been cut out of the stucco, more to illuminate Beléna than to give a view of the world beyond. Fitting, Imari mused, as she squeezed through that small crack and landed in the palm grove outside.

She'd forgotten how sharp fronds could be.

Imari waited amidst those unforgiving fronds as she assessed the narrow slip of land between Vondar and its surrounding wall. Silhouettes stood along the ramparts, surveying all that moved in and out of the main gate. Mostly all that moved in. They were not particularly concerned with anyone going *out* at this hour.

And, as fate would have it, Imari recognized one of the guards from her morning rounds.

Imari dusted herself off and adjusted her clothing, so that she didn't look like she'd just been sneaking all over the palace rooftops, and approached the three guards with confidence.

Perception was everything in these sorts of situations.

One guard spotted her, and then all three turned.

"Alma Sable," said the guard Imari recognized. He looked pleased to see her now. "Good evening."

Imari smiled, all charm. "Good evening. I've just realized I left my jar of soprese during my rounds this afternoon."

"I'll have someone fetch it for you." He sounded very eager to help.

"That's all right. It's a nice evening, and I could use the fresh air."

"Of course, mi alma." The guard did not hesitate. "Would you like me to come with you?"

"No, thank you. I prefer being alone."

He dipped his head. "Yes, mi 'alma."

She smiled and walked on.

Just like that.

Wards, if only things had been so simple in Skanden.

A sand-flecked wind pushed against her, and she clutched her shawl close. People walked the city streets, trading and chattering beneath the amber glow. Laughter echoed, a timpani drummed nearby, and palms rustled in the breeze. All of it wove around Imari like some tapestry of sound, pulling in close and wrapping her tight. Imari stopped and breathed in the spice and dust and warmth. A scent that belonged only here—one she would bottle up and keep forever if she could.

Imari pulled her heart from that exquisite and living tapestry, and kept walking. Away from the light—the life—and toward the reason she had snuck away in the first place.

The lure she could not cut.

The sounds quieted and the shadows stretched the farther she walked from the market, while her heart drummed faster. She should not be here—she knew—but she needed to see. She needed to know and understand this gnawing hunger inside of her. Finally, she arrived at the edge of E'Centro: Trier's slums.

Where the Sol Velorians lived.

Imari gazed down E'Centro's dark main street, clutching her shawl close. The world faded here, where the city lights and music did not reach. Where instead of incense and pink jasmine, the air festered with sweat and disease and human waste, and the crumbling structures looked one sandstorm away from total collapse.

That boy lives a better life here than he would anywhere else, Ricón had said. *At least here, in Istraa, they can earn wages... It's enough for them to buy food and water, and a roof over their heads...*

Imari breathed in one deep and shuddering breath. This was not life. Not at all.

Two wiry figures limped down the main street. Their heads were shorn close, as the boy's had been, but these were adults, one man, one woman. They ducked into a dark doorway and out of sight.

Imari took one glance over her shoulder, made sure her shawl was secured, and started down the path.

Into E'Centro.

Two rats scuttled along the street's edge, and flies buzzed over a dark and suspicious mass off to one side. This could have been her life, had she not been born to a sar.

But I have been born to a sar, so what now? she wondered. How could she use her position to help these people?

She padded forward upon the hard dirt, avoiding the damp patches as she scanned the dark windows and the cracks between buildings—searching for what, she couldn't say. Had she really hoped to find the boy? At this hour? It wasn't like she could ask anyone where he lived; she didn't even know his name. Perhaps tomorrow, when she returned to the Qazzat. She could find his name, and then...

And then what? Sneak out again? Did she dare make a habit of this? Truly?

And to what end?

Imari's next breath felt tight and shallow as she gazed at this crumbling empire of human deterioration. *Her* people.

Maker, what do I do? she prayed to the stars. How do I help them?

But the stars did not answer.

Imari sighed and turned to leave when she spotted a silhouette at the end of the street. A limping and scrappy silhouette.

Of a boy.

She knew the moment he spotted her because he stopped in his tracks. Imari felt that strange stirring in her belly again. And then the boy bolted.

Imari cursed. "Wait!"

She sprinted after him, but he was too quick. Like a mouse, skittering away, intimately aware of every hole and crevice in this pile of rubble. He scrambled over a crumbling wall, which had once belonged to a building, and by the time Imari reached the top of it, the boy was nowhere in sight.

She cursed again from her perch, scanning the broken frames and the dark path beyond, and then she leapt down to the other side, where a shine caught her eye. Imari took four steps and crouched. It was the small jar of soprese she'd left on the stool at the Qazzat.

She grinned. That little thief.

She picked up the jar, slipped it into her pant pocket, glanced around, and kept walking. Deeper into E'Centro. She searched every crack and doorway, sensing eyes watching her from the dark windows. Finally, she stopped where a slip of a path separated two taller structures.

The path ended at a doorway strung with old wooden beads.

The power in her belly stirred yet again, and Imari realized she could *hear* the beads' lingering vibrations. A sound she should not have been able to hear.

Curious, she crept forward and stopped at the beads. Up close, she could see that they were actually chips of cactus wood and shards of rock. "Hello...?" she called out, gazing into the darkness beyond.

No answer.

"Excuse me, but I believe you dropped this," she said.

Nothing.

Imari frowned, and was just setting the jar upon the floor when the boy appeared through the beads.

He stared at Imari. Wards, those eyes. They were so familiar.

Imari smiled, set down the jar and stood. "Hi. I'm...Sable."

The boy's eyes narrowed. First on the jar, then on Imari.

"I can help you," Imari said softly. "The soprese will stop infection, but it won't ease the pain. This does." She withdrew the jar of salve she'd brought, and gestured to his back.

Still, he regarded her, and then, suddenly, he said, "I'm Saza."

Imari's smile widened, and a string plucked in her chest. "Nice to meet you, Saza."

The boy—Saza—picked up the jar with wide and dirtied hands. He would grow tall someday, Imari noted.

Saza tilted his head, motioned for her to follow, and disappeared into the shadows. Imari pushed through the beads and stepped inside.

FROM THE ROOFTOPS, an owl watched. The girl had not seen him follow her all the way from Vondar, curious as to where she could possibly be headed at this hour.

But he never would have expected this.

It was too perfect. Almost...supernatural in design.

He would have smiled, had he been in human form. Instead, the owl pushed off the roof's edge and soared into the night, thinking, perhaps, that there was hope to be had after all.

13

Niá watched her client climb out of her tousled bed and pour himself a glass of nazzat. The brazier light danced over his naked form—a form she had come to know well these past six months.

For she was his favorite.

He downed the nazzat and promptly poured himself another glass. Not much fazed this client, but he was agitated tonight. Considering what he'd just confided, while lying naked and vulnerable beside her in the facsimile safety of her bed, she was not surprised.

And now she needed him to leave.

She slid from her bed of silk and seduction, put on her robe, and walked to the narrow window framed by red gossamer. The window was nothing more than a small cutout in this room that wasn't hers, though it had been given to her for the goddess's celestial purpose. Ashova, Istraan goddess of fertility. Istraa's beloved. This was *her* temple, where Istraan men and women worshipped the goddess with their bodies, hoping she would fertilize their land in return.

Where Niá had resided this past year, after a kahar had

spotted her shucking wheat and deemed her too beautiful for the task.

Maker curse that day.

Niá gazed absently out the window, to the courtyard below. Behind her, fabric shuffled as her client dressed.

"You're quiet," he said.

"You do not come here for conversation," she teased, though the words tasted sour in her mouth.

He moved behind her and touched her hair.

Her attention focused on the courtyard's center, where Ashova's statue arched in eternal pleasure, drawing power from her nakedness. Her femininity.

As Niá had learned to do.

"I like conversing with you," her client whispered, his voice sultry as his nose pushed into her hair. As if he wanted her again.

"And it is an expensive conversation."

He had spent a small fortune on her. A sum that would have easily purchased a real life for her. But he never wanted her to have a real life, despite his romantic professions in the throes of passion. He just wanted control. They all did. Everything else was illusion.

With that thought at the forefront of Niá's mind, she handed him back his jerkin while resisting the urge to throw it at him.

Her client looked at the jerkin, at her. For a moment, she feared he would stay. Pay the sum. Exhaust his allowance to take her again—he'd done it plenty before. He had never abused her. She'd seen the bruises other temple servants had borne; she knew she was more fortunate than most.

But what did that matter, bruised or indulged? They were all vessels, their purpose only to bring pleasure. Used until they could be used no more, and then they were promptly discarded.

She'd seen that too. This morning, in fact.

"You have a very busy day tomorrow," Niá reminded him.

He inhaled through tight lips and finally took the jerkin.

Niá turned back to the window.

"Not a word, Niá," he whispered.

She hated when he called her by name. As if it meant something to him.

"You know I never do," she replied.

Once he had finished dressing, he walked over to her and gently pulled the curtain of dark hair away from her neck and planted a kiss there at the bend.

As if that meant something too. As if all of this were more than silk and lust and need.

She stood perfectly still, eyes fixed on the goddess reveling in her power.

"I will see you tomorrow," he whispered upon her neck.

Boards creaked as he crossed to the door. Niá waited, the door opened and closed with a soft click. Still, she waited, in case he changed his mind. But he did not return, and she was grateful, because the shiva did not like to be kept waiting.

Niá drew her gossamer draperies closed and blew out the candle beside her rumpled bed. She found the golden pin atop her nightstand, where her client had pulled it from her hair with practiced ease. He had given it to her two months ago, and it was elegant, dipped in gold and adorned with small, gleaming rubies.

Niá stabbed the pin into her arm.

Pain pricked and blood pooled, welling like one of those crimson jewels. Niá dropped the pin into her client's empty glass, dipped her finger into the blood, and painted a small symbol upon the doorframe. Her door bore no lock—not from the inside. This enchantment would not lock it either. That would be too obvious, but this *would* give her warning.

And she could not be caught.

She whispered a word. The symbol flared like moonlight then faded just as fast, dissolving the blood with it, though the enchantment remained—stacked on top of all the others, though invisible to the naked eye.

It was an enchantress's mark, and only an enchantress could see it.

Niá hurried over to the vanity and painted another, different symbol upon the glass—a symbol tied to a sister marking, activated by her blood. The mark flared and the glass rippled like a mirage, then the image slowly cleared and sharpened, until it was no longer her reflection in the glass.

It was the shiva.

A heavy cowl shadowed most of his warded face, though his black eyes gleamed like two pools of ink. Behind him, Niá spied only darkness and stone. The shiva had never visited her in person. His mere appearance would have marked him for what he was: Liagé. Specifically *shiva*—a restorer—and a very powerful one. No, this *shiva* had sent a servant when he had somehow discovered Niá.

That day, the shiva had given her purpose, and for Niá, that purpose was water over parched soil.

It was hope.

And he paid handsomely too. It would not be long before she could afford to start a life away from this place. For all three of them.

"You're late," the shiva said without preamble.

"I know," Niá whispered, glancing briefly at the door. To be sure. "Sur Kai just left."

Those dark eyes flashed. "Have you confirmed the girl's identity?"

This was what he had wanted. From the moment he'd learned of Sur Ricón's return, the shiva had wanted to know every little detail about the stranger Sur Ricón had brought back with him.

"Yes."

The shiva waited.

For some reason, she found it difficult to utter the words. Difficult to believe them, even though they'd come from the younger sur himself. "She is Sar Branón's bastard. Surina Imari Jeziél Masai—alive, all these years. And she is Liagé. It wasn't the flute after all."

The shiva did not react. He did not shed an ounce of surprise as Niá had done when the younger sur had explained the situation. In fact, the shiva looked more like a man satisfied at having his suspicions confirmed.

"Where is she now?" the shiva asked.

"In Vondar. They will not announce her yet. She is to assume Gamla's role as Trier's healer."

"Indefinitely?"

"No. They're hoping to wait until they catch you—for her safety, as much as Branón's. They're worried the rois and roiesses will think she is...well, *you*. In the meantime, Sar Branón is seeking an alliance with Roi Naleed through betrothal to his son, Fez. Roi Naleed has two thousand able men."

There. Niá caught a small spark of intrigue in those cold black wells.

"Is Naleed receptive?" the shiva asked.

"Sur Kai thought so. They're in negotiations and plan to announce the betrothal once they announce Imari."

"And Naleed knows what she truly is?" the shiva gave weight to the word *what*.

"Yes."

The shiva digested this, then asked, "Did he mention anything about the Wolf?"

This was another part of Sur Kai's story that had surprised Niá, and she was equally shocked the shiva already knew. Perhaps she shouldn't have been. The shiva had ears everywhere.

"The Wolf is the one who contacted Sur Ricón. He...let her go." It hadn't made sense to Niá, or Sur Kai, but again, the shiva did not look surprised. Sur Kai still suspected the Wolf of deception, and that his easy release of Imari was a trap to place Istraa out of favor with the other Provinces.

"Where is the Wolf now?" the shiva asked.

"In Corinth, though Sur Kai did not know of any continued correspondence with King Jeric, so it's possible…"

The shiva's head tipped to the side, as if he'd caught a sound.

"*A'prior*…" Niá started, leaning closer to the glass. Master. "When will you act?"

The shiva looked back at the glass. Light gleamed off the large rings stretching his long earlobes.

"If the girl truly is Liagé, aren't you concerned? They want to use her power against you, to find where we—"

"Learn everything you can about the sar's bastard," the shiva cut her off. The glass rippled, marking the end of their conversation. "Where she eats. Where she sleeps. Who she spends her time with."

"Of course, but…"

The shiva was gone before she could finish her question. Leaving Niá alone to stare at herself.

"Who can fathom the Maker's perfect designs? For he created the heavens and the earth, and orchestrates all things to work together for his greater purpose. So let us draw nearer to him in times of trial, for he bears our pain and our struggle, and promises to deliver us."

~ *Excerpt from* Il Tonté,
As recorded in the First Verses by
Juvia, Liagé First High Sceptor.

14

Imari ascended a dark and uneven stair, while Saza waited at the top, holding aside a cloth that served as a door. The room beyond was small, about the size of Imari's room at Tolya's, but here there were no windows, not unless one counted the gaping hole in the mudbrick ceiling. The plastered walls peeled, exposing the palm logs beneath, and a candle burned in one corner, illuminating three straw pallets spread upon the floor. Saza crouched beside one, where an old woman lay shivering and moaning beneath a shoddy woolen blanket.

Imari stopped in her tracks. For a split second, she saw Tolya, with her stern brow and wild mess of gray hair.

The old woman's foot stuck out from the end of the blanket. The foot itself was swollen like a melon, and a deep gash oozed from her heel, the surrounding skin black and necrotic.

Imari's heart sank and she gazed down at Saza, who sat devotedly beside the old woman. Wards, Imari hated this part of her trade. When she knew tonics and herbs would never be enough.

When she had to say it out loud to the people it would hurt most.

"Is she your family?" Imari asked, buying time as she knelt beside Saza.

"She's my oza."

Grandmama.

"Does anyone else live here with you?" Imari gestured to the third pallet, hoping it meant someone else would be able to look out for him. Hoping he wouldn't be alone.

"My sister Niá, but...she's at Ashova's." His gaze dropped as he admitted this.

Imari's chest squeezed. She knew what fate awaited Ashova's "servants." Saza would be left alone.

"How long has your oza been like this?" Imari asked instead.

"A week," Saza said quietly.

Many laborers couldn't afford shoes, so injury wasn't surprising, but this... The old woman had been infected with a heaping dose of something particularly foul.

"Where does your oza work?" Imari asked, pressing at the tight and spongey skin around the wound, and Saza's oza moaned.

"Ajadd," Saza replied.

"Ah."

The Ajadd district housed Istraa's infamous color vats, and it also explained the vermillion stain upon the old woman's calf. Imari recalled that some of Ajadd's vats served to soften leather, and to achieve this, workers brewed a cauldron of pigeon poop and goat urine. If the old woman had stepped into that fetid concoction with an open wound...

These were the sorts of issues Gamla had always tended, before they turned severe—like this. No wonder Saza had stolen the soprese. But he was too late. The infection had reached the old woman's blood, and she was dying.

"You can help her?" Saza asked.

"I..." Imari started, but the hope in his eyes broke her. Hope, when he already suffered. Hope, when Fenuk had tried to whip it out of him.

Hope, that Imari couldn't bring herself to take now.

Imari remembered her papa's words, how he believed Restorers—Liagé healers—still existed in Istraa, but if one lived in Trier, certainly he or she would've already helped this woman. Either way, there was no time to find one now.

Imari looked back at the old woman, into this face that reminded her so much of Tolya, and determination rose swift and sudden. Like a single note of purpose resonating through her soul, singing louder and louder, demanding to be heard, and her belly tingled.

Imari had no idea what she was doing, but she had to try. She'd used her voice before, specifically to calm Jedd in The Wilds, and then Jeric, when he'd been recovering from shade poison and kept suffering those horrible nightmares. Both instances had happened *before* she'd unlocked her power. Perhaps she could do more now.

Still, she didn't dare expose herself.

"Is there water nearby?" Imari asked.

"There's a well—"

"Go."

Saza didn't need to be told twice.

Imari waited for the beads to clatter, then waited a moment more. "Help me heal her," Imari whispered to the one who had helped her before. "If I truly have influence over souls, then help me save this one."

Imari put her hands upon the blanket, over the woman's slow heart, and shut her eyes tight. She inhaled deep, feeling that breath fill her lungs and expand her chest until it brushed against the tingling in her belly, and she exhaled with song. Her notes rang hesitant at first. She tumbled over uncertain intervals, not sure where the melody should go, while fearing that at any moment, someone might walk through the door and see her.

146 | BARBARA KLOSS

Realize what she was, and proclaim it to the world. But Imari persisted, giving more breath to her voice, while her notes climbed over the lines and spaces of an empty staff, slowly filling it with melody.

And then the melody began to guide *her*. As if it had always been there, written upon her heart.

It drew from her breath, faster and faster. The notes consumed the empty staff as if rushing to fill it with predetermined song.

Imari didn't stop—couldn't stop. A voice inside warned her to slow. To clamp her lips down on the song before it drew all of the breath from her lungs. Suddenly, the tingling in her body surged.

It crashed over her in a rushing tide, drowning her in light and heat. Imari's chest seized, her lungs depleted, and then there was fire—a searing, unquenchable fire that swallowed her whole. The world flashed white—a blinding, blistering white—and she was weightless, floating through a cloud of haze, and she could not turn her gaze. She had no eyes with which to see, or head to turn. She was simply consciousness floating through this endless expanse of white, insubstantial and fading.

Fading and drifting.

In the distance, a bass drum beat softly.

Imari knew that drum was her heart, and somehow she knew that if it faded completely, she too would fade away forever, and so her thoughts—this strange ethereal existence—latched onto that sound. That steadily beating drum. As if it were an anchor, her thoughts the tether, keeping her consciousness from drowning in that expansive nothing.

She felt a burning, though she didn't know how it was possible to feel without a body, but she held on to that beat—centered all focus upon it, this single substantial piece of her hazy white world. Slowly that beat grew louder.

And stronger.

Finally, the white nothing took shape, shadows formed and made contrast, until she could see the room again—with *her eyes*.

And then there was pain.

A great, tearing pain, as though her soul were being ripped from her body, and Imari cried out.

"Quick. Fetch water."

Imari just managed to glance over. To her surprise, the old woman was awake—wide awake, and looking much healthier than she had any right to look, but she hadn't given the command to Imari. She'd spoken to Saza, who stood agape at the door. His eyes were saucers, and an empty pail lay in a puddle of water at his bare feet.

Imari wondered how much he had witnessed, but then her body convulsed, and she suddenly couldn't breathe.

"Hurry!" the old woman hissed, pushing herself to sit.

Imari tried to tell the old woman to lie back down, but a scream hissed through her teeth instead.

Burning wards, it hurt!

The old woman cursed and rifled through her straw pallet, then produced a small knife. Imari didn't have a moment to wonder. The old woman carved into her palm, blood welled, and Imari turned her head and vomited. Not from the blood, but from the pain.

Maker have mercy!

Imari vomited again, and the tearing sensation intensified. It was going to rip her in two.

"Where's that boy…" the old woman hissed, painting blood on her forearms.

Imari vomited again, but this time, nothing came up.

"Bring it here," the old woman commanded.

Footsteps hurried close, Saza handed over the bucket, which the old woman promptly dumped over Imari's head. Imari gasped from the shock of it and then started to tremble uncontrollably. Saza spoke, but his words muffled together. Murky, as though he were underwater. The old woman dabbed Imari's face dry with her blanket, and then she began painting blood on Imari's cheeks.

Imari meant to refuse, to pull away, but she could not stop shivering. Little but firm hands grabbed her shoulders and held her steady while the old woman finished painting, and then the old woman spoke a word. Just one, a command.

Imari felt a burst of air—a sudden gust of wind, localized to this room. It doused the heat on impact, like water over hot coals. Imari's racing heart slowed, her chest relaxed until she could breathe again, and for a long moment, Imari simply sat there, focused only on filling her lungs with air.

In and out.

In and out.

"Wards, girl! You can't go bringing people back to life without your *talla!*"

Her...what?

"I don't know what..." Imari started, but her temples wrenched and she shut her eyes, waiting for the pain to pass.

"Didn't my sister teach you anything?"

Imari tried focusing on the words. They should matter—she knew—but she was having a very difficult time forming complete thoughts.

The old woman sighed and tilted her head back against the wall. "Get some more water, Saza." Whatever the old woman had done to help Imari, it had exhausted her.

Saza snatched up the pail and left.

The old woman gazed at Imari through half-lidded eyes. "Tolya's gone, isn't she."

Imari's chest heaved and she stared at the old woman who shared Saza's dark and familiar eyes. This woman had reminded her so much of Tolya, because...

The world tilted and Imari swayed.

The old woman sighed. "Just breathe, girl."

"You're...she..." Imari's throat felt like it'd been scrubbed with pumice, and her mouth tasted like ash. "I had no idea..."

"You might have said *something*," the old woman murmured, but Imari didn't think those words were meant for her.

Imari coughed and bright red blood splattered the floor.

"You'll be all right," the old woman said, noting Imari's alarm. "Just too much fire in your throat, that's all." A pause. Those dark eyes—so familiar, but in a different face—skewered her. "*Never* do that again."

Imari still wasn't sure what she had just done.

"I'm Taran," the old woman said. "Tolya's twin. The smarter one, I'll have you know."

Stars above!

Not only had Tolya had a sister but she'd had a *twin*, and she lived *here*, in Trier. And Imari had walked right through her front door.

What were the odds?

"The Maker has a funny sense of humor, doesn't he?" the woman—Taran—said, mirroring Imari's own thoughts, then eyed her. "Branón doesn't know you're here."

"No..." Imari managed, thankful Taran had sent Saza for water. The lingering taste of ash and blood made her feel like vomiting again.

"So how in all the stars did the good Maker coax you through my front door?" Taran asked.

"I saw Saza...in the Qazzat."

"Ah," Taran said. "Bleeding heart in you. It's a wonder you survived The Wilds, though Tolya did say you were headstrong."

"She's one to talk," Imari said, and Taran barked a laugh. "What did you...do to me, just now?"

"You mean *kehtan*?"

It was almost the Istraan word for suppression—*kehtané*—but oftentimes "almost" between Istraan and Sol Velorian dialects lent very different meanings.

"That blood painting and…" Imari winced as another throb pulsed in her head, so she waved a hand at the rest of her words.

"*Kehtan* is a spell that momentarily cuts off your connection to the Shah, and saved your life," Taran replied sharply. "You can't just open yourself to the Shah like that, girl. Not without your *talla*."

That word again.

"My *what*?" Imari asked.

Taran sighed as if she'd just been handed a burden she didn't want to bear. "Your *talla*. Please tell me you know the four talents."

Imari did, but only vaguely, and what little she knew had come from her limited travels with Tolya. Liagé power was divided into four major categories: Restoration, Enchantment, Guardianship, and Sight. They had Liagé names for it, of course, but this was how Imari had always remembered it. Ventus had been a Restorer—*shiva*—though healing was only one aspect of his particular brand of power. Necromancy was another. Tallyn had Sight—*ziat*—but he had been created alta-Liagé by Azir, and could therefore access other branches of power. But true Liagé did not choose which of these powers they inherited; they were simply born with one, and trained how to use it.

"Yes, from Tolya," Imari said. "But I only know basics."

"Well, at least you didn't completely waste your time," Taran scolded her sister's ghost, and then to Imari she said, "Your *talla* is a kind of talisman. An object specific to *your* talent, so you can safely channel your power. The Maker gave us access to his power, but it is still *his* power, and far too great for our mortal bodies to withstand. To channel it directly, as you've just done…."

"But I've seen others use it," Imari cut in. "Without these…tallees—"

"*Talla*, and no, you haven't. People might do small things at no risk to their person, but you can't channel the amount of raw power needed for *bringing back the dead* without a talla, or you'll burn up quick as summer wheat."

Rasmin had never told her this, but then he'd also never asked her to use her power without her flute. Everything he had attempted to teach her had been with the expectation that she'd be using the flute.

"You didn't use anything just now," Imari said.

The old woman gestured irritably to her forearms, which she had painted with blood. The blood was gone, but an inflamed outline remained, as though the skin had been burned, specifically in the shape of a glyph that looked very similar to one carved into a stone atop Skanden's warded wall.

"I am *voloré*," Taran continued. Enchantress. "My *talla* is language. The world was created by Word, and by Word we enchantresses—and enchanters—manipulate it. I would never open my body to the Shah without giving it a Word anchor. Something to hold the brunt of it. We are not the vessels, child. We are vectors. We direct power from the well. We don't *become* the well."

Imari thought of Ventus and his silent—Tallyn, too—who had borne markings all over their skin. She'd always assumed the markings had given them power, and while that was partially true, the more accurate purpose was to anchor the Shah. Those markings allowed them to safely draw upon that well of power, and use it how they needed.

It didn't explain Rasmin, but then he'd always been buried in heavy wool. No telling what marked him in places she could not see. And this woman had already told her more about using the Shah than Rasmin had ever done. Wasn't this precisely what she'd been looking for? Someone to teach her how to use her power? Someone who didn't have vested interest in using it for themselves?

"Teach me," Imari asked.

Taran looked sharply at her.

"Teach me how to use my power," Imari said, before the woman could refuse, "and in exchange I will do whatever I can to help the people of E'Centro, just...teach me how to use my power. *Please.*"

Taran didn't speak. She didn't seem to breathe. And then, "Those are big words coming from someone who will be lucky to keep her life once all of Istraa learns the truth."

"And if I *do* keep my life," Imari persisted, more certain than ever that she had been led here, for this very reason, "then you have someone in Vondar who will do everything in her power to help your people." A beat. "*Our* people."

Taran's eyes were a fire, searing through Imari if to burn all impurities away. To see what her heart was really made of.

Just then, Saza returned with the bucket. He set it before Imari, but Imari wasn't thirsty anymore.

Saza whispered to Taran, and Taran sat up at once. "The city guards are making rounds."

Imari frowned. The guards had just finished evening rounds when she'd arrived, which meant...

She glanced at the hole in the ceiling, shocked to find the black had softened to a deep gray. Sunrise was near. How was that even possible?

Imari cursed, standing and swaying to her feet, but already, her energy was coming back. Which surprised her. It had taken Imari two weeks to recover from her fight with Astrid, and she had used her flute then—her *talla*.

Taran was more powerful than she'd let on. And she still hadn't given Imari an answer.

Instead, Taran gestured to the hole in the ceiling. Imari felt the sting of disappointment, and Saza crouched beneath the hole and threaded his fingers together to give Imari a boost.

"Oh, I almost forgot..." Imari dug into her pocket. Her clothes were still wet, but thankfully desert air never let cloth remain wet for very long. She withdrew the little jar. "This is for your back. Apply it morning and night, and it'll help the skin heal."

Saza's expression brightened, but Taran sat quiet, studying Imari with those hard and unyielding eyes. So like Tolya's.

Imari set the jar on the floor, then placed her foot into Saza's threaded fingers and he pushed up as she jumped and caught hold of the hole's rough edges. With a grunt and a very determined strain, Imari hoisted herself through the opening and clambered onto the flat mud roof. She gazed out and spotted three silhouettes moving at the end of the street, then peered back into the hole. Taran and Saza gazed up at her.

"Will you come back?" Saza called from below, loud as he dared.

Imari looked to Taran. "If that is all right with your oza."

Will you teach me and let me help? Imari's words still lingered in the space between them.

And then a smile cracked Taran's lips. "Just don't get caught, girl."

Imari found herself grinning too. "I won't."

And then Imari tugged her shawl over her head, took one last glance at the approaching guards, and was gone.

15

"Think of yourself like that bucket," Taran said the next night, as Imari lay heaving on the floor.

Imari had played, as Taran had instructed. She'd tried to channel the heat and tingling from her belly into her arms, and down her fingertips. She'd tried pushing it into the flute, but it had come like the tide and drowned her, leaving her gasping for breath on Taran's stone floor.

Thankfully, Taran had not been forced to use *kehtan* again. She'd wrested the flute from Imari's grip before reaching that dangerous point.

"Reach into that well of power and draw only what you need," Taran continued. "When you run out, you draw more, but remember each draw—each pull—is a physical strain on your body."

"That's what I'm doing—"

"No, you're still trying to take the whole stars-forsaken well," Taran snapped. She picked up Imari's flute from where it had rolled, and for a moment, Imari thought Taran might hit her over the head with it.

Taran held it out instead.

Wincing, Imari sat up and grabbed the little glowing flute. Her intestines were like rope, twisting and pulling and knotting within.

"That well *is* the Shah, girl, and we *all* draw from that power. Take what you need, and *only* what you need, and you won't drown."

That's what she'd *tried* to do. What she thought she'd done.

Imari lifted the flute to her lips—again—but hesitated. "You're sure no one can hear this?"

Taran looked insulted. Before they'd begun Imari's lessons, Taran had drawn enchantments around the door and ceiling to contain the music to this room. "You can always go home, if you're concerned."

Imari pressed her lips together, then closed her eyes, arranged her fingers, and pushed a ragged breath into the flute. An A stretched slowly, demure in the aftermath. Again, her power stirred like a cauldron in her belly. Again, she held that A steady, while focusing on that tingling where her power was contained.

Imari shifted her fingers and gently pushed her A into a B. The tingling in her belly rose like steam into her chest. She pictured her chest like a bucket, slowly filling it with that tingling steam until the pressure pushed against her ribs, and then she stopped drawing from her belly and instead vented the pressure into her fingertips. Let it drip into her flute. Her B grew bolder and stronger, rounding out at the edges, like a balloon filling with hot air.

Emboldened, Imari vented more power from her chest into her flute, but then the cauldron in her belly erupted in a wave of searing heat. Imari cried out and dropped the flute.

Taran simply looked at her.

"I'm trying!" Imari clutched her belly, which burned and cramped and twisted.

Saza watched from near the door, chewing on a fig Imari had

brought.

"That's enough for tonight," Taran said at last.

"But we only just started—"

"No."

"Maybe if you told me where to guide my power once I push it into the flute—"

"The first lesson in Shah manipulation is gaining control of one's power. It's something small children know how to do."

Imari decided not to be offended. "How long does it take them to learn?"

"Well, you're a good bit older," Taran answered, without really answering at all. "Your Shah is more developed, therefore more difficult to control, but not impossible. And *that* is what you must learn." Taran jabbed a turquoise-stained finger at Imari. She'd returned to work the vats today. "You've got to secure that anchor so your power won't fly wild and lash out on everything in its path."

Imari sighed and dropped her head in her hands.

"It might take you a few weeks," Taran continued. "So don't lose heart yet."

However, the next night she didn't fare better, nor the next, or the one after, and by week's end, Imari was growing quite discouraged—and exhausted. All these attempts to control her power left her physically weary, and the late nights coupled with the long days spent healing Trier's sick left little time for rest.

Taran sat forward, rubbing her temples, and Imari lay on the ground, staring up at that cursed hole in the ceiling. Saza set a cup of water beside Imari's head—a cup she'd given them just the night before. Imari opened her mouth to say thank you, but all that came was a strangled grunt. She sat up and took a sip, letting the water cool the fire in her belly.

"Well," Taran said at last. "There is one good thing coming out of all of this. Our people haven't been this healthy since Gamla."

Though Imari couldn't do much about their living situation yet, she'd brought whatever herbs and salves she could, adjusting contents to match the Sol Velorians' needs, per Taran's reports. Of course, news of Taran's late-night visitor spread, though Taran never disclosed her source, and the people were so grateful they didn't push the old woman for answers. Still, a few *did* come to see Imari in person, and Imari cherished those visits, dangerous though they were. She loved getting to know and care for these families, and it only reinforced her resolve. Once she was able to claim her title as her own—a surina of Istraa—she would find a way to free the Sol Velor of Istraa's golden shackles.

But for now, she would have to be content with getting them healthy.

Imari lowered the cup. "Did you know my uncle well?"

Taran glanced up at Imari.

Imari sensed she'd touched upon something bleeding and raw.

"I did," Taran replied quietly.

Imari regarded the old woman, and suddenly more details clicked into place. A missing piece from the puzzle leftover from her conversation with her papa, when she'd first arrived.

Gamla had known Tolya. Because he'd known Taran first.

"*You're* the reason he sent me to Tolya," Imari said.

Taran held her gaze steady.

Imari set the cup down as a dozen more questions crowded behind her lips. "Did you tell him you were *voloré*?"

Taran didn't answer immediately. "He...figured it out."

Gamla must have spent a lot of time here. "Tolya was *voloré* too, wasn't she?"

Taran tilted her head. "Yes."

She knew it. Tolya *had* used enchantments to hide Imari all those years, but when Tolya had grown weaker, her enchantments had grown weaker too.

Imari wondered what else Gamla had known.

"Papa said the rois and roiesses believe Gamla suffered an accident on the road," Imari said.

Taran barked a laugh.

Imari sat forward. "I see you disagree..."

"Gamla didn't suffer some accident," Taran said, as if the very idea were an insult to Gamla's memory. Her gaze shifted to the hole in the ceiling. "No, someone took him."

Imari remembered her conversation with her papa. "Is it related to this...Liagé leader?"

Saza looked up from his bowl of figs.

And Taran smiled. "Now you are asking the right questions, girl."

"So it's true then? There's an uprising?"

"It's true. And it isn't."

Imari frowned.

"We're here, aren't we?" Taran asked rhetorically, gesturing at herself, at Saza. "Do we look like we're rising up to you?"

"Well, no, but there are rumors about—"

"Bah." Taran batted a dismissive hand. "There are always rumors."

"So...you're saying the rumors aren't true?"

"I didn't say that. I said there are always rumors. The Deceiver's greatest delight is sowing discord."

The Deceiver. The ruler of all darkness and corruption, according to the Sol Velorians.

Taran's expression sobered, and when she spoke again, her voice took on a reprimanding quality. "But to answer your question: Yes. There is someone sowing weeds in the Maker's good garden. You know them by their fruits, or lack thereof. And I do not rise up for them. I rise only for one."

Taran reached into her tattered dress and produced a small book about the size of Imari's hand.

"Oza..." Saza started, sounding nervous.

Taran hissed sharply at Saza, and held out the little book to

Imari. It was leather bound, worn from decades of use. A stamp was the cover's only marking—a stamp of a tree within a circle, its long branches and roots reaching out and around the circle, becoming part of the circle.

Imari remembered the tree from her nightmare, but only because they were both trees. This emblem was nothing like that fearful vision.

Imari took the little book from Taran. The leather felt soft and pliable, and its edges cracked from wear. Imari trailed her fingers over the stamped tree, feeling the ridges and bumps.

"It is Asorai's mark," Taran said.

Imari's fingertips stopped.

Asorai—The Maker. The god of the Sol Velor.

She glanced up at Taran, but Taran was looking at the little book with reverence.

"*Il Tonté*," Taran whispered. They were the verses inspired by the Maker himself, recorded by the First Liagé, from which the Sol Velor had based their faith.

The verses by which Azir had claimed superiority and tried to destroy the world with his four Mo'Ruk generals.

To have this book was treason. Taran had taken great risk showing her this.

"It is yours if you want it," Taran said levelly. "Read it. Find your answers. See for yourself who the Maker truly is and not what all these imposters claim."

Just as Tolya had urged, and Tallyn too.

We are masters at manipulating truth to suit our desires, Tallyn had said. *Don't condemn the Maker for the sins of man.*

Saza's worried eyes slid from Imari to Taran, and Imari gazed down at the book, wondering how something so small and so innocent could be the source of so much pain.

Imari wrapped her hands around the soft leather. "Thank you."

Taran regarded her. "It's late. You should get going. We'll try again tomorrow, but keep that hidden."

"I will." Imari hated to leave, but Taran was right. Imari tucked the verses into her satchel, stood, and approached the hole in the ceiling.

There, she stopped. "Gamla found something. Didn't he?"

Taran gave her a kind of sad smile. "Gamla was always seeking information, much like you. But there are some things that do not wish to be found." A pause. "Be careful, girl."

"You seem...different," Ricón said to her the next morning over breakfast.

Imari looked up from her bowl of yogurt and fruit to find him studying her. She couldn't imagine what he saw. This past week, Imari had survived mostly on adrenaline, and last night she'd stayed up particularly late, reading the little book of verses Taran had given her.

It had been like opening a door to another world—a brighter world, full of hope and goodness and love. Not at all what Imari had expected, though if she thought about it, she wasn't sure *what* she'd expected. Condemnation? Judgment? A call to arms? She found none of that. Every word was like sweet nectar, satisfying a craving deep in Imari's soul and filling a hole she hadn't realized was there.

It also made her wonder what Sol Velor had looked like, before the war had ripped it apart and left it in ruin. A few passages mentioned cities and architecture that Imari couldn't quite fathom, and it wasn't because she lacked experience with Liagé construction. The Wilds' infamous bridge—The Crossing —had been built by the Liagé of old, defying nature as it spanned a deep gorge and connected that frigid snowscape to the Five Provinces. The bridge had impressed her every time she'd laid eyes upon it, during her annual circuit with Tolya. How much more could those same skilled Liagé hands do for an entire city?

Imari hadn't stopped reading until Ricón had knocked on her door for breakfast, and then she'd promptly shoved that little book under her pillow.

Even though it was hidden, and he had no reason to go into Gamla's small room and search the bed, she felt it there, burning a hole in her periphery.

"Well, perhaps I grow better in the desert," Imari answered with a grin. Her skin *had* grown darker the past month, and the regular meals had already smoothed the hard lines of hunger The Wilds had created. "Where's Kai?" she asked, wanting to change the subject.

"Saints, who knows." Ricón took a long sip of tea. "Freedom is the luxury of the second-born prince."

Imari chuckled, and then asked, quietly, "How is Anja?" Imari had hardly seen the Sura after her explosive exodus before the private council. Since then, the sura had kept mostly to her private chambers, and when she did leave, it was only to go to Jadarr to pray.

Ricón sighed and returned the tea to its saucer with a soft clank. "Still bitter and angry, and not your problem." He looked pointedly at her.

Imari disagreed, but Ricón had persisted in convincing her otherwise.

"I'm hearing good reports from Seb about you," he said suddenly, thumbing his tea. "Even Bayek isn't complaining."

"Oh?" Imari said, popping a fig into her mouth.

Ricón stopped thumbing his tea and eyed her. "I'm also hearing murmurs from E'Centro. Some of the workers are talking about a...moonlight healer."

Imari choked on her bite.

So that's what they were calling her? Huh. She sort of liked the name.

Ricón continued eyeing her while she swallowed and washed down the fig with tea, and when she finally lifted her gaze to Ricón's, his eyes burned.

"Dashá, Imari, you promised," he hissed.

"Ricón, I can't pretend they aren't there!" Imari hissed right back. "And Gamla healed them—"

"*You're* not Gamla!" Ricón leaned forward. "What do you think happens when the rois hear, and you know they will—"

"I really don't care—"

"You should! Have you considered how this looks? They'll think you're the leader, which is exactly what we've been trying to avoid—"

"They are *suffering*, Ricón! You think we're better because we pay them, but our *wages* are scat. It's not nearly enough to live, and I can't sit here and leave them to suffer when I can do something to help—"

"So instead you sacrifice *us*."

She'd opened her mouth to argue, but her tower of words collapsed. Ricón had pulled the foundation right out from under them, and now her argument lay broken and scattered upon the floor.

Because he was right.

Doing this thing—sneaking out as she'd done, and being a small hope to an oppressed people—she had risked her family. But by *not* healing the Sol Velorians—also her family, of a kind— she sanctioned their suffering, which went against the very fabric of her being as a healer. No matter which path she chose, someone suffered.

"Our papa has risked *everything* for you," Ricón continued. His expression softened a little, seeing that she understood both sides of the dilemma. "And you repay him by doing the one thing we asked you not to do." A muscle tightened in his jaw. "You spit on his sacrifice, Imari."

Imari turned away as frustration welled in her throat.

Ricón sat quiet, letting his words and disappointment stand. Imari wasn't sure which struck harder: the impossible dilemma, or Ricón's disapproval.

"Ricón, I don't know how to be both," Imari whispered.

She did not need to explain. He already understood.

"Just be *one*," he pleaded, leaning forward and grasping her hands. "We'll figure out the rest later, but Imari...you can't keep this up."

He was right. Wards, she knew he was right.

"I'm sorry," she whispered. "I didn't mean to put you or Papa in danger, I just..."

"I know," he said. He squeezed her hands briefly, let go, and then stood. "I'm so sorry to leave like this, but I'm already late."

Imari watched him as he snatched his coat from the back of a chair.

"Where are you going?" Imari asked.

"Jeol needs my help in Zappor today. He doesn't think Casta is being honest about his numbers and hopes a little pressure from Vondar will fix the problem."

Imari eyed him. "Maybe you should send Tarq."

Ricón chuckled. "Not a bad idea, actually."

Casta owned the olive groves in Zappor, and was, therefore, Istraa's main supplier of oil. It was also a day's ride from Trier, located where the Sivon dumped into the Yellow Sea.

"How long will you be gone?" Imari asked.

"Just a few days." Ricón walked around the table, bent over and kissed Imari's forehead, then pulled back and looked at her. "I love you. I hope you know that."

"I do."

He searched her. "And we're agreed?"

Imari inhaled deep. "Yes."

And they were.

But she would return tonight—one last time. Because Taran and Saza deserved to know why.

16

"You doing all right?" Braddok asked, ducking into Survak's cabin.

Jeric had finally stopped retching this afternoon, thank the gods, because he was fairly certain his ribs couldn't take anymore.

Jeric tipped his head in acknowledgment.

"How is he?" Braddok asked.

"Same."

Tallyn had not miscalculated. He'd successfully slowed Stanis's infection, but every day at sea, Stanis had grown a little paler and the black reached a little farther. It almost brushed his shoulder now.

"Go on. Get some fresh air." Braddok nodded at the door. "I'll stay with him for a bit."

Since they'd departed Felheim, Jeric had rarely left Stanis's side, and the rocking confines of Survak's small cabin had made that no simple task.

Nothing Jeric didn't deserve.

But Jeric had refused to leave. Too clearly, Jeric remembered the pain and crushing loneliness. The overwhelming urge to give in to it, and he would have, had it not been for Imari's iron will, her voice...

"Wolf."

Jeric glanced up.

Braddok looked concerned.

"Worried about me?" Jeric asked wryly.

Braddok snorted. "Worried about getting my tavern."

Jeric grinned as he tipped his head back and closed his eyes. He heard Braddok sigh, and wood groaned as his packmate sat beside him.

"Survak says we'll arrive in about two hours."

"Thank gods," Jeric murmured, as a wave of nausea churned in his stomach.

"So, what's the plan?"

Jeric leaned forward, rested his elbows on his knees, and let his hands dangle between them. "Well, Stanis is our first priority. Hopefully, Imari put in a good word for me, and Branón won't kill us on sight."

"Hopefully, she didn't put in *too* good a word, and Branón decides to kill you anyway."

Jeric chuckled lowly.

"Think we'll beat Astrid there?" Braddok asked.

"Gods, I hope so, or we won't make it past Vondar's gate."

Braddok watched Stanis, considering. "We *should* get there first. There's enough snow in the passes to slow her down."

"She could've skipped the passes and taken the Fallows."

"Well, we've had unusually strong winds."

Jeric grunted. "Tell me about it..."

Braddok chuckled, then asked, "You excited to see Imari?"

Yes, he was, and though he didn't turn, he could see Braddok in his periphery, waggling those bushy brows.

"I'm excited to get off this godsdamned boat," Jeric said instead.

Braddok smirked with a shake of his head. "Whatever, Wolf."
He looked back at Stanis. "You really think she can heal him?"

"I think we'll find out soon enough."

Braddok pulled a flask from his coat, unscrewed the top, and took a long swig. He offered it to Jeric, who shook his head and immediately regretted it when his world spun again.

Stanis gave a sudden cry. His body tensed, ramrod straight, and Jeric jumped to his feet, fighting down the nausea as he rushed to his friend and pulled Stanis's tunic back. The black now grazed Stanis's collarbone. Braddok and Jeric exchanged a glance.

"I'll get Tallyn," Braddok said, ducking outside.

But Jeric knew there was nothing else Tallyn could do.

He needed Imari.

"Hold on, Stanis," Jeric said, begging the gods—or whomever would listen—to intercede. To slow the spread. "We're going to get help, just...hold on."

Footsteps pounded on deck and Tallyn appeared, followed immediately by *The Lady*'s captain. Survak took one look at Stanis, and all the color drained from his face. Tallyn bent over the cot, pressed his palm to Stanis's sweaty brow, and gazed heavily back at Jeric.

Tallyn did not think Stanis would make it.

"No," Jeric said through his teeth. "He's not gone yet."

Tallyn's lips thinned. He glanced over his shoulder, at Survak. "Ready your crew. We have to move fast."

They reached the Istraan port in a little more than an hour, where Zappor guards waved them to an empty dock. Jeric spotted two imposing figures dressed in black cloth, long scims crossed at their backs.

Saredd.

He hadn't expected to see them here. Similar to Corinth's Strykers—the ones Jeric had almost joined—saredd kept near the throne, and the one occupying it.

"We'll wait here," Jeric said to Survak. "Find out if Branón is here."

Because if Branón was not here, and these saredd discovered a Wolf and his pack, Jeric could be detained for gods knew how long. And Stanis didn't have a second to spare. Jeric could see that Survak wasn't keen to take orders from his cargo, but the wisdom in Jeric's command kept him amenable.

Survak nodded once, then looked at Tallyn. "You should probably wait too."

Tallyn didn't disagree; his scars wouldn't hide well. So Tallyn, Jeric, and the others squeezed into Survak's cabin, while Survak spoke with the saredd at dock. Jeric watched from the port window.

"How's it look?" Braddok asked.

"Well, no one's drawn a scim..." Jeric frowned, then cursed. "They're coming up." Jeric ducked away from the window.

"So what do we do now?" Chez asked.

"We wait," Jeric said tightly, meeting Tallyn's concerned gaze.

As it turned out, they didn't wait very long. Five minutes later, the cabin door flew wide open and two saredd strode in, followed by Survak. Jeric had to admit: the saredd looked impressive wrapped in shadow and steel, with only their eyes visible. Perhaps he'd mention it to Hersir. See if they could improve the Stryker uniforms. Make them more imposing.

The saredd appraised the six of them, though the one closest kept looking from Braddok to Jeric, where his dark and predatory eyes finally rested.

Hunters always had a sense for other hunters.

"Who are you?" that saredd asked in Common, his Istraan accent thick.

Jeric had already considered his options, and only one of them did not require casualties. "Jeric Oberyn Sal Angevin of Corinth. We're on our way to your sar, and we're in a bit of a hurry." He gestured at Stanis, who lay moaning on the bed.

Jeric didn't say more. He didn't know what Sar Branón had shared about Imari, if he'd shared anything at all. So far, Jeric had not heard of any announcement, and he'd be damned before he put Imari in any more danger.

"The *Wolf*." The saredd said it like a curse.

Jeric flashed his teeth. "The very one."

The saredd's expression darkened. "We don't do business with wolves."

"Fortunately it's not your business."

It was, of course, the wrong thing to say, and behind them, Survak pinched the bridge of his nose as he bowed his head.

"*Corazzi* filth." The saredd spat on the floor at Jeric's feet and took a small step nearer.

Jeric's men drew their weapons.

The saredd drew theirs.

Jeric held up a fist to hold off his men, while he looked straight at the saredd before him. "I didn't come for a fight. If I had, I certainly would have come with more than four men."

The saredd didn't look convinced.

Normally, Jeric would have been flattered.

"Take me to your sar," Jeric said lowly. "Escort me yourself, if you must, but I will see him."

The saredd stared long and hard at Jeric, and just when Jeric thought he'd have to employ other tactics—those involving casualties—the saredd said, gruffly, "Just you."

"Like hells—" Braddok started.

"It's all right," Jeric cut him off.

The saredd's eyes narrowed and he gestured for Jeric to exit.

Jeric ducked through the cabin and stepped out into the salty air. Wind caught his hair and clothing as he followed the saredd past the watchful crew and onto the dock, where more city guards waited, distinguishable by their tan breeches and tunics, and long crimson waistcoats. Jeric's sea legs nearly tripped him twice, and both times the saredd reached for their scims.

Jeric had to hand it to them. Their reflexes were almost as fast as his.

Gulls squawked, and the air stunk of smoke and salt and dead fish, which did nothing to quell Jeric's nausea. Merchants and fisherman eyed Jeric as they passed. His fair complexion marked him as a foreigner in this land of sepia, and his high-profile escort made them wary. Finally, the saredd turned down a narrow alley that stopped at a dead end.

On second thought, perhaps he shouldn't have dismissed Braddok's concern so easily.

The saredd approached a small and storm-weathered door, nestled into the chipped stucco, and rapped three times. A few breaths passed, and the door cracked open. The saredd spoke fast and low to whomever stood within, and then the door flew wide open and Ricón stepped through.

Ricón's surprise mirrored Jeric's own, and then—to the saredd's acute surprise—Ricón beamed. "Sicta..." Ricón reached Jeric in three strides, and the two men embraced. "Wasn't expecting to see you here," Ricón continued, in accented Common this time. "Shouldn't you be at your coronation?"

"Probably," Jeric replied.

Ricón pulled back and took in the fullness of Jeric's wild appearance. His easy demeanor vanished, only to be promptly overcome with unease.

Jeric jerked a chin at his baffled escort, and Ricón leaned closer.

"Astrid escaped," Jeric whispered.

"*Dashá*..." Ricón raked a hand through his hair. "When?"

"Nine days ago. When did you leave Trier?"

"Early this morning."

The two men exchanged a long, worried glance.

"Did you come alone?" Ricón asked sharply.

"No. My men are still aboard the ship. One of them took ill."

Ricón nodded a fraction. "How many?"

"Six, including me."

Ricón barked orders—in Istraan—at the bewildered saredd, demanding they see Jeric's men safely off of *The Lady*, and then he instructed the city guards to secure additional camels and supplies.

"My man can't ride," Jeric said.

Ricón looked at Jeric, considering. "We'll need a sledge," Ricón called after the guards, and then motioned at Jeric to follow him through the door.

Beyond was a small antechamber occupied by a low table, cushions, and one saredd. The saredd followed Jeric with his eyes, as Jeric strode after Ricón and up a wooden stair in back.

"Where are *your* saredd?" Jeric asked, as the boards creaked and groaned.

"At Vondar. With her."

This should have brought Jeric comfort, since Ricón had left his best with Imari, but it did not.

When they reached the landing, Ricón turned through a doorway and into a bedroom. Waning daylight bled through the decorative screen, throwing patterns of light upon the floor. Jeric gazed through the screen's holes and to the harbor beyond. From here, he could see the edge of dark and bulbous clouds brooding over Ziyan—the Forgotten Wastes. The ever-present storm left over from a people who had more power than they'd known what to do with.

A people who shared Imari's blood.

Hopefully that blood would protect her now, if Astrid reached her before they could warn her.

"How did Astrid escape?" Ricón lifted the lid of a large cedar chest and rifled through its contents, while Jeric explained what had happened.

"Wolf." Ricón shut the lid with a loud *thunk*. "Bringing Stanis here, in his condition...you're putting my people at risk—"

"He's not lost yet."

Ricón sighed and faced him square. "Imari cannot do this."

"You have no idea what Imari can do."

Ricón stopped, and his lips pressed into a line. "Your faith in her abilities is commendable, but it's selfish to ask this of her. It'll expose her for what she—"

"What do you mean, *expose* her?" Jeric interrupted. Ricón didn't answer, but Jeric understood, and he took a single step forward, feeling a sudden flare of anger on Imari's behalf. "You're still hiding her. That's why you haven't made an announcement—"

"It's for her own safety—"

"The safest thing you can do for her is let her be who she is. She needs your rutting support—"

"Don't tell me what she needs, *Wolf*." Ricón's eyes flashed. "Your family is the reason we had to hide her in the first place."

"And *I let her go*," Jeric growled. "*With my blessing.*"

"This shouldn't come as a surprise to you, but a Wolf's blessing means very little around here."

Jeric looked straight at Ricón, and said, lowly, "I am not my father."

Ricón regarded the Wolf King. "No, you're not," he replied at last. "But it's still Tommad's Corinth, and until we—"

Just then, someone rapped on the door.

The men exchanged a glance, and Jeric ducked behind a changing screen, angling himself so that he could see the door as it opened, and whoever stood beyond.

It was the saredd from the antechamber below. He whispered a few low words to Ricón, who nodded and closed the door as Jeric reemerged from behind the screen.

Their unfinished argument strained the quiet between them.

"We'll have to continue this later," Ricón said tersely. "It's time to go. But first, you and your men need to put these on."

· · ·

WITHIN THE HOUR, Jeric and his men had shed their Corinthian wool in favor of loose Istraan cotton, and tied wide scarves around their heads. Of course, if anyone looked closely, their light complexions would give them away, but at a distance, they blended in well enough.

They gathered their belongings from *The Lady*, but at the top of the ramp, Jeric stopped beside Survak. Both men watched Braddok and Aksel carry an unconscious Stanis between them.

Jeric glanced sideways at the old captain. "You know him."

It wasn't a question.

Survak took a long pull from his pipe as his eyes followed Stanis's unconscious form. "No," Survak said at last, exhaling a plume of smoke. "I don't know that man at all."

And then Survak turned away from the rail and retreated back to his cabin. Jeric's earlier suspicion nagged, but now wasn't the time to chase old threads, so Jeric walked on and joined Ricón at the docks.

Ricón led them to stables, where the city guard had readied half a dozen camels, two horses, and a sledge. Some of them would be sharing a mount.

"Easy," Ricón said, amused, as his saredd watched Jeric's men struggle with the camels. Ricón leaned forward, forearms crossed over his saddle. "They need a moment to warm to you."

"A moment, my ass," Braddok cursed. Every step he took toward his camel, the camel took a step back.

One saredd chuckled.

"Maybe he doesn't like the smell of akavit," Chez mused.

"Assuming he can smell anything over his own godsdamned breath..." Braddok mumbled.

Jeric ensured Stanis was comfortably secured to the sledge, and then he approached the camel harnessed to it—the one he would be riding. She towered over him as he gazed up into her rich brown eyes framed by thick black lashes. She looked curiously back while her enormous mandible slowly worked over an old meal.

"Saluté," Jeric said, then held out a conciliatory hand. *Hello.*

The camel snorted, her ears flickered, and she turned her head away.

Behind him, Braddok cursed after the camel who had turned around completely and was walking away from him. Ricón's guards hooted and hollered.

"I brought you something." Jeric grabbed an apple he'd packed and offered it to the camel. She turned her head back to him, curious now, and her long lashes blinked slow. In one bite, she took the apple from his palm, chomped it with an impressive set of blocky teeth, and then nudged Jeric's face with her nose.

Gods, her breath. He thought he might vomit again.

"Sorry. I don't have any more." Jeric opened his hands so that she could see his empty palms. She grumbled in annoyance and nudged him again with her nose.

"Touch her hind. She'll sit for you to climb," Ricón said, looking mildly impressed.

Slowly, so as not to startle her, Jeric rested a hand on her hind, just behind the saddle. She belched loudly, but sank upon all fours.

Braddok folded his arms and glared. "Rutting showoff."

Jeric winked, then climbed onto the saddle, wincing a little as his wound pulled. The camel rose, and Jeric caught on to the motion, leaning back and following the camel's momentum as she stood upright.

A saredd returned with Braddok's camel, and helped Braddok climb on, despite the loud protestations of both rider and mount.

Ricón looked to Jeric. "Ready?"

Jeric glanced back at Stanis, who lay tied to the sledge, unmoving, and nodded once.

"Viama!" Ricón yelled to the others.

And Jeric prayed to whatever god would listen that they'd reach Trier in time.

17

I mari lowered herself through the hole in Taran and Saza's ceiling, and they both glanced over: Saza, with delight. Taran, with suspicion.

That woman was sharper than a suture needle.

"Saza...get us some water," Taran said.

Saza's shoulders slumped, but he did as Taran bid. Imari tossed him a fig, which he caught with a grin, and he ducked out through the door.

"You came to say goodbye," Taran said once he left.

Imari faced her square and breathed in deep. She hated this. Hated. This.

That she had to choose. That no matter what she chose, someone suffered. That she had to abandon two people who already meant so much to her—who already felt like family.

"You don't need to explain," Taran said. "I warned you not to get caught." Taran's gaze flickered over her, and Imari thought she detected a bit of sadness there too. "Well? Back for one more try?"

"I didn't bring my talla."

Taran's dark eyes sharpened. "We're not practicing without—"

"I've been reading the book you gave me."

That was clearly not what Taran had expected Imari to say.

"There's a passage I wanted to ask you about," Imari continued.

Taran drew back, eyeing her.

They hadn't spoken much about Imari's particular talent this past week, because Taran had resolutely focused on Imari learning control. But the passage Imari had read last night had wormed into her brain, and she could not pull it free.

"It says that in the beginning, Asorai ruled the heavens with his five most trusted."

"The Divines," Taran said carefully.

Yes, the Divines. Imari had always pictured them like Asorai's supernatural guard, and each Divine was said to encompass an aspect of Asorai's power. In fact, it was this model Azir had used for his attempted reign, appointing the most powerful Liagé from each of the four Shah talents to serve as his high commanders— the Mo'Ruk, he'd called them, and together, they had terrorized the land. And it was the power of the original four Divines that had leaked into Sol Velorian soil, creating those four Liagé talents as they now knew them.

But there was just one problem.

Imari had always known them as the *Four* Divines; the verses claimed there had been *five*.

"There were five Divines. Not four," Imari said. And the fifth had been a sulaziér—singer of souls.

Taran's eyes glittered, but she did not deny it.

"What happened to the sulaziér?" Imari asked, because this was the question she could not shake. She remembered her nightmare of the tree, and it filled her with a fear she could not explain. "The verses did not say anything more about the fifth Divine. I checked, and—"

"They wouldn't," Taran said, sighing. "Well, not in that form, I should say, because the fifth isn't referred to as a Divine. But the details as to why, you'll find only in the teachings of Moltoné, though I haven't seen that book in a very long time."

Imari didn't understand what Taran meant. "And what do Moltoné's teachings say about the sulaziér?"

Rasmin had told her each generation produced only one with her particular power. She did not know if that were true, but it seemed to follow, considering she'd never heard of anyone else with this talent. She'd never even heard the word until Ventus.

Taran pressed her lips together. At last, she said, "The sulaziér fell."

"What do you mean, fell? He died? He—"

"*She*," Taran interrupted. "They called her Zussa. She was... Asorai's most trusted companion."

"And what happened to her?" Imari asked.

Taran shrugged. "She wanted more."

"More what? More power?"

Taran inclined her head.

"Oh." A chill moved over Imari. "So she *turned on* Asorai."

Taran noticed Imari's growing trepidation. "Understand, child, that the brighter the light, the stronger the darkness pulls. For what does the darkness care for a flicker? But if it can smother the one who illuminates the world...well, then, it owns the world."

And the sulaziér had been the strongest Divine of all.

Again, Imari thought of the tree, the nightmare and that horrible voice. Would it be the same for her? Would darkness call to her as it had lured Zussa?

"What did Asorai do?" Imari asked.

"Well, according to the teachings, the other four Divines took Zussa's talla and destroyed her with it. The process alone disintegrated their physical forms, but their power leaked back into the soil and—"

"That's what made the Liagé," Imari answered.

"Yes."

And then, "What was Zussa's—" *talla*, Imari meant to say, when the beads clattered.

Both women looked to the doorway, expecting Saza, but only silence followed. No footsteps trudged up the stairwell. There was nothing at all.

And then Imari realized that Saza had been gone a very long time. Taran realized this in the same instant and started to rise, but Imari said, quietly, "Wait here."

"*No*. You stay here," Taran said, climbing to her feet. "If you're discovered—"

But Imari ducked through the doorway before Taran could finish. She crept down the dark stairs, fear prickling her senses, and just before she reached the bottommost step, she stopped in her tracks.

A marking shone above the door, on the inside. A ward, just like those atop Skanden's wall, but this had been drawn directly on the plaster, invisible unless activated.

Imari's heart pumped faster. She knew who had made it, but what had set it off?

Saza.

Imari grabbed the beads to quiet them as she slipped through, and a tingling swept over her body, like the brush of silk. It was the power imbued in Taran's ward. Imari could feel it now, this steady pulse of Shah energy.

Its warning.

Imari crept forward, sticking to the shadows. When had the night turned so quiet? And so...dark? Imari reached the end of the short alley and peered around the corner.

"There you are, sulaziér."

18

An inky silhouette materialized from the shadows, about a dozen paces away. The silhouette was human in form, but Imari found nothing human in the person occupying it. The body was emaciated and hollow, and one shoulder slouched, as though the muscles holding it together had detached. The wool covering was ripped and tattered, and one bare foot twisted inward, bending the skinny leg unnaturally. The head drooped as though sheer willpower held it aloft.

"Astrid..." The name tumbled out of Imari's lips, and her heart pounded with sudden fear. Not because of the creature standing before her.

But because of what Astrid's presence meant.

"Where's Jeric?" Imari demanded.

She could almost feel Astrid's cruel smile.

Astrid limped closer, dragging that twisted foot behind her. "She cares for a wolf." It was a legion of sound, warped and otherworldly. An off key to the pure and natural tones of this world. "How...sweet."

"*Tell me where he is.*"

Shadows slid beneath Astrid's pale skin, and something like a finger pushed against her face from the inside, distorting her cheekbone. "Your *dog* is dead."

Imari's heart seized, and she suddenly couldn't seem to draw enough air.

No.

He couldn't...

Not Jeric.

"You're lying," Imari snarled, though fear clawed through her body.

"Are we?" Astrid's black eyes gleamed with unnatural light, delighting in Imari's anguish. "Perhaps we should have saved him for her, so she could have heard his screams."

Imari wanted to believe the demon lied, but another truth wheedled its way in: Jeric would have warned her. Unless Astrid had taken his life before he'd had the opportunity.

Imari's body hummed with fury. She was a bell struck too hard, the vibrations so strong, they nearly cracked her surface.

"Such anger," the legion said, and that unnatural light in Astrid's eyes shone brighter.

Imari took a step forward. "I will *destroy* you."

"Delicious." Astrid licked her lips. "Give us more, little sulaz-iér..." And then Astrid looked past Imari where, to Imari's horror, a silent stepped into the street, dragging someone behind it.

Saza.

Her heart lurched as Saza screamed and lashed, trying to break free.

Imari did not know how in the world a silent could be here, or what business it had with Astrid, but none of that mattered seeing Saza in its clutches.

"Let him go!" Imari demanded.

But the silent did not let Saza go, and so Imari turned back to Astrid, beseeching. "*Please!* He has nothing to do with—"

"You will leave this place, demon," said a new voice, and Taran stepped into the street, standing straighter and taller than

Imari had thought possible. Wild hair framed her fury, and her hands dripped fresh blood. She was wrath and judgment manifest, how Imari envisioned a Divine, come to earth to exact her perfect vengeance.

Astrid hissed like a cat, hackles raised. "*You.*"

"Get back, girl," Taran snapped at Imari as she strode right past to stand between Imari and the legion.

Before Imari could wonder, Astrid opened her mouth wide—much too wide, as though her jaw unhinged—and she vomited darkness. It poured from her lips like a fountain, pooled onto the ground and slithered toward Taran.

But Taran was drawing fast upon the ground—in her blood. She painted symbols like the one above her door, like those upon Skanden's warded wall. Astrid's darkness crashed into them like a tide, Taran's symbols flared bright, and the darkness broke against the moonlight barrier with a horrible wailing. It recoiled, slithering back to its master, where it frothed at her feet.

"Who brought you back?" Taran snarled, swaying a little.

Imari noticed.

So did the legion.

The legion smiled viciously with Astrid's black teeth and pushed her palms forward. That darkness swept forth again, this time in a rush. It crashed into Taran's wards in an explosion of air that knocked Taran on her backside. Almost outside of her warded circle.

Astrid crept closer, a lion stalking its kill. "You're weak, *prior*. The years have not been kind to you."

"And you call what you're doing to that poor girl's body a *kind*ness," Taran hissed, climbing to her feet.

Imari distantly registered their words as she gazed back at Saza, struggling in the silent's grip. Now was her chance; the legion was distracted, *and* it wanted Imari alive, which could work to her advantage.

Imari sprinted.

She had no idea what she was going to do, but she had to do something.

The silent eyed her, completely unconcerned, but Saza redoubled his efforts. He kicked and thrashed and screamed, and the silent jerked Saza up by the shirt, holding him eye level. Saza's feet dangled as he ripped and clawed at the silent's immoveable arms. Imari took the opportunity and jumped onto the silent's back, wrapped her arms around its neck, and squeezed with all her might.

The silent snarled and stumbled back, slamming Imari into a wall—so hard, bits of plaster came away with her. But she did not let go, and the silent slammed her back again. This time, her skull struck stucco and she tasted blood, but when she looked back, Saza was gone. The silent held only his tunic.

And little Saza was sprinting—shirtless—down the street.

"Go!" Imari screamed, as the silent rammed her against the wall again.

Imari cried out, stucco ground into her back, but she held on tight, trying to give Saza every possible advantage. And then she heard a scream. A horrible, gut-wrenching scream, like a heart being ripped from its body, and her gaze followed the sound to where Taran collapsed. Her wards flickered out, and she lay in her circle of dark blood, staring up at the night, unmoving.

Gone.

"*No*," Imari cried.

In Imari's distraction, the silent wrenched her arms from its neck and threw her to the ground. She collided hard, rolling and tumbling until she smacked into the wall opposite.

Taran.

Imari shoved herself up just in time to see one of the legion's inky tendrils lash out and catch Saza's ankle. The darkness pulled like a whip, yanked his feet out from under him and dragged him back to Astrid as he screamed.

"Saza!" Imari cried out.

Suddenly, a powerful beating of air sounded overhead, and something clattered to the ground a few paces away.

Her flute.

Imari lunged for it, but a force barreled into her side, knocking her to the ground. The silent. It stamped a heavy foot upon her back, pinning her down.

Imari yelled through her teeth and tried pushing herself up, but the silent would not budge. The air beat again, and this time, the silent screamed. The pressure at her back lifted, and Imari scrambled to her feet. She pitched forward and snatched her flute as a giant black owl raked the silent's face, ripping and tearing at its eyes.

Rasmin.

He'd taken one of the silent's eyes, and was diving low to take the other.

No time to think, Imari lifted the flute to her lips. The tingling and heat rose immediately into her chest, as if it'd been waiting for this moment.

And she played.

Notes poured from her flute, her fingers flying fast. She vented her power into the instrument, but just like every other night these past few weeks, the blaze raged through her chest like an inferno. Imari cut the note short before the fire consumed her.

Saza cried out, and Imari glanced over to see the darkness weave around him like a cocoon, while the silent battled Rasmin's sharp talons.

Imari raised the flute again, and played.

Saza screamed as the darkness pulled higher and tears welled in Imari's eyes. That inferno raged through her chest, but she did not stop. Saza needed her *now*.

The owl screeched as it was thrown against a wall, and the silent, thus freed, rammed into Imari again, knocking her back to the ground. The flute flew from her hands, and the silent flipped Imari onto her stomach, while Imari bucked and thrashed, trying—and failing—to throw the silent's insurmountable weight.

The darkness reached inky fingers into Saza's mouth.

"Saza!" Imari screamed, struggling to break free.

Saza's scream turned into gurgling.

Nononononononono....

"Saza..." Imari cried as hot tears leaked from her eyes."No... Saza..."

Saza jerked and convulsed. The blackness moved under his skin, spreading through his innocent face until his eyes filled with pure black. There, the darkness welled and dripped from the creases like tears of ink, and Saza's head lolled to the side.

Dead.

"*No...*" Imari choked on a sob and sagged beneath the silent. Her fight gone.

Astrid approached, slow and steady, stepping over Saza's lifeless form as if he were nothing more than a hole in the street. The demon's pure black eyes fixed on Imari, who lay pinned and crying quietly.

"You can't escape us, little sulaziér," said the legion. "This is your destiny—"

Thundering footsteps sounded, and a man yelled, "Stop where you are!"

Astrid's eyes narrowed as she looked farther down the street, while the silent grabbed Imari's arms and jerked her to a stand. The silent's face was mangled and covered in blood, and a gruesome hole remained where one eye had been. Rasmin had come so close to taking the other.

Five city guards approached, including one very large saredd.

Tarq.

Tarq spotted Imari in that same moment, and when he noticed Astrid, he stopped in his tracks. The others stopped behind him. One made a sign to the saints.

"Tarq, get out of here!" Imari cried through her tears. "Warn my—"

The silent clamped a hand over her mouth, stopping the rest of her words.

"Get the healer." Tarq gestured at two of the guards, who immediately rushed Imari and the silent. The silent shoved Imari at the first guard and whirled on the second with impossible speed.

But it had let her go.

Imari knew she had mere seconds to act.

She untangled herself from the first guard and launched for her flute, leaving the guards to the bloodied and one-eyed silent. In her periphery, Astrid's inky serpents took down the other two guards, sucking the life from them as she'd done in Skyhold's great hall. And just like in that hall, those serpentine tendrils slid back toward their master, *into* her body, and Astrid shuddered as she ingested their life force.

And then Tarq moved in.

He didn't see the metallic glint in Astrid's hands, because he was coming up behind her.

"Tarq, look out!" Imari screamed.

But Tarq did not hear her, and in a sweep of ink and smoke, Astrid moved behind Tarq and stabbed him through the back with the scim of a fallen guard.

Tarq stopped and stumbled forward in surprise, the point of his fallen fellow's scim protruding through his abdomen.

Astrid smiled, while her eyes glowed with that strange light. The other two guards, who had fought the silent, lay on the ground bleeding life onto the dirt. Dead or unconscious, Imari couldn't say, but the silent staggered forward, dripping blood.

"Come with us, sulaziér, and no one else needs to die," the legion said with unnatural calm.

Imari's flute pulsed warm in her hand.

"Hand it over." Astrid held out her hand.

Wings flapped again, and the owl dove, clawing at the silent's face as the silent screamed.

Rasmin had just given her one more chance.

Imari raised the flute and played. Notes flew into the night, desperate and searching.

Slow. Clear your mind.

The voice.

The one she'd heard in Skyhold's underbelly, and again in the great hall. It spoke into her mind, just as calm and steady and clear as it demanded she be now.

Steady, Imari.

Imari forced her mind clear despite her racing pulse and trembling fingers. She threw out every errant thought and fear, and focused only on that voice.

Steady, the voice repeated.

This time, miraculously, the tingling stayed back. Her mouth was a dam regulating the flow of power pushing against it, but the tingling remained calm and steady. Contained.

Well done.

Imari's next note rang strong and clear, and she opened that dam just a little, allowing power to drip into her fingertips.

And the world...changed.

She didn't understand what she was seeing at first. Her world became little points of light and the shadows in between. She saw the buildings like constellations, outlined in light, as if she were standing in the heavens, and the stars had taken shape to outline a city. Imari's note hitched with surprise, and the stars nearest flickered like candles stirred by a soft breeze.

Responding to her music.

Suddenly, Imari understood. Those lights—those stars—were the Maker's own essence woven into all of creation. A kind of spirit plane, and the brighter stars were actually *people*. The citizens of E'Centro gazing out of their windows and doorways.

And then she saw Astrid.

Or, more accurately, it was what Imari did *not* see that showed her where Astrid stood, for in that place, only darkness existed, just as it had been in Skyhold. Cold and infinite and vile, like some tear in the fabric of this world.

Find the tension, the voice urged in her mind.

Imari did not know what *finding the tension* meant, but the voice had not led her astray yet, and so she took a breath and held her note firm. She listened to every layer of that tone now pouring from her flute, following the note to its edge while watching those little points of light vibrate all around her.

Reflecting her sound.

She'd experienced something like it before, when she'd hummed in a small enclosed space and the surrounding walls had caught hold of her specific tone and reflected it back, amplifying it like a harmonic. Similarly, these stars resonated with her note, amplifying it, but one tone stood out from the rest: a dissonant timbre to the pure harmony of creation. And that tone was coming from the points of light which brushed the perimeter of Astrid's darkness, as if those stars had warped, infected with her evil.

Find the tension, the voice repeated, and the fire in her belly breathed.

This time, Imari knew exactly what the voice meant. She needed to catch that off key, those infected stars, and tune them back to purity.

She pushed her D to the lowest edge of an E, to match Astrid's dissonance, and those little points of light surrounding Astrid— the ones at the edge of the tear, distorted by the legion's evil— began to vibrate faster than the rest.

Imari felt a surge of hope.

"No..." the legion growled. Astrid tried to take a step, but her feet would not move. All those little points of light around her fixed into a solid barrier of tone, keeping her contained.

Imari pushed her note farther to bend the sound. Not

changing notes, but *tuning* them. The stars around Astrid shone even brighter, caught with Imari's music. Waiting for Imari to guide them back to purity, like tuning the strings of an oud.

Imari bent the tone even farther, and the stars surrounding Astrid flared bright and began pushing *against* the darkness. As if Imari's flute was a needle, her notes the thread, slowly weaving the light back together again.

Weaving the darkness out.

"NO!" Astrid wailed. In one vicious and desperate burst of strength, Astrid broke through the net of collapsing stars.

But Imari did not stop. She played to those little points of light, pulling them closer and closer. Astrid snarled, teeth bared as her bloodied hands clawed at the air, and with a final burst of breath, Imari ended the piece and stitched the tear closed.

Binding out the void.

Astrid wailed so loudly, all of Trier would have heard it. In fact, all of Trier might be there now, Imari noticed, because a crowd had gathered—saredd and city guards and citizens alike— and many more faces looked on from E'Centro's dark windows.

Imari heard the sharp snap of metal, and Astrid collapsed to the ground in a heap—completely still. Liagé cuffs now bound her wrists and pulsed with ward light.

Tarq stood over her, his shoulders sagging and belly soaked in blood. His gaze met Imari's and he stumbled back. He would have fallen if guards had not caught his arms. Imari ran to him, but more saredd blocked her path. One was a man she'd helped just a few days ago in the Qazzat.

"He's bleeding out!" she snarled, feeling slightly dizzy from the power she'd just channeled. "Let me help him!"

The saredd exchanged an uncertain glance, looking from Imari, to her glowing flute, to Tarq, and then—finally— they backed away to give her space. Imari dropped to her knees beside Tarq, distantly aware of more footsteps approaching.

Imari pressed her fingers to Tarq's wound, and he winced.

Wards, he'd lost so much blood. Too much. It was a good thing he had a lot of it.

Tarq mumbled something she couldn't make out.

"Shh," Imari insisted. "Stay with me, Tarq. I will fix this."

And she rutting would fix this.

"What happened here?" shouted a new voice, though it was one she recognized. Sebharan, and he'd brought a dozen more city guards with him.

Was all of the Qazzat here too?

Imari did not answer, but instead ripped the wrapping from Tarq's head and pushed it to the gaping wound. "Hold this here to staunch the flow."

Sebharan stopped behind her and took in the scene. "Saints above..."

"Get Tarq to Gamla's," Imari said. "I can still save him."

Sebharan snapped his fingers and gave a command, and two city guards helped Tarq to his feet. Tarq weighed so much, a third came to assist, and together, they dragged him toward Vondar.

Imari spotted the silent on its knees, totally blind and covered in blood, and surrounded by guards.

"What do we do with him?" a guard asked Sebharan.

Sebharan looked to Imari.

"Kill it," Imari said.

"And what about...her?" Sebharan asked, gesturing at Astrid.

Imari was about to request they let her kill Astrid, but reconsidered. She needed answers. Silent couldn't speak, but Astrid could. "You still have the Liagé holding cells?"

A handful of such cells had been constructed during Azir's time, in the dungeons beneath Vondar, with the help of Liagé who'd sided with the Provinces. Just to be ready, in case they'd captured Azir, or his Mo'Ruk.

"One, yes," Sebharan answered.

"Lock her in it."

No one moved.

"Well? You heard her," Sebharan barked.

Still, no one moved.

Imari couldn't blame them. It was like walking up to a night-mare. So Imari approached Astrid herself, while the guards and saredd watched in silence. She could feel more eyes watching from the dark windows.

Imari couldn't imagine what the citizens of E'Centro must think of her now, someone they'd come to know as a moonlight healer who had just wielded Shah power against a demon.

And had failed to save Taran and Saza.

Imari clenched her hands into fists as she stopped beside the demon and gazed down at its emaciated shell. Wards, the smell. Imari could hardly see Astrid's skin anymore through all the filth and blood. Her hair was thin and matted, and chunks of it were missing, as if she'd ripped clumps right out of her scalp. She nudged Astrid's body with her boot, but the demon did not stir.

It would be so easy to end it all right now.

But.

Then Imari would never know what Astrid had wanted.

"I've weakened her," Imari said sharply, addressing Sebharan. "But I'm not sure how long it'll last, and I *need* to help Tarq if he's to survive."

"Go on," Sebahran said. "We'll handle this."

Imari glanced over at Taran's still body, and Saza's. Her chest constricted so painfully, for a moment, she couldn't breathe. But Imari didn't have time for grief just yet. Though she hated to leave Saza and Taran like this, there was still one more life she might save, if she hurried.

Imari tore herself away, and sprinted.

I mari caught up with Tarq and his escort, and the five of them rushed through a city that no longer slept. What had happened in E'Centro had woken all of Trier. People spied through doors and high balconies, searching for the source of the commotion.

There would be no hiding as Sable, not anymore; too many people had seen her use her power. She'd worry about that later.

She hurried with Tarq and his escort up Vondar's stairs, which proved challenging, as Tarq had an increasingly difficult time supporting his own weight. Imari preceded them through the main gate and into an atrium full of more city guards, where she spotted Sar Branón speaking rapidly with Bayek and Avék.

Imari cursed inwardly. Avék would not be happy with her. She'd snuck away on his watch.

"Pa... Sar Branón!" Imari called out, catching her error at the last second. Wondering—distractedly—if it even mattered now.

Sar Branón stopped talking and looked at his daughter. Relief filled his face, and she was in his arms a second later. "Saints, you're all right." He pulled back and looked her over as if needing to be sure that she was truly unharmed. "When Avék said you weren't in your chambers, I thought—"

"I'm fine," she said, briefly snagging Avék's furious gaze. "But I have to go. Tarq needs my help."

Sar Branón glanced at Tarq then, whom the guards struggled to hold upon his feet. His gaze settled on the wound. "Do what you need to do," he said, then added, quietly, "Where is the demon?"

"Sebharan's taking it to a holding cell."

"Holding cell?" Bayek approached. "We can't afford to keep that thing in Vondar. It's too dangerous—"

"We need it for questioning," Imari interjected. "Someone sent it here, and if it's working for the Liagé leader, perhaps we can—"

"That isn't your decision to make, *healer*." Bayek said her title like a reprimand. "And what were you doing in E'Centro at this hour, anyway?"

"She's right," Sar Branón said.

Bayek fumed. "But mi sar, this—"

"If the demon knows anything, this could work in our favor," Sar Branón said pointedly, then added, "And Imari has exposed herself to too many eyes."

Meaning, her secret wouldn't be *secret* much longer.

"I'll go with her," Avék said, to Imari's surprise. He'd sidled closer, and his hand rested upon the metal claws dangling at his waist.

Sar Branon nodded at Avék, then looked back at his daughter. "I'll find you later."

Imari nodded and pushed on, not sparing Bayek another glance.

"You should have told me," Avék said, once they left the atrium.

"Would you have let me go?"

Avék did not reply. They both knew the answer.

Thick drops of blood stained the path all the way to Gamla's door, where Jenya waited. She was fully dressed in sarred attire, and fully armed, with her hair pulled back neatly in a long rope, and she glanced from Imari to Avék with a frown.

Imari shoved the door open, and the others followed her inside. The chimp-shaped lantern still burned, and a book about antidotes lay open before it—a book Imari had told Avék she would be retiring early to read, as she'd done every night. Avék looked at the book, at Imari.

"Someone start the fire."

Avék gazed at her a second longer, and then started for the firebox.

Imari began clearing a place on the table, and Jenya moved to help her. "Lay him here."

The guards carried Tarq to the table and laid him down just as the door opened again and Kai stepped through. He still wore yesterday's clothes, though they appeared rumpled and his tunic was untucked. Imari did not think he'd been sleeping.

She didn't really want to think where he'd been.

"What in all the saints..." Kai started, eyes wide as he looked over Tarq.

"Hotter," Imari said to Avék.

But Avék was staring at Tarq, who moaned.

"Avék!"

Avék snapped to attention and heaped more coals into the box.

"Make sure he doesn't roll off," Imari said, then rushed over to Gamla's shelves. She rifled through the jars, and insects, searching for the little opaque vial she'd spotted just the other day.

"Where are you..." she mumbled, furiously shoving bottles aside, when her fingertips grazed the cork.

Ah!

She snatched it up, shook the vial, and the contents sloshed gloriously. Suspension of Verra Root. Worth a sar's ransom.

Imari pulled the cork free, and the pungent odor of rotten eggs struck her at once. She hopped down from the counter, grabbed the bottle of Rosaca, and returned to her patient.

"Hold him steady," Imari said, setting the Verra Root on the bench.

Two guards secured Tarq's hands, while Avék and Jenya each grabbed one of Tarq's enormous boots.

"What happened?" Kai asked, stepping dazedly into the room.

Imari grabbed the sopping headwrap from Tarq's midsection and tossed it at Kai's feet. It landed with a wet slap, and Kai paled as Imari swiveled back to Tarq and ripped open his covering.

The room fell silent.

It was a nasty wound, at least four fingers wide, just below his left ribcage, and blood oozed with each pump of his heart.

Not good.

She unscrewed the Rosaca and poured. Tarq's body clenched, but the others held him firm while the antiseptic bubbled and fizzed and pulled the dark clots away.

"I have to cauterize this." Imari looked at Jenya and held out a hand. "I need your scim."

Jenya's eyes hardened. She glanced down at Tarq.

Imari couldn't believe that even now, with Tarq lying at death's door, that Jenya wouldn't trust her—

Jenya produced a scim, hilt first.

Imari took it, then poured Rosaca over the metal and rushed it to the firebox. The coals weren't as hot as Imari would have liked, but there wasn't time to wait. Imari shoved Jenya's scim into the hot coals, waited until the metal was hot enough, then ran back to Tarq.

"Your belt." She looked sharply at Kai. "Put it in his mouth."

Kai blinked, then seemed to remember himself. He tugged his

belt free, which wasn't difficult since he hadn't secured it properly, and handed it to Avék, who set it between Tarq's teeth.

"Hold him," Imari warned.

The others braced themselves.

"Stay with me, Tarq," Imari pleaded, holding the hilt of the fire-hot scim. She splayed her fingers upon Tarq's broad and muscled abdomen, steadied her hand, and with a quick prayer to the Maker, she touched the hot metal to Tarq's bleeding wound.

Skin sizzled and Tarq thrashed as he screamed through Kai's belt. Imari moved Jenya's scim out of the way just in time. The wound was too wide to close in one pass, so she repeated the process a second time, finally sealing the wound shut.

"Turn him over," Imari said, plunging the dagger back into the hot coals. She heard Anja's voice just beyond the door, and the sura stopped in the threshold. All the commotion undoubtedly woken her, but—Imari noted—not even sleep had kept the sura from dressing in mournful black. Kai hurried over to his mama and whispered fast, briefing her on all that had transpired.

Imari ignored them and repeated the process on Tarq's back, and when she finished, she handed Jenya the scim. Jenya took it, staring at Imari as if seeing her clearly for the first time.

Imari grabbed the vial of Verra Root off the bench. "Help me roll him onto his back."

No one hesitated this time.

Imari walked around the table, and the others moved out of her way. Tarq was no longer panting. He wasn't moving at all, and fine beads of sweat glistened upon his forehead. Imari put a hand to his face. Wards, he was so cold.

"Stay with me, Tarq," she demanded, then used her thumb to wrench Tarq's jaw open by the teeth. She poured the entire contents of the vial into his mouth, slammed his jaw shut, and prayed the black liquid would go down.

Tarq's throat bobbed.

Imari waited.

The silence labored.

Tarq, please…

Finally—gloriously—Tarq gasped. One long, wheezing inhale, as if he were breathing his soul back into his body. And then a guard cried out as Tarq rolled off the table. Avék and Jenya lunged, catching Tarq just in time.

"This is all your fault."

The words had come from Sura Anja.

Imari looked back at her papa's wife. Really looked at her—at this woman who carried nothing but hate and resentment, who wore it like armor.

"You bring death wherever you go." Anja's voice trembled, her knuckles blanched as she clutched her black shawl.

She wasn't wrong.

Imari crossed the room and opened the small door to Gamla's private chamber. "Bring Tarq in here."

"Don't ignore me, *beram*."

Bastard.

Imari gazed back at her step mama, and then she approached. The others looked on, quiet, while the sura drew herself upright, her features set with self-righteousness, as if to ward herself against the abomination that was Imari.

Imari stopped before the sura, gazing upon this woman who had never accepted her into their family—never given her a chance—and Imari suddenly felt so tired. "I haven't ignored you a day in my life, mi a'sura, and that's part of the problem."

Anja stared, her cheeks splotched with indignation, but before the sura could utter another word, Imari strode right past her and a gaping Kai, then stopped briefly at the door.

"Keep an eye on Tarq," she said to the guards. "I'll be back soon." Then Imari gestured at Avék and Jenya to follow her as she ducked out of the room.

Where she stopped and exhaled a long breath.

Avék and Jenya stepped into the hall. Imari couldn't be sure, but they almost looked pleased.

"I need to have a word with our prisoner," Imari said, glancing at them. "Will you come?"

NIÁ CREPT ALONG THE SHADOWS, away from Ashova's seductive lights. Her client had left in a hurry, his passions harshly interrupted by an insistent messenger from the Qazzat. Normally, Niá wouldn't have given it a second thought. Her client would return, and she'd lure the information from him later. Her bed of nazzat and pleasure always loosened his tongue.

Except she'd caught the word E'Centro, and Niá's heart—that shriveled organ in the dark cavity of her chest—had suddenly flared to life and pounded hard.

With fear.

Niá held her shawl close. She'd grabbed a garment of nondescript cotton, because the good citizens of Trier did not like to see their favorite pets wandering free. Twice, she stopped as a handful of city guards hurried past with a couple saredd in their midst.

Never, in all Niá's seventeen years, had she seen so many guards running about the city, especially at this late hour. Someone had kicked the hornet's nest. But who? Certainly the shiva would have warned her if it were time.

Niá made it to E'Centro's edge and peered around the corner, into those filthy recesses where her people dwelled—where her family dwelled.

Those spaces were not dark this night.

Torchlight chased the shadows away, and guards and saredd alike gathered, speaking in hushed tones while citizens of E'Centro watched discreetly from their crumbling windows.

Niá moved to get a better view of the street, and her heart stopped.

She spotted the wild hair first, splayed about a vacant and familiar face, dark eyes staring at the night—unseeing—and a chill swept over her.

No...

Niá touched her fingers to her mouth. *Oza.* She lay in a heap, surrounded by blood-drawn glyphs—glyphs that had burned and died. Their energy had been used up and overwhelmed.

Niá's fear intensified as she scanned the street, hoping and praying that she would not find what she expected to find.

And she did.

On the opposite side of the street lay another body. Her little brother, Saza. His eyes were pure black, and a web of black veins stained his precious torso and face.

"*No...*" The word wrenched from her chest as her eyes burned. If she had doubted she had anything left of her heart, she did not doubt then, for it was tearing in two.

Niá did not realize she had started running toward Saza, and then she was beside him, dropping to her knees. "Saza...my little star... Not you..."

But he did not hear her.

He was gone.

Gone.

"*Why!*" Niá screamed. "Why him? He was just a boy! Why couldn't you take *me*?" And then she collapsed over his body and drew him into her arms, holding him tight.

"Saza..." she sobbed, rocking him gently as she did when he was a boy. When he had trusted her to protect him, and when she had promised she always would.

Instead, she had been in bed with a man.

Niá could hardly breathe through her tears.

Hands grabbed at her to pull her away, while Niá sobbed and screamed and clawed for Saza in desperation. Until her throat was raw. Until she couldn't fight anymore.

Until they dragged her wretched body away.

20

Imari made her way to Vondar's dungeons with Jenya and Avék following close behind. Vondar had not been constructed with dungeons in mind, for the gods' laws were clear, their punishments swift, therefore their Istraan ancestors had never considered the value of holding life ransom.

Until Azir.

Azir's war had changed everything. It had turned loosely affiliated colonies into five distinct provinces, with individual governances and a treaty to hold them all accountable. The war also convinced Istraa's sar of that time that, perhaps, there was advantage to be gained through ransom, and so he recast a section of Vondar's sewers for this purpose. Their best architects worked with Liagé enchanters and enchantresses to construct cells akin to those beneath Skyhold, equipped with warded chains and skal doors, and those cells had proven pivotal in leading the Five Provinces to victory—or so Vana, Imari's kunari, had always taught.

"They even held one of Azir's Mo'Ruk," Vana had said once.

The Mo'Ruk: Azir's four prized generals, each the strongest in their class of Shah power. Imari didn't know much more than that, because the stories surrounding the Mo'Ruk's war crimes had been too gruesome and frightening for little Imari, and Vana did not like to lose sleep.

But as the years following Azir's war passed, and fear lost potency to pride, the Liagé holding cells were abandoned and dismantled, though her papa had retained *one*. Imari suspected it was more for sentimental value than anything else.

And this cell was where Imari found her papa now, speaking in hushed tones with Sebharan amidst a handful of city guards, all standing before Istraa's last warded skal door. A door that looked so similar to the one beneath Skyhold, though this lacked the wounds of a temple collapse. Imari thought of that door, and how it had not been enough to hold Astrid, and her heart constricted.

Stars, she hoped Astrid had been lying about Jeric.

At Imari's approach, both Sar Branón and Sebharan glanced over.

"He's stable," Imari said to Sebharan, and Sebharan visibly relaxed. "Is she secure?"

"I believe so," Sar Branón said quietly, "though she's unresponsive."

Imari gazed upon the door, feeling that strange tingling of Shah energy push against her. "I still want to try to talk to her."

Sar Branón gazed upon his daughter a moment more, and then nodded at his Qazzat master. Sebharan approached the door and withdrew a key, which he inserted into a tiny hole at the door's center that Imari had not noticed until then. The door clicked and swung inward, revealing darkness beyond. But it wasn't total darkness. Astrid's glowing binds diffused the shadows and cast eerie light over everything.

Imari stepped through the door and into the roughly hewn domed chamber. Shah energy tingled in the air. In fact, as Imari breathed in, she detected a slight burning, like smoke from a distant fire.

The chamber itself had been carved right out of Vondar's

bedrock, and four skal-black chains as thick as Imari's arms had been bolted into the ceiling's arch. Wards had been carved along each individual link, giving the impression that the chains were comprised of glowing strings of text, which converged upon a hunched figure at the room's center.

Astrid.

She sat upon the rocky floor, her silhouette illuminated by the chain's light, and thick cuffs clamped around her wrists and ankles. Her legs were folded before her, her head drooped, and a snarl of hair hung forward, concealing her face. In a perfect circle around her, as if she were at the center of a target, larger wards had been etched directly into the floor. It reminded Imari of the blood circle Taran had painted in haste, which had failed her.

Imari took a step forward. "Astrid."

Nothing.

"I guess I shouldn't be surprised you didn't answer. It's not your name."

Still, nothing. The chains did not rattle. The air did not move, though it tingled as the Shah actively diffused whatever power existed within Astrid's emaciated frame.

Imari took another step forward, while the others watched her from the doorway. At the edge of that warded circle, Imari stopped and crouched upon the balls of her feet, regarding the creature at eye level. Dark shapes slithered beneath Astrid's pale skin, but nothing pressed against the surface.

"Look at me, demon," Imari commanded.

Silence.

"I said *look at me.*"

And Astrid laughed. It was a quiet sort of sound, deep and gurgling, and it sent a shiver over Imari's skin.

"She is angry with us," the legion said with amusement.

"Oh, what I feel toward you runs much deeper than anger."

Astrid's head lifted just a little, those black eyes piqued with delight. "Good, little sulaziér. Very good."

Imari glared at this depraved creature. It took every ounce of willpower not to kill it right then. "Where is Jeric?"

The legion smiled through Astrid's chapped and bloodied lips. "But we already told her that her precious dog is dead. Does she want more?"

"I want the truth."

Astrid licked her bloodied lips, delighting in the taste of her own blood. "His bones snapped so easily in our hands. Perhaps we should have brought one for—"

"*Enough,*" Imari snarled. "Why did you come here?" She didn't know if the demon was being truthful about Jeric—or if it *could* be truthful—but Imari would not torture herself with these gruesome potentialities about his fate any longer, nor would she indulge the demon's sadistic pleasures.

But Astrid only looked at her, a gleam in those black eyes.

Imari tried again. "What do you want from me?"

Astrid's lips curled in a cruel smile. "What we want matters not, little sulaziér."

Imari frowned, remembering Taran's words: *Who brought you back?*

"Then who sent you?" Imari asked.

Astrid's smile broadened, revealing black and bloodied teeth. One canine had cracked in half. But still, she did not answer.

Imari ground her molars together. "I will get what I want, demon. I will find out why you're here, and then you will pay for all you've done. Even if it kills me, by the Maker of all creation, *I swear it.*"

Astrid's eyes glittered.

Imari abruptly stood and backed away. She didn't trust herself to stay in the legion's presence any longer. She had just reached the door, when the legion said in a rasping voice, "The tree beckons us too."

Imari stopped in her tracks.

"What are you talking about?" Imari asked, feeling a sudden

spike of fear. She was very aware of everyone watching from the door.

The legion continued, eyes alight as it gazed in wonder at the domed ceiling. "Always calling us home. Calling us. Calling us." Those black eyes landed on Imari again. "The time is near, little sulaziér."

And then her eyes rolled back in her head, leaving only whites, and her lips moved in a steady and chanting whisper as she rocked back and forth.

Back and forth.

Imari inhaled a shaky breath, strode out of the room, and pulled the door shut behind her. The others stood around, quiet.

"What tree is she talking about?" her papa asked.

Imari gazed at the door, which Sebharan locked. "I have no idea." A lie.

But they believed her. It almost made it worse. That she was so good at lying.

And that she was lying to them.

"You have three days, surina," Sebharan said heavily, turning back to face her. "And then she will go to the Kourana for execution."

"Of course. I understand."

The Qazzat master had already lost four guards, and he had almost lost one saredd. Three days was generous. But a large part of Imari feared that, perhaps, three days might even be *too* generous.

You are mine, *sulaziér...*

Imari woke with a start, her hand on her chest where the tree's branches had speared her heart.

Just a dream.

But it was the same dream, that black tree with diseased flesh, its bare branches reaching like tentacles—searching, for her.

Always calling us home. Calling us. Calling us...

Imari breathed in deep and rubbed her temples. The little chimp-shaped brazier flickered innocently beside her, illuminating the open pages of the verses Taran had given her, where she had sought comfort and answers late into the night. Imari cursed at herself. Stupid, stupid, stupid! If anyone had walked in here and seen her with this...

Imari shut the little book, shoved it into her tunic and stood, then looked toward the screen, where a rising sun painted the screen's decorative holes pink.

Burning wards, it was morning.

Imari crossed the room and shoved the verses deep into a cupboard, grabbed fresh bandages and the bottle of Rosaca, and went into Gamla's private chambers to check on Tarq.

A lantern burned beside the small bed where Tarq slept peacefully, thank the stars. He wasn't quite snoring, but he was a heavy breather, and Imari thought his crooked nose was probably to blame. She knelt beside him, lifted last night's bandages, and checked his wound. The skin looked raw and angry, but the cauterization had done the job. The bleeding had stopped. She would still need to make sure infection didn't set.

She looked back at his square face, so tranquil with sleep, and finally set the Rosaca down. Perhaps she'd wait a few hours. It seemed cruel to wake him now.

Just then, voices erupted down the hall. Many of them, by the sound of it. Someone was speaking quickly with Avék, and even through the door, she knew that voice. She hadn't expected to hear it for at least two more days, however, and she was just rushing for the door when it flew open and Ricón stepped through, followed by their papa.

"Saints, you're all right," Ricón said, rushing to her, and pulling her into a tight embrace.

"Papa told you about Astrid?" she whispered.

"Yes." Ricón pulled back and searched her, and now that her

shock had worn away, she noticed the huge bags beneath his eyes, and the wild state of his hair and clothing.

"Wards, did you ride all night from Zap—" Imari started, when another figure stepped into the room.

Imari's heart stopped.

Jeric.

21

Imari forgot what she had been about to say. She forgot everything as her world came to a sharp and sudden focus on the man filling the doorway. The wind had pushed Jeric's short hair back, his cheeks flushed with exertion, and when his storming blue eyes landed on her, she suddenly couldn't breathe.

He was alive. Maker be praised, Jeric was *alive*!

And he was *here*.

A soft whimper escaped her lips, and her feet were running before she could spare another thought. Jeric intercepted her in two strides, drawing her swiftly in his arms and crushing her close.

Wards, she had missed him—so much it physically *hurt*, and she hadn't realized the extent of that ache until just then.

"You're all right," she whispered. His arms felt so solid around her, like an anchor in her wild world. "Wards, you're all right, I was so worried when she..."

Jeric pulled back and looked fiercely into her eyes. "I was a fool to let her live. I put you in danger, and I'm sorry."

"She is not your fault, Jeric. There's no way you could have known."

"I *should* have." His gaze moved back and forth between her eyes. "And I am so sorry. I was—"

"*Wolf*. Godsdamnit, stop flirting and help me," grunted a new but familiar voice.

To Imari's swift disappointment, Jeric released her, but she snagged her papa's watchful gaze before looking to the door, where Braddok struggled to carry...

"Stanis." Imari gasped, bewildered as she moved nearer. His face was pasty-white, his straw-colored hair lank and clinging to his sweaty forehead, and his body twitched involuntarily.

"What in the wards—" Imari started.

"He got nicked by a shade," Jeric said tightly, wedging his arms through Stanis's to shoulder some of the weight. "We've got another hunter in the Blackwood." A grunt. "Apparently."

Oh, no.

That meant Astrid had made more than the three she'd smuggled into Skyhold.

Together, Jeric, Braddok, and Chez heaved Stanis into the room, with Aksel and Avék following. And then another figure ducked through the door, bearing scars that disfigured half his face.

Imari could hardly believe her eyes. "*Tallyn*...?" He was alive too! But how were they all together, and what were they—

Tallyn gestured to the table.

Right.

Imari rushed over to where they'd laid Tarq just the night before, and started clearing off the medicinal books she'd piled on. "Lay him here."

Ricón hurried over to help, taking the heavy stacks of books and setting them on the counter, while Jeric and his men hoisted Stanis onto the table. In her periphery, she noticed Tallyn close the door, which was none too soon, because Stanis yelled and his body seized. Jeric, Chez, and Braddok fell over him, clamping him to the table with their hands and body weight before he could roll off. Still, Stanis was strong—unnaturally strong, from the poison flowing in his veins—and Aksel rushed over to add his weight too.

Four men to hold him down. And not just any men—four *wolves*.

Jeric had two hands pinning Stanis's left arm to the table, and even that required most of Jeric's weight to keep it there. Leaning forward, Jeric looked sharply—desperately—back at Imari. "I hate to ask even more of you, but will you help him?"

She saw Gerald all over again, haunting Jeric's memories. Imari had no idea how she could possibly help Jeric with this, or why he thought she *could*, but Imari could not bring herself to deny him. Instead, she looked to Tallyn, but Tallyn only shook his head. Of course, if Tallyn had been able to procure more antidote, he would've done so by now.

"Do you know how to make more?" she asked.

"No, Imari. This has to be *you*." His one eye glittered with meaning.

He meant her power—her music.

She opened her mouth to argue, but stopped. She'd healed Taran's wound, hadn't she? Imari hadn't a clue how she'd done that, but if her metaphysical power had the ability to heal a physical infection, it certainly should be able to heal a metaphysical one.

Stanis's scream cut off her racing thoughts. His back arched and Chez cursed, losing his grip. Stanis would have slipped right off the table if Ricón hadn't jumped in to help.

Ricón looked furiously at Jeric, using all his strength to hold Stanis down. "I told you she can't do this—"

"You *can*," Jeric said through his teeth, looking only at Imari. "I know you can, Imari."

Just then Stanis's teeth bared, and he bucked so hard, the

force of it sent Chez and Aksel flying. Stanis gnashed his teeth, and his eyelids flew wide open. The whites yellowed even as Imari stared, and his pupils shrunk to pinpricks.

He was Changing before their eyes.

"Imari, get out of here," her papa said, stepping forward.

"Grab his feet!" Braddok yelled.

"Dashá!" Ricón hissed, falling forward to grab a boot.

Avék lunged to help, but Stanis screamed and kicked him in the face. Avék cursed and stumbled back.

"Avék, get her out of here!" Sar Branón ordered.

"It's too late for him, Wolf!" Ricón hissed, struggling to hold both of Stanis's feet. "Imari can't fix this! You need to end this *now*, and if you don't, I will!"

Imari's gaze snapped to her brother.

Imari can't fix this.

Imari can't.

Can't. Can't. Can't!

Imari pulled the flute from her belt. The little glyphs flared to life, drawing everyone's attention. Ricón looked at her with exasperation, but Jeric's expression remained fierce and steady.

You *can*, his eyes insisted.

And then Imari noted the quiet. Stanis was not fighting. He lay perfectly still on that table, beneath the weight of five men.

Looking at her.

Those yellow eyes focused, predatory and cruel, and his lips curled back with a snarl.

She might not be able to cure him, but burning wards, *she would try*.

She lifted the flute to her lips and played. Notes poured from her flute, and she was very aware of everyone watching her. Especially Stanis, whose pinpricked pupils locked on her as he snarled and thrashed, trying to break free of his human binds. He snapped and he bit, trying to sink his teeth into Jeric and Braddok, who kept dodging. Imari played on, focusing on the warmth in her belly, guiding it into her chest, and let it drip into her flute. Just as she'd done in E'Centro.

Stanis screamed in fury.

Imari's notes swelled, yawning open inside this little chamber, filling it with pure sound. A small part of her wondered what Ricón and Avék and her papa would think. They had never seen her use her power before; they had never seen this half.

A half Ricón would be forced to reckon with now.

But Imari no longer cared.

She followed the melody on her heart, her notes eating up space and time against a backdrop of Stanis's furious screams. And then, just like before, when all of E'Centro had become a canvas of stars, Gamla's room turned into light and dark. Stars, and the dark spaces in between. Where Jeric and the others stood, she saw light. They were constellations, the brightest stars just over their hearts, like miniature suns.

Jeric's burned so brightly.

But where Stanis lay was mostly darkness, as if a black fog had settled in his chest, slowly blotting out the stars of his life. It writhed over his heart like some bulbous spot of ink, tendrils flaring out and reaching, snuffing out the other stars in his body. With Astrid, there had been no light, and so Imari had woven the surrounding stars around her back together, blocking it out. Mending the tear in the world. But with Stanis, who wasn't gone yet, somehow she knew that she needed to draw *him* out. Make his miniature sun burn brighter, and burn all the darkness away.

Find the tension.

"Hurry!" Braddok yelled.

"Avék, I said get her out of here!" Sar Branón demanded.

Imari ignored them all. The thrashing and screams, Avék's hesitation, Ricón shouting at Jeric, and Jeric shouting back. She played and focused only on that sputtering sun buried inside of Stanis's black fog. To it she played, sifting and searching.

There.

Though she could not see the little sun through that darkness, she heard the faintest resonance—the tone it had reflected back, amplified. Distorted.

Imari held that tone firm, pouring more breath and power into it, as if to give that star the strength it lacked. And then she bent the sound, just like before, slowly tuning it back to its proper pitch, and finally—*finally*—the star over Stanis's heart flared.

In her mind, something horrible screamed. A sound from a darker world.

In the real world, Stanis wailed, a blood-curdling scream that nearly made Imari lose her note, but still she played. She moved beyond that single tone, now drafting melody in the key of Stanis's heart, bringing out the tones of each and every point of light in his entire body. Weaving them into her song. Those stars shone brighter and brighter, and with the help of his miniature sun, their combined light burned the darkness away.

With a final scream of pain and defeat, the inky blot vanished. The stars over Stanis's body shone bright and pure, still vibrating and humming with that defiant tone.

Imari stopped, and her vision returned to normal as she lowered her flute.

The room was silent.

All eyes stared at her, though she only looked to Jeric, who gazed at her with a mixture of wonder and gratitude.

Suddenly, the tingling in her fingertips flushed over her in a single, powerful wave, and her entire body trembled. The room tilted, she couldn't seem to fill her lungs with enough air, and she became distractedly aware of a pair of strong hands grabbing hold of her. And then her entire world went black.

JERIC CAUGHT Imari in his arms.

"Gods...she did it," Braddok said, gawking at Stanis in disbelief. "She actually did it!"

But Jeric's concern had shifted to the woman in his arms. He crouched low and scooped her up, ignoring the sting as her head rested against his burn. "Tallyn. Imari needs your help."

Sar Branón rushed forward. "What's wrong with her?"

Tallyn moved toward them and placed one hand against Imari's cheek. "She's all right. Just exhausted from the power." He removed his hand and looked at Jeric, at Sar Branón. "She needs rest."

"Where should I take her?" Jeric asked Sar Branón.

Sar Branón considered his daughter, then his audience. Jeric sensed the Istraan king wasn't keen to leave the Wolf's pack unattended. Especially with the old alta-Liagé.

"You stay," Sar Branón said to Avék, who promptly touched two fingers to his temple.

Jeric exchanged a quick glance with Braddok, who nodded. "Don't worry about Stanis. We'll stay with him."

Ricón waited by the door, holding it open as Jeric maneuvered Imari into the hall, careful not to bump her dangling legs against the narrow doorframe.

"Are you all right carrying her?" Ricón asked, to which Jeric returned a look of annoyance.

Sar Branón joined them in the hall and closed the door on the others. The sar had not been particularly thrilled when he'd first intercepted the Wolf in Vondar's halls, and even less so following Ricón's hurried explanation. But neither of those compared to the dark look the sar gave him now, seeing his daughter in the Wolf's arms.

Jeric adjusted to hold her closer.

"Stay close," the sar said curtly, and kept walking.

He led them quickly through Vondar's quiet halls, past guards and servants preparing for morning's demands. Sar Branón paused briefly to give orders to a Sol Velorian servant, who bowed and rushed off with a basket of linens, but he did not stop again until they reached Imari's chambers.

Sar Branón pushed open the engraved wooden door to a dark room.

"One moment," Ricón said, striding past them both. He heaved heavy draperies open, though instead of open windows, as Jeric had expected, a decorative wooden screen stretched between the adjacent walls. Shafts of morning light shone through the screen's tiny, crescent-shaped holes, dusting patterns upon the travertine floor and illuminating the large bed off to the side.

Jeric carried Imari inside, and when the sunlight brushed her face, she shifted against him. Curled in closer, murmured against his chest.

Suddenly, he didn't want to let her go.

Jeric stopped beside the bed, holding Imari while Ricón turned back the silk sheets. Then Jeric laid her down, thinking what a fitting picture this made. Imari, the princess of Istraa, covered in dirt and old blood, lying atop a bed of fine silk.

Two sides of a perfect coin.

Jeric carefully slipped off Imari's shoes and set them on the floor, and Sar Branón pulled the blankets over his daughter. The softest sigh escaped Imari's lips and she turned onto her side, relaxing into the sheets while her thick, dark lashes settled peacefully upon her bronze cheeks.

Jeric's chest tightened. Gods, she was beautiful.

A clump of hair had fallen across her face when she'd turned, and Sar Branón leaned forward to push it back. For a moment, Jeric was struck by the image, because it was not a king, but a *father* looking over his daughter. As if he meant to draw her pain into himself so that she did not have to bear it any longer.

Jeric's father had never looked at any of them like that.

Jeric didn't fully understand Branón's reasons for sending

Imari to The Wilds, or his reasons for perpetuating secrets now, but he knew one thing for certain: It was not for lack of affection.

Not wanting to intrude on the moment, Jeric moved about the room, taking inventory of the vast and open space. He stood before the screen, admired the craftsmanship. It was a fine meshwork of sunlight and smooth wood. Not particularly impenetrable, however. He crossed the room and opened the small door off to the side. A circular washroom lay beyond, with a mosaic floor and claw-footed tub, and a handful of empty pots meant for plants. High, square windows had been cut out of the stucco to let in more light. Trier was The Wilds' opposite in every way, and Jeric felt a sudden and unexpected sadness for the woman sleeping on the bed behind him.

"I believe the last we saw each other, you had a woman on each knee," Sar Branón said sharply, in Istraan.

It was the last thing Jeric had expected the sar to say, and he almost laughed at the intended slight, but Sar Branón wasn't wrong. The last time they'd seen one another had been two years ago, when Branón had come to Skyhold to negotiate potential trade of Istraan oil for Corinthian timber, and being that Jeric's father never wasted the opportunity to display Corinth's wealth, he'd held a feast in Branón's honor. Of course, Jeric had been a mere Wolf back then, not a king, and so he'd endured the diplomatic posturing the way he usually did.

"You have a good memory," Jeric said in perfect Istraan, as he turned around. "And if *I* recall, you kept dumping your akavit into a potted plant, thinking no one noticed." Seeing Sar Branón's surprise, Jeric winked and added, "I never said a word. I hate the scat myself, and honestly, I was impressed by your fortitude. I see where she gets it." Jeric nodded in Imari's direction.

Ricón glanced away, fighting back a grin.

Sar Branón, however, did not find humor in Jeric's words, and he also looked annoyed that Jeric could speak his language so well. His eyes hooded slightly. "You were so...engaged, I'm surprised you noticed."

Jeric smiled, all teeth. "I notice everything."

"Except a Liagé right beneath your nose."

Jeric held his smile firm. "Except a Liagé right beneath my nose."

"Have your senses dulled then?" Sar Branón continued eyeing him. Searching for the smallest crack in Jeric's hard veneer. "Or am I to believe the Wolf of Corinth has truly lost his appetite for Liagé blood?"

Jeric considered the sar. Gods, he hated these kinds of conversations. This dancing around the sharp point of a sword until someone finally tripped and fell upon it.

He sat upon the divan and leaned back, one arm stretched along the armrest, one ankle crossed over his knee. "I'm not my father, Branón. If you have a point, make it."

Sar Branón regarded Jeric.

"*What he means*," Ricón answered for his father, looking between them both, "is that we're concerned, Wolf. It's no secret Corinth doesn't take infractions of Provincial law lightly, and we want to know if you'll demand that Istraa honors it."

It was on this point they had argued in Zappor. Because Provincial law demanded Imari's death, and a swift punishment to the one who had hidden her—in this case, Sar Branón. The law was drafted during Azir's time, so that no single territory would hold too much power over the others.

Jeric looked from Ricón to Sar Branón. "Why would I send her home if I was going to hold you to Provincial law?"

"To confirm guilt and complicity while you ally the other Provinces against..." Sar Branón's words trailed, and he frowned. "I'm sorry, is this amusing to you?"

"Very."

Sar Branón's gaze flickered to Ricón as if Ricón might interpret Jeric's unexpected and un*kingly* behavior, but Ricón merely shrugged as if to say, *See what I've been dealing with?*

Jeric sat forward. "I have no intention of fulfilling the law on the point of Imari...however. You do have a problem on your hands. A big one. Brevera knows, and just before I left, Davros sent a messenger seeking confirmation."

All that Jeric had said was true. News of this sort traveled fast —both ways. Brevera had learned about Astrid, which was another reason Jeric's jarls had been angry that he hadn't righted the offense immediately. Jeric wondered if, when he returned, he'd even have a throne to return to. It might solve a lot of problems if he didn't. Let his rutting vultures have at it, may they forever tear themselves apart.

Sar Branón's lips thinned. "What does Brevera know, exactly?"

Jeric looked straight back. "More than your own godsdamned people."

Just then, someone knocked on the door.

"I'll get it," Ricón said, then crossed the room and cracked the door open.

Jenya stood on the other side, speaking to Ricón in a hushed tone, and then Ricón closed the door and turned back to his father with a shake of his head.

Sar Branón exhaled irritation, and Jeric got the impression he had missed an earlier conversation.

"Let me speak to Mama," Ricón urged quietly. "I'll convince her to spare one."

Sar Branón considered. "Why not keep Jenya?"

"Jenya's not kunari, Papa."

Ah. Sar Branón had requested one of his wife's maids, now that Imari's secret was out, but Sura Anja had refused. Jeric thought it an odd thing to quarrel over, but jealousy had the unique ability of turning everything into a competition.

He'd seen that with his own brother.

Ricón said something else Jeric could not hear, Sar Branón

grunted a response, and Ricón left, closing the door behind him. But not without first giving Jeric a quick warning glance.

"Why didn't you tell Istraa the truth?" Jeric asked in Common this time, cutting right to the point.

Sar Branón turned back to him, and said, in Common, "Out of all people, I would think the Wolf of Corinth might understand why announcing the return of my Liagé bastard is a challenge."

Jeric decided he hated that word: bastard. "But you have Corinth's support."

Sar Branón smiled. "I'm not really in the habit of trusting *Corazzis*."

Which was exactly what Ricón had said, but Jeric refused to take offense. "As I said: I'm not my father."

"No, you're worse. You're a wolf, and you've somehow managed to seduce my dearest lamb."

Jeric sat forward. "*Dearest lamb*? Horsescat. You shipped her off to *The rutting Wilds*—"

"To protect her against *your* family—"

"And I've offered my protection, but you're *still* forcing her to hide—"

"Protection?" Sar Branón cut back. "You call sending a demon to my front door *protection*?"

Jeric clenched his hand into a fist, fighting to regain his composure. "I never meant for Astrid to reach Trier. Hells, I never meant for her to leave her rutting cell."

"Thrones are not built on intention, Wolf," Sar Branón said lowly. "They are built on blood and steel. You failed, and that error cost me four guards, nearly one saredd, and almost my daughter."

Jeric stared hard at the Istraan sar. "Yes. I made an error. A grievous one. As it turns out, I've made many. I've ruined more lives than I care to admit, and this time, I wanted to save one. My —own—sister. Had I realized the depth of Astrid's depravity, maybe I would have chosen differently, but what's done is done. And you're a godsdamned fool if you think your lies are protecting Imari."

"My *lies* are the only thing keeping her alive—"

"*She* is the only thing keeping her alive," Jeric snapped. "And she needs your *support!* To be *who she is.* You can't keep treating her as halves, Branón. Choosing which part to keep and which to hide. Imari is *both*, and stronger because of it, and she is the *only* reason you didn't lose more than four guards last night. She doesn't need your rutting protection. Hells, she doesn't even need Corinth's. We need *hers.*"

Just then, Imari moaned softly and shifted on the bed. Both men immediately stopped talking and looked over at her. Her head turned to the side; she sighed once more and fell deeply into sleep again.

Sar Branón sat down in the chair opposite Jeric and leaned forward. "You think you know because you've hunted them, but you *don't know.* You have no idea what it is to be hunted. You don't know what they are together, or how deeply my people fear them, because you were just a squirming babe suckling his nursemaid's breast when *better men than you* stopped a war before it took hold. When better men than you suffered."

Jeric gazed back at Branón, his posture deadly still. "I was seven. And that war took my mother, so *please* tell me again why I have no right to a rutting opinion."

Sar Branón's lips pressed together tightly, and he sat back, considering Jeric.

"Ricón told me what's happening in Istraa," Jeric continued. "It sounds exactly like what happened in Corinth, and now Trier knows the truth about Imari. So what now, Branón? Do you still think the answer is marrying her off to the son of some gods-damned roi?"

A shadow passed over Sar Branón's face. He clearly hadn't

expected Ricón to mention his plans to Jeric. "It's really none of your business."

"It's absolutely my business. Your roi will use her. Maybe even against the Provinces. Just like my brother and Rasmin tried to do."

The sar's eyes flashed. "This is not Corinth."

"You're right. Your rois are their own men, with their own ambitions. Don't think I didn't spend all those years in my father's court ignoring the machinations of his blood-sucking jarls. They're all the same. Every godsdamned one."

Sar Branón tapped his fingers upon the end of the armrest, regarding the Wolf with a king's practiced stoicism. But Jeric knew he had gotten under the sar's skin. Sar Branón had expected a king's duel and been bitten by a wolf instead.

"And who, might I ask, would you recommend?" Sar Branón said lowly. "Certainly you're not offering *yourself* as an alternative."

Jeric would be lying if he said the thought hadn't crossed his mind. It had. More than once. For what better way to unite the Five Provinces than allying Corinth and Istraa—the two most polarizing factions—through a marriage?

He'd also be lying if he said that was the only reason he'd considered it.

However, he already faced bountiful enmity from his people. How much worse would it be for Imari? Obliterating generations of prejudice would be a long and difficult road for Corinth—and all the Five Provinces— assuming Imari would even agree to leave Istraa.

And with a Wolf.

Jeric could not ask that of her—would not. And he would never force her into anything she did not want. She'd been forced into far too much already.

Also, she deserved so much better.

"No, I'm not suggesting that," Jeric said, though Sar Branón didn't look convinced. Honestly, Jeric wasn't convinced either. "But I think you should wait before making arrangements. Let the people see her and know her first—for who she truly is. And then decide, though I'd definitely consider her opinion. She has a lot of them, and they're usually right."

Sar Branón looked irked. "You endured your father's court. You just said it yourself. So how, exactly, do you expect me to do that without putting my entire family at risk?"

Jeric smiled, all bite. "You were the sar when men better than me stopped a war. I'm sure you'll figure something out."

Sar Branón bristled.

"Branón. You have Corinth's support," Jeric continued in earnest. "I swear on my life. I will stand with Istraa if and when this matter is brought before the other Provinces, and you know *in this* that Corinth's word holds power."

Sar Branón stared at Jeric a very long moment. Then, abruptly, the door cracked open and Ricón returned. He hesitated just inside, as if expecting carnage from a slaughter. Seeing that both his father and Jeric were seated—and completely intact—he exhaled and stepped into the room, followed by two Istraan kunari. The kunari were wrapped in cloth the color of wine, their heads bowed as they held baskets of colorful clothing between them.

Clothing meant for Istraa's surina.

Per Ricón's direction, the kunari carried their baskets into the washroom. A second later, Jeric heard the groan of a lever followed by a burst of water.

"Come," Ricón said, interrupting Jeric's running thoughts. "I'll take you to see your sister."

22

Niá did not know how long she stood in total darkness. Her legs trembled with fatigue and her knees ached, but she could not give them relief.

Not in this prison.

It was Ashova's forgotten room—the punishment for delinquency, for the kahar would not inflict gross physical damage. They didn't dare mar the outer shells of their favorite toys.

But they did not care how they ruined what lay within.

Niá's fingertips tightened, crusted with blood from when she'd clawed and raked at this tight, claustrophobic hole. She stood within a compact cylinder of stone, carved out of the sandstone beneath Ashova's temple, her only exit a trapdoor high above.

She didn't bother with enchantments, not that they'd work. Ashova's kahar had kept the Liagé wards intact, knowing full well the gamble they played by using the Sol Velor as they did, and Niá had spied the marks of suppression upon the trapdoor.

Some of the same marks her oza had used in her circle of blood.

Niá's chest clenched. Grief and horror were her only

companion in this foul place. It should have been her, lying dead in that circle.

It should have been her.

And little Saza...

Niá bit her bottom lip so hard she broke skin, but she did not cry. She had no tears left to shed, only rage. Pure, unadulterated rage, because what had attacked Saza and her oza was a demon. A very specific kind of demon that feasted on souls of the living to draw strength and power. A *leje*—legion—that could have only been summoned by a powerful *zindev*—necromancer.

And Niá happened to know one powerful enough.

All of her oza's warnings rushed tragically back to her—warnings Niá had been all too eager to ignore. Niá had been so desperate for a savior, and the shiva's ample coin had finally pushed her over that uncertain edge.

Coin Niá had hoped to use in order to start a new life for the three of them, far away from this place.

"You warned me," Niá whispered. "I'm so sorry I didn't listen."

Oza had known the moment Niá had offered her some of that coin, which she'd refused, and then she'd immediately suspected Niá's involvement with the rumored Liagé leader.

"Fortune is an easy lure," her oza had said. "But in time, you will know him by his fruits, my little Ni. There are many who come in Asorai's name, but they are servants of the evil one."

"He's going to free our people!" Niá had defended. "We will finally have freedom—*real* freedom."

"But at what cost?"

"Does it matter?" Niá had shot back. "Look what they've done to us. If this is our chance at a real life...for Saza's sake, I will do whatever it takes."

"Oh, it matters, my little Ni," her oza had replied with sadness. "It matters more than any other thing."

The memory played like another horror, and Niá ground her teeth so hard she thought they might crack. The shiva had *used* her. He'd lured her with money and promises, and she'd taken the bait. He did not care whether she lived or died, only that she provided the information he needed, and she had provided that aplenty. All her nights with Sur Kai in her bed. Oh yes, Niá had been very important indeed.

Until she wasn't.

Until the shiva's *leje* had escaped its prison and come to extract his prize. And Niá had given him all the information he had required to pass on to his next good and faithful servant.

But what Niá still could not comprehend was why that prize —why Imari—had been in E'Centro with her oza and little brother. Why had her oza died defending the bastard surina, who had befriended a Wolf?

The trapdoor opened and light flooded the chamber so brightly it hurt. Niá shut her eyes, and the end of a rope smacked her face.

"Time to come up, my little serpent," drawled Kahar Vidett, a man for whom Niá held a special place of loathing in her heart.

He was the Kourana's most devoted pet, Ashova's precious proctor. The one who had discovered Niá in the fields that fateful day, and then ushered her to Ashova's and taken it upon himself to break her in. *To prepare her for the goddess's holy work*, he had said.

Niá grabbed the rope's end and wrapped it tightly around her wrists. Kahar Vidett tugged the rope to make sure she had hold, and then he pulled. The rope burned into her wrists, and her body scraped and banged against the walls. Soon enough, hands grabbed and pulled her out of the chamber completely, and helped her sit upon the floor.

Kahar Vidett crouched before her, his pristine red robes pooling on the polished white tiles, like blood. He looked over her naked body and his lips curled. His fingertips brushed her face, and the only thing that kept Niá from breaking those fingers was pure exhaustion.

"You know how I hate doing this to you," he said, then slapped her cheek—hard.

Niá toppled to the side, her cheek stinging.

"Give her a bath. The Kourana will be here within the hour."

He had sent for the High Priestess.

Of course he had sent for the High Priestess. Her oza had just revealed that she'd been an enchantress. The Kourana would want to know if Niá had inherited it too.

Hands dragged her out of the room and down the hall, while her temple sisters and brothers peered out from behind draperies and columns. For Niá had become a favorite, and favorites were not usually punished. It wasn't good for business.

The lesser kahar—two men and one woman—dragged her to the bath and, without ceremony, dumped her into the cold water. Niá gasped from the shock of it, and they scrubbed the filth from her skin and hair.

She wished they could scrub away the rot within.

They toweled her off and dressed her in sheer red silk, brushed and plaited her long, black hair, and when they finished, Kahar Vidett stalked in to appraise her. His dark eyes lingered unabashedly on her breasts, which were visible through the sheer silk of her clothing. And then, abruptly, he grabbed them and squeezed hard. Niá gasped in pain.

"You belong to *this* house," the kahar said lowly, his eyes boring into hers. "Do not leave it again." He let go, then motioned to the door.

Niá held her head high and stepped through. She followed the kahar to his office. A place she tended to avoid, when she could help it, but the Kourana was here. There was no avoiding it now.

Kahar Vidett opened his door.

Niá did not look at him as she stepped through, to where the Kourana waited. Kourana Vidéa, grand mistress of Jadarr and all the temples, keeper of the kahar, and the sole intercessor between the gods and Istraans.

May she burn in Shael for all eternity.

The Kourana wore her familiar white in contrast to the kahar's red. Like a goddess surrounded by her angels of blood and death. Let them do all her dirty work, so her robes could remain pristine. Black hair fell like a sheet around a severe and angular face, and her gaze was dark as a moonless night. Hard and cold as the tile beneath Niá's feet.

The door closed with a soft slick.

Niá resisted the urge to squirm.

"This is the one?" the Kourana asked, appraising Niá but speaking to Kahar Vidett.

"Sei, mi a'Kourana."

"On your knees, girl," the Kourana said.

Slowly, Niá dropped to her knees, but she did not drop her head. She stared straight at the Kourana. It was a subtle defiance, but a defiance, nonetheless.

The Kourana arched a brow. "You know the rules. What were you doing?"

"I was out for a walk—"

The Kourana slapped her. The sound cracked through the little room, and Niá's other cheek now stung. Behind her, one corner of Kahar Vidett's lips turned upward.

"Don't waste your lies on me, ascáb," the Kourana hissed. Scab. "The only reason you still have your pretty head is because you happen to be Sur Kai's favorite, but do not think for a moment that favoritism will protect you forever." The Kourana squeezed Niá's chin and forced her to look up. "I'll ask again. What were you doing in E'Centro?"

Niá swallowed a lump, hating the woman who stood before her, and everything she represented. "Sur Kai was here, but someone from the Qazzat came to get him. I overhead mention of E'Centro and...I worried for my family."

"Why?" the Kourana hissed. "What do you know?"

"Nothing, I—"

This time, the Kourana grabbed Niá's braids and pulled her head back. Painfully. "Did you go to meet their *heretic* leader, whore?" The Kourana spat. "Is that why you left?"

"No, I swear..." Niá strained against the pull in her scalp and neck. "I just...went to see my family."

Niá would not cry. Not here. Not before the Kourana and her vipers. She would not give them the pleasure of knowing their favorite toy was already broken.

Irreparably.

"You mean your *voloré* grandmama?" the Kourana snarled, staring hard at Niá. She was searching. Looking to see if Niá had known.

If Niá was *voloré* herself.

"I did not know," Niá lied. The Kourana twisted her hair, and Niá gasped. "I swear, I did not..."

The Kourana glared down at Niá, her expression hard and full of disgust, and then she released Niá with a shove. Niá fell forward, catching herself on her hands.

"Where are the bodies?" the Kourana asked Kahar Vidett.

"Burned this morning."

Niá shut her eyes tight, and her fingers curled into fists upon the tile.

"Good. Keep a tight leash on your whore. I must speak with Sur Kai and see what is to be done."

Because the Kourana did not dare harm Niá without Sur Kai's permission. But Niá held no delusions that Kai would defend or protect her.

Kahar Vidett bowed his head. "As you wish, mi a'Kourana."

The Kourana cast Niá one more scathing look, and Kahar Vidett escorted her out. The two male kahar grabbed Niá's arms, hoisted her to her feet, and escorted her out of Kahar Vidett's office to her room. There, they left her, and the lock turned a second later.

Niá strode to her narrow window. It wasn't wide enough for her to climb out, of course, but she could still see the courtyard. Numbly, she looked on as the Kourana spoke to Kahar Vidett near Ashova's marble statue.

He would come to her later. Of that, she had no doubt.

Niá wrapped her arms around herself, and her gaze settled on Ashova, arched in eternal pleasure. And then she picked up the emptied nazzat she had shared with Sur Kai just last night and threw it at the wall. The bottle exploded; glass shards rained. Niá stood there heaving fast, unable to contain the rage and grief twisting inside of her. Desperate, Niá crouched and picked up a shard, and carved it into her palm.

Blood rose to greet her—her only constant companion, it would seem. The color looked so vivid in her grim world. She clenched her hand into a fist, felt the blood well and trickle and burn, and then she painted on her mirror, not bothering with the door this time.

They already suspected, and if Sur Kai agreed to let the Kourana perform her tests, there would be no hiding what she was.

"Where are you..." Niá hissed lowly, staring at the image in her mirror. Not a reflection, but of a dark stone room. There was no light this time, which struck Niá as unusual. The shiva always kept a black candle burning for her.

Niá gripped the edges of her vanity, not a care for the blood she smeared on the polished mahogany. "*Where are you?*" she snarled as loud as she dared.

But only silence answered. It was an empty and complete sort of silence, and without his power to feed their connection, the portal didn't hold. Already, the image warped like a mirage. Fading, and fading, leaving Niá to stare at herself.

The shiva was not there. Which meant he had begun. And he hadn't even thought to tell her.

Fortune is the perfect lure.

Niá rested her forehead against the vanity, and cried.

TALLYN STOPPED at the courtyard's edge. The great temple of Jadarr rose magnificently before him. Vondar might be Trier's heart, but Jadarr was its lifeblood, where the Kourana and her devoted kahar dwelled. They deemed themselves the physical tether between man and the gods; the intercessors for Istraa's people. A gilded statue of Asiam, ruler of all the gods, crowned Jadarr's dome, while his celestial brides guarded the grounds below. Nián, goddess of fate, Beléna, goddess of beauty, and Ashova, goddess of fertility. Each held their own temples throughout the city, but here, in Asiam's courtyard, they stood together as part of the whole.

A construct to control mankind.

It had been the same since the dawn of man. Different versions, of course, depending on the region, but all the same. As if man could trap fate, control it, and bargain one's way to prosperity and blessing while ignoring the very ones they were commanded to serve.

Vanity. All of it, vanity.

There was only one god with any power, and he could not be contained or controlled. Every so often, a generation would be brought to its knees in remembrance. It had happened with the Sol Velor.

It was about to happen again.

Tallyn knew the signs, for he'd survived them once. Perhaps this was why the Maker had spared him all those years. To give him another chance.

To show his perfect mercy.

Tallyn's gaze followed a pair of kahar walking through Jadarr's bronze doors of judgment. He had told Sar Branón that he wanted to investigate Trier, to see if he could find traces of Shah that Branón's saredd had missed. None of that had been a lie, and Sar Branón had given his permission. But motivation, Tallyn had found, often came with layers, and he'd only given Branón the most superficial one.

The second was what had led him here, specifically.

Tallyn passed through a low bridge connecting two buildings and proceeded down a worn, cobblestone path made narrow by tightly clustered facades. The city was quieter here, where the buildings' high backs provided a barrier against sound.

Which was why this path had long been a favorite.

Tallyn reached the small, whispering fountain at the path's end, where four bronze basins burned with hot coals. This fountain had been dedicated to Torat, god of serenity. Or, what he and very few others had called the god of whispers.

Tallyn stood before the fountain, watching the water burble over Torat's placid marble face. Coins glimmered in the deep— offerings, to be collected by the kahar, or some dauntless beggar. They were always caught eventually, and the Kourana was not kind to those who stole from her kahar.

Wings beat behind him, and the air stirred, rippling Tallyn's cloak, but he did not turn. He did not need to.

"How did you know?"

It was a voice Tallyn had not heard in a very long time. Hearing it now set him on edge. "I sensed you the moment I stepped foot in this city."

A beat. "So your scars did not sever it completely."

"No, they did not." Tallyn still could not decide whether that was a blessing or a curse.

Another, longer beat. "I have already seen your face, Muzretall. You need not hide from me."

"If you'll recall, I came to you, Rasyamin." Tallyn turned around sharply and faced the one who had made him...this.

Rasyamin looked the same as Tallyn remembered, but also less. A shadow of what he'd once been, emaciated and hollow, and a new scar cut his owlish brow in half. Though, as Tallyn reflected, the decades had done this to them all—stolen their might, sucked the marrow from their bones, and left them a brittle echo of what they'd once been.

It was nothing they didn't deserve. They had been Azir Mubarék's secret weapon, and he had employed them ruthlessly to serve under his Mo'Ruk.

"Why do you not conceal it?" Rasyamin asked, his dark and fathomless gaze moving over Tallyn's thick scars.

"So that I never forget." A pause. "Though I understand regret is not an emotion you comprehend."

If Rasyamin felt offense, he did not show it. Instead, his gaze took on that familiar distance, his features slack. So it was with the Sight, and Rasyamin had been the strongest *ziat*—Seer—of this age. Even more so than Lestra, Azir's Mo'Ruk Seer.

Rasyamin's focus returned a second later, piercing Tallyn with keen interest. "You killed the others."

There was no condemnation in that voice. Only open curiosity.

"I did."

"And then you traveled to Corinth to warn the Wolf King, but Astrid had already escaped. So you changed course." Rasyamin spoke as if watching the past replay itself before him.

"What a gift you have," Tallyn said with spite. "Seeing what isn't yours to See so that you might take what was never offered to you."

"Says the man wielding a power he was not born with."

"I didn't take it," Tallyn snarled. "You *gave* it to me. I never had the choice."

"There is only one choice for the dying," Rasyamin said simply. "Because of me, you had another."

"And what about all the choices you *stole*, Head Inquisitor?"

"I took only what was necessary for our survival," Rasyamin replied in his way. Always circling the truth to make one forget where it was. "Sometimes we must accept the lesser evils of this world in order to save it from the greater ones."

"Ah, yes. How could I forget? Your view of the Maker has always been so small. As if he needed *your* wretched hands to accomplish anything."

Rasyamin's eyes narrowed so slightly. "*Everything* I have done has been with the girl in mind. Without her, our fight is futile—you know this. And if it weren't for me, she would have fled The Wilds as a demon's puppet."

Tallyn knew that pinning guilt on Rasyamin was a futile endeavor; he felt none. He had always been too arrogant for error. So Tallyn changed course. "Where have you been?"

Rasyamin regarded him. "I was in the Baragas. Searching, to see if I could find anything about our elusive Liagé leader."

"Why not use your Sight?"

Rasyamin's dark eyes glittered. "My Sight has been some-what...erratic these past few months. The present and future are hidden to me." A pause. "It is the same for you."

It was both question and statement.

"Yes," Tallyn admitted, watching Rasyamin with growing unease. "Who is tampering with our Sight?"

But the real question that hovered between them: Who was powerful enough to interfere with *Rasyamin's*?

This time, Rasyamin turned to the fountain and gazed at their burbling reflections. "That is precisely why I left, but I found nothing. Still, I sense it."

Tallyn sensed it too. "So there are two."

Rasyamin glanced sideways at him.

"A *ziát* and a *shiva* must be working together." A Seer and a Restorer. Tallyn had initially suspected one mind behind it all—one power that had summoned the legion and set the gears of a Sol Velorian uprising in motion. And perhaps it had been one mind in the beginning, but now there was obviously another. Because any *shiva* powerful enough to summon that demon was not also strong enough to block Rasyamin's Sight. Only a true Seer could do that.

"Yes, I believe there are two," Rasyamin answered quietly.

"But who could it be?" Tallyn asked. "Anyone with so strong a tie to the Shah could not have hidden from you this long."

Rasyamin's cold eyes sparked. "I know."

Tallyn studied his old master. "You suspect someone."

Rasyamin did not answer immediately. "I've come across this...particular connection only once in all my life."

Rasyamin did not need to say more. Tallyn knew he was referring to Azir's Mo'Ruk, but all of them had perished with Sol Velor.

"That's not possible," Tallyn whispered.

"They never buried Azir's *shiva*. They never found the body." And Azir's *shiva* had been uniquely horrible.

Tallyn stared at Rasyamin. "You think...*Bahdra*?"

Rasyamin's brow furrowed. "I suspected it under Saád, though his mission died before I could be certain."

Saád Mubarék. Azir's many-great grandson, who had come to finish what his great grandfather had started: to set the Liagé as supreme rulers over all the Provinces. Saád's rebellion did not gain much traction, however, because he was betrayed in its feeble beginnings—by his own sister. Sar Branón, Kormand of Brevera, Tommad of Corinth, and Jezié—Saád's sister—had laid a trap for the hungry usurper, and slit his throat while he slept.

"This *feels* like Bahdra," Rasyamin continued with an intensity Tallyn rarely heard from his old master.

Tallyn considered all that Rasyamin had said, and then added, "We have a problem."

Rasyamin looked straight at him. "Yes, we do. And Imari will not listen to me."

"You sound surprised," Tallyn said dryly.

Rasyamin gave him a thin smile. "Work with her, Tallyn. She needs to understand what she is, and what she faces, so that she does not fall."

Like every other sulaziér before her, he did not add. He did not need to. They both knew Moltoné's teachings very well.

And they had both already witnessed one fall.

"The Deceiver has ensnared very capable servants in his web this time," Rasyamin continued. "I know you sense it too. Imari must be prepared if she is to have a chance. If any of us are to have a chance."

Tallyn rested his palms upon the fountain's edge and leaned forward, staring at his rippling reflection. Rasyamin was right. Imari needed to know what she was, what she faced. All of it.

But that meant showing Imari so many other things Tallyn wished for no one to See. Especially her.

"I will be nearby, should you need me," Rasyamin said. "I will keep searching, and in the meantime, I suggest you share your Sight. Help her understand her role in all of this." His black gaze flickered over Tallyn. "I am glad to see you, Muzretall."

Tallyn did not return the sentiment, but Rasyamin did not seem to expect him to. He whirled his cloak, wool swirled into feathers, and black wings flapped. The great owl hovered above him, hooted once, and flew away.

Tallyn sighed and closed his eyes. "Oh, Maker give me strength."

23

I mari stood in the middle of a storm. It obscured everything, this angry tempest of wind and sand that ripped at the ground and reached for the sky, as if it meant to swallow the world. Shadows shifted within, wailing as they called out to her by name. They drew nearer and nearer but vanished before Imari could make sense of them.

You are mine, sulaziér.

The words were thunder, rumbling through her body, all bass and vibration. The wind ceased abruptly, as if the moment had frozen in time. Each particle—each infinitesimal grain of sand— suspended, hovering in midair. Imari reached out, marveling at them all, and touched a single grain.

Her touch was a spark, spurring the gears of time back into motion. The sand collapsed, and Imari saw a tree.

The tree.

It stood alone atop an endless stretch of sand, black and gnarled and diseased. And Imari approached.

Everything inside of her screamed to run away, but her feet carried her steadily forward. She lacked control of her body. The tree shuddered as she neared, and its oozing black trunk swelled in and out, like lungs. Breathing.

Rasping.

Sick and diseased.

Imari stopped a few paces from the tree. Its branches arched high like readied spears, and one dipped low and curved upward.

MINE, snarled that voice, more bass than sound.

And the spear pierced right through her chest.

Imari jolted awake.

She clutched at her chest, trying to catch her breath as the pain ebbed. It took her a moment to make sense of her surroundings, and then she realized she was in her chambers. Her *real* chambers—not Gamla's—though she had no idea how she'd come to be here. A few lanterns burned, the wood stove glowed with heat, and the screen's decorative holes were black with night.

"Surina?" A figure stepped through the washroom door, giving Imari a start.

It was Dasi, one of Sura Anja's kunaris, and it looked as though she'd been preparing a bath. It suddenly dawned on Imari that Dasi had called her surina. Not healer. Not Sable.

Surina.

And then everything else came rushing back to her. Jeric. Stanis. The shade poison.

Jeric.

She hadn't realized she'd whispered his name aloud until the kunari said, "Excuse me?"

"Nothing. Um." Imari's throat felt raw and scorched, and tasted like ash. "Never mind." Imari threw back her silk sheets, feeling a moment's regret at dirtying them with her filthy self, and then she slid her feet to the animal-skin rug and stood. Her world tilted, and she grabbed onto the bedpost for support.

Dasi rushed forward to help, towel in hand.

Imari waved her off. "I'm all right. Just...give me a second."

Imari paused, almost afraid to ask her next question. "How...long have I been sleeping?"

"Nearly twelve hours."

Twelve. *Hours.*

Imari supposed she should be thankful time hadn't been quantified in *days* like the last time, but she still hated knowing that Jeric had been here almost an entire day and she'd missed all of it.

A wave of nausea rolled through her, and she tore across the room, nearly tripping on a hassock, before making her way into the washroom and vomiting into an empty planter.

"Shall I call for Sur Ricón?" Dasi asked quietly from the doorway, offering the towel.

Imari shook her head, immediately regretting the motion, and gripped the planter's edge to brace herself against another upheaval. Thankfully, nothing came, but her mouth still tasted like ash and vomit. "Water... Please."

Dasi left the towel and stepped away, returning with a glass of water.

"Thank you." Imari took the glass, swished the water around her mouth, and spit into the planter before taking a real sip. She suddenly recalled the strong hands that had caught her before her world went dark. "Did Ricón carry me here?"

"No. It was...the Wolf, mi a'surina." Dasi's tone was neutral, but her eyes were not. She did not approve.

Imari found she didn't care.

"Where is he?" Imari asked.

"In the dining hall with Sar Branón, mi a'surina."

Imari wanted to inquire about Stanis, but Dasi wasn't the one to ask, and being that she'd been Sura Anja's kunari first, Imari did not trust her either.

But.

Jeric was here.

In Trier.

Here.

Suddenly, her world did not seem so bleak.

Dasi brought the kettle from the wood stove and dumped scalding water into the tub, mixing hot with cold. The sweet scent of orange blossom rose with the steam.

"Would you like assistance, mi a'surina?" Dasi asked, setting the kettle down.

"No, thank you."

Dasi clasped her hands and bowed her head. "I'll leave a fresh nightdress on your bed."

"Clothes, please. I plan to join Papa."

"Of course, mi a'surina," Dasi said, and left, closing the washroom door softly behind her.

Imari quickly stripped down, but not too quickly, because she was still unsteady on her feet, and then she tossed her ruined clothing to the floor and climbed into the claw-footed tub. The heat felt glorious against her skin, and she sank low, until the water lapped at her chin and steam filled her nose, drowning her in sweet orange blossoms. She tipped her head back and closed her eyes as her joints relaxed and muscles loosened. Reveling in the heat and comfort and *quiet*. She could have soaked in that tub all night, but...

Jeric was here.

Imari dunked herself completely in the water once, then grabbed the pumice Dasi had left and scrubbed the blood and dirt from her skin. Her skin felt raw by the time she'd finished, but she'd made quick work of it, and the water was still warm as she climbed out and dried herself with the fringed towel. With wet hair and feet, Imari padded into her room and noticed Dasi had already stripped the bed, undoubtedly to wash the sheets Imari had ruined. Lying on top of that bare mattress—as promised—were fresh clothes.

Not clothes for a healer, but for a surina.

Imari did not know what this would mean for her, or the

whens and hows of her papa's inevitable announcement to the rois and roiesses, which would come very soon now. And Imari still had no idea how to navigate being both Istraan and Liagé in a world that only accepted the former, but she decided not to worry about those things right then. Futures were built on moments, and *this* moment was all that mattered now. She would leave the rest to the Maker.

The soft-cream dress was simple, knee-length and sleeveless, with a neckline that plunged to her navel and hung equally low in back. Wide straps hooked over her shoulders, and, to keep the neckline modest over her breasts, a single ribbon stretched across her sternum, holding the fabric in its proper place. An embroidered, golden sash looped around the waist to give the dress shape, and a single high slit had been cut into one side of the draping skirt.

It was elegant in its simplicity. Far more exposing than Imari had grown accustomed to, but so very Istraan. It crossed her mind that Jeric would see her in this dress, and she hesitated with her hand resting upon the soft silk. A part of her wanted him to see her in it, and that part surprised her. But there was an equal part that worried he might think she was *trying* to get his attention, which was something a man as striking as Jeric was undoubtedly used to. And she did not want what existed between them—whatever this was—to be reduced to...that.

"I'm being ridiculous," Imari scolded herself.

She was a surina. Of course she would wear this.

And so she shoved that concern deep down and dressed. She strapped on sandals, combed her damp hair, slipped on the golden bangles Dasi had left, and glanced in the mirror. She still looked a little pale, but the bath had brought color to her cheeks and life to her hazel eyes.

Imari took a deep breath, and stepped out into the hall.

Jenya, who stood guard just outside her door, took one look at

Imari and her eyes widened. "You look...like a surina. Mi a'surina."

Imari smirked. "Thank you...?"

Jenya gave her a small, knowing grin. Then, anticipating Imari's next question, Jenya said, "They're in the dining hall."

Imari closed the door. "How's Stanis?"

"Good. Sleeping in Gamla's chambers." Before Imari could ask, Jenya added, "We moved Tarq to the Qazzat."

"He could walk?" Imari asked, surprised.

"He was a damned bear, but we managed."

Imari chuckled, Jenya grinned, and she felt a wall crack between them.

"I'll escort you," Jenya said, and together they walked down the short stair and through Vondar's airy halls, Jenya's long, segmented ponytail swishing behind her. Jenya was the only saredd who did not wear the traditional headscarf, instead wearing her femininity for all to see.

And Imari admired her more for it.

The evening was warm and quiet, the lanterns burned with buttery light, and Imari's nerves churned. It was with no small effort that she restrained herself from running straight to the dining hall. They turned down the corridor leading to Gamla's chamber, and Imari spied Avék standing guard outside the door.

"Did you want to check on Stanis first?" Jenya asked.

Imari gazed past Avék and the swaying palms, in the direction of the dining hall. Even from here, she could hear those rattling notes of a mizmar dancing on the breeze, beckoning to her. But she couldn't come up with a reasonable explanation for bypassing her patient, since he was literally along their way.

She felt Jenya watching her as she answered, "Yes, I probably should. It'll just take a moment."

Avék's eyes brightened as they approached, and he inclined his head respectfully. "Good evening, surina. You look well."

"Twelve hours of sleep and a hot bath will do that."

Avék grinned.

"I wanted to check on Stanis."

"Of course." Avék pushed the door in and stepped aside, and Imari passed through the doorway and into Gamla's room.

And stopped.

Jeric was *not* in the dining hall. He was here, and sitting shirtless upon a stool at the counter's end, bending over a sheet of parchment while clutching a reed pen in his hand. That chimpshaped lantern burned beside him, casting a warm glow over his strong profile. His pants were fresh and fitted, and one long leg stretched upon the floor while the other propped on the stool's supports. He looked completely at ease in a way that made Imari feel as though *he* were sar here, and she his guest.

He'd bathed as well, his hair damp and dark and combed back, though a clump of it had fallen forward as he worked, but hearing the door open, his pen stopped, he glanced up, and that sharp blue-eyed gaze landed on her.

Imari's heart skipped a beat.

"Surina," Jeric said. His rich cello carried across that space and strummed every string inside of her. "How are you feeling?"

Jenya excused herself and—to Imari's surprise—shut the door. Leaving the two of them alone, with Stanis's snores rumbling faintly beyond Gamla's small door.

Imari took a step forward, though the motion felt unsteady, and it had nothing to do with her twelve-hour nap. "Surina...?" she teased. "I haven't seen you in a month, and I've already become a stranger with a title."

One edge of Jeric's mouth curled. "In my defense, you've carried so many different titles, it's hard to keep them straight anymore. Sable. Healer. Thief." His eyes glittered on that last one. "Surina seemed...safest."

"Since when were you ever concerned with social graces?"

Jeric's lips stretched in a slow smile that showed his teeth, and nearly stole Imari's breath in the process. "Yes, you're definitely feeling better."

"I am, thank you."

They looked at each other across the room, and the quiet magnified until it became almost awkward. Or maybe it was just Imari feeling awkward, because Jeric seemed perfectly at ease—maybe even a little amused, as he held her gaze—while Imari became hyper aware of herself, how her hands hung limply at her sides. What did she normally do with her hands? She suddenly had no idea.

Thankfully, she remembered why she'd come here in the first place. "How's he doing?" she asked, and started for Stanis.

"Good," Jeric replied two seconds later, and she heard the reed pen *plink* into the inkwell. "Still sleeping, but the poison is gone."

"Mind if I –" She gestured at the door.

"Go ahead."

Imari cracked the door open and peered inside. Stanis slept peacefully, his snores loud and steady. Someone had removed his tunic, leaving his chest bare. Like Jeric, he bore a collection of scars, but Imari saw no black. Not a single, wicked trace of it.

Imari stared with astonishment. Her music had worked, and even now, she could *feel* his life force—the energy generated from the plane of stars visible only to her. The air hummed with it, like the lingering vibrations of a bell.

"Thank you. For saving his life."

Imari turned around in the doorway.

Jeric watched her from the stool, his expression serious. "It wasn't fair to place that burden on you, with him." A crease formed between his brows. "He hasn't been kind to you. I realize that."

"I'm glad I *could* help him," Imari replied, and she meant it. She closed the door and approached Jeric slowly. "But I hope you know that you don't need an excuse to visit next time. This shade-poisoning act is starting to become excessive, and it shows a real lack of imagination on your part."

Jeric's eyes gleamed, a grin playing at his lips. "You wound me, healer."

"That is, in fact, the exact opposite of what I do."

This time, Jeric laughed.

It was a full sound, deep and resonant, and Imari wished he laughed more. "Anyway, I hope I didn't interrupt anything...?" she asked.

"No, not at all." He sat back and he gazed down at the parchment before him. "I was just writing to Hersir."

"I'm impressed you could focus with *that* going on." Imari nodded in Stanis's general direction.

"Well, I *am* impressive, in case you hadn't noticed."

Imari snorted.

Jeric winked, then picked up the parchment and rolled it as Imari stopped before him.

"Now this is an impressive piece of craftsmanship." Jeric pointed at the lantern with the rolled parchment. "Is it supposed to be a chimp?"

"Made by Uki Gamla, in my honor." Imari gestured at herself with a flourish.

Jeric's gaze flickered over her, and suspicion sharpened the strong angles of his face. "Suddenly, your thieving adventures in Skanden make infinitely more sense."

Imari smirked. "I'll have you know that Vondar didn't prepare me for ice and snow very well. I slipped and fell from many rooftops in my more primitive years."

Jeric grinned while his fingertips skirted the lantern's face, searching for a way to open the grate.

"Here." Imari reached past him. Her hand brushed his as she pushed the little lever, and the grate-belly hinged open, exposing the burning innards.

"Ah," he said. "Clever."

"The cleverest."

Jeric picked up a wedge of wax and held it over the coals while Imari leaned against the counter, watching him. Even though she was standing and he was sitting, they were almost at eye level.

"Hersir is your Lead Stryker?" Imari asked.

"Yes." Jeric looked pleased that she'd remembered, and then let the wax drip onto the rolled seam. "I temporarily left him in charge of Corinth."

"That's a tall order."

"Thankfully, Hersir's a tall man."

"Not as tall as you, however."

Jeric smirked. "Which was why I thought I should probably let him know I'm not dead, much to my jarls' chagrin, and also make sure I still have a throne when I return."

Corinth had been a volatile place when Imari had left—that much had not been lost on her. She'd hardly seen Jeric in the days that'd followed Astrid's imprisonment, because he'd been so busy assuaging his jarls. How much more volatile had it become when Jeric announced his plan to free all of their Sol Velorian slaves?

Assuming he had done it.

Ricón's words came back to her.

"Because you're attempting to liberate all of their labor?" Imari asked, hating that her brother had sowed those seeds of doubt into her mind.

"Yes, but that's not all of it." Jeric stamped his ring into the wax, leaving an imprint of Corinth's wolf insignia. Imari was relieved to hear that Ricón had been wrong. "I liberated the ones in the city, though I'm not sure if it's done more harm than good."

"Why do you say that?"

"They don't have anywhere to go, and the jarls won't spare land for them. I've offered competitive wages, but Godfrey says we can't afford them."

"Is that true?"

"I don't know." Jeric replied with a sigh. "Godfrey's always been a stingy son of a bitch, and it's hard to know truth from self-interest."

"Well, that's true no matter where you go."

Jeric quirked his brow in agreement and slipped the rolled parchment into a leather sleeve. "Maybe I should send our Sol Velor here, where you pay wages."

Imari leaned forward. "Have you actually *been* to E'Centro? Those aren't wages. Those are little crumbs of virtue that makes Istraa feel better about itself."

Jeric looked at her. "Little crumbs of virtue. I like that. Maybe I'll use it on my jarls next time."

"If they're anything like my papa's advisors, they won't like it very much," Imari warned.

"They'll like it more than the other names I've called them."

Imari laughed.

Jeric caught her gaze, mischief in his eyes, and then he closed the cap on the leather sleeve, buckled it, and set it on the counter.

Beside an empty amphora of nazzat.

"Now *this*..." Imari picked up the bottle. "This is impressive. An entire bottle of nazzat, all by yourself, and I don't even smell it on you."

Jeric smiled, all teeth, and he leaned so close that she could see the chimp's reflection burning in his eyes. "If I'd known I was going to see you tonight, I would have waited to share it."

Imari stared at him, wondering at his words while trying not to take more from them than he'd probably intended, but then he stood.

Jeric was tall—she knew that, yes—but this close, with all that bare and muscled chest right in front of her...well, it was a lot. *He* was a lot. And despite her best efforts to keep her gaze fixed on his face, it dropped to his chest, which was also when she noticed the bubble of angry skin over his sternum.

"Burning wards, Jeric!" she exclaimed.

"Funny you should use that particular phrasing…"

Imari touched his chest, and Jeric stilled beneath her fingertips. "Seriously, how did this happen?"

"A burning ward."

Imari glared up at him.

"I'm serious," he defended with a grin, palms out. "I was wearing a warded necklace, and it sort of…disintegrated."

Imari regarded him flatly.

"Imari, really," he said with a soft chuckle. "It's fine."

"It's *oozing*." Which was probably why he'd left his tunic folded on the counter beside the empty amphora.

"I've suffered worse."

"I have to treat this."

"No, you don't, and you've already—"

"It wasn't a question, Jeric."

He looked straight into her eyes. "How did I ever miss that you're a surina?"

"I don't know. Maybe you were distracted?"

Amusement flashed in his eyes, and she suddenly realized what she had said.

Also, he didn't deny it.

"Wait here." Imari poked a finger at his chest, feeling suddenly flushed. "I'm going to get something for…" She waved a hand over him. "*This*."

Jeric only grinned in reply, as if he noticed her discomfiture and was enjoying every second of it.

Imari moved alongside the cupboards, taking the opportunity to gather her composure. Her gaze trailed the shelves, searching for that little jar she'd spotted just a few days ago…*ah*. She remembered. It had been tucked away upon one of the higher shelves. She started to climb onto the counter, but hesitated, realizing the compromising position this dress put her in.

And then Jeric was there, stopping her with his long arm. "Let me help."

Imari was about to argue, but Jeric turned toward the shelves and blocked her out completely. "So what are we looking for?" he asked, scanning the jars.

Imari tried not to admire the broad sweep of his strong back. "Gurga paste." She pointed. "It's a little black jar on the top shelf. No...? Okay, lower...no, that's not it. I said *black*. No. *Black*, Jeric. That's green. Oh, just..." And then she realized Jeric was purposefully grabbing all the wrong jars. "You ass."

He smirked and held the little black jar out to her, which she took. And then she promptly whacked him on the head with it.

"Gods..." Jeric ducked with a chuckle. "Do you normally attack your patients?"

"No, but I'm happy to make an exception in your case."

Jeric flashed his canines, as if he welcomed it.

Imari rolled her eyes, then gestured at him. "Stand there."

Jeric did as instructed and leaned back against the counter, his palms squeezing its edge, while Imari untwisted the lid to the paste. The room seemed very quiet just then, and when she set the lid on the counter, the sound echoed, unnaturally loud.

Imari was just reaching into the jar when Jeric said, suddenly, "Ricón took me to see Astrid."

Imari looked up at him, but his gaze was fixed past her, unfocused. "And?" she asked.

Jeric's chest expanded with a deep inhale, his features tight. "Nothing. Not even a glance. She just sat there rocking back and forth." His nose twitched. A nervous tic. "Gods, I hardly recognize her anymore."

Those last words came out pained.

Imari lowered her fingers from the jar and placed them over Jeric's hand instead. "You can't keep blaming yourself, Jeric."

His hand flexed beneath her palm, his gaze met hers.

"What happened to Astrid is horrible, and I am so sorry you

have to deal with the consequences of it, but the legion is not your fault. *You* didn't pull it from the dark. *You* didn't send it into your sister, and you certainly could not have stopped it had you known."

A muscle ticked in his jaw, but he didn't look away. "But I should have—"

"Sometimes terrible things happen to good people," Imari continued, giving his hand a gentle squeeze. "All we can hope is to do the best we can in the time given to us, and that is exactly what you are doing. And what you will continue to do. I know you will."

Jeric's brow furrowed and his gaze dropped. She knew he was thinking about all of the things he had done in the name of his gods, and so Imari lifted her hand from his and touched his cheek instead, lifting it to force his gaze back to hers.

Where anguish ran deep.

"I meant what I said the day I left," she continued. "You are a good man, Jeric Oberyn Sal Angevin, and the people of Corinth are lucky to have you as their king. I'm lucky to call you my friend. Even if I really want to hit you sometimes."

Jeric slowly grinned, and they stood there like that, with her hand on his face, gazes locked, and Imari remembered their kiss. When she had been Sable, and he had been Jos. But then Jeric's features tightened again, and he turned his face away. She dropped her hand, feeling a stab of disappointment, so she looked down at the gurga paste instead.

But honestly, what had she expected? That Jeric would kiss her? *Here*? When anyone could walk in? And then what would her papa say? No, what would he *do*? The relationship between their nations was strained enough already.

And that was assuming Jeric even *wanted* to kiss her. It was quite possible her feelings for him were entirely one-sided.

"There was a moment," Jeric said suddenly, interrupting her thoughts. "In Corinth. I thought it was her. She was at the sewers' exit." He paused, and eyed her. "The same place *you* were supposed to escape on my horse with one thousand crowns to start your new life."

Imari raised a brow. "I could still do it, you know."

"Really? And here I'd half expected you'd given it all away to some charitable cause."

Imari feigned surprise. "You know what, that's a fantastic idea! Why didn't I think of this sooner?"

Jeric regarded her flatly.

Imari chuckled, and waved the little jar before him.

Jeric planted his feet apart, and Imari moved to stand between his legs, forcing herself to focus on her job, though she couldn't help admiring this beautiful weapon on full display before her.

"I didn't think Astrid would still be there," Jeric continued. His words were so close. *He* was so close. "She'd had a good head start, but when we reached the rocks, she was just standing at the water's edge like she'd been waiting for me." A beat. "It was *her* voice, Imari."

Imari caught his gaze. "You think she's still in there."

"I don't know." Jeric pressed his lips together. "It was only a moment, but it was her voice, I swear to the gods. And then the ward started burning."

"Wards do that when they're overwhelmed," Imari said. It had happened to Skanden's on occasion, but Skanden had the advantage of numbers. Jeric had only brought the one.

"Where did you get the ward?" Imari asked.

"Rasmin's office."

Imari eyed him. "Well isn't your inquisitor just full of surprises."

Jeric grunted in annoyance.

"He's here, by the way."

A deadly stillness fell over Jeric, his features hardened, and his head bent forward. A hunter on a scent. "What."

"I haven't technically seen him," Imari continued. "He left me a note when I first arrived in Trier. In my room—"

"In *your room...?*"

Imari gave him a look to keep his voice down.

Jeric's eyes narrowed. "You didn't tell anyone?"

"No, and I'm fine. *Clearly.*"

Jeric was not pacified in the slightest. "What did the note say?"

"That he wanted me to practice, but I burned it and threatened to put archers on my balcony if he ever tried to contact me again." At this, Jeric chuckled softly. "Anyway, tell me more about this ward you were wearing." She dipped her fingers into the paste. It tingled on her fingertips.

Jeric flexed his grip on the counter's edge. "It belonged to my father's grandfather."

"Tommad the first?"

"The very one."

Yes, Imari had heard of that warded necklace, given to King Tommad the First by a very powerful enchantress. It was said to have protected him against Azir and the Mo'Ruk. She was surprised his family had kept it.

"It probably lost potency after the years," Imari said. "They do need to be maintained, but it was smart to try."

"I told you, I'm impressive—" Jeric started, but then Imari touched the paste to his wound, and he sucked a curse through his teeth.

"Sorry." Imari smirked, and Jeric grumbled. "I should have warned you."

"Why start now?" he said wryly, and Imari chuckled.

She dipped her fingers into the paste again and gave him a warning glance. He only narrowed his eyes in return, and she grinned as she spread more upon the burn, noting the faint symbol within. "Actually, I think I can see the enchantment." Imari squinted and leaned closer to study the mark that had burned right into his skin. "Yes, it's safe to say you've been branded."

"Rutting fantastic," he murmured.

"What's this?" Imari pointed to a mark just above his waist that looked like a hastily patched-up stab wound.

"It's just a cut."

Imari gave him a patronizing look, and he flashed his teeth.

"It's fine," he insisted with an edge of irritation. "Tallyn stopped the bleeding with his...whatever it is that he does."

So it *was* a hastily patched-up stab wound. "Well, that explains the strange hatch pattern of young skin. Looks like he tried to speed up the healing process," Imari mused, then she spotted the three black lines from the Changling. "These look good. Any issues?"

"No."

Imari eyed him.

He rolled his eyes to the ceiling and sighed. "They tingle at times. When I'm in close proximity to other shades."

"Did you tell Tallyn?" she asked as she smeared more paste into the wound that Tallyn had healed.

"No. I haven't told anyone."

She didn't miss the concern in his voice, faint though it was.

"Well." She stood upright and set the paste back on the countertop. "You're not going to spontaneously Change into a shade. It'll be interesting to see if Stanis shares any similar side effects, but in the meantime, consider it your own special Liagé talent." She turned back to face him.

Which was a mistake, because she'd forgotten how close they were standing.

She quickly looked away, reached past him, and plucked a bandage from the bottommost shelf. "Speaking of Tallyn, how in all the stars did you find him?"

"He found us," Jeric replied. "He *says* he's been in Tül Bahn." A pause, and then, more quietly, he added, "He killed the others."

Imari stopped, bandage draped across both hands. "*All* of them?"

"All but two."

Imari had known the old alta-Liagé was powerful. Of course, she hadn't known this when she'd initially agreed to stay with him in his home, hidden just outside of Craven. No, if she'd glimpsed the breadth of his power, she never would have trusted the man. He had wisely kept it hidden until Riverwood, when Ventus had caught up to them. Tallyn had come to their rescue, and his power had been a wonder to behold.

I was Azir's second for a reason, Tallyn had told her then.

And he had singlehandedly returned to Tül Bahn to finish off Ventus's silent. Except for two, it would seem.

"So what was Tallyn doing in Corinth?" Imari asked.

"Tracking those two silent." At the look of surprise on Imari's face, he added, "They came to help Astrid."

Imari felt her lips fall open. "*What...?*"

Jeric gave her a knowing look.

"Why would they be helping her?"

"I don't know," he replied heavily, glancing past her, deep in thought. "But I lost a scout to a shade in the Blackwood. Astrid knew about it."

Those wards should have prohibited all forms of communication in and out of the cell. Imari thought of Astrid here, in Trier's warded cell, and she could tell Jeric was thinking about that too. "Did you tell Papa?" Imari asked.

"I did."

Imari did not like this. She did not like it at all, and neither did Jeric, judging by the expression on his face.

"Arms out," Imari instructed.

Jeric held out his long arms.

Imari breathed in deep and leaned forward, suddenly aware of every inch of him as she reached past his laterals to wrap the bandage around his broad chest. Once. Twice. He smelled deliciously of cedar and spice and heat, and she had to force herself not to breathe him in too deeply.

She tucked the end of the wrapping into itself, near the pit of his arm, but as she pulled away, Jeric grabbed her wrist and looked straight at her, his eyes dark as monsoon clouds. "You will not face the Provinces alone, Imari. I told your father this, and I'm telling you now. You have every resource I can spare. Corinth will stand with you."

Imari stared at him. "Thank you." Her words fell out at a whisper.

"It's the least I can do."

Imari glanced down, feeling suddenly overwhelmed, and he let go of her hand.

Finally—reluctantly—Imari took a small step back so that she no longer stood between Jeric's legs, and then she grabbed the lid to the jar.

Still, she felt Jeric watching her, but she didn't turn to look. She didn't trust herself, because she wanted...

She...*wanted.*

"Are you glad to be home?" Jeric asked.

The question caught her off guard, and she felt his attention burning through her as she twisted the lid into place. "Sometimes I wish I'd just taken your thousand crowns, settled in some distant village, and made a life myself."

"Sometimes I wonder if I would have joined you."

Imari glanced curiously at him, but then he turned his attention to the little jar and picked it up. It looked minuscule in his large hands—hands that had carried her to her room last night, Imari remembered.

"This is incredible. I hardly feel the burn anymore," he said, studying that little jar. "What's it made of?"

Imari blinked and looked at the jar. "You don't want to know."

His sharp gaze landed on her. "Trust me, I do."

"Almond essence, aloe, scorpion venom, and...bat droppings."

Jeric's features expanded with new appreciation, and then he gestured at the shelf, silently asking if she'd like him to return it.

"No, leave it. I'll need to do this again tomorrow."

Jeric set it down and pushed off the counter. He stood so close, he towered over her as he gazed down into her eyes. "I look forward to it, surina."

Voices sounded in the hall, and the door flew open a second later.

Ricón strode in. He'd been saying something to Braddok, who walked in behind him, but then he caught sight of Jeric and Imari, standing hardly one foot apart, and he stopped in his tracks.

Braddok's lips broke into a big smile. "There she is."

Imari couldn't help but smile back at Jeric's enormous friend.

Ricón, however, was not smiling. His gaze slid from Imari to Jeric, where it settled, and Jeric stared straight back.

Braddok, who seemed happily oblivious to their silent stand-off, stalked toward Imari with heavy strides, pulled her away from Jeric and into an enormous embrace.

It never ceased to amaze Imari how the strongest men had the softest interiors.

"Good to see you, little thief," Braddok said, releasing her to ruffle the top of her head.

"Good to see you too." Imari sniffed at the air. "I see you found the nazzat."

"And I see you found a Wolf." Braddok's gaze swiveled to Jeric. "I was wondering what took you so long. Should've known better."

Imari caught Ricón's piercing stare, and she swiftly looked away just as Chez and Aksel waltzed through the door.

"Surina." Aksel tipped his head toward her. His freckles were more pronounced than she remembered. Probably due to Istraa's brighter sun.

"Good evening, Aksel. Chez." Imari grinned to each in turn.

"Glad to see you're up and about," Chez added. "You look well." His beard was fuller—not longer, just fuller, and she spotted flecks of sand in it. Actually, there were flecks of sand all over him.

"And you look like you've been in the desert," Imari said in good humor.

Chez chuckled. "Tell me about it. Godsdamned sand gets everywhere. I'll probably be picking this scat out of my—"

"Chez," Jeric snapped.

Chez smirked, winked at Imari, and then took a seat at the table.

"So...no changes for our sleeping princess?" Braddok gestured toward Stanis's door, where the snoring still rumbled.

"I'm glad you're feeling better," Ricón said to Imari, drawing her attention back to him. "If I'd known you were awake, I would've sent dinner."

"Thank you. I'm not really hungry anyway."

Ricón's gaze flickered briefly to Jeric, before adding, "Papa went straight to your chambers."

Assuming Imari would be there, his words implied.

Imari cursed inwardly. "I'll go now."

Ricón looked at her like that was probably a good idea.

"And if it's all right with you," Jeric interjected, snatching the leather sleeve off of the counter, "I need to send this to Skyhold."

"Of course," Ricón said. "I'll take you to Hayit now. I thought I saw him around here somewhere..."

Jeric snagged his tunic, slung it over his shoulder, but then turned to Imari. There he stopped and looked at her. That mischief returned to his eyes, followed by something deeply wolfish, and then he leaned forward and kissed her cheek.

Imari's breath hitched as Jeric's soft lips lingered against her skin. "Goodnight, Surina Imari," he whispered, more breath than sound, and a shiver moved over her, head to toe.

Jeric pulled away. His eyes burned with something like a

promise and a challenge all wrapped into one, and then he brushed past her and strode out the door, not sparing the others so much as a parting glance. His men didn't seem to notice. They all appeared conveniently preoccupied.

Except Ricón.

His jaw flexed, his gaze slid back to Imari. "I'll see you in the morning," he said at last, and then he left.

Braddok cleared his throat, and when she glanced back, he winked at her. "Night, Surina."

"Good night," she said, then left through the door, and started for her chambers, where her papa waited.

24

I mari intercepted her papa in the hall outside of her chambers. His hair fell free, and bits of it strayed, untamed. In contrast to Imari, who had slept the day away, he looked as though he hadn't slept at all. Heavy bags pillowed his eyes, and the lines in his forehead carved deep.

"There you are." He sounded tired too. "I was about to go looking for you."

"Ricón said you were here," she said as her papa grabbed her arms and looked her over. She caught a whiff of heshi on his clothes, and the sour tinge of body odor. "I was just checking on Stanis," she said. Which was true, but she left out the rest.

"Is he awake?"

He sounded eager for this inevitability.

"No, not yet, but the poison is gone."

He let go of her arms. "You were kind to help him."

Imari did not know if it was a compliment. It wanted to be, but missed the mark. Self-interest often interfered with basic human values, Imari had learned.

"Well, I wasn't going to let him suffer, if I could help," she said, as if to remind him of those values.

He looked at her. She didn't think he agreed.

"I wanted a word, if you're feeling up for it," he said.

Imari had the sneaking suspicion that whatever those words might be, they were *needed*, and not necessarily *wanted*.

It set Imari on edge. "Of course, Papa."

He gestured in the direction of her chambers, and together they walked back to her door, where two saredd stood guard. She glanced sideways at her papa, and he gazed steadily back.

Because this would be her life now. Guarded, monitored, and controlled.

Sar Branón nodded at the saredd. One—a shorter fellow with a beard trimmed to a point—pushed into the room and vanished. He reappeared thirty seconds later.

"All clear," he said.

Her papa gestured for Imari to go ahead, and she strode through the antechamber, where Dasi was mending the clothes Imari had ruined while fighting Astrid in E'Centro. The woman sat upon a sleeping pallet, Imari noticed. Apparently, Dasi would be staying here too.

Imari's chest suddenly tightened, her breathing turned quick and shallow, and she felt the sudden, inexplicable urge to flee.

"Leave us," Sar Branón said to Dasi.

Dasi bowed, set down her mending, and left through the main door, closing it after her. Her papa strode into the bedchamber, while Imari followed slowly, forcing her steps steady.

Sar Branón stopped just inside, arms akimbo as he glanced around, taking in the space as if seeing the past in her furnishings. Finally, he looked back at her. There was a deep sadness in his eyes, but then it was gone so fast, Imari wondered if she'd imagined it.

"I never thought I'd see you here again, in this room," he said quietly. "I'm glad I was wrong."

Imari didn't really know what to say, because she didn't know if *she* was glad. She'd thought coming home would give her more freedom and a sense of belonging, but that was quickly proving not to be the case. She had comfort, yes, but anonymity in The Wilds had given her freedom she would never have in Istraa.

"So what is to happen to me now?" Imari asked.

Sar Branón sat heavily upon her high-backed, brocaded chair. He looked at her, and one edge of his lips curled into a satirical sort of smile. "You always see through everything."

"It's kept me alive."

She didn't say it to be rude; it was simply the truth.

His smile turned wistful and he leaned forward, elbows on his knees as his hands dangled between them. "Obviously you can't continue being Sable."

"I know." Imari took a seat on her divan. A plate of fruits and flatbread had been left upon her table, reminding her that she hadn't eaten, and so she reached forward and tore off a piece of flatbread.

"You will be introduced to the rois and roiesses next week."

Next week.

She knew it was inevitable, but...

Next week.

This was what she'd wanted, wasn't it? To be Imari? To finally open that forbidden door and shed light on the truth?

Imari licked her lips, gripping the flatbread in her hand.

"I've spent most of the day responding to their inquiries about you," he added, glancing in the direction of her wood stove.

Burning wards.

It had only been one day since she'd used her power before all of E'Centro and Trier's guards, but that news had already reached the rois' ears.

Imari leaned back and turned the flatbread over in her hand. "Word travels fast."

"You have no idea."

Imari brought the flatbread to her lips. It tasted like sand as she tore off a bite and chewed. "And...do you have any indication as to how it's...how *I* am being received?"

Her papa leaned back and draped his arms over the chair's, his fingers tickling at the air. "Well. Out of my eleven, three are demanding I abdicate my throne, five want your blood, two are willing to take this to trial, and one seems intrigued."

Imari pressed her lips together as she processed this. "Are you still glad you were wrong?"

Her papa gave her a small smile. "Absolutely." His fingertips stopped dancing. "It's not as dismal as I'm making it sound, Imari."

Imari chuckled darkly.

"I mean it. I've been in meetings with my private council for most of the day, and Bayek is securing an arrangement."

At his words, Imari froze and looked straight at her papa. "What sort of arrangement?"

Sar Branón leaned in the chair, not really meeting her gaze. Which did not help her mounting anxiety.

"Roi Naleed has promised support and reinforcements," he said at last. "And if you recall, Bisra Tai is home to nearly two thousand able men."

Yes, Imari remembered. Bisra Tai was Istraa's largest locality, because it bordered the sea and stretched over a wide river, and in this desert climate, access to water provided vast economy. Roi Naleed had often tried using that economy against her papa, and it was only thanks to the unanimous support for Sar Branón that the roi had not succeeded.

Support which, it seemed, her papa no longer possessed.

An alliance with Roi Naleed made sense.

However.

Imari's eyes narrowed. "You've promised me to his son, haven't you."

The transformation from papa to sar was immediate—a learned defense against emotions that would interfere with his ability to rule, unbiased. Imari watched as those loving lines hardened into duty and resolution, and before he spoke another word, she knew her argument was lost.

It had been lost before she'd started. "Papa..."

"Imari." He sat forward, and his dark gaze bore into hers. "Even without all of the existing complications, you had to have known this would eventually be your reality. Ricón will inherit this throne, assuming I can keep it, and he will marry. Vondar is not large enough for two suras."

Imari clenched her teeth and glared at the floor, at the narrow lines between tiles while her heart beat furiously. She felt like one of Gamla's mice trapped in a cage. A pretty cage, but still a cage.

She thought of Jeric.

"I know you just arrived," her papa continued, somewhat softer than before. "And part of the reason I was so keen to keep you as Sable was so that...so that I did not have to rush this. But I will not risk your safety, Imari—"

"*My* safety?" Imari's head whipped up and she fixed that glare upon her papa. "No, this isn't about me. This is about *you*. Otherwise, you would have given me a choice in this matter, but you've chosen *for* me. Just because you're in a loveless marriage, don't think that I—"

Sar Branón raised a hand, and Imari flinched in expectation. But he did not strike.

Instead, his fingers curled into a trembling fist. "You have no idea, Imari." His voice was low and full of rare emotion. "*None.*"

And she knew this was about her mama. Her *real* mama.

"Then help me understand!" she pleaded, throwing her arms.

He shook his head, lowered his fist and closed his eyes. "I can't."

"You *won't.*"

His eyes opened, he looked at her. "I won't."

"*Why*, Papa?"

His gaze moved over her face, but Imari had the strangest sensation that he wasn't looking at her at all. That he was seeing someone else. And then his eyes refocused on *her*, and his expression turned serious. "You need to stay away from your Wolf, Imari."

Imari felt herself harden. "He's not *my* Wolf."

Her papa looked doubtful, and also angry. "He will leave, and that's the end of it. Don't make this more difficult than it needs to be."

Imari stood abruptly. "*Difficult*? You want to talk about *difficult*, Papa?"

Her papa also stood, and he was a good head taller. "*Don't*, Imari. Don't say things you'll regret."

"The *only* thing I regret is believing I actually had a home here."

Her papa's lips pressed firmly together. "This will always be a home for you, Imari. That's not the issue. The issue is that it's no longer a home you want."

Imari did not have anything to say to that.

He was right.

Trier was the same. Nothing had changed.

But *she* had.

Her papa sighed, his shoulders sagged. "Try to rest. We have a long road ahead of us, and this is only the beginning."

Imari felt suddenly numb, and her gaze dropped to the antechamber where Dasi waited just outside the door. "She's staying here now, isn't she."

"Yes. And until I can secure your safety, I will not leave you unattended."

She looked sharply at him. "It didn't stop you from sending me to The Wilds."

A muscle flexed in his jaw. He looked like he was about to say something else, but stopped himself. "Goodnight, Imari."

Imari didn't respond. She watched her papa walk to the door, watched him stop in the threshold, shoulders tight, and then he pressed on, shutting the door behind him.

IMARI DID NOT SLEEP well that night. Partly because she'd already slept for twelve hours straight, but mostly because her mind would not shut off. Her thoughts kept wandering down hazy paths of a future she could not see, nor was it hers to determine.

She dreamed of Roi Naleed, or at least her memory of him. She dreamed of his son, though the face was a smudge of shadows and blurred features, but she woke feeling revulsion at being touched by a man she did not love. She dreamed of Jeric too, in which she watched him from afar as another woman kissed him in the way she so badly wanted to. She hated that dream almost more than the first, and it left her in a fury.

Unable to take anymore, Imari slid out of bed, grabbed her shawl and wrapped it around her shoulders, and then she pushed through her screen door and stepped out onto her veranda. From here, she had a sweeping view of the city, sleeping in the pre-dawn light, though a few lanterns still burned below. A soft glow rose behind the Baragas' broad backs, and a cool breeze kissed her skin. Imari closed her eyes and breathed in deep, trying to expand her tight lungs and dull the nerves that sleep had tortured.

Maker have mercy.

Her insides were in knots, coiling tighter and tighter. She didn't think she could untangle it if she tried.

She supposed, bitterly, that one good thing might come of this. With Roi Naleed's forces behind her, it might actually be possible to exact change for the Sol Velor, sooner than later. Naleed had the resources, the financial stability. If she persuaded him to restructure their labor and pay more competitive wages, the other rois and roiesses would follow suit.

But...

"How can I marry another man when I feel these things for you?" she whispered to the dawn, as if Jeric were standing right there beside her. But the moment that confession left her lips, she knew she had a problem.

She clutched the shawl close and watched the sun rise over the Baragas, igniting the sky. There was nothing like a desert sunrise, and the sight of it struck a chord deep within her.

"What do I do?" she whispered to the sky, as yawning daylight swallowed the stars in brilliant fire.

She so desperately wished the Maker would give answer, and she stood there waiting for it. Waiting and waiting, and that was how Dasi found her.

"Ah. There you are, surina."

Imari turned.

Dasi had changed into a simple lilac gown this morning, though her features sharpened as she gazed disapprovingly over Imari. Not that Imari expected any different. Dasi had first belonged to Anja, and Anja had never hidden her disapproval where Imari was concerned.

"They're breaking fast below," Dasi continued, all stiff politeness. "Unless you'd rather take it in your chambers."

It was obvious which option Dasi preferred. So Imari chose opposite.

"I'll go below, thank you."

There was a tick in Dasi's cheek. "Of course, mi a'surina. Shall I ready your bath?"

Imari almost laughed. She'd bathed more in two weeks than she had in the past two months. "No, that won't be necessary."

Dasi bowed her head. "I'll leave clothes for you on the bed."

Imari waited another moment, until she was certain Dasi had returned to the antechamber, and then strode back into her room, where Dasi had left a sapphire-blue gown upon Imari's bed. Though as Imari made sense of the garment, she realized it wasn't a gown but two pieces: a cropped and fitted top with cuffed sleeves, and a pair of loose pants to match, cinched only at the waist.

At least Dasi had chosen something more functional this time.

Imari dressed behind the screen, and even though this outfit had been made of considerably more fabric than the dress she'd worn yesterday, somehow it felt...less. The top hugged her chest so tightly, it lifted her breasts in a way that made her seem larger than she was, and the embroidered hem ended at her ribcage, leaving her waist exposed. The pants were comfortable at least, the silk soft and billowing, giving her a wide range of motion. She strapped on her sandals, combed her hair and pinched color into her cheeks, and then met Dasi in the antechamber.

Dasi gave her a once-over, looking satisfied and irritated at the same time, and then opened the main door.

Where Jenya and another saredd stood guard.

Jenya stepped forward immediately. "I'll take her."

Imari smiled in gratitude.

The two of them walked quietly through the halls. Wide palms fanned the breeze, and cinnamon spiced the air.

"Tarq asked me to thank you, by the way," Jenya said.

"He's very welcome," Imari replied. "I'm glad he's doing well. Maybe I could check on him later today?"

"I think we could arrange that," Jenya replied, then added at a whisper, "Though we might need to bring him here. Sar Branón has given strict orders that you're not permitted to leave Vondar."

Imari curled her hands into fists and glared at the next column they passed by. "Of course he did."

"It's for your own safety, surina," Jenya said gently.

"That's what everyone keeps saying."

Jenya didn't say another word.

Neither did Imari.

Her nightmares were still too near.

They reached the hall to find the doors hanging wide open.

Imari spotted a few dozen guests within, dining at various tables. The hall often entertained Trier's prestigious citizens, and this morning was no different. Servants moved about, replenishing food and beverage, and a handful of saredd stood watch at the open archways, guarding the morning.

Imari spotted Jeric immediately.

He stood out in this room of Istraans. Not just because he was Corinthian, but also because he was so uniquely striking, and somehow managed to command a room just by being in it. Even now, he lounged at the end of a table, seated beside Sebharan while turning a chalice in his hand. So at ease. Natural, even, as if he were master here, despite the looks of disapproval he received from some of the other guests. But Jeric didn't seem to notice, or care.

He wore fitted dark breeches and a loose cream tunic, left untied at the neck, and he'd left his bronze hair elegantly tousled. The sun had given more color to his cheeks, and his eyes shone bright.

The desert suited him well.

Jeric glanced up then, met her gaze. Even though he looked at her from across the room, even though a crowd spread between them, she felt that stare to her core, and Imari's chest filled with butterflies.

Yes, she had a very large problem, indeed.

"Good morning, mi a'surina."

Imari had not noticed the servant beside her. A Sol Velorian woman. It was a rare promotion for a Sol Velorian to be assigned a position in Vondar's main hall, but it did happen.

"Sar Branón reserved a place for you," the servant continued, gesturing toward another table, where Sar Branón sat at the head with Bayek, Jeol, and Kai.

Kai looked very pale, and very tired.

Anja wasn't anywhere to be seen, but that came as no surprise.

Her papa waved a hand at her, and Kai moved over, creating space between himself and Bayek. Imari caught Jeric's gaze once more before making her way toward her papa, and she felt that gaze burning through her back even as she sat down.

Jenya moved off to the side to speak with one of the saredd standing guard.

"Good morning, surina," Bayek said, casting an ersatz smile.

Which Imari returned. "Where's Ricón?" she asked.

"With the Kourana," her papa said, lifting a chalice of pomegranate juice to his lips.

Imari frowned. "What's happened?"

He swallowed, and set the chalice down. "We've apprehended—"

"Are you sure we should be talking about this here?" Bayek cut him off, glancing furtively about. His gaze snagged on the Sol Velorian woman.

Sar Branón gave him a look. "It's not exactly a secret."

Kai tensed beside her.

Sar Branón looked at Imari. "We've apprehended a woman from Ashova's."

This time, Kai's hand flexed upon the table.

Imari looked sideways at her brother, their gazes met, and Imari knew: Kai had known the woman they'd apprehended.

She remembered him the night she'd saved Tarq. Kai had arrived fully awake, and fully dressed, with his clothing rumpled.

Because he'd come straight from Ashova's.

Kai's jaw set and he glanced away as a dozen more pieces clicked into place. She'd known Kai frequented Ashova's, but how many others had known this and capitalized on Kai's habit? And what could they have learned? Was that how Astrid had known where Imari had been that night?

And then she remembered that Saza's sister worked at Ashova's. She wondered if the two were connected.

"A servant or kahar?" Imari asked. Though she already speculated, she needed to be certain.

Her papa quieted as a servant reached past and set another chalice on the table before Imari, along with a plate, and walked away.

"Servant," Sar Branón said.

Imari did not miss the look he gave Kai.

Kai pulled the cloth napkin from his lap and tossed it on the table as he stood. "Excuse me," he said. "I have business to attend."

A lie. Everyone knew it, but no one corrected him.

He strode briskly out of the hall, and Imari looked back at her papa.

"Kourana Vidéa believes this woman was feeding information to...their leader."

The *Liagé* leader, but he would not chance that word here. That *would* draw attention.

She held her papa's gaze level. "About me."

"About you."

Imari processed this. She suddenly didn't feel very hungry any more.

"That's not all," he continued.

Jeol cleared his throat, and he and Bayek exchanged an irritated glance. Clearly, they still didn't approve of having this conversation right now.

"Another temple was burned down this morning," her papa said quietly. "In Bal Duhr."

Bal Duhr was a city that lay a few hours south of Trier.

Imari watched her papa as he took a long sip. She didn't think a destroyed temple was the end of it. "What else happened?" she asked quietly.

He set the cup down, ignoring the warning looks both Bayek and Jeol were giving him. "Near one hundred of Bal Duhr's Sol Velorians are missing. The laborers, and their families."

Imari felt her eyes widen, her thoughts reeling. "How many have we lost, in total?"

"Since First Sow... About two thousand."

Imari gasped. "Two thous—"

"Ah, ah," Bayek said sharply, glancing about them. He gave Sar Branón a pointed look.

Two thousand Sol Velorians were missing, and Imari didn't have to think long to understand why. This Liagé leader, whoever he or she was, was building an army. And even if only one tenth of those missing Sol Velorians were able to fight...

The Qazzat employed and trained one hundred fighters—both saredd and city guard.

She looked at her papa. "And how many able men can Trier spare?"

He looked pleased with her conclusion, and her question. "Maybe three hundred."

That made four hundred, total. But those numbers would not matter if the Sol Velorians had Liagé in their midst. No wonder her papa wanted Roi Naleed's forces.

"What happened to the citizens of Bal Duhr?" Imari asked.

Jeol shifted in his chair.

Bayek's eyes darkened. "They were barred in the temple with the kahar, and burned alive."

Imari's lips parted in horror. "All of them?"

"Every man, woman, and child."

Imari suddenly felt sick.

Someone laughed in the hall, the sound incongruous with this horrible news.

"Sebharan's scouts reported it late last night," Sar Branón continued, glancing about them. "He's sending sarred later today. Ricón will join them."

"Have you spoken to Jeric about this?" she said without thinking, and the use of his familiar name garnered her swift disapproval from her papa, and Bayek. "He's the best tracker in the

Provinces," Imari continued, defending her mistake as best she could—with truth. "He might have insight, especially since Corinth dealt with something similar."

These events had to be related.

"That's why Sebharan's speaking with him now." Her papa glanced in Jeric's direction.

Imari took the opportunity to glance over to where Jeric and Sebharan sat. She also noticed the small group of women—all daughters of Trier's wealthiest—who had slowly pressed closer, making eyes at the Corinthian king. Apparently, not even a century of Provincial enmity could keep them from admiring him. Imari couldn't fault them for it, but it didn't stop the unexpected prick of jealousy. Jeric didn't act as though he noticed them, but Imari knew he noticed everything.

And then Jeric caught her gaze. His eyes shone with something wolfish, and then he looked to the group of women—at one, in particular—and flashed a disarming smile.

The woman smiled in return, her cheeks flushed.

Jeric looked back at Imari, winked at her, and then turned his full attention back to Sebharan.

That arrogant, pompous...ass.

"Imari," her papa said.

She didn't think it was the first time he'd said her name.

When she finally looked back at him, her suspicions were confirmed.

"I need you to stay within Vondar's walls for the time being," Sar Branón said.

"Jenya mentioned it," she replied curtly, more from irritation at Jeric than her papa's command. "Now I understand why."

He looked satisfied. "Good." He stood, rounded the table's edge and placed a heavy hand on her shoulder. "I'll visit later. I need to speak with Ricón before he leaves." He bent forward and kissed the top of her head. "Be careful, Imari."

Careful.

As if being locked in her chambers would keep her safe. No, the best way she could be "careful" was to practice her flute and be prepared to defend herself should battle come to Vondar.

And she knew just the person who could help.

"Have you seen Tallyn?" Imari asked.

"Yes, he was with Sebharan, but left this morning to investigate E'Centro again. You should ask Sebharan to be sure."

"I'll do that," Imari replied, eager for an excuse to walk over to Jeric.

But when she looked back, the Wolf was gone. And so was one of the ladies.

IMARI NAVIGATED the rest of the day with increasing agitation. She told herself it had nothing to do with Jeric, and everything to do with all of the news her papa had relayed. Soon after their conversation in the hall, Ricón had stopped by to say goodbye, but hadn't stayed long. He was in a hurry to hunt the enemy's tracks while they were fresh, and so he essentially left her with the platitudes of an adoring oldest brother: *I love you, be careful,* and *I'll see you soon.*

Guards followed Imari everywhere, which did not help her mood, and when she attempted to visit Astrid, she quickly learned she'd been banned from further visitation. Apparently, her papa had put the pieces together, and so long as the demon had a mysterious way of communicating through warded skal doors, he intended to keep his daughter as far from it as possible. The only reason the demon's execution had not been expedited was because they were all too busy with the events surrounding Bal Duhr.

Jenya joined her sometime near midday, noticed Imari's irritation, and sent the other guards away, but with Jenya as her sole guard, Imari was able to check on Stanis. Jeric wasn't there, not that she'd gone there looking for him specifically. No, she definitely had not. Aksel said Jeric had gone with her papa and Sebharan to the Qazzat, to discuss whether or not to bring the other Provinces into this.

Imari was irked they hadn't included her when she knew she could help.

She was also irked Jeric had left the hall without saying a word.

Actually, she was just irked at Jeric.

She snatched *Il Tonté* from Gamla's cupboards, slipped it into her pants, and returned with Jenya to her chambers, where two saredd stood guard. Jenya gave her an apologetic look, but there was nothing she could do; Sebharan had requested Jenya's presence at the Qazzat. And so Imari was left with two strangers and a kunari who insisted on staying *inside* Imari's chambers.

"They are Sar Branón's orders," Dasi insisted.

Still, Imari argued, and eventually Dasi agreed to keep to the antechamber.

Imari plopped on her bed and read from the verses, though even those hopeful words could not pull her from her dark mood. She'd read the same passage five times in a row before she finally put the book away and reached for her flute, deciding she might as well practice. Do something physical. She padded into the washroom and closed the door, so no one would overhear, but she couldn't focus there either. Her notes were mechanical and completely uninspired, and everything just sounded...angry.

So she hammered out a few finger exercises instead. She was pushing one tone to the edge of its fullness, when the small jars of bath salts toppled from a high shelf and shattered upon the tiles, spilling scented salts everywhere.

Imari froze, eyes wide.

Dasi ran in two seconds later.

"I'm fine," Imari said, her chest tingling with Shah energy. "Everything's fine. It was just an accident."

Dasi looked from the jars' remains to the glowing flute, which Imari quickly hid behind her back.

"Really, it's fine," Imari insisted, as the tingling subsided. "I'll clean it up."

Dasi's eye twitched. She pressed down the fold of her dress and left, closing the antechamber door. Imari glanced down at the flute, at the broken jars. Maybe now wasn't the best time to practice.

She put the flute away, and had just finished cleaning up her mess when Dasi returned to the washroom. Dasi's gaze went immediately to Imari's hands and, seeing them flute-less, looked relieved.

"There is a...man here to see you," Dasi said.

Imari frowned.

"He says his name is Tallyn."

Imari gasped, anger forgotten as she rushed for the door. She opened it to find Tallyn standing in her hall, flanked by Jenya and another saredd in addition to the two saredd already standing guard outside of her door.

At the sight of Imari, Tallyn smiled. "You look well. Your color has definitely returned."

Anger tended to do that, but she didn't say that out loud.

"I feel better, thank you," she said.

He arched one hairless brow. "Sebharan said you wanted to see me?"

"I did... I do." Her gaze flitted to the saredd before landing back on Tallyn. "I wondered if we could speak in private."

"Whatever you need," Tallyn said.

Behind her, Dasi cleared her throat.

Imari looked back.

"Excuse me, mi a'surina, but you are forbidden from being alone with any man who is not an immediate relation, especially in the confines of your bedchamber."

Imari smiled tightly. "Of course," she replied, and an idea bloomed. "I know just the place. Jenya? Would you..."

Jenya grinned and stepped forward while Imari faced the other saredd. "You're relieved for now. Jenya will attend me."

The saredd looked at Jenya, then at Imari, bowed their heads, and walked on.

Imari gave Dasi her most brilliant smile. "There, you see? Problem solved. I'll be back, but don't wait up for me."

25

"Follow me," Imari whispered to Tallyn and Jenya.

They followed her down the steps, through columned walkways and past swaying fronds. Servants were just beginning to light lanterns as evening descended in full.

They had almost reached Imari's destination when Jenya said, "Ah." There was a smile to that one word.

Imari stopped before the door to the small prayer room and pushed it in. A dark lantern sat beside the marble statue of Peloti, Istraa's beloved emissary god. The room was small, equipped with a table for prayer and offering, and a single bench just wide enough for the two of them to sit.

Tallyn appraised the space and closed the door behind them. "I never would have known this was here."

"You're not alone there." Imari grabbed a candle from the hall, and touched it to the lantern. Light blossomed. "I used to come here as a girl. To hide from my kunari."

Especially during the monsoons, when the rooftiles were too slick to climb and she needed to get away from Vana's strict demands. She'd suspected Ricón knew about it, but he never told anyone, and no one ever found her, because no one seemed to remember this was here. Most people, Imari had found, preferred their prayers to be heard by men rather than gods, and this little room could not put their righteousness on full display.

"And you're still hiding," Tallyn said.

He didn't mean offense, and she wasn't offended.

"Yes, I supposed I am." She set the candle back in its holder and returned to the prayer room. "I thought you were dead."

"I nearly was."

"And then you took on all of Tül Bahn's silent," Imari said. "By yourself."

To his credit, he did not shrink away from the truth. "I did. They are evil, and a danger to this world."

"And yet you—one man—killed them all."

"All but two. Thankfully, your Wolf killed one, and the saredd finished the other."

Imari did not miss where Tallyn had placed the possessive determiner.

But there was no guilt in his words, no conviction. Not even pride. Tallyn had spoken matter-of-factly, as though what he'd done was simply a necessity.

"But why were they working with Astrid?" Imari asked. "I thought they only answered to Ventus."

Tallyn sat down on the bench and folded his hands in his lap. "That, my dear, is an excellent question."

He sat quiet with his thoughts, and Imari waited.

"Imari," Tallyn continued at last. "There are many weeds in our good Maker's garden, and the shoots will not stop until the root dies. Ventus was only one evil shoot from a much darker and insidious root. Someone very powerful summoned the legion, and sent Azir's chakran after you. I believe that same someone called to the silent—through Astrid." He looked straight into her eyes. "All to get to you."

"But *why*?" Imari asked. It was the question that kept blaring in her mind. "Rasmin said I have power over hearts and minds, and I know Hagan intended to use that power to take back Corinth's old capital, but I've never used my power in that way. I've only used it to...block out darkness. I have no idea how to do what they're suggesting, and I can't imagine ever wanting to."

Tallyn considered her, quiet with his thoughts. And then, "What do you know about Azir's war?"

Imari's sighed and sank onto the bench beside him. "I know that he was the most powerful Guardian of that time." Guardianship was the branch of Liagé power devoted to enhancing bodily strength and manipulating the physical world, and, consequently, it made them unstoppable weapons in battle.

Tallyn nodded. "So you're also acquainted with the four Liagé talents."

"Yes, but not in any depth," Imari replied. "I was...well, I met someone in E'Centro, and she was starting to teach me, but..." Imari's voice trailed.

"Taran."

He said the name with fondness. With familiarity.

Imari looked at the alta-Liagé. *You knew her?*"

"Not technically, no," Tallyn said. "I knew Tolya. Quite well before you came along. And so, I knew *of* Taran."

Imari's gaze fixed on that little marble emissary. "Tolya never mentioned her to me."

Tolya had never mentioned a lot of things.

"I've no doubt she would have," Tallyn said quietly, watching Imari with that single pale eye. "I think she'd grown so used to having you there that she was afraid to lift all of her protective enchantments and let you go. Risk...losing you."

Imari inhaled through tight lungs and gripped the bench's edge.

"If I may, how did you end up crossing paths with Taran?" Tallyn asked.

Imari explained what had happened to Saza at the Qazzat,

and how she'd snuck out at night to find him. "I suppose it was luck," she added.

"Do not mistake luck for supernatural design." When Imari did not comment, Tallyn said, "So Taran worked with you on your power?"

Imari sat forward. "Mostly on trying to harness it. She explained about *tallas*, and tried to teach me how to channel the Shah through my flute."

"And you were successful?"

"No," Imari said tightly. "Not until it was too late."

Not until *after* Taran and Saza had died.

"Do not be so hard on yourself, child," Tallyn said quietly, sensing the direction of her thoughts. "You're a good deal older than most when they learn to channel their power—"

"Taran died." Imari looked sharply at Tallyn. "Protecting *me*, and if I hadn't been there...if I hadn't snuck out every rutting night—"

"Yes, if you hadn't snuck out every night, you still wouldn't know how to use your power, more people would have died, and you'd most likely be with the demon now," Tallyn said, looking hard at her. "You were there for a reason, Imari. Taran knew it too. The Maker's plans are too great for us to understand—"

"You're saying the death of an innocent child was the Maker's *plan*?"

"No." He gazed steadily at her. "But there is evil in this world, and so long as there is evil, there will be pain. We cannot possibly fathom the Maker's ways, but everything works together in the end—for good. You must trust in that, Imari. When the world is darkest, when you feel as though you are surrounded by enemies on all sides. Do not lose hope. Do not give in to bitterness and hate, for there is one who stands *for* you and beside you, who is greater than *everything*. Only he has the power to right these wrongs, and he will. In his perfect time. Until then, we must do our best to trust in him, to be a light in this world, and hope to be of service when he calls."

Tallyn placed his hand on the bench, between them.

That scarred and ugly hand.

"I will show you what I know," Tallyn said so quietly. "If you like."

Imari stared at that hand, remembering the last time he had shown her his memories. She reached out and let her hand hover over his only a moment, and then she rested her palm atop the back of his. Tallyn curled his thumb back over her fingers.

And the world flashed.

Wards, she'd forgotten how fast and how overwhelming the pressure, as though her body were being squeezed through a small orifice. Her lungs compressed, thrusting all the air out of her body, and then it was gone. All of it, as quickly as it had come. Thankfully, Imari remembered to step at the last second, and she caught herself before she fell.

It took her a moment to make sense of their surroundings. She and Tallyn stood within an impressive domed atrium built of smooth sandstone bricks, its walls abbreviated by archways from which corridors branched. It reminded Imari of the nave of a cathedral, but there were no windows. No natural light. Only dozens of flickering candles, staining these walls with soot, and Imari suspected they were underground.

"We are in the catacombs beneath the Mazarat," Tallyn said, confirming her suspicions.

"The Mazarat..." she repeated. "The Liagé temple in Assi Andai?"

"Yes."

Assi Andai had once been Sol Velor's capital, rumored to be the most beautiful place in all the world, with the Mazarat temple at its heart. It was where the Liagé had trained and studied their respective Shah talents. Of course, no one in Imari's limited acquaintance could confirm that beauty since the

Mazarat—and all of Sol Velor—had been destroyed during Azir's war.

But.

Tallyn had been created during that war; he would have seen it with his own eyes before its destruction. And even these catacombs were a wonder. This veritable garden of gleaming marble sarcophaguses, with rose petals sprinkled like garnish. Silence pervaded—the thick blanket of silence given only to the dead.

"I wanted to show you this first," Tallyn said, gesturing for her to follow.

She did.

She spotted two robed figures talking quietly in the shadows off to one side, though she couldn't make out their words, and they did not seem to be the reason Tallyn had brought her here.

He'd stopped before a wall. No, a *mural*—an enormous and very old mural that filled the wall's entirety, illuminated by bronze basins of burning coals and flickering sconces. More rose petals dusted the platform before it—some old, some fresh.

Imari's gaze trailed the magnificent painting, which had faded from time in some places. It wasn't just a painting, but a story. A chronological story of the histories, beginning in the upper left corner.

With light.

When the Maker had created the heavens and the earth. She followed the story with her eyes, but did not make it far before stopping at one picture in particular.

"The Five Divines," she said. "I'd always learned there were four. It wasn't until...recently that I learned there had been five."

Tallyn stood in quiet confirmation, nodding for her to continue.

So Imari moved on, watching the moment the Maker had sent his Five Divines to their world, to govern and watch over the people. But as the story progressed, one of the five grew darker and darker in shading, as if the artist had painted that particular figure with deepening shadow, until it was nothing more than a blot of ink amidst the brilliance of the mural.

"Zussa," Imari said, staring at that blot of ink.

"Ah, so you know."

"Taran told me. But we were interrupted before I could ask more."

Tallyn gazed upon the blot. "Zussa was Asorai's most trusted, and most powerful. But eventually that power was not enough for her—or perhaps it became too much for her—because she turned on Asorai."

Imari stared at that blot of ink. "Taran said the brighter the light, the greater the pull of darkness."

"Taran is not wrong," Tallyn replied. "We don't truly understand why Zussa eventually turned, but it is widely understood that she did." Tallyn gestured to the next image, which depicted battle and death. Bodies piled, cities burned, and that smudge of ink hovered over them with a band of similar smudges, victorious.

And then Imari's eyes fixed on a little aberration in that smudge, for it wasn't an aberration at all, but an intentional line. A protrusion, clutched in Zussa's inky black hands. Tiny, silvery whorls had been painted along its breadth.

A chill swept over Imari, head to toe. "Is that...a flute?"

A beat. "Yes. It was Zussa's talla."

Imari stared at Tallyn with growing fear. "Is that *my* talla?"

But Tallyn only gestured at the picture and said, "Keep reading."

Imari's thoughts spiraled in a thousand directions, but she stepped closer to the mural, following the story with hungry eyes. Watching as the other four Divines took that flute—Zussa's talla, which looked exactly like Imari's own—and used it to hold her, destroy her. It took all four of them, with Asorai's help, and they used that flute to make a tear in Asorai's pure light. Like a single black seam amidst a world of brilliance and color, and there they exiled Zussa. Using the flute again, they sewed the seam back together, weaving her out of their physical world, though a thin stitch remained. Like a scar upon the Maker's beautiful creation.

The process destroyed the other four Divines—burned them up like an overwhelmed ward—and their power rained back to the earth. The mural depicted this event as little points of light, like a localized shower of stars, and where the stars watered, a tree grew.

Not the tree from her nightmares, but the one embedded onto *Il Tonté*'s cover.

Imari stared at that mural for a very long time, and then she looked at Tallyn. "I have Zussa's flute."

He looked back at her. "It would seem so."

Imari's next inhale shuddered, and her head felt light. "How do I have it?" Ricón had always insisted he'd purchased it off of a bazaar merchant. Nothing extraordinary. And she did not think he would lie.

"I do not know," Tallyn said. "Suffice it to say that you do, and I do not believe it to be accidental."

Imari took a dizzying step away from the mural.

"You mentioned you had only ever learned about Four Divines," Tallyn continued, gazing wistfully at the mural, "and that is because Zussa is not considered a Divine to the Sol Velor. Her choice separated her from the Maker forever, and so she presides over darkness—where the Maker is not. In the verses, you will have seen her mentioned as the Great Deceiver."

So that was what Taran had meant when she'd said the verses mentioned Zussa, but not by the name Imari had expected.

Tallyn's gaze lingered on the painted tree. "Many believe it was the Deceiver's power Azir sought, during his war. He'd certainly suffered enough casualties to prompt him to construct us." Tallyn gestured at himself. "But still, he saw the futility in his endeavors. His losses were unsalvageable, and so many of our brothers and sisters had turned against his cause. Azir grew desperate and turned to other measures."

"You think he tried to open the tear."

"Yes. And that is what inevitably destroyed Sol Velor."

Imari considered this. "But his chakran was bound in Corinth. How is that possible? If he'd been in Sol Velor trying to open the tear, wouldn't he have been destroyed with it?"

"You're assuming Azir was the one trying to open the seam."

Imari frowned, but before she could ask, Tallyn said, "Ah. Here we are." He nodded toward a group of figures ahead.

Imari spotted the younger Tallyn immediately.

With Rasmin.

Rasmin was much younger. His eyes were that same fathomless black, his brows owlish, but this Rasmin wore his jet-black hair long.

Imari looked at the present, older Tallyn, and drew back, suddenly wary. "You knew him."

"Of course I knew him," Tallyn said, still walking. "He created me."

"You said *Azir* created you."

"He had me created. Rasmin knew how. And those other three figures are the enchanters who helped him."

Imari did not know how to feel about this new information as she followed the alta-Liagé through the wide and cavernous corridors beneath the Mazarat. She had known Tallyn had been created, but to see him with Rasmin—to see him walking comfortably beside him—she couldn't help thinking of the Tallyn she had seen fighting Ventus. The one wielding a power she had never guessed at.

The one who had terrified her.

The Tallyn walking beside her was undeniably different from the one ahead of them, but what had changed?

They ascended a broad stair, and Imari wondered why Tallyn had not shown her this before, or why he had not explicitly mentioned his connection to Rasmin. But the answer arrived with the question: Imari never would have given him a chance. She studied the old and present Tallyn, whose gaze lingered upon his younger self with something akin to pity.

Perhaps this was difficult for him. Imari could only imagine living through her memories where Sorai had lived, and died. Past was past for good reason. Imari had thought Tallyn's ability a wonderful gift, but she'd failed to see how torturous it could be. Reliving one's personal nightmares without any power to alter them.

The stairs ended, their corridor opened, and Imari felt her eyes open wide. They stood in an enormous round chamber crowned by a magnificent, golden dome with an open oculus at its center that allowed a shaft of warm light to pass through. Along the far side of the chamber were four broad archways, like open mouths. Gilded stones lined each archway, all of them engraved with Liagé markings—the largest symbols rested upon the cornerstones, which all shone faintly with wardlight.

Four archways, one for each Liagé talent: Restoration, Sight, Enchantment, Guardianship.

And at the center of this chamber, in the shaft of daylight, stood a tree.

The Liagé tree.

Somehow similar to and entirely different from the one in Imari's nightmare.

It rose from an elevated round stage, as if this chamber had been built to hold it. The trunk was thick and strong, and a bevy of brilliant, golden leaves cloaked its branches while its fat roots tucked deep into the soil as if to anchor this celestial plant to the human world. A breeze pushed through the chamber, and the leaves tingled like bells.

The sound struck a strange chord within Imari, reverberating through her very soul.

Tallyn stood beside her, admiring. "The tree of the Divines."

Imari stood mesmerized. Terrified. She remembered the mural. "This is where they perished?"

"Yes, or so we believe. There is no other tree like this one. The Mazarat was erected around it, though the temple has known many forms over the centuries." Then, "You've seen this tree."

Did she tell him what she'd seen? If this was truly the Divine's tree, the one in her nightmare could not be the same. This tree was beautiful and shimmering and pure, and yet...

Yet.

She could not shake the off key from her nightmare. Not entirely. Like some faint, dissonant pitch just beyond her hearing.

"I have," Imari said at last, watching those little golden leaves shimmer with a melody that thrummed through her core. "But it didn't look like this. It was diseased and leafless and...*alive*. And it wasn't inside of a temple. It was rooted in sand."

Tallyn's pale eye focused on her, but then he caught sight of the group passing through a set of engraved double doors. "We should keep going," he said quietly, walking on, though she could tell that her words had bothered him.

They hurried after the group, through the Mazarat, and finally stepped through the main doors and into light.

Imari stopped in her tracks.

It was a city made of sand. As if the desert itself had been contoured and solidified, then cast with magic to hold shape. It stood taller than it had any right to stand, and a maze of bridges connected third and fourth stories. Various pools glittered throughout, as though the city had been set with sapphires.

Oh, yes, The Crossing bridge paled in comparison to this.

"Wards, this place..." Imari gasped in wonder. "How is this even possible?"

"This city was built by the Guardians and Enchanters of their age, sustained by Shah. Not all Guardian power is...destructive. I believe the Maker's intended design was very *con*structive."

No wonder the Sol Velorians had grown inflated with superiority. Wards, look what they had built! What they had achieved! Nothing in all the world compared, and, as she'd suspected, the verses could not possibly do it justice. Words and drawings could never quite capture the scale of a place.

The scene was dappled with color throughout, from banners and garlands, and enormous pots glazed the color of the sea. Palms reached for the heavens, their fronds waving in a breeze Imari could not feel.

No...

She *could* feel it, whispering across her nose, though it did not ruffle her hair. She realized it was Tallyn's memory of that breeze, the sensation of wind that she was experiencing. Not the wind itself.

That was new.

"You're more open to the Shah now," Tallyn said. "So my memories are clearer to you. Fuller. And you will continue to grow more open to it, as you use your power."

Wards, she could smell—yes, she could *smell* the spice and heat and...energy. She didn't know how else to describe it, but there was an *energy* to the air. Like some tingling perfume as constant as the blazing sun above. And people were everywhere.

Sol Velorians.

All Imari's life, all she'd known of Sol Velorians was their oppression. How they walked with heads bowed and shoulders bent to appear less. To *be* less, so that their superiors would not beat them.

But here, in this place, they were resplendent.

They walked tall, faces turned toward the sun. They wore luxurious wraps and robes, and some wore nothing at all, though their bodies were so covered in inked glyphs, Imari could hardly see their bare skin. Everyone bore glyphs in some fashion, Imari noticed as she looked closer. Upon hands or foreheads or necks. But the one thing they did *not* wear was shame.

"I wanted you to see what it was like," Tallyn said quietly. "I wanted you to know what we lost." And Tallyn extended a hand.

Imari hated to leave this place, but she extended her hand.

Another flash. Pressure, and then...

She and Tallyn stood at the edge of a plateau. Portentous clouds brooded and churned above, and Imari realized she knew where they were.

Just over the distant ridge lay Trier, but she was not looking at the ridge. She was looking at the valley below, where two massive forces collided.

Istraan and Sol Velorian.

Imari had seen death and fighting, but she had never seen war. She had never seen two nations stand against each other with ultimatum between them.

She had never seen disunity collide.

And she stood there, watching in horror, as men turned animal and ripped each other apart.

Body after body fell with chaos and nonsense—so much life wasted, discarded like chaff. Blood painted the ground, and the ground drank its fill, while vultures and crows circled above. Arrows flew as shields clashed and swords pierced, and men screamed. It was a maelstrom of death, a symphony of horror and blood, accented by the screams of the dying.

Tallyn stood quiet beside her.

Imari could not find words to ask him why he had brought her here.

She saw the Liagé. They were easy to find, with their crimson robes and inked skin, using Shah power to set fire, to destroy. To tear men apart. Guardians, she guessed. Liagé who had the ability to manipulate Shah energy within a physical object. In Assi Andai, they had used that energy to build and construct.

Here, they used it to destroy. Only to destroy.

Covered in inked glyphs and wielding enchanted scims, they laid waste to those around them. On both sides. Imari watched two guardians—one fighting for Istraa, the other against—collide in a burst of air and blue light, both thrown back a dozen paces from the force of it.

Drawing Imari's attention to a group of Liagé wearing midnight black robes, seated upon horses at the edge of Sol Velorian ranks.

There were four.

"Are those the Mo'Ruk?" Imari whispered.

Tallyn's eye narrowed on them. "Yes."

Imari's inside turned cold. She watched as one of the Mo'Ruk moved apart from the others. She could not see his face from their vantage, but there was something...particularly dark about him. A shadow that clung to him like a second skin.

The figure crouched and dug fingers into the soil. Inky darkness seeped from the earth like snakes, and slithered down into the battlefield. Imari watched in horror as it latched onto the dead, filled their still bodies with corruption, and pulled them back to their feet.

"That is Bahdra," Tallyn said quietly. "Azir's *shiva*."

Shiva, the Liagé term for Restorer—someone with healing magic. But Imari remembered one specific subset of Restoration.

"He's a necromancer," Imari said, staring at this Bahdra as his long fingers curled and twisted, this master of puppets. She looked sharply at Tallyn with growing trepidation. "What happened to Bahdra?"

Tallyn looked at her. "We don't know. All of Azir's Mo'Ruk were accounted for when he fell—all except for Bahdra."

And Bahdra would have been a master at evading death.

"There is speculation that he helped Saád Mubarék during the second rising, around the time you were born, but that revolution ended before anyone could be certain."

That sense of trepidation grew stronger. "Is Bahdra responsible for Astrid?"

Tallyn did not answer her immediately. "I believe so."

Imari watched Bahdra wield his puppets through the chaos—
Istraan and Sol Velorian alike. They were all his for the taking,
for manipulation.

"This is...your memory," Imari whispered, looking sideways
at Tallyn. "You were here."

His eye looked glassy and she followed his gaze into battle,
where a young Tallyn grabbed an Istraan head between his
hands and twisted hard, breaking the Istraan's neck.

Imari's chest squeezed as she watched the Istraan fall.

"If you no longer trust me after this, I will understand," Tallyn
spoke quietly. "But you needed to see. To understand. Even if it
compromises your opinion of me. Because what is happening
now is so much bigger than I am." And then, "There—" Tallyn
pointed. "This is why I brought you here."

Imari peeled her gaze from the frightening younger Tallyn, to
where a man stood at the edge of the battlefield. Tall and broad
shouldered, his expression severe, his long black hair pulled to
one side and shaved on the other like some god of war.

"That is Azir Mubarék," Tallyn said.

Azir Mubarék.

The start of it all, the bitter seed of hatred and fear that had
buried deep into Provincial soil and caused so much suffering for
generations to come. All because—like Zussa—he had wanted
more. He had wanted *everything*, and so he had taken everything.

And then Imari noticed the woman beside him.

Unlike Azir, she wore all black and no weaponry, her long
black hair plaited down her back, her expression beautifully
austere. "Who is that?"

"That is Fyri. The sulaziér of Azir's time. And his lover."

Azir's...lover?

Imari's gaze fixed on that woman, this sulaziér, and a string
anchored to the very depths of her soul pulled tight.

"*Watch*," Tallyn said.

The woman—Fyri—dismounted and stalked toward the

battlefront. The mere sight of her impressed Imari, this unarmed woman striding fearlessly into battle. She passed through the fringes, stepping over dead bodies, her purpose unwavering. A few Istraans noticed her, and changed course *for* her, but she did not spare them a glance. She raised a banded wrist instead.

Imari heard sound. A single, ringing tone that she should not have been able to hear from where she stood, through the din of battle. No, she didn't hear it with her ears; she felt it in her heart as it reverberated across that battlefield.

And the man closest to Fyri slit his own throat.

Imari froze, eyes wide with shock and horror as she watched every Istraan man within a dozen paces of Fyri kill himself.

"That is the power you hold within your being, Imari," Tallyn said. "Just as Guardians can use what the Maker intended for good, so can you wield your light for dark."

Fyri stopped and crouched, head bowed and eyes closed. She was a single, solitary point of calm at the eye of a storm. And then there was silence. A complete and unnatural kind of silence, as if all sound in the battlefield had suddenly been drawn into the figure at its center, leaving a total absence of sound.

And then Fyri threw back her head, arms out and palms wide.

All the sound she had drawn into herself was suddenly thrown back at the field in one concussive burst. So powerful, the ground shook with it, fissures cracked, the birds scattered—gone. Feathers rained. The bodies nearest Fyri soared through the air, landing in broken piles nearly fifty feet away, while others scrambled beneath them, unsteady upon the rolling earth.

"She is the one who tried to open the tear," Tallyn whispered.

Imari had always wondered what kind of force could have destroyed a nation, and the answer crouched in beautiful severity upon that field.

A flash.

Imari hardly felt the pressure as Tallyn's power released her back to the prayer chamber, and she staggered back to the bench and sat, bewildered.

"I'm to be a weapon," Imari whispered.

Tallyn crouched before her so that they were eye level. "Only if you allow it, Imari. No one else gets to decide who you are unless you let them." He paused, searched her face. "Your gift is a strength. But our greatest strength can also be our greatest weakness. I showed you this so that you would see the extreme. So that you might...better understand the line you walk, so that no matter who pulls on you, you keep your gaze fixed above. On the Maker's goodness and light. Focus there, and you will not fall."

"Though the binding of the Great Deceiver overwhelmed the Four Divines, their power rained back to our soil—untouched. From this, we received the tree of wisdom, the tree of life. A gift from Asorai himself, so that we would still know the perfect way he intended, and find comfort in his promise to deliver us from the evil one."

~ Excerpt from the teachings
according to Moltoné,
Liagé Second High Sceptor.

26

Rasmin perched atop the guardwall, gazing upon this sleeping city, and unease nagged at him. It was a still moment before a storm, before the clouds released their fury, when the air charged with kinetic power, waiting to strike. But he could not See in this form, and he dared not Change. Not here, atop this post where saredd stood watch. And owl eyes were better suited for night, besides.

Rasmin pushed off the wall, wings spread wide, and Vondar fell away beneath him as he soared over the city. The hour was late, the night dark, and rain had urged Trier's midnight wanderers to shelter. Everything was quiet—peaceful, almost, as rain whispered.

And yet.

Rasmin could not shake this foreboding.

He scanned the empty streets with his owl eyes, searching for one.

Bahdra, you old fiend, where are you?

Rasmin had sensed Bahdra's presence the moment he'd landed in Trier, that fetid aura lingering at the edge of his awareness. It was a presence he had not felt since Azir's war, like a warped and corrupted signal distorting the Shah's pure energy. Rasmin had searched each night, though he found nothing that pointed him to where Bahdra could be hiding. He'd flown deep into the Baragas, fought their tumultuous currents until his wings could not hold him aloft any longer. Still, he'd found nothing, but that did not mean Bahdra wasn't there. Bahdra had always been like an infection, creeping and insidious, showing no superficial signs until the host was sufficiently compromised.

It was how he'd earned his rank as a Mo'Ruk.

Oh, how Azir had prized his necromancer, and for good reason, Rasmin reflected. Bahdra believed in the Maker's power more than he believed in the Maker himself, and there was nothing Bahdra wouldn't do to see Azir's world come to pass.

Even now, over one hundred years later, Bahdra was still trying. But something felt different this time.

Rasmin drifted higher, letting the air currents carry him, while memories of the past chased him like a ravenous beast. It had all been so long ago, and yet it was always there, haunting him in the quiet.

Rasmin soared over Trier's outer farms, and the tall grasses swayed beneath him, the little homes and stables like islands amidst a dark and rippling pool. Even the livestock had tucked away for the night. He exited the outskirts and glided over the open sands, his owl eyes fixed ahead, in the direction of the Baragas, though he could see nothing.

His owl eyes locked, focused.

Wait...

Suddenly, a surge of Shah power jolted through him like an electric current. His body shuddered with it, his wings jerked—erratic—thrown off course. He flapped desperately to right himself, straining to stay airborne, but it was like flying through sludge. The air was thick as mud and smelled of burning.

He'd struck a Sight veil. A kind of visual blockade, woven of Shah power—a talent known only to Seers. This was one of the strongest charges he had ever felt and it carried a vividly familiar watermark.

Lestra.

Rasmin would have cursed, if he'd had lips. Instead, he tried to push deeper into the veil, to see through the Shah forces holding it together, but Lestra's power was too strong. Too everywhere. And it tangled him up like a fish in a net.

Rasmin squawked and twisted, giving his wings a solid flap. Finally—*finally*—he broke free, turned back and raced for Trier upon frantically beating wings.

RASMING COULD NOT SEE Lestra standing behind the veil she had woven, watching the owl retreat with bemused interest. "We have been spotted," she said.

"What is your command, my lord?" asked Kazak—the second-greatest Guardian this world had ever known.

But Bahdra did not answer. Though he had dragged them out of the darkness from which they had been bound these hundred years, he was not their lord. That title belonged to the man standing beside him.

Azir Mubarék.

Azir gazed at the city he had tried—and failed—to take over one hundred years ago. He would not fail this time.

"It is time," Azir looked to Bahdra.

Bahdra stepped forward. He crouched low, his black robe pooling at his feet as he dug long, inked fingers into the sand. Bahdra closed his eyes, breathed in deep. Beetles and centipedes wormed from the ground, scuttling around him as he spoke the incantation. Air pulsed from his hands, sending a shockwave of sound rippling across the sand.

Heading straight for the city.

It struck the fields first, pushing through the tall grasses like a gust of wind. Goats bleated, and birds scattered in a screech of fright. Lanterns bobbed in the streets, palms swayed, but no one would know it for what it was. For Shah power worked in a different plane, and only those tied to that plane could sense it.

Like the few in E'Centro, who had been watching for this sign.

But Vondar's guards did not know what it was, and did not think anything amiss when that wind slipped down their dark tunnels.

To where Bahdra's most faithful servant awaited command.

The spell rippled through the warded skal door. The etchings flared bright and died with a hiss—overwhelmed. Like water thrown over embers. The spell slipped through the hairline cracks around the door, leaking like smoke to the other side, as it reached for the figure hunched at the center. The warded circle flared then died, and Astrid's matted hair stirred.

A beat.

The liagé binds holding the leje flared bright, and brighter —blinding.

The air stunk of burnt flesh and hot metal, and with one final and desperate flash of wardlight, the chains disintegrated. Flecks of skal ash rained down all around, settling to the dungeon floor.

Astrid's eyes snapped open, and she smiled.

27

"I think that is enough for one evening," Tallyn said, standing. He looked weary, and Imari wondered if reliving those memories had exhausted him more than the power required to experience them.

"Thank you," she whispered. "For sharing your memories."

"You are welcome, surina." He paused, and looked at her. "I would...understand if you did not trust me after this."

Imari took a deep breath and stood. "Tallyn. I take people as they are. Not who they've been, or who they want to be. That is for the Maker to decide. The present is for us." They were Tolya's words, spoken to Imari ages ago.

Tallyn seemed to recognize them at once, marked by the small, sad smile now touching his lips.

"I don't know the man in those memories, but I do know *this* one." Imari pointed at him. "I believe who people *show* me they are, and you have shown nothing but a devotion to what is right and good. I trust you. And I am grateful you are helping me make sense of all this."

Tallyn's expression faltered beneath her words. As if the weight of them was too much to bear. "And I will do my very best to help prepare you for whatever lies ahead. My knowledge and power are at your disposal."

"I appreciate that, Tallyn. Thank you." Imari walked to the door and cracked it open to a quiet and mostly empty hall. Jenya stood watch outside her door, and she spotted two more guards on patrol, farther down.

Imari glanced back at Tallyn. "Have you told my papa about Bahdra?"

"Not of my suspicions, no," Tallyn replied. "But he would remember the name from Saád's attempted war."

"May I tell him?"

"You may relay *all* of it, if you wish."

Meaning, she had his blessing to disclose the parts that incriminated him as well.

Imari considered Tallyn. This grossly scarred man who wore beauty on the inside, where it mattered most. "You are not our enemy, and I'll not divide his attentions when concern is unwarranted. I will leave you out where I can."

Tallyn gazed long at her, and Imari stepped into the hall.

"Surina."

She glanced back.

"If she'd had your constitution, Sol Velor would not have fallen," Tallyn said, standing in the doorway of the prayer room. "Perhaps you might save them still."

Tallyn bowed his head respectfully and strode on, and Imari stood there looking after him, wondering at his words. Which was how Dasi found her.

Dasi was flanked by two guards—one of which was Avék—and Imari's senses immediately went on alert.

"There you are, mi a'surina," Dasi said, breathless.

Imari looked from Dasi to Jenya and to Avék, where her gaze settled. "Where's Stanis?" Because Avék was supposed to be standing guard outside of Gamla's chambers.

"With the Wolf and his pack in their bedchambers," Avék

replied, and noting Imari's confusion, he added, "Stanis is awake."

"Oh."

Imari had not expected that, and to her surprise, she felt a stab of disappointment where she should have felt relief that Jeric's man was healed. Because her papa had made it very clear that Jeric and his men would be leaving Trier once Stanis was well enough to travel, and Imari couldn't bear to think about Jeric leaving just yet.

Dasi continued, "Sar Branón asked that you retire to your chambers for the evening, as it's late."

Imari briefly met Jenya's apologetic gaze.

"I left dinner in your chambers," Dasi continued. "If you'll follow me..." She started down the hallway.

Left with no other alternative, Imari followed Dasi back to her chambers, with Jenya and Avék and the other guard following close behind. All lanterns and braziers had been lit, though a damp chill slipped through the open halls, promising rain. Imari crossed her arms over her bare waist, trying to keep her body heat close until they finally reached her door.

Avék and Jenya took position on either side, while the third guard moved to stand across the hall, and Imari followed Dasi through the antechamber and into her bedchamber. As promised, a tagine of spiced vegetables and flatbread waited on a table, alongside a small carafe of water, and a fire burned in the wood stove. The draperies had been drawn over the rear screen wall, trapping the stove's heat inside, and the air felt pleasantly warm. Dasi crossed to the wardrobe, pulled out a nightdress, and draped it on the end of Imari's bed.

"May I get you anything else, surina?" Dasi asked, approaching the washroom. "A hot bath, perhaps?"

"No, thank you," Imari sat upon the divan. "I want to be alone tonight, so you may go." She lifted the tagine's lid, and hot, spiced steam touched her nose. She should be hungry, but she felt strangely numb, and the aroma did nothing to awaken her appetite.

And Dasi was still standing beside the washroom door.

Imari was not in the mood for this—for *her*. Especially tonight. Her papa could station all the saredd he wanted outside her door, but *dashá* she would sleep alone tonight.

"Dasi, there are three saredd outside my door," Imari said sharply, setting the lid down. "I'll be fine."

Dasi clearly did not agree.

"And I'm not going anywhere, if that's what you're all concerned about." Imari's words came out with more bite than she'd intended. "It's nearly impossible to climb these rooftops when it rains."

Dasi's lips parted with scandal.

"It was a joke," Imari said flatly, and picked up the carafe and poured water into a chalice. "I won't be sneaking out anymore. You may go."

Dasi gazed at Imari, at the closed draperies. Trusting neither of them.

"That is an order, Dasi." Imari set the carafe down with an emphatic clank. "And I take full responsibility for that order. *Goodnight*, Dasi."

Imari glared her into acquiescence, until Dasi finally—reluctantly—bowed her head. "Goodnight, mi a'surina."

Dasi crossed the room and left through the antechamber, then closed the outer door with a click. Imari stared at that door a long moment, and then she sank back upon the divan and closed her eyes with a sigh, chalice in hand.

"Honestly, I'm disappointed you didn't take her up on that bath."

Imari nearly dropped her chalice. Her eyes snapped open and she whipped around to see Jeric slipping out from behind her draperies. He wore a heavy cloak, and his hair was damp with rain.

"Wards, Jeric!" Imari hissed. A little thrill went through her at the sight of him, and all of her anger from earlier suddenly diffused. "You nearly gave me a heart attack!"

"I do seem to have that effect on women."

Imari snorted. "Well, I did see you flirting with your little troupe of admirers this morning..."

His blue eyes pierced. "Jealous?"

Imari glared at him, to which he smiled wolfishly, and then she plucked the round pillow off the divan and chucked it at his head.

He ducked, and the pillow sailed right past and hit the draperies instead. "See? So violent for a healer."

"You have no idea."

"Oh, I do. I was expecting the chalice."

"I'm still considering it."

Amusement curled his lips. "So much fire for such a little person. Maybe I should go ahead and start that bath for you. Help you put it out."

Imari's lips parted, hardly believing what he had just said.

But before she could respond, Jeric took a small step and asked, with complete seriousness, "Is it all right that I'm here?"

Was it all right.

She was afraid to tell him just how *all right* it was. How...he had become this anchor of stability and calm when the rest of her world seemed to be spinning out of control.

How her heart ached at the sight of him.

"How did you get in?" she asked instead.

Jeric flashed his canines. "You're not the only climber around here, little thief."

She felt her brows rise. "You climbed the rooftops...*in the rain*?"

He looked at her, his hair curling with effortless beauty in contrast to the hard lines of his face. "Well, obviously the conditions aren't optimal, and while I do have the uncanny ability to get what I want, I haven't figured out how to control the weather yet. It'll come, I'm sure."

Imari laughed.

Jeric eyed her, a smile in his eyes. "You still haven't answered my question." He took another small step forward, though he might have touched her by the way her body responded. "I heard you say you wanted to be alone, so I'll leave if you—"

"No, *stay.*" She cut him off—strongly. So strongly, in fact, that his lips curled like his hair. "But I should probably close that." She gestured at the door to her antechamber, then looked sideways at Jeric. "Though you did kiss my cheek quite scandalously in front of my brother. Maybe you *want* to get caught in my bedchamber."

Jeric's eyes lit with something Imari couldn't pinpoint. "Sadly, I'm not looking for scandal this evening."

Imari felt an unexpected stab of disappointment, but she grinned anyway and started for the antechamber door. "Good, because I'm betrothed, you know."

"So I've heard," Jeric said behind her, as she closed the antechamber door. "And here you are letting strange men into your chambers in the middle of the night." He made a tsk-tsk-tsk sound. "I'm no expert in marriage, but this doesn't sound like the best start to yours."

Imari grinned over her shoulder at him. "Thank you for that non-expert opinion."

Jeric smirked as he unclasped his cloak and tossed it over a chair. He was still wearing the attire he'd had on this morning: the cream tunic and fitted breeches. More Istraan than Corinthian in style. The sleeves hugged his broad shoulders, and Imari couldn't help but admire his backside as he turned to take inventory of her walls and shelves.

Wards, he was beautiful.

"Have you actually met Fez?" Jeric asked, picking up the small statue of Beléna.

Imari blinked and slid her gaze from his backside to his face. "Who?"

Jeric looked at her and set the statue down. "Your betrothed. That *is* his name, isn't it?"

Imari felt her cheeks warm.

"Fez." Jeric said the name as if it were a piece of food he was trying to fling out of his teeth. He was still looking at her too, and there was something teasing and deeply arrogant in his gaze that she decided she didn't like very much.

"I have met him once," she said, feeling a sudden defensiveness as she took a step forward.

"How old were you?" His amusement was thick, as if he already suspected the answer and that answer was far from adequate.

"Seven. No..." Imari looked to the ceiling as if her answer were somewhere in the rafters. "No, I *was* seven. It was just before my eighth birthday."

"Fez must've left quite an impression." He flung that name again.

"Would you stop it?"

"Why? It's his name."

Imari looked at him.

Jeric smiled wide and brilliantly, and Imari rolled her eyes.

"All right, all right..." Jeric raised his palms. "I'll stop."

When he raised his palms, his tunic pulled on the bandage beneath—a bandage she'd *intended* to replace this morning with fresh gurga paste.

"Stars, I was supposed to change that," Imari said, her healer feet already moving toward Jeric.

He glanced down at himself and lowered his palms. "I think I'm going to live, Imari."

"Let me see it." She reached for him.

"Always trying to take my clothes off..."

She eyed him.

He chuckled deeply, and then seeing that she wasn't budging on the matter, he sighed and lifted his tunic up and over his head, then tossed it atop the cloak. He stood tall and faced her fully.

Maker.

Have.

Mercy.

For a second, Imari completely forgot what she'd asked him to do because the only thing she wanted to do was run her hands all over him.

Her breath suddenly seemed very loud, and she was aware of his breathing too, as his chest expanded with a slow inhale, but neither of them moved.

"What should I do now, healer?" Jeric asked in that deep cello.

Imari didn't know what Jeric was talking about anymore, but she didn't meet his gaze just then.

"Lift your arms," she said quietly.

Jeric lifted his arms just a little, and Imari began to unwind the bandage.

"Nothing happened with any woman this morning, by the way," Jeric said, his voice resonating in the slip of space between them. "One followed me out, but she learned very quickly that I was not interested."

Imari didn't look up at him. "Why are you telling me this?"

"You looked upset."

"You're imagining things."

"Am I? I thought I lacked imagination."

Imari still didn't look up at him, not even as she tossed the bandage atop his shirt.

"*Fez*," Jeric whispered.

Imari glared up at him then.

His eyes glittered.

"I'm regretting the chalice," Imari said.

"I bet you are."

Not knowing what else to do with him, she turned her attention to the burn. It looked much better this evening. The skin wasn't angry anymore, and the oozing had stopped, though she would have liked to rub one more dose of gurga paste into it.

"So...? Am I going to die?" Jeric's voice was low and teasing.

"Not by your burns, but I might kill you."

Jeric chuckled lowly. They stood so close, the sound rumbled through her body, strumming every string inside of her.

"It does look better though." Her eyes moved over his body again. She couldn't seem to help herself. "You'll have a scar, but I suppose it's just one more to add to your impressive collection."

"I *did* say I was impressive."

Imari grunted.

"Should I get dressed?" Jeric asked. "Or did you prefer me half-naked? Though I'm not sure Fez would approve..."

Imari looked up at him, and he gave her a wicked grin. She had the sudden, inexplicable urge to kiss that grin off of his handsome face.

Instead, she smiled. "Honestly, I prefer you like this," she said, and his eyes widened. He hadn't expected that response.

"But you're right," she continued, all innocence. "Fez would not approve, and I can't afford the scandal. Best put your shirt back on."

She gently patted his bare chest, turned, and walked away.

Quiet.

"How'd it go with my papa and Sebharan?" she asked over her shoulder.

Jeric didn't answer immediately. "Good." He cleared his throat. "Fine. I got a tour of your city, and Sebharan took me to see the Qazzat. I'm going to write Hersir again tomorrow to see what arms Corinth can spare."

Imari sat on the divan at an angle and glanced over at him as he—regrettably—pulled his tunic back over his head.

"So you're going to help him hunt," she said.

He adjusted his tunic. "As best I can."

Imari folded her arms along the divan's back and leaned forward. "Corinth hasn't helped Istraa in over a hundred years."

Jeric's blue eyes found hers. "I know. That's part of the problem, and the core of our discussion." He crossed the room, and Imari's gaze trailed him as he rounded the divan and sat beside her. He sat at an angle so that they were mostly facing each other, but he draped one arm along the divan's back so that his hand rested just behind her shoulders. "The Provinces have sustained walls for too long." A pause. "And I've helped sustain them."

Imari tucked her feet beneath her, so that her knees rest near Jeric's leg, but not touching. Almost, though. "I *think* Istraa is going to need more than steel," she said carefully.

Jeric looked at her. "Explain what you mean."

Imari chewed her bottom lip. "Have you heard of Bahdra?"

Jeric's gaze sharpened on her. "*The* Bahdra? Azir's Mo'Ruk necromancer?"

Imari nodded. "Tallyn believes Bahdra is the one behind this."

"That he's the Liagé leader?"

Imari inclined her head.

Jeric frowned. His fingers tapped right behind her. "He told you this specifically?"

"I was with him just before I came here."

Jeric considered this, his gaze sharp as his mind worked. "I remember rumors of Bahdra's involvement during Saád's time, but nothing was proven, and it's also very hard to believe."

"Why?"

He looked at her. "It's been over a hundred years."

"And? Someone pulled Azir's spirit back to this world after it had been bound for over a hundred years," she reminded him.

Jeric's lips pressed into a line.

"Bahdra's the only Mo'Ruk they never found," Imari said.

"Imari." He sighed, and looked at her. "I have spent my entire life hunting Liagé. If it were Bahdra, I would have discovered *something*."

"I don't mean to be rude—" she started, and Jeric gave her a skeptical look. "But you didn't know about *me*, and you spent two full weeks in my presence."

He waved a hand. "That's different."

"How is that different?"

"You...weren't using your power."

That wasn't his first answer.

"All I'm saying is that if you didn't detect anything about *me*, it's entirely possible that someone as gifted as a Mo'Ruk could have hidden their power all this time."

Jeric thought this over while those long fingers tapped. "Then why now?"

Imari shrugged. "No idea, but *someone* is behind the legion and the chakran that *you* actually had in your body—"

"I remember." Jeric turned his face away and dragged his teeth over his bottom lip. "So Tallyn believes Bahdra is to blame."

Jeric still had doubts. Imari could see them all over his face.

She sat forward just a little, and her knees edged closer to his leg. "Do you remember how I told you Tallyn showed me his memories before?"

His piercing gaze shot back to hers. "Yes...?"

"Well, he showed me more," she continued, and Imari proceeded to explain everything Tallyn had shown her.

As she spoke, Jeric watched her intently, tracking every word with a predator's acuity. At some point, her knees came to rest against his thigh. Imari didn't know how that had happened but neither of them pulled away.

She didn't want to, either.

When she reached the part about Fyri drawing sound into herself and throwing it back in an explosive wave, Jeric inhaled deeply and his brow furrowed.

"I've always wondered what sort of power could have physically ripped a nation apart," he said. His lips parted then closed, and his fingers stopped tapping behind her.

She sensed a question on his lips, but he had stopped himself.

"You want to know if I can do that," Imari said.

He looked straight into her eyes. Sometimes that gaze was so penetrating, the force of it startled her, like now. "I am not afraid of you. I hope you know that."

"Maybe you should be."

His gaze slid over her face and then his fingertips absently moved to her bare shoulder and lingered there, sending a shiver through her body.

"We don't inherit the sins of our ancestors, Imari," Jeric said. "Those sins might influence our circumstances, but the future is *our* responsibility. *Our* choice. You have shown nothing but self-lessness, so no. I am not afraid of you. In fact, we should all hope to be more like you."

The words were genuine and unexpected, and they made Imari's chest swell. She wondered if he really understood how much his faith in her meant, how she cherished it.

He pulled his fingertips away, reached behind him, and withdrew her flute.

Imari gasped. "How...?" Her eyes narrowed as she recalled that he had already been in her chambers when she'd arrived. "Who's the thief now?"

He chuckled, but his attention shifted back to the flute as he held it, studied it. It looked so tiny in his large hand.

"This is a fascinating object," he said, trailing his fingertips over the holes hers had hammered upon earlier.

And as he held that little flute, it was as though he were touching *her*. As if his fingertips were sliding over her skin rather than her flute, and her body started humming—pulling inexplicably toward him.

Imari swallowed hard, feeling herself flush, wondering at this new sensation and the surprising intimacy of this moment.

"Ricón never found the merchant?" Jeric asked.

She could have sworn she felt his breath over *her* skin as it brushed the flute.

"No." The word came out at a whisper.

"If it did belong to Zussa, I'm glad it made its way to you. Perhaps it can have a second chance at life." He looked at her.

Imari gazed back at him, and she didn't think he was talking just about her flute anymore.

And then he held the flute to her.

Imari reached out to take it from him, and the moment her fingertips touched the little instrument, the symbols flared, bathing them both in moonlight.

But Jeric hadn't let go.

Imari tensed. It was an innate response because of the reactions she'd received from everyone else who witnessed those little glyphs burning with ward light. A swift reminder of what she was, of the Shah power that flowed in her veins—that she was different. Even Ricón, who had tried so hard to hide his unease, could never hide it completely, and so she had kept her flute hidden where it wouldn't make others uncomfortable.

None of this was evident in Jeric's expression as he looked in wonder at her flute, with the moonlight reflecting in his eyes. He simply looked over it, his hand touching hers as they held her flute together.

"Does it feel warm for you?" he whispered, awed.

"Yes." She could hardly find her voice.

"I feel..." Jeric tilted his head, studying it. "It's almost like pulses of energy."

Imari swallowed, not trusting herself to speak further as she stared at him. Waiting for the rejection that had become an unfortunate habit, and fearing it would devastate her when it came.

It didn't.

He looked at her—right into her soul. "Play for me."

Imari's heart pounded, her breath stuck somewhere in her chest.

He didn't let go of her gaze, or her flute. "I want to hear you play, Imari."

Did he know what this was doing to her? What his words meant? How his belief in her was simultaneously putting her together and tearing her apart?

Because he was the only thing she wanted, and the only thing she couldn't have.

"The guards..." she managed.

"I think they'd be far more concerned about my voice than your playing."

True. In fact, the playing would probably keep them away.

Jeric pushed her flute gently but firmly toward her, and let go. Imari couldn't be certain, but it almost seemed as though the light dimmed the moment he'd pulled his hand away.

Jeric watched her intently, the moonlight glow still reflecting in his eyes. Like lightning within monsoon clouds.

"Play," he whispered, but the word brushed all over her skin.

And Imari relented.

She closed her eyes and raised the flute to her lips, feeling his attention burning through her.

"I trust you," he said quietly.

Those three little words meant more to her than he could ever know.

So she inhaled deep, and played.

She didn't choose the notes consciously, but let her heart guide her fingers. She felt awkward at first, knowing Jeric sat right beside her, watching, but the notes soon swept her tangled thoughts up and into the rafters, soaring through the heights of her tall ceiling. Power stirred in her belly, but it lay contained and content. Reminding her it was there, should she want it, but satisfied in slumber.

Distantly, she felt the cushion shift. It was a subtle shift, and

Jeric had probably moved, though she knew he was still there beside her. That steady calm within her storm.

She suddenly wondered if her betrothal would have bothered her as much had she not known Jeric. If she hadn't known the ache in her heart when he looked at her, or the fire when his skin brushed hers.

When he'd kissed her.

She remembered that kiss now, when she had been Sable and he had been Jos. When she hadn't known the truth, and felt the draw to him all the same. A draw that had only grown stronger with time, and now she couldn't bear the thought of him leaving. Of spending the rest of her life without him, because...

Because she loved him.

Completely and irrevocably.

Warm and solid hands wrapped around hers, cutting Imari's melody short, and her eyes snapped open.

Jeric was right in front of her, with only the flute's length between them, and he gazed at her with an intensity that made her heart pound hard and fast. Slowly, deliberately, he peeled the flute from her hands, and, without turning his gaze from hers, he set the little instrument on the table beside them.

Imari's heart drummed louder, her breath stuck.

What was happening?

Was this...had *she* done this, with her power?

Jeric's gaze moved over her face, as if memorizing each and every turn, while Imari's pulse drummed faster and faster.

"Gods, you are so beautiful," he said, more breath than sound. He reached up and slid his hand into her hair, cradled the back of her head. "I don't think I've told you that."

He hadn't, and Imari's chest squeezed hearing those precious words, but they weren't *his* words. *She* had forced this, without realizing. Somehow those longings of her heart had poured into her notes, making him...

Jeric tipped his head closer; his lashes slid low.

Imari squeezed her eyes tight, feeling acute physical pain at what she was about to say—what she *needed* to say. "Jeric, *stop*."

And he did.

Immediately.

Jeric went perfectly, impossibly still. Even his breath seemed to freeze on her lips.

"Don't do this," she whispered.

The quiet stretched, tense and charged, and Imari felt that tension strain the hand he still had wrapped in her hair.

She felt him pull back, though he kept his hand in her hair, and when she opened her eyes, his face hovered one foot from hers, those blue eyes storming. She watched as his features slowly hardened, severing any vulnerabilities he had just let slip through.

Imari couldn't stand the way he was looking at her then. How he'd walled himself off before her eyes.

"I'm sorry..." she whispered. His hand began to slide out of her hair. "I don't *want* to stop you, Jeric, but you're not yourself."

His eyes narrowed, cutting through her completely.

"It's my music," she continued, trying to explain and also horrified by what she'd accidentally done to the one real friend she had in this world. "I didn't think... I didn't know that it would..."

Slowly, his expression relaxed, brick by brick, and something else began to light his eyes. "Ah."

"I know," she said. "And I'm so sorry. I swear I didn't mean to do it...not to you. Never to you."

Jeric tilted his head so that he was gazing up at her from beneath his firm brow. "You think your music compelled me to want to kiss you."

Imari bit her bottom lip, and Jeric's gaze dropped to that lip before lifting back to her eyes.

"It did, and I'm so sorry," she said.

One edge of his lips curled up. "You're not making me do this."

"You can't know that."

He leaned closer and slid his hand into her hair again, gripped it more firmly this time. "I do."

"But what if that's just my music—"

"Fez."

Imari blinked.

He grinned, but this time, there was something predatory to it. "See? I'm completely myself." He leaned closer still—so close his lips just brushed hers. "Imari, I've been wanting to kiss you from the moment I stepped through Gamla's door."

Imari could hardly think, hardly breathe. "So why haven't you?"

His mouth moved to her jaw. Not kissing her, but just trailing his lips upon her skin. "Because I needed to make sure you wanted me to."

Imari's heart pounded so loudly, she was certain he could hear it. "I do," she breathed.

His mouth moved to her ear, and a shiver moved over her, head to toe. "You do...what?"

Imari felt another sort of tingling in her belly, and it had nothing to do with her power.

"I need to hear you say it, Imari," he whispered, his breath hot against her ear. "I need to know what you want from me."

Because there would be no coming back from this. Imari knew that deep in her bones. They were both standing at the edge of a cliff, ready to jump. Not knowing if the other person would follow, or if the fall might kill them.

She suddenly didn't care if it did.

"I want you to kiss me—"

Jeric crushed his lips to hers, stealing her words, her breath.

And Imari let herself fall.

And fall.

His lips were both firm and velvety soft, and Imari sank into him, every other thought obliterated as she breathed him in deep. The rain on his clothes and the heat of his skin, the sweet taste of nazzat on his tongue as it pushed greedily into her mouth. Claiming her.

By the wards.

This was so much different than when they'd kissed in Gavet's cellar. That had been unexpected and confusing, the both of them accidentally tumbling over a line neither of them had intended to cross. But this...this time they were not kissing despite, but *because*, and it felt like the start of something rare and beautiful.

His hand slid from her hair and down her back to her bare waist, holding her tight. Those hard-earned callouses scraped over her skin, but Imari liked the feel of them. So raw and real and sharp, and so perfectly Jeric.

Imari moved her hands into his hair—that beautiful, thick hair she'd cut months ago. It had grown long enough for her to grip between her fingers, and so she did, holding his mouth firmly against hers. As if she could freeze this moment, trap him there for all eternity and survive off of his lips alone.

Jeric groaned against her mouth and turned toward her completely, one long leg stretched on the floor, the other bent upon the divan, and suddenly his lips weren't enough. She wanted to feel every inch of him against every inch of her, and so she rose onto her knees to scoot closer. Jeric seemed to have the same idea, because he grabbed her hips and drew her into his lap, but before he could pull her down completely, Imari climbed over his legs and straddled him.

Her pants were thin—very thin—leaving nothing to the imagination. She felt *everything*, and his desire sent an unexpected jolt through her body. She kissed him harder and rocked her hips forward, hardly conscious of what she was doing, only that her body naturally wanted to move against him.

A deep, guttural sound escaped Jeric—half growl, half moan. His kisses turned ravenous, and he squeezed her waist firmly as he rocked back into her.

Imari moaned, heart racing and body on fire. He was everywhere, and yet there was still too much space between them. She craved him with a very physical need, desperate to close every gap, and so she started pulling at his tunic.

"You really need to make up your mind, surina," he said, kissing her deeply.

Imari bit his bottom lip, and he chuckled, but slid his hands from where they'd crept beneath her top to help her remove his. He tossed his tunic behind him without a care as to where it landed, and had his hands and mouth on her again before his tunic had even reached the floor.

Maker have mercy, she would never have enough of this. Of him.

They were a tangle of ragged breath and heady kisses as Jeric ran his hands all over her body, squeezed her thighs and held her tight—so tight. Yet somehow the more Jeric kissed her, the more he touched her, the more of his touch she wanted.

"Jeric..." she said through his kisses.

"Mm." His palms pressed flat to her bare stomach while his fingertips tickled the underside of her breasts, driving her crazy.

"I want...I want you to do more than kiss me."

"I need you to be more specific, surina." That last word slipped over her skin like velvet.

"I want *you*," she said, all breath.

"That's still not very specific..." He pressed his lips to her jaw, her collarbone, while his fingertips teased higher.

Imari groaned in both frustration and desire, and pulled his belt as she squeezed his legs between both of hers.

"Ah." His breath feathered along her neck. "You mean this..." He grabbed both of her her thighs and dragged his thumbs along the creases.

Every string in her body coiled to near breaking, and a gasp escaped her.

Jeric chuckled lowly. "I should stop. It looks like I'm about to give you another heart attack."

"I don't want you to stop." Imari grabbed his face in her hands and kissed him hard, back into the divan.

Jeric groaned, surrendering to her lips, but only for a moment before he dragged his lips away, breathing hard. When he looked back at her, his eyes were huge and dark. Wolfish. He pressed a palm to her cheek. "We need." A breath. "To stop."

She sensed his words were more for himself than for her.

Imari frowned, panting, with her hands on his bare shoulders. "Why?"

"Imari." Those wolfish eyes burned as they looked at her, and his thumb trailed over her lips. "I am *seconds* away from throwing you on that bed, and if your saredd *do* decide to come in, it's going to be very difficult explaining why their precious surina is pinned beneath me, naked."

Imari stared at him, her pulse speeding out of control. Her heart was a rolling bass she could not calm. "What if I don't care?"

He closed his eyes, his expression strained. "You're not helping."

"*You're* the one who snuck into my room in the middle of the night."

"I know." Jeric's eyes opened again, but only halfway. "I said I was impressive. Not perfect."

Imari eyed him, her lips pursed.

He tipped his forehead against hers. "And should they walk in, it's much easier to stop kissing you than it is to hide—" He pressed his palm to the small of her back, and pulled her hips against his again. "*This.*"

Imari looked at him and sighed, breathless and frustrated and totally unsatisfied. "So what now?" she said like a challenge.

He looked straight at her, his palm still blazing against her bare lower back. "Come back with me."

Imari stared at him, wondering what he meant, and also afraid to hope he meant what she wanted those words to mean.

Jeric dipped his head and caught her mouth. Kissed her once. Twice. "Come with me to Skyhold."

"Jeric, I'm practically betrothed."

"Betrothals can be broken." A third time. "Also, you're not really acting like someone who's committed to another man."

She gave him an annoyed look, and he grinned and kissed her mouth a fourth time.

"Is that even possible?" Imari asked.

"You know that's not a question I ask," he said on her lips.

Imari pressed her hands to his face. His stubble scratched her palms as she held him there and looked at him directly. "Jeric, I'm serious."

He looked fiercely back and placed his hand over hers. "So am I."

Imari gazed at him, heart pounding and swelling and feeling suddenly too large for her chest.

"Jeric, how would we—" Imari started, when the screen door slammed open and a gust of wind tore into the room, startling them both.

Her lanterns sputtered and dimmed, but then the wind was gone as fast as it'd come, and the flames burned calmly again.

But a strange tone echoed in her mind—a distant off key to the natural harmony of this world—and it did not fade.

Jeric had gone rigid, his gaze fixed on the screen door, which hung wide open to a starless night and falling rain. Jeric gave her a weighted look, and then grabbed her waist and slid her from his lap, gesturing for her to wait as he started for the screen door.

Imari sat up and adjusted her top, which had climbed halfway to her neck, when she felt a wash of tingling that lingered in the air.

The hairs on her arm stood on end.

"Someone is using the Shah," she whispered with growing concern.

It wasn't Tallyn or Rasmin. She couldn't say how she knew that, specifically, only that they had both used their power around her, and it had never felt like this.

Jeric stopped at the door and looked back at her, eyes sharp. "How do you know?"

Imari stood, her gaze fixed on the open door as she approached. "I feel…"

She strode past him, through the door and onto her covered veranda, hardly noticing the damp chill as it cut over her skin. She stopped at the railing and gazed upon Trier through the veil of rain, where darkness settled like a black fog. Even the city lanterns struggled to bring light.

"Could it be Tallyn or Rasmin?" Jeric asked, joining her at the rail. He was a predator on the hunt.

She noticed he'd tucked a dagger into his belt. She didn't bother asking where it'd come from. They always seemed to sprout from his body.

"I don't think so," she whispered. "This feels different."

"*There*," Jeric said suddenly, pointing.

Imari followed his trajectory to a bird flying over the merchant district. She initially mistook the bird for a bat, given the erratic way it flew, but the body was much too large and its wingspan too wide.

Rasmin.

And he was racing straight for them.

"What is *he* doing here?" Imari started.

Rasmin soared up and over Vondar's wall.

"Get behind me." Jeric didn't wait for a response. He pushed Imari behind him, and Rasmin landed in a violent twist of wool and feathers. Rasmin had hardly completed the Change, and Jeric had him bent over the rail with a dagger at his skinny throat.

How frail Rasmin looked, as if all the consequences from his horrible deeds and unnaturally long life had finally caught up to him and drained him of his humanity, leaving him a bird. His eyes were wild, his nose beakish, and his thick tufted brows curled past his temples. Rain splattered his face, but he didn't seem to notice. He only spread his palms in surrender—both of which were covered in inked glyphs, Imari noted.

No longer hiding what he was.

Or, perhaps, this was simply another act. Another role he'd decided to play to fit the circumstances surrounding him. To garner their trust.

"What *in the rutting hells* are you doing here, you godsdamned snake?" Jeric hissed, pressing the dagger so hard against Rasmin's neck, the skin puckered.

To Rasmin's credit, he did not flinch. He only endured. Which, Imari imagined, was probably what he had done for the entirety of his pathetic life.

"You better talk, before I—" Jeric started.

But Rasmin's black eyes landed on Imari, his palms trembling as he said, "He's here."

28

Imari was about to ask Rasmin *who*, but the answer dropped into her mind before she could form the words. *That* was the surge of power she'd felt, the wind that had ripped into her room. The off key that persisted like some perversion of the Maker's pure and perfect melody.

Imari's blood turned to ice.

"*Who's* here?" Jeric demanded.

"Bahdra," Imari whispered, drawing closer.

Jeric's gaze shot to Imari. He didn't lessen the pressure at Rasmin's neck.

"That's what I felt a second ago," Imari said with growing horror.

"And he's...not alone," Rasmin managed. "He's brought reinforcements."

Jeric's lethal gaze cut to the city and beyond. "I don't see scat."

"Sight Veil..."

Imari frowned at the former Head Inquisitor. "Sight Veil...?"

"A Seer's spell used to hide things they don't want anyone to see," Jeric said through his teeth, holding that blade firmly at Rasmin's neck. "It's what Tallyn used to hide Survak's ship in my harbor. The *problem* is that Bahdra is a necromancer. Only a Seer could hide an entire army behind illusion, and it just so happens that I've caught one..."

"Wasn't...me..." Rasmin strained beneath Jeric's sharp blade, and he held his palms wider. "*Lestra.*"

Jeric's entire being tensed, his focus as sharp as the blade in his hand.

Imari did not know the name, but she got the distinct impression she should.

"You're lying," Jeric growled, but Imari detected an edge of concern in his voice.

"I wish I were," Rasmin continued. "I tried to...fly through the veil, but I couldn't..."

Crows startled in the distance—*hundreds* of them—lifting midnight perches, and the sky echoed with rattling cries and beating wings.

Jeric cursed.

He pulled his blade from Rasmin's neck, and turned his sharp gaze on Imari. "We should go to..." His words trailed off as a sphere of flaming white-blue light shot from the sands like a cannonball.

The flaming sphere arced over Trier's farms, casting them in an eerie pale glow before crashing into a cluster of residential towers at the city's edge.

The towers exploded in a violent cloud of fire, debris, and thunder. People screamed, and Vondar's outer wall came alive with shouts and movement. Just then, Jenya, Avék, and the third guard burst through Imari's opened screen door and onto the veranda. They spotted Imari and stopped in their tracks, taking in the scene, and the guard promptly drew his scims.

"It's all right!" Imari held up a hand to hold them off. "*I'm* all right."

Jenya's gaze narrowed on Jeric, with particular emphasis on his bare torso, and then she looked suspiciously at Imari. Behind her, the screaming and shouting crescendoed. Trier was wide awake now.

"Who are you?" Jenya spat in Istraan, pointing her scim at Rasmin, who leaned against the veranda rail for support.

A second sphere lobbed from the sands, only this time, the sands were no longer dark. Along Trier's edge, limning the outer farms and fields, stretched a line of torches that illuminated an armed force at least a thousand strong.

"Saints above..." Avék gasped. "Who's that?"

Imari met Jeric's gaze as realization dawned between them. "The Sol Velor."

But there were so many more than Imari—or anyone—had expected, and it made her wonder if the Sol Velor had been assimilating well before they'd started vanishing from Istraa and Corinth. Regardless, Trier was not prepared for this—not in the slightest.

A great, bellowing cry rose from beyond the fields, and the Qazzat bell pealed in alarm.

Imari looked to Jeric. "Your men..."

Together, they started for the door.

"Imari, you have to get out of here!" Rasmin called after them. "Trier has no means to fight this, and you are not ready!"

"You are not in a position to give me orders, *Inquisitor*," Imari snarled, and then slammed the screen door on him.

And the Qazzat bell rang.

"We need to get you to safety, surina," Jenya said.

But Imari was at her wardrobe, throwing on a coat and shoes, and then she plucked her flute from the table. It earned her a few curious glances, especially as that moonlight flared, but she slipped it into her coat pocket and faced them all. Jeric had thrown on his tunic and strapped two daggers to his belt.

Jenya started for the door. "Let's get you to the cellars."

"I'm not hiding, Jenya," Imari said.

Jenya stopped, her lips pressed in a line. "Surina. Your safety comes first—"

"The safety of Trier's citizens comes first, and you need help," Imari said as another explosion rocked the night. "You can't fight that fire with your scims. I'm coming."

Imari did not know what she was going to do, but she couldn't leave. She wouldn't hide. Especially when she might be able to help.

Jenya looked pleadingly at Jeric to intervene.

"The surina said she isn't hiding," Jeric replied, in perfect Istraan, "so I'm not sure I understand the issue."

Jenya's nostrils flared with breath, and Imari strode through the antechamber, threw open the door, and started down the hall. Palace guards sprinted toward the main entrance, while servants and guests rushed by in a frenzy, many sobbing as they hurried to find shelter within Vondar's cellars.

Imari rounded a corner and nearly bumped into her papa, who was fully dressed and fully armed, flanked by three saredd. He had never looked more like a sar than he did in that moment.

Sar Branón took in Imari's deadly escort, and to her surprise, he didn't seem shocked that Jeric was already with her. Even more startling was that he looked relieved.

"I was just on my way to find you," he said.

"Bahdra's here," she replied.

Her papa looked straight into her eyes. "I know."

Imari's lips parted. "How did you—" she started, but her papa grabbed her shoulders, held them tight.

The Qazzat bell rang and rang.

"Imari, listen to me." His gaze focused on her as his saredd waited behind him. "You have to get out of here."

Imari drew back. "What? No. Papa, I can *help*—"

"Not this time."

"I'm *not* hiding—"

"No, you're *leaving*."

Imari blinked. "Leaving? Papa, you can't—"

"You know what to do," Sar Branón said to Jenya, ignoring Imari's protestations.

A crease formed between Jenya's brows. Her gaze flickered to Imari and she nodded once.

"Papa—no! I won't run when I might be able to help—" Imari started.

"You are not ready for this, Imari." Sar Branón looked fiercely at her. "I don't say it because I don't believe in you, but—"

"That's *exactly* why you're saying it—"

"*You. Can't. Stop. This.*" He shook her with each word. Not very hard, but in desperation. As if he could shake her into understanding. "He's come for *you*, and you are not strong enough to fight him. *Trust me*, Imari. It's why I sent you away in the first place, hoping you would have the time to..." His expression pained, and then his gaze settled with resolve. "*Go*. Get far away from here. Learn how to use your power to the very best of your abilities, and when you're ready, come back. Come back and end this once and for all."

Imari trembled in his grip. "Papa, no. I won't—"

"It's not a request. It's an order." It was the sar speaking to her now, unyielding and firm.

And the Qazzat bell rang.

Imari's eyes burned. "*Please* don't do this..."

Sar Branón looked sharply at Jeric. "Do you love her?" he asked, in Common.

Imari stilled and gaped at her papa. At Jeric.

But Jeric didn't flinch, didn't shy. He held Sar Branón's gaze firmly, steadily, before settling on Imari as he replied with an unwavering, "Yes."

Imari forgot to breathe.

Sar Branón regarded Jeric a moment more and nodded, satisfied. "And you will protect her?"

Still, Jeric looked only at her as he said, "With my life."

Imari was frozen—trapped somewhere between a need to fight and the desire to hold on to this moment forever.

Jeric looked back at her papa, and something passed between the men.

"Good," Sar Branón said at last. He looked at Avék and the other guard, and in Istraan, he said, "You two, come with me."

Sar Branón then looked back at Imari. His expression broke, and he drew her into his arms, swift and sudden, crushing her to his chest. "I wish we had more time. I love you, Imari. More than you will ever know."

Imari did not want to hear those words. Not right now, and not like this. They sounded too final.

Her papa kissed the top of her head and let go.

"I *will* see you when this is over," she said. Needing to believe it. Needing *him* to believe it too.

Her papa touched her face, as if he would take this picture of her with him to the afterlife, and then he nodded at Jeric and fled down the busy hall at a jog with the guards running after him.

"Saints be with you," Avék said. He held something out toward her.

A little snakeskin sheath, made irrefutably from the viper she had killed along their journey here. It encased a blade with a bone hilt.

She met Avék's gaze, and he winked.

"It has been a pleasure, surina," he said, touching two fingers to his temple before he fled down the hall after the others, and Imari felt a painful prick that she would never see any of them again.

SURA ANJA GAZED out of her window and watched her beautiful city burn. Wicked blue flame consumed the towers and palms like a savage beast, tearing down the pride of her ancestors, while Trier's feeble arms could do nothing to stop it.

You did this, Branón, Anja thought with fury. *You did this when you betrayed me for a whore.*

Oh, that she would have staged an accident all those years ago. She'd considered it, and now her cowardice would be their ruin.

The air rumbled, the ground quaked, and her vase of verbena toppled and shattered upon the tiles.

"Sura...?" said Atti, her kunari.

"Give me a moment."

"Sei, mi a'sura."

Anja sensed Atti leave, and closed her eyes, breathing in deep as she clutched the sacred beads at her neck. The air smelled of ash and burning, and everywhere, in all directions, people were screaming.

Dying.

This was not war; this was a massacre.

Anja's hatred twisted inside of her, gnashing and coiling and vicious. *It isn't fair.* All her life, she'd devoted to the gods, and to the good people of Istraa. She had been faithful to her husband, and for what? So that he would sire a child on some Scab whore, and destroy everything Anja held dear?

Anja felt such anger, her body trembled with it.

The air exploded, the world shook, and the great Qazzat bell dropped like an anchor, crashing through the barracks below, never to sing again.

And the cries of battle drowned out the world.

A presence entered the room, and Anja knew it was time to go.

"I'm coming, Atti." She opened her eyes. "I just..."

It was not Atti.

The Corazzi princess stood before Anja's door. Tattered and soiled clothing sagged off of her skeletal frame, and dark shapes slithered beneath her skin, distorting her features, as those soul-less black eyes fixed on Anja.

Saints above...

Anja took an involuntary step back, clutching her beads tighter. Anja had only caught a quick glimpse of the Corazzi princess when the saredd had first carried her to Vondar's dungeons, but it was not until this moment that Anja truly believed she stood in the presence of a demon.

The demon took a step in the Corazzi's body. No normal body could have sustained such damage, and Anja knew it was the demon's power alone that held it together. The world beyond was a symphony of death and chaos, but Anja hardly noticed for the horrible creature standing before her.

"What do you want?" Anja asked in a trembling voice.

The demon slunk forward another step, dragging a twisted foot behind it, and the shadows in the room deepened.

"So much hate." The demon licked bloodied lips, and shuddered with ecstasy. "It has eaten her heart."

Anja took another step back but bumped into the wall. "Is it the girl you want?" she asked in desperation. "The bastard? I'll tell you anything you want to know, just *please* do not hurt my family."

The demon regarded her with those empty black eyes, as the outline of a face pressed against her cheek from within. "Who is the girl?"

Anja blinked with a moment's confusion. It was not a question she'd expected. "I do not know, I—" The demon took another step. "Saints as my witness, I do not know. Branón never told me who birthed her, though I begged. I swear it..."

Another step. The shadows in the room darkened further as the battle waged beyond.

"Please. I know nothing more than that. He was gone for over a year during Saád, and he returned with a baby. She's staying in the southernmost tower. There are three saredd guarding her door, and one of my own kunari is staying inside with her."

The shadows began to leak like ink. They seeped from the corners, pooling at the demon's feet, and an eerie white shone within the demon's black eyes. "Where is the flute?"

"With her, I believe. No, I'm sure of it," Anja babbled as that darkness crept closer. "She keeps it with her at all times, though I don't know if she's used it again since—"

A tendril of darkness whipped out and poured into Anja's mouth in a shock of horrible cold, and the last thing Anja saw was the demon smiling viciously.

29

"We must hurry, surina," Jenya said urgently.

Imari didn't want to leave, didn't want to run. She was so tired of running, and she didn't want to lose the family she had just got back.

"I need to find my men," Jeric said.

Jeric's words brought Imari back to the present, and she quickly slipped the snakeskin sheath and blade into her coat pocket, right beside her flute. "We find his men first," Imari said to Jenya, who did not argue.

They sprinted down Vondar's hall and toward the west wing. Imari couldn't stop thinking of all those innocent people in the city at the complete mercy of this power they could not stop. Trier might have been able to stop it at one time, but they had since destroyed any artifacts that could have saved them now.

This would be a slaughter.

Imari remembered Fyri. Wards, if she could just channel *that* —or some form of it, because Imari couldn't imagine using her power to kill as Fyri had done—Trier might stand a chance. And if Bahdra had brought a Seer, a Guardian, and an entire army to catch Imari, he'd probably worried she could channel that power too.

They intercepted Braddok and the rest of Jeric's pack before they ever made it to the west wing. They were all dressed and ready for battle—even Stanis, though he still looked a little pale.

"Gods, there you are," Braddok said, taking in their small group at a glance. Braddok tossed a baldric and sheathed sword at Jeric, who snatched it from the air.

His sword with the wolf hilt.

"Bahdra's here," Jeric said, pulling the baldric over his torso.

Jeric's words brought his men up short.

Stanis looked between Imari and his alpha, who was now busy strapping his sword into place at his belt, beside the other two blades.

Jeric looked like a veritable weapon rack.

"As in the Mo'Ruk?" Chez asked.

Jeric pulled a strap on the baldric, securing it. "The very one."

Braddok loosed a long breath that carried a few curses in it.

Stanis's sharp gaze narrowed on Imari.

"And here I thought you were the only one collecting powerful enemies," Braddok said to Jeric, who winked.

"So what now?" Aksel asked.

"We get the surina to safety," Jenya said, in Common, and gave Imari a hard look.

Braddok looked at Jenya, as if finally noticing her, and then stood tall, puffed out his chest, and a big-toothed smile cracked open his beard. "Whatever you say, beautiful."

Jenya had the curved edge of her scim at Braddok's throat before Imari could blink. Chez snickered. But Braddok's smile only widened.

"Call me beautiful again, *Corazzi*, and I will cut you into a thousand tiny pieces," Jenya hissed.

Braddok's eyes gleamed, her threat seeming to have the opposite effect of what she'd intended, but Braddok smartly kept his big mouth shut. Vondar's walls suddenly shook, and Jenya jerked her scim away.

"Follow me," Jenya said, casting Braddok one more threatening glance before pressing on.

"I like her," Braddok said.

"Strangely, I don't think the feeling's mutual," Chez said, smacking Braddok on the shoulder.

Imari exchanged a glance with Jeric, who only shook his head, and they followed Jenya down the halls. The palace guards had fled to join the battlefront, leaving Vondar's corridors mostly empty, though a few servants rushed for the cellars. Jenya pushed through the doors of Vondar's inner courtyard and stopped in her tracks.

"Godsdamnit," Braddok hissed.

Astrid stood at the courtyard's center, gazing upon the statue of Asiam and looking worse than ever, but also *more*—more of the festering evil inside, less human, and darkness frothed at her feet.

Those last images of Taran and Saza flashed in Imari's mind —especially Saza, as Astrid's darkness leaked into his body and stole his precious life—and Imari felt a flare of white-hot anger.

Astrid's head turned then. Her black eyes shone with strange inner light as she smiled wickedly. "We knew you'd come, little sulaziér," the demon hissed in that warped dissonance, and took a small step in Astrid's body.

Jenya drew both scims, and Jeric and his men drew their swords.

Astrid's eyes narrowed. "Ah, we see you found our little dog," the legion said.

"And you're a liar," Imari said, sliding her hand into her pocket, where her flute lay.

"Are we?" Astrid took another step. "Or, perhaps, we were telling the little sulaziér what is to come..."

"I'll ask you once more, demon," Jeric cut in lowly, blade in hand. "Release her."

Shapes slid beneath Astrid's translucent skin, warping her features. "Your hope is too little, too late. And how we feasted upon her horrors. There were so many of them. So many delicious atrocities that your own brother committed while you were away—"

Silver flashed, but Astrid vanished into smoke and reappeared two paces away from the place she'd been standing, and Jeric's dagger struck the statue instead.

Astrid's vicious smile stretched her bloodied lips too wide. "Always too late. Never enough."

And Astrid lunged.

She moved in a blur of snarls and smoke, but Imari had anticipated it, and notes were already flying out of her flute. This time, her power rose to her call immediately, the connection between mind and Shah plane growing tighter—stronger. Almost involuntary. She channeled that tingling sensation from her belly, down her fingertips and into her flute, and a hundred points of light flared to life, filling the air around them. The courtyard had become a world of miniature constellations, vibrating in resonance to Imari's pure tone. Imari focused on those notes surrounding Astrid, just like before, searching for their specific tone. She found it in an instant, warped slightly from the darkness in their midst. Imari bent her pitch to match, and those stars shined brighter in response. And just like before, Imari continued bending her tone, catching those stars in her music, tuning them until they surrounded Astrid like a cocoon.

The darkness snarled. It was a writhing, shrieking hole of ink at the center of Imari's starlit world, but Imari held fast. Pushing her tone and tuning those stars until her lungs ached for breath. But Imari still had not completely recovered from what she'd done in E'Centro, and again with Stanis. She needed breath, and she needed it now, and Imari broke her note to draw air. But in that split second, the darkness burst through the collapsing cocoon of light and scattered Imari's stars in all directions.

The force of it flung Imari right back into Braddok, and her flute slipped from her hands.

Imari cursed, scrambling after the flute while Astrid lunged for her. Jeric moved to intercede, but Astrid snarled and threw out her hand, and a burst of inky darkness struck him square in the chest. It knocked him back, right into Chez and Aksel, and Astrid was just lunging for Imari again when a shadow flew out of nowhere. Feathers whorled into wool, and a solid figure slammed into Astrid.

Rasmin.

They collided, and went flying into a bed of palms and giant ceramic pots.

"*Go!*" Rasmin yelled. "Get out of here!"

Astrid threw Rasmin back into the statue of Asiam. The marble cracked from the force of it, but even as Rasmin's body was sliding to the ground, he changed form and flew back at Astrid, talons extended as he raked and clawed at her face.

Imari snatched her flute just as Jeric grabbed her arm, panting.

"He can handle it," Jeric snarled, pulling Imari across the courtyard, while Astrid and Rasmin battled in a blur of ink and feathers and inhuman shrieks.

They sprinted through the opposite arch at breakneck pace, Jenya taking the lead. Toward Sar Branón's private chambers, Imari soon realized.

Jenya reached the door, kicked it in, and ushered everyone inside.

"Block the door," she commanded, and Jeric—with Braddok's help—dragged a wardrobe before the door, while Jenya rushed to the mural along one wall: a life-sized portrait of Istraa's very first sar.

"Gods have mercy..." Braddok murmured. All humor had fled

from his voice as he stared out the window.

Imari followed his gaze, and her heart nearly stopped.

Her city—her beautiful city—had become a cauldron of fire and smoke and death in a matter of moments. With so much Liagé power at Bahdra's disposal, the tides of war were completely imbalanced. Trier was a calm and tranquil shoreline being struck by a hurricane.

And it was ripping them apart at the seams.

The Sol Velor were almost upon Vondar's wall.

Another flaming sphere of guardian fire launched from somewhere *inside* the city, near the merchant district, and collided with the Qazzat bell tower. Rock and plaster exploded, bodies sailed in the air, and the great bell crashed to its death.

Somehow the bell's silence rang louder than its alarm.

And without that alarm, the night was left to screaming.

All of this—*for me*, Imari thought grievously.

"*Jenya...*" Jeric said through his teeth.

"It's stuck." Jenya was pressing a specific place along the lip of the mural's frame.

Jeric stalked forward and slammed his wolf hilt against the frame. Something clicked; the mural unhinged. Jenya cast him a quick but grateful look, then motioned at Imari as she swung the frame open like a door. "Hurry!"

A dark corridor lay beyond—a secret passage between Vondar's thick walls.

"Well, I'll be damned," Stanis said.

"You might just get your wish sooner than you were expecting," Aksel mused.

"We need a light..." Jenya looked back at their group.

"No need." Imari withdrew her flute, and the little etchings flared.

There was a split second of quiet as all gazes fell on that little Liagé artifact.

"Lead the way," Jeric said simply, looking at Imari in the way he had looked at her in her room, when he'd asked her to play for him. Trusting her completely.

And Imari ducked inside.

The air smelled old and stale, and a blanket of dust covered the floor. A cockroach scuttled away, out of the wardlight, and once everyone was inside, Jenya closed the mural behind them.

Muting the din of battle.

"Where does this lead?" Imari asked as they walked the tight and winding passage. Jeric kept pace right behind her, because the path was not wide enough for them to walk abreast.

"Just outside of the bazaar," Jenya said from the back.

So not entirely out of the city, but behind the brunt of battle.

"We'll have to be careful, but between all of us, we should be able to get you out of here," Jenya added.

Jenya meant to be reassuring, but Imari found no relief in her words. Only the crushing weight of responsibility.

Their passage ended at a solid wall and a hole in the ground. The ends of a wooden ladder stuck out from that hole, fastened by iron clasps, and reached straight down into the darkness.

"Ah. So we're going *beneath* Trier," Aksel said.

"I'll go first," Imari said, and when Jeric looked as though he were about to argue, Imari said, "I've got the light."

"I'm coming down with you."

"Fine."

Imari started down the ladder, tested its weight, and kept going. The ladder bounced and groaned as Jeric stepped onto the uppermost rung, and there he waited, making sure it could support them both.

So far, so good.

He looked down at her, nodded once, and together, they descended. The ladder ended about five feet above a dirt floor, and Imari jumped down the rest of the way and looked around.

"It's another tunnel," she said to the others, who waited some twenty feet above. She could just see their faces, all leeched of color from the moonlit glow of her flute.

Jeric jumped down after, and Imari held her flute high while the others descended. Unlike the passage above, this tunnel had been carved directly out of bedrock.

The earth trembled again, and chunks of rock rained.

"What if it's caved in?" Chez asked.

"There are two potential exits along this tunnel," Jenya answered in Common as she gazed into the darkness. "Though we should avoid those if we can. They're still too deep in the city."

Jenya ran on, and the rest followed, keeping to the silvery halo of Imari's light. Occasional rumbles shook the ground from above, and more rock rained down upon them.

More lives destroyed.

They hadn't been running long—Imari guessed they were probably below Syccor, where the wealthiest lived—when she spotted the cave-in ahead.

Aksel cursed behind her as Jenya's footsteps slowed.

"Oh, good," Braddok said. "I was starting to worry we were gonna get out of this without seeing any action."

Jenya's lips pressed into a line. She looked back at Imari, then Jeric, then gestured for everyone to follow. They backtracked a few paces and turned down a narrow crack in the tunnel that Imari had not noticed before.

"This leads just outside the Qazzat," Jenya said with obvious unease.

"Isn't that where the bell just collapsed?" Chez asked.

Where Tarq still lay, recovering.

"Yes."

"Rutting fantastic."

They soon reached the tunnel's end, as well as another ladder, which led *up*.

"Should be an old supply room," Jenya said, gazing into the darkness above.

The ladder's bottommost rung hung suspended about four feet off of the ground, and before Imari even reached for it, Jeric grabbed her waist and hoisted her up.

Hand over hand she climbed, and the ladder shook as Jeric climbed on behind her. She reached the top to find the exit blocked by a wooden hatch, and so she set the flute between her teeth, placed both palms to the hatch, and shoved.

Nothing.

She shoved again.

Still nothing. It didn't even budge.

Jeric climbed higher, until his body was flush with hers. He held on to the ladder with one hand, and pressed his other to the hatch.

No luck.

He looked at her, nodded once, and together they shoved. Something large toppled and the hatch gave. They pushed the hatch open a crack, and Imari climbed through Jeric's arms just enough to peer out. Sure enough, dust and storage crates and old weapons coated the floor beyond.

Imari shoved the hatch open completely and clambered into the small space, and without the ground's thick insulation, those harsh sounds of battle expanded to full volume.

Imari felt a sudden wave of panic. Her papa was out there. And Kai and Avék, and so many others, like Sebharan and Tarq. Fighting and dying—because of her.

Jeric climbed through the hatch, and Imari held her flute over the opening, giving light to the others as they ascended. Jeric approached the narrow door and pressed his ear to the wood, listening, while Stanis and Chez scavenged the abandoned weaponry. Aksel shoved a rusted scim into his belt.

Imari had the fleeting thought that the rust might do more damage than the scim.

"Is it clear?" Jenya asked Jeric.

"As clear as it's going to get," he answered. His eyes met Imari's, and then he opened the door.

It was as if he'd opened the door to hell.

All Imari could see was smoke—smoke and shadows and flame against a symphony of screaming and shouting and crumbling rock, with the occasional quake beneath her feet. The sound arrested her, gripping her chest as the magnitude of it all squeezed her lungs tight, and she suddenly couldn't draw a full breath.

And then Jeric was squeezing her shoulders, holding her firmly before him, his gaze locked on hers. "Imari."

Behind him, smoke curled and screams echoed.

"We're going to do our best to get you out of here." He did not say it would be all right. He did not say it would be easy. He said only what was true—that he would do his best against an enemy that was far greater than any of them.

So that she would be safe.

While an entire city burned.

"Stay close to me," Jeric said to her, then he exchanged a glance with his men and Jenya, who had fallen quiet, weapons ready.

Jeric stepped into the street, took quick surveillance—though how he could see anything through the smoke and shadows, Imari did not know—and gestured for the others to follow. Imari slipped out of the doorway after him, the others close behind, and they all followed Jeric along the street. Smoke and burning filled the air, making it difficult to breathe, and behind her, Chez coughed. Jeric stopped at a cross street, eyes narrowed, and Jenya moved to stand beside him.

"Which way?" Jeric asked.

"That depends. Can you see anything?" Jenya asked quietly, flexing her hand around her scim.

Jeric considered. Pulled a dagger. "There's movement over there." Jeric gestured left.

Jenya looked curiously at him, then glanced right. "All right. This way."

The six of them followed Jenya forward, hugging the fractured walls while keeping to the shadows. Broken brick and burning remains lay everywhere, and Imari was just stepping over a chunk of debris when she realized the debris was actually a body. A woman, near her age, but the woman's chest had been completely crushed, and blood saturated the ground around her. Imari swallowed a hard lump and kept going.

Past more bodies. Men and women.

Children.

Her eyes burned, and not just from the smoke.

"Keep your eyes up, Imari," Jeric said beside her.

But it didn't matter where she kept her eyes. Bodies lay everywhere, draped out of windows, slumped in doorways and against walls. Many were still burning, and the stench of seared flesh soured the air.

Imari thought she might be sick.

So much death. So much *waste*. She had thought Tallyn's memories a difficult thing to bear, but this...

Nothing could have prepared her for this. The raw brutality of it. Seeing so much life tossed aside and left to burn, and for what?

Was this justice?

Jenya stopped abruptly and looked back at Jeric. "Two men, one woman." She gestured around the corner.

Jeric and Jenya exchanged a glance, and then both moved in unison. Braddok grabbed Imari's arm and held her back while Jeric and Jenya slit the throats of the three Sol Velorian warriors, adding them to Bahdra's casualties.

More blood.

More death.

Jenya urged them on through side streets and steadily away from Vondar proper, stopping only as they intercepted fringe Sol

Velorian fighters who'd been working to secure parts of the city Bahdra's forces had already demolished. It was during one such skirmish that Imari heard a cry down an alley, and she left Jeric and the others to investigate.

A family of three stood at the alley's opposite end, their exit blocked. No, a family of *four*. Imari spotted the father lying on the ground, unmoving, as two Sol Velorian warriors approached the mother—their backs to Imari—while a cloaked figure blocked the family's exit.

The cloaked figure ripped the toddler from the mother's arms.

The mother screamed and tried to go after her baby boy, who was also screaming now, but the two Sol Velorian warriors grabbed the mother's arms and jerked her back. The eight-year-old girl started after her baby brother, but the cloaked figure raised a fist, spoke a command, and a wall of air punched the girl.

Imari's heart seized.

The girl cried out, flew back, and struck a wall, while her mother screamed and sobbed.

Imari's breathing came hard and fast, and her world zeroed to a focal point. All else faded away in that moment—the fighting and shouting, the flames and shadows—and a single voice cut through her tumultuous thoughts: *I am with you.*

It was the voice from before. The one who had spoken to her in Skyhold and lent her strength where she had failed.

It lent her strength now, and the tingling in her belly surged.

"*Imari!*" She heard Jeric hiss behind her—their skirmish with the Sol Velorians having ended—but Imari was already running down the alley. Through the smoke and beneath lines of burning laundry as she drew the little dagger from its snakeskin sheath. Purpose narrowed her focus, as fury gripped her heart.

Enough, she snarled in her mind.

The Liagé was focused on the screaming toddler, the two Sol Velorian guards focused on the mother, and none of them noticed Imari until she'd slashed her dagger across the backs of the Sol Velorians' hamstrings.

They yowled in pain and collapsed as Imari shoved right past them, her gaze fixed on that Liagé. A woman, Imari realized. Ink covered her face, and wisps of long, dark hair curled out from beneath her cowl. Seeing Imari approach, the Liagé woman hissed a word. Energy pulsed, and a wall of air struck Imari this time. Imari cried out, her dagger flying from her hands as she slammed against the wall and bounced to unforgiving ground. Pain lanced through her shoulder, but Imari snarled and shoved herself back to her feet, and pulled her flute free. The little glyphs flared moon-white.

The Liagé's eyes narrowed, and she shoved the toddler aside as Imari let her notes fly.

The Shah plane became visible at once—that unique world of stars and all the spaces in between. Imari saw the alley not with her human sight, but in that other plane of energy. Millions of tiny stars burned all around, shining most brilliantly where the Istraan family cowered, and where the Liagé woman blocked the alley.

Where...the world suddenly seemed to exist outside of natural time.

Because Imari could *see* the stars' undulating vibrations—a motion that should have been too fast for her human eyes to comprehend. And as she marveled at the sharpness of her starlit world, as her heart guided each note into the next, she felt a tug on her belly. As though someone had pulled upon the line connecting her spirit to the well of Shah power that all Liagé drew from.

Imari watched as a strange, glowing haze poured into the brilliant star that shone over the Liagé's chest, filling it with more power. She watched as that star swelled with it, creating space for the energy the Liagé had drawn. And in that slowness of time, Imari heard the command, though it was not a word as it had been before. In this plane, it was a tone. An F sharp, in fact, that hummed through the span of little stars between them—a ripple of sound, igniting each light in its path, as it arced straight for Imari.

But time still moved unnaturally slowly, and Imari dropped her note to match. She caught the rippling F sharp before it struck her.

The Liagé's command froze, and the world expanded.

Imari didn't know how else to describe it. Darkness and stars warped, elongated and strained out from her, as if she were a central point—an anchor—and the world around her stretched, elastic. Imari smelled an edge of something like pepper, but she held on to that note. Held it firm against the pull of power and time, as the line between her and the Liagé woman strained from the torque.

And then Imari let it go.

The power whipped back toward the Liagé, and a line of stars ignited like a bolt of lightning. That light struck the Liagé woman hard and fast, her inner sun flared white, and she went soaring like a shooting star.

Imari's vision returned to normal, only to find the Liagé lying in the street beyond the mouth of the alley, her body splayed and unmoving.

Imari glanced down at the mother, who sobbed beside her dead husband while clutching her two babies.

"Go," Imari urged. "Get out of here. Hurry."

The woman looked up at Imari with huge and frightened eyes.

"Go!" Imari hissed.

This time, the woman grabbed her children and ran.

"Imari."

Jeric stood right behind her.

Imari turned around to face him, her flute in hand. He was looking past her, where the Liagé lay—dead or unconscious,

Imari did not know and she was too afraid to find out—and then his gaze settled back on her.

He looked...she couldn't read the look on his face.

"We have to go," he said. He reached for her, but she stepped back.

"I can't, Jeric," she said.

A muscle ticked in his jaw. "I know this is difficult, but—"

"Difficult? They're *dying* because of me!"

"*No*," he said fiercely. "They're dying because of Bahdra—"

"And they don't have any way to fight back!"

"Imari, you're just one person!" Jeric didn't say it because he didn't believe in her, but out of fear *for* her. Yes, that was the expression on his face. "Do what your father asked—*please*. I will help you fight this, but we need to prepare. We need to—"

"I'm not running, Jeric."

Jeric stopped—everything about him stopped—as he realized she would not be moved.

"I might not have the power to stop Bahdra," she continued, as Jenya and the others jogged into the alley, "but I can at least give you *time*—"

"Imari—"

"Get out of here!" Imari persisted. "I will do what I can to distract him, so that you can warn your people and prepare your guard, and send word to the other Provinces—"

"Imari, *please*—"

Imari grabbed Jeric's tunic, fisted it in both hands, and then pulled him close and kissed him hard. She kissed him for all the times she hadn't, for all the times she wouldn't, for a life they would never share.

If there was any one thing that might shatter her resolve, it was this.

But she knew that even if she ran, if she gave in to Jeric's plea, it would only be a matter of time before Bahdra caught up to them. Before Bahdra used Jeric to get to her.

And Imari would die before she let that happen.

Finally, Imari pulled back—though it nearly killed her to do so—and she gazed into his storming blue eyes. "I love you, Jeric," she said, and his expression broke. "I'm sorry, but I won't let you die because of me."

She let go of his tunic, turned away from him, and sprinted down the alley.

Straight for Vondar.

30

Niá stood at the window of her room and watched Trier burn. She had known Bahdra was coming. She had felt his power sizzle through the air. It had woken her from a nightmare, one where she'd drowned in all the coin Bahdra had given her.

Coins smeared in Saza and her oza's blood.

Niá had slipped out of bed and hastened to the window, sensing something off in the quiet. The silence had not been natural, the darkness too thick, and Niá knew immediately it was the work of a Seer, and an unusually gifted one.

So, it's time, she had thought.

Bahdra had completed his task, and he had come for his reckoning.

Niá carried no notions that he would come for her; she held no delusions of importance. She had served her purpose, and like any toy rendered useless, she had been discarded.

The first rumble passed through the city. Niá could not see the source from her bedchamber, but she felt each ripple of Shah power, tinged with heat and fury.

Saredii—Guardian magic.

The Shah connected all things, and through that invisible plane, most Liagé had a sense for others using it. When saredii magic was invoked, it stirred a physical response—a call to action. Saredii magic was unique in that way. But Niá had never felt so strong a call before. This permeated the air, heady and intoxicating.

Voices sounded in Ashova's halls; a door shut below. Lights flickered on in the city as people woke to see what had rattled the earth.

Defenseless. All of them. Because time had blurred memory, altered truth, and the people forgot the vital lessons their ancestors had died learning. They had forgotten that steel was nothing to Shah power, and in their pride, they had destroyed every artifact that might have shielded them from this.

Bahdra would not have to work hard.

A flare of light appeared in Niá's periphery, and she saw the sphere this time. A flaming ball of white-blue light, arcing down upon Trier and crashing into a cluster of buildings in Syccor, the wealthy district.

Where a few of her clients lived.

She secretly hoped they were there now, sleeping.

The world quaked, people screamed, and those flames stuck like tar, eating up everything around them.

Guardian fire.

Niá had never seen it before, but she knew what it was. It had been used by Kazak—one of Azir's four Mo'Ruk—in the war against the Five Provinces. He'd destroyed a dozen cities with that fire before the Liagé who'd allied with the Provinces finally conjured a way to stop them. Trier had no such resources now, and so Istraa's pride burned.

Niá wondered if a sphere of Guardian fire would land on Ashova's.

She wondered if she cared.

She also wondered where a Guardian with this amount of

power had come from, or where Bahdra had found him or her, because someone with this strong a Shah mark could not hide easily.

The city bell rang, a constant pealing wail through the explosions and screaming. Citizens fled, fighting erupted in the distance, and Niá spotted groups of saredd and soldiers sprinting through the streets.

To their death, she knew.

All this, for the surina. The sulaziér.

Niá had thought Bahdra wanted the sulaziér in order to take Trier. That he needed her power to attack. Watching this battle unfold, Niá realized just how little she'd been told.

But then, why had he wanted the girl?

And why had her oza and little brother been trying to help her?

The answer to the latter began to take shape and fill with color.

Oza Taran had believed in a world where Liagé and the Provinces lived in harmony. That the Maker's gifts weren't just for them. That Sol Velor and Liagé were not elect, but that *all* humanity was elected and loved by the one who had created them. And it had always been her oza's hope that one day the people would see the Maker's goodness—his true intention, where people placed others above self.

Where people loved one another as he loved them.

To that end, Oza Taran would risk anything. Even her own life, if she thought it would help the Maker's perfect world become reality.

So what had Oza Taran seen in the sulaziér?

Ashova's temple shook so suddenly and so violently, Niá pressed a palm to the wall for balance. She spotted a group of Sol Velorian fighters push into Ashova's courtyard, and within moments, they cut down the men and women standing out front, dressed only in robes and fear, and burst into Trier's favorite temple.

Niá heard the screaming. The thuds and shatter of glass, and horrid cries of dying. And then her door burst open and three Sol Velorians stood there, two men, one woman. They wore a mixture of culture, from Davros embroidery to Breveran cloth to thick wool from The Fingers.

But these Sol Velor belonged to the Provinces no more.

They looked at her, and she them, and then the woman tossed Niá a scim.

It landed at Niá's feet. They nodded and pressed on.

Niá looked at that scim, the curved edge stained with blood. She stepped forward and picked it up. And then she stepped through her door and into the hall.

Blood smeared the wall, the floor. Bodies lay on the floor—clients, and kahar. One kahar slumped beside her door with his skull bashed in.

Niá kept walking. She stepped around the bodies, slipped past another one of Bahdra's warriors, who was on his way upstairs, and she stopped at the landing.

Kahar Vidett lay on the steps, on his stomach, his hand reaching as if it were his one last attempt to reach his gods so that they might deliver him. His fingers twitched, his breath gurgled.

He was still alive.

Niá walked down those stairs, eyes narrowed on him, and she knelt at his side. His black eyes swiveled to her, and focused.

"Niá..." he rasped, more blood gurgling upon his lips.

Niá plunged her scim into his back, right over his heart.

He gasped, his body jerked once, and then he died.

Niá's entire body trembled. "You deserved so much worse," she said through her teeth, and then she got up and walked on, stepping over his still body and out of Ashova's temple for the very last time.

31

I mari ran down the street, through the smoke and flames, intent on Vondar. She did not know what she was going to do, only that she needed to try. That she needed to do *something.*

That she would never be able to live with herself if she ran away while this city burned.

She heard shouting and voices to her left, and ducked into the shadows as she scanned the street. The smoke made her eyes burn, though she spotted three figures emerging from a building opposite—Sol Velorians. Two women, one man. These were not dressed for battle. Just servants of this city. The woman wore a simple smock, the men colorless breeches and tunics, and two of them weren't wearing shoes, though the one who did wore a pair of sandals in far too good condition. Imari thought he'd probably pinched them from his former master. That master was probably dead, judging by the blood staining their simple clothes.

As the three Sol Velorians moved on, Imari slipped out of her hiding place and kept running while her mind worked fast. She wasn't stupid enough to think she could face someone like

Bahdra, or this Lestra that Rasmin had mentioned, but there were other Liagé fighting within Bahdra's forces, like the one she'd fought in the alley. If she could find those and take them out—not necessarily kill them, but render them unconscious—it might give Sebharan's forces a chance.

If there was anything left of them. She'd seen the Qazzat. It was nothing more than a pile of rubble now, and she wondered if Tarq had gotten out in time.

Imari moved through the shadows like a ghost, slipping along the fringes unseen, just as she'd always done in Skanden. She reached out with her power, casting it out like a fishing line, searching for little tugs like the one she'd felt in that alley.

There.

And there. And there.

Imari counted fifteen Liagé interspersed throughout the city, pulling on that infinite well of Shah power. Five drew upon that well with much more force than the others—two of them were most likely Bahdra and Lestra, but who were the others? Rasmin? Tallyn? Even so, that only totaled four.

Imari felt the weak pull of one Liagé just a few blocks over, and she headed straight for it. The sounds of fighting crescendoed as she neared, and that tug on her line of Shah power grew steadily stronger.

She was getting close now.

Imari gripped her flute tight. The little instrument warmed in her hand, and she ducked through the open doorway of a broken building, scurried through rubble and beneath fallen beams, until a hand gripped her arm and yanked her back.

Imari whirled, prepared to strike, only to find herself staring into a pair of familiar deep blue eyes.

"Jeric!" she said, and Jeric pressed a finger to his lips. Warning her to be quiet. "You're supposed to be leaving!" she hissed in a whisper.

"She's so cute," Braddok said, stepping out from the shadows, with Jenya right behind him, who said, "You know I'm not leaving this city, surina. Or you."

Imari understood why Jenya had stayed. Jenya would die before she abandoned this city, but Jeric...

"And you should also know by now that the Wolf never does what he's told," Aksel said, striding in after them, with Chez and Stanis on his heels.

"Which, consequently, is why we stick around," Chez said with a wink. "His piss-poor decisions make us pretty damn rich."

Jenya rolled her eyes to the ceiling as she strode for the narrow doorway in back that Imari had been about to walk through before Jeric had arrived.

"Jeric, *please* take your men and go—" Imari started.

"You've made your choice. I've made mine." He spoke firmly, his expression unyielding.

"But Corinth needs you!"

"Corinth needs Trier to stand," Jeric said lowly. "And it's about rutting time our people worked together again. So." Jeric turned his gaze to the smoke-hazed street beyond. "What's your plan?"

Imari pressed her lips together. She looked to Jeric's pack, but they only gazed expectantly back at her.

Imari relented with a sigh. "Bahdra has about fifteen Liagé in this city."

Jeric's gaze shot back to hers. "How do you know that?"

"I...*feel* it."

She felt Jeric's men watching her—Jenya too—though she didn't turn to look.

"Five of those fifteen are significantly stronger than the rest," she continued, "and I suspect two of those five are Bahdra and Lestra."

Braddok grunted. "Well, hells. This almost feels like cheating."

"Your favorite pastime," Chez mused.

"Oh, that's hardly my favorite pastime," Braddok said, waggling his brows at Jenya, who looked like she might just gut him with her scims.

"Well, however she knows it," Jenya said sharply. "It will be highly effective in keeping us alive."

Jeric tipped his head, studying Imari. "You want to find the Liagé first."

"Yes," Imari answered. "If I...if *we* can subdue some of them, maybe Sebharan will have a chance to fight back."

Jeric's features sharpened, and his gaze settled back on the street. "Where's the nearest one?"

"Just over there." Imari pointed. "One block over."

Jeric nodded once. "We'll cover you."

Imari glanced at Jeric's pack, expecting at least some resistance, but she found none. They all focused on the smokey world beyond, armed and ready.

Imari exchanged a glance with Jeric, and then she slipped out of the building and into the smoke and shadows. Jeric kept right behind her as they crept across the street, through the rubble and past more bodies—Istraan and Sol Velorian. Mostly Istraan.

She stopped at the end of the street and peered around the corner. Jeric peered around as well, his head just above hers.

Ahead were a dozen Sol Velorians, wearing a patchwork of leather and cloth, and bearing a single inked symbol upon their heads. They fought against six city guards, while two women—a mother and daughter—cowered against a wall. Another figure stood off to the side—a woman, covered in inked glyphs, with a plait of black hair that fell to her waist—flinging concussive spells that knocked a few guards down.

A guardian.

Jeric tapped Imari's shoulder twice.

He wanted to know if she was ready.

Imari clutched her flute tight. Jenya and his men waited behind them, while shouts echoed one street over, and the ground shook with a distant explosion. Was anyone ever ready for war?

Imari pressed her lips together and nodded.

Jeric squeezed Imari's shoulder once, encouragingly, and then he stepped out into the street.

"Hey!" someone yelled in thick Sol Velorian, spotting Jeric immediately. The other Sol Velorians, who had just finished off the remaining city guards, looked over. The Liagé guardian, who had begun walking away, back toward Vondar, paused and glanced over her shoulder.

"It's a *Corazzi*," said one of the Sol Velorians.

Someone...Imari recognized. A man who worked the smithy, and she'd treated him just last week for a bad burn.

"*Idri...?*" Imari called, stepping out into the street.

Idri froze. He held a crossbow. "Ah, the moonlight healer..." His gaze fell to the flute glowing in her hand, then darted back to her face. "You didn't tell us that part. That you're one of us. Lucky you're a sar's bastard, I guess."

"Idri, please. I was trying to help—"

"Tell me, *healer*, how was it visiting us in the slums knowing you could go back to your bed of silk every night? Was that Corazzi filth waiting for you—*don't move or I shoot!*"

Jeric had resumed walking forward, but stopped mid-step. The other Sol Velorians fanned out behind Idri, and the Liagé had turned back around and was slowly approaching.

"Tell your *Corazzi* to drop his weapon." Idri looked down the sight of his crossbow.

"Idri, don't do this—" Imari started, but then Idri aimed his crossbow at her.

Jeric dropped his sword. It landed on the ground with a clank and a small cloud of dust.

"It's her," Idri said to the Liagé. "We'll handle the Corazzi."

And the Liagé snapped a command.

Imari felt a sharp tug on that line of Shah power, as though a whip had lashed out and coiled tightly around her flute.

And pulled.

The glyphs on her flute flared white, and Imari growled, holding tight and digging her heels into the ground. But the force dragged her feet forward. Her knuckles blanched, the flute shuddered in her grip, sliding though her sweaty palms. Suddenly, the pressure released, and Imari went stumbling backward on the rebound, nearly tripping over her own feet.

She looked over to see what had stopped the Liagé so abruptly, only to find a dagger—Jeric's dagger—hovering in midair, inches from the Liagé woman's face.

The woman hadn't been able to divide her power, and so she'd redirected it at Jeric's blade. It was just the distraction Imari needed.

And she lifted her flute and played.

Her vision turned to stars, and she focused on the place the Liagé stood. Where that haze of light both poured into and out of the star shining brightly over her heart, where she directed that force at the dagger, aiming it right back at Jeric.

Imari heard the Liagé's command like a tone—a single pitch ringing in this world of contrasts, just like before. Imari entangled it with her melody and held fast. The stars trembled, caught between two forces.

But Imari's was stronger.

Imari bent her note, torqued her line of power as she forced the Liagé woman's tone to match her own—taking command of it —and Imari thrust that dagger's hilt at the Liagé's skull. Imari didn't turn the blade; she didn't want to kill the Liagé. The hilt struck hard, and the Liagé collapsed—unconscious—as the dagger clattered to the street.

Imari ended her song, time and sight returned to normal, and Idri looked both stunned and furious.

"You picked the wrong side, bastard." Idri turned the crossbow on Jeric, and fired.

"No!" Imari shouted, but Jeric somehow had another dagger in his hand, cut hard and fast, and knocked Idri's bolt aside.

The bolt struck the wall instead and clattered to the ground.

Pure shock momentarily arrested the Sol Velorians. They exchanged uncertain glances, and then the foremost warrior attacked.

Imari raised her flute, but before she'd even loosed a breath, Jeric had toed his sword, kicked it into the air, and snatched it up, impaling the Sol Velorian who descended upon him.

Imari stood briefly stunned as Jeric jerked his sword free and shoved the dead Sol Velorian into the next two attackers before whirling on a third who charged him from the side. He severed that man's arm in one stroke. The Wolf was a choreographed masterpiece of death, cutting through each attacker with singular focus and precision. They ran at him, but the Wolf remained steady. Each step strong and perfectly timed, each stroke bringing calculated death. One Sol Velorian man wielded a scythe, which the Wolf knocked free in one swift punch. He caught the weapon on the rise, brought it around, and gutted the man in a spray of blood and intestines.

Jeric turned and caught Imari's gaze, his face splattered with blood. None of it was his.

But their battle had drawn attention, and more figures ran into the street, none of them Istraan—a dozen ahead, and a dozen more behind. Including another Liagé. An older man this time. He had no hair, and inked glyphs covered his scalp and face.

"Oh, good," Braddok said, stepping out from behind the corner. "Can't let you have all the fun..."

"I'll handle the Liagé," Imari said, eyes locked on the older man, who was already moving steadily toward her.

And chaos exploded.

Jeric, Jenya, and Jeric's men clashed with the Sol Velorian fighters, and Imari let notes fly. Her world became light and dark, but now the man was sprinting toward her. He hadn't thrown any power for her to catch hold of, and she didn't have time to weave her stars around him—perhaps he'd sensed her intent—but then she got an idea.

From something she'd unwittingly done before, a very long time ago.

She focused on the star situated over his chest as he ran at her. She could see the natural vibrations, and it was there she focused her music. Finding his tone, matching it with her own, catching hold and slowing down the vibrations of his heart.

Slower.

Slower still.

His star dimmed and he collapsed.

Imari's vision returned to normal as she heaved a breath, a sheen of sweat dampening her forehead. The Liagé lay sprawled on the ground, eyes closed and unmoving. Not dead, but sleeping deeply. Now if she could just do that to the rest of them...

Around her, Jeric and the others fought on, working in impressive synchrony and tossing weapons between them. They moved as one body, each an extension of the whole with Jeric the mind. Jenya fought with them, easily holding her own as she wielded both scims, and Imari raised her flute and kept playing.

One by one, she fixed on the stars situated over the Sol Velorians' hearts, finding each warrior's natural resonance, and, she used her notes to slow them down. Slowly dropping them into a deep sleep. One rose behind Jeric, and she caught his heart's light and slowed its vibrations.

The man collapsed.

Imari wove her music all around their fighting. She was able to separate Jeric and the others from the Sol Velorians. How, exactly, she couldn't say, only that she *felt* where they were standing. The familiarity of their resonance, as though their individual tones were written upon her heart. She tried to drop two Sol Velorian fighters at once, but her breath strained and her note turned brittle, so she focused on taking them down one at a time.

Down.

Down.

A sharp cry—down—and she was just moving on to the next bright star when she felt an immense surge of power.

It hadn't come from her.

It charged the air like static before a lightning storm. So strong, the air warped with it, and a humming filled Imari's ears. Louder and louder until it strained her eardrums, as if all the stars were vibrating out of control, overwhelmed. And through the smoke, with her normal vision, Imari spotted a figure dressed in heavy midnight robes. Like some harbinger of death moving steadily toward them. Even from where she stood, with the Shah still fueling her blood, she knew she was no match for the one approaching.

This was one of the five.

And *wards*. The strain this Liagé put upon the well of Shah power was suffocating up close. Imari might have been impressed if she weren't suddenly terrified.

Desperate, Imari lifted her flute and played.

But.

She could not see her stars.

It was as if this figure's presence had completely snuffed out the light in the section of street where he or she walked, like a massive black hole in the Maker's starlit world.

"Jeric!" Imari yelled, her heart pounding with new panic.

Jeric glanced over, totally covered in blood as he drew his sword from a man's back. He followed her trajectory, and stopped cold.

"Pull back!" he yelled, and his men started to look over.

The figure raised a hand.

Imari felt an abrupt jerk on the line connecting her to that infinite well of Shah power—so strong, it made her physically lurch forward. And beside her, one of the dead stirred.

Imari felt a rush of horror. "It's Bahdra!"

All around Imari, the Sol Velorians that Jenya, Jeric and
his men had just killed began rising—impossibly—to
their feet, and their eyes shone with milky light as they
dragged weapons with them.

"What in the actual hells...?" Braddok said, taking a bewildered step back.

"Sort of how I imagined hells, actually," Chez said, as they
gathered together, backs to one another with Imari at the
center.

Bahdra's dead now surrounded them.

Jeric wiped the back of his hand across his forehead. He was
tired. Imari could see the strain on his features. On all of their
features.

"Not how I thought I was gonna go, honestly," Aksel
commented.

"You giving up that easily, Aks?" Stanis drawled, licking his
lips as he turned over his sword.

"All I can say is that you're gonna be paying me for the rest of
my life for the mental damages this nightmare is gonna cause,"
Chez said.

"What about *my* mental damages for putting up with your sorry ass?" Braddok said.

Imari couldn't believe they were joking right now, but they all fell quiet as Bahdra drew closer.

Soulless black eyes shone from the depths of Bahdra's heavy hood, and his skin was so covered in ink, it looked as though he'd been created from it. The air around him warped and blurred, like heat rising off Majutén sand, and Imari wondered how in the world she had ever thought that she could possibly help Jeric against *this*.

So we meet at last, sulaziér.

The voice exploded in her mind. She wasn't unfamiliar with this kind of communication. Ventus could speak in her head, but this was worse. It forced out every other independent thought, overwhelming her sense of self, and rattled her skull.

Imari ground her teeth, straining against the sharp and sudden pressure in her head. "What do you want?" Imari snarled aloud. She would not talk to him in her head. That felt too much like surrender.

The dead sidled closer. Jenya and the others raised weapons, ready to fight, but the dead did not attack. Not yet. They dangled at the end of Bahdra's invisible strings, awaiting their puppetmaster's command.

You, Bahdra spoke simply, in her mind.

Imari winced from the pressure, and she remembered Fyri. "I'll die before I help you."

I don't think that's true.

And then Bahdra curled his fingers into a fist, and his dead attacked.

Imari was ready for it. She let notes fly as Bahdra's dead clashed weapons against Jeric and the others. But she did not play for Bahdra's dead.

She focused her attention on the source: Bahdra. On that thick black cloud of shadow.

She was distantly aware of Jeric and the others fighting, brutally hacking and cutting to disable men and women that no longer felt pain. Imari looked to the stars struggling at the fringe of Bahdra's massive black cloud.

No, a *poison*.

Imari could taste it on her tongue, the cadaverine taint of rot and decay. It nearly made her gag, and her trill hitched, but she pushed on. Harder and harder, trying to find the tone of those lights at the fringe. Trying to find the stars Bahdra had snuffed out with his evil.

But *wards*. The more she pushed into that cloud, the more she tasted acid and corrosion. The more it pushed down her throat, as if simply by touching it with her notes, she connected her line of Shah power to his, and she could not draw on her power without drawing his poison with it.

Suddenly, the line between them snapped taut.

He knew what she was trying to do, and he was pulling *back*.

Imari's lungs pinched, and a sharp pressure pushed through her core, as if Bahdra's line had latched on to her stomach and was dragging it out through her mouth.

Imari cut her note short, unable to bear the pressure anymore. She bent forward, lungs burning and chest aching, and suddenly, a tentacle of inky darkness lashed out from Bahdra's inked palm, right past Jeric and the others, and whipped around Imari's wrist.

Imari cried out as it cinched tight. She clawed at it with her free hand, but her fingers slipped right through. The inky tentacle was somehow both substantive and immaterial.

Another tendril lashed out from Bahdra's palm, coiled around her ankle, and yanked her foot out from under her.

The flute flew from her hands, and Imari braced herself for impact with the ground, but the tether jerked her upward, suspending her upside down in midair. Jeric yelled her name, but he couldn't get to her. He was surrounded by Bahdra's dead, while Imari desperately reached for her flute with her free hand.

A third tendril caught that free wrist. Imari yelled through her teeth, wriggling and writhing, kicking her free leg while Bahdra's inky black tendrils held her suspended.

"Let me go!" Imari yelled.

You will help me, little sulaziér. Or you will watch them die.

Imari could not physically break Bahdra's tether, nor did she have her flute to help her, so she did the only thing she could think of.

She hummed.

Just one note, holding it steady despite her panting breath, and she focused her thoughts on the well of Shah power within. Willing the heat to rise and burn Bahdra's bindings away.

Immediately, a flare of fire shot through her chest.

Imari gasped in surprise and pain, and she lost the note as heat licked down her arm. The tendril coiled around her right hand ignited in a sudden burst of blue flame, and disintegrated into ash.

But her hand was free.

Yes!

Imari was about to hum again when more voices sounded from an alley to her right. She glanced over as a handful of saredd and—

"Papa!" she screamed, simultaneously relieved that he was alive, but also horrified that he was here. He was covered in blood from head to toe, and a deep, ugly gash dripped fresh blood down his cheek.

But he was alive.

He spotted her and stopped in his tracks. She watched him follow the tether to Bahdra. And then she watched him run.

At Bahdra.

Inexplicable fear seized her heart as he pushed through the dead, his gaze fixed on the Mo'Ruk shiva. He moved with singular purpose, hacking and shoving through any dead who got in his way, while his saredd fought with Jeric and the others, and Imari dangled over them all like a sacrifice.

Imari would have been impressed by her papa's speed and agility, had she not been simultaneously overcome with fear. She expected Bahdra to stop her papa any moment, but Bahdra simply stood there, watching the sar fight his way toward him.

Four paces.

Sar Branón ducked from a dead man's sword, shoved another back and kept running.

Three paces.

Two.

Sar Branón yelled and swung his sword.

And Bahdra shot a spear of inky darkness right through her papa's heart.

"*No*," Imari gasped.

Her papa froze, sword high. His eyes widened, and he staggered back as his sword slipped from his grip and clattered to the stones.

And he collapsed.

"*NOOOO!*" Imari screamed.

That one word shattered through space and time, punching through the street in a single, concussive blast of air. It exploded with such force, it knocked Jeric and the others to the ground, while Bahdra's dead exploded in sprays of blood and body parts. Bits of loose plaster rained from the building's facades all around them; cracks splintered the walls. Searing heat tore through Imari, and in the next moment, she was on the ground with ash floating all around her.

Bahdra's tendrils were gone.

But Imari hardly noticed as she shoved herself to her feet and sprinted past the unconscious forms of Jeric and the others, through the blood and gore.

Straight for Bahdra.

She would kill him. She would kill him with her bare hands.

Bahdra whipped out a hand, and another tentacle of inky darkness shot out. But this time, his motions seemed sluggish. She could see the tentacle arcing toward her, follow its trajectory, and she easily dodged its path. It struck the stones beside her.

Bahdra's black eyes narrowed.

He loosed another. And another. She twisted and dove. She was three paces from him.

Two.

And then she struck an invisible wall so hard, the force sent her flying back half a dozen paces. She landed on her rear, rolling over four times before her body finally stopped. An invisible grip caught hold of her before she had the chance to climb to her feet, and then that force whipped her upright and lifted her until her feet dangled inches from the ground. That same force spun her around, and she found herself face to face with a nightmare.

It wasn't Bahdra.

She had never seen this man before. If power had a form, it was this. Like a god, he stood present and yet removed from this world. In it, but not *of*. Power leaked from his pores—so strong, the air around him shimmered with it, and all the world fell silent, as if his very presence absorbed ambient sound. Strong bones composed his severe and angular face, and he had no hair, no brows or lashes. Only more inked glyphs where hair should have been. And as she gazed into his obsidian eyes—those cold, contemptuous, and cunning eyes—she spotted something wild within. Some writhing monstrosity hidden just behind this steel visage of power.

And yet, as she stared at this stranger, she couldn't help but feel that he wasn't a stranger at all.

There was something...familiar.

Imari's lungs burned as she strained to breathe against that invisible vice, while the figure held her effortlessly before him.

Those cold eyes bored into hers. "It is good to finally look upon you with my own eyes, little sulaziér."

Her blood ran cold.

That voice. She *had* heard that voice before.

When it had belonged to the chakran.

"You..." Imari gasped, strained against her hold. "*Azir...?*"

That was why he had seemed familiar. Bahdra had given the chakran his body—or *a* body. Azir looked different than the memory Tallyn had shown her, and yet there was also a hint of that man.

Azir's eyes gleamed. "Clever girl. But not so clever. You should have listened to your dear papa."

Imari whipped her head forward and slammed her forehead into his nose.

Azir reeled back a step, hands clasped over his face. His eyes flashed with rage, and suddenly that pressure around Imari squeezed so tight, she choked on air.

"Careful, little sulaziér," Azir said, dropping his hands. Blood trickled from his nose. He didn't bother wiping it away. Not even as it slipped into his mouth. "One more move like that, and he will suffer for it."

He gestured to Jeric, who was now conscious and being shoved to his knees by three Sol Velorians. Jenya and the others were awake and being rounded up as well. Imari hadn't even realized more Sol Velorian fighters had entered the street, and it was then she realized how quiet the entire city had become.

The fight for Trier was over, and Trier had lost.

"What shall I do with them, my lord?" Bahdra asked, those soulless eyes fixed on Jeric.

Imari's vision started to swim, and Azir released the pressure just enough for her to breathe again.

"Hold them for now. They might come of use," Azir replied, and then he smiled at Imari. "Welcome to my new world, little sulaziér."

"Their hearts no longer sought to follow Asorai's perfect will, and so Asorai gave them over to their depravity."

~ *Excerpt from* Il Tonté,
As recorded in the First Verses by
Juvia, Liagé First High Sceptor.

33

"Lestra," Azir said sharply.

Lestra.

The one Rasmin had mentioned. The Seer who had made the Sight Veil, who was powerful enough to instill fear in both Rasmin and Jeric. Watching her approach, Imari understood why.

Lestra's face was a patchwork of skin, as if she'd been pulled right out of the ground where she'd rotted and then stitched together, old skin and new. Some of the seams still bled. Her features were overly sharp, her chin tapered to an unyielding point, and white eyes gazed out from beneath a heavy hood.

Suddenly, horribly, Imari understood.

Lestra was a Mo'Ruk. One of Azir's four, just like Bahdra. Which meant...

Bahdra had brought them *all* back. Those were the five points of enormous power Imari had felt straining the well of Shah power.

Maker have mercy.

She should have listened to her papa. She didn't have the power to fight this. She didn't know if she *ever* would.

Lestra stopped before them, but Imari looked past, at the slumped form of her papa. The strings of her heart pulled tight, and her eyes burned.

I'm so sorry, Papa...

"Lock her beneath Vondar," Azir said to Lestra. "Learn what you can."

Lestra bowed her head. "Yes, my lord. What of the Wolf and his dogs?" She had a voice like a serpent, more hiss than tone.

Azir considered, those obsidian eyes fixed on Imari, while Imari still struggled to breath, suspended in midair.

"Throw them in the cages," Azir said with dark amusement. A flicker of madness shone in his eyes.

"It will be done, my lord," Bahdra said.

Without warning, the pressure released around Imari, and she dropped like a stone. The second she hit the ground, firm hands grabbed her arms and hoisted her back to her feet.

"And this?" Lestra had retrieved Imari's flute, but Imari noticed the Mo'Ruk Seer did not touch it with her bare hands. She'd pulled her sleeve over her fingers to hold it.

Azir's hand twitched, as though he meant to reach for the object, but stopped himself. "Hold on to it, for now."

"I won't help you," Imari snarled. "Whatever it is you're planning, I won't do it."

Azir regarded her. "I think you will."

Imari felt a slight shift of pressure, a push of air, and Jeric gasped, clutching at his throat as if he suddenly couldn't breathe.

Imari thrashed—futilely—against her captors. "Stop it!" she yelled, but Azir did not stop. "Stop—please!"

"So it *is* true," Azir said simply, watching her with those cold, black eyes.

Jeric's neck corded; his lips turned blue.

"No, please!" Imari cried. "Let him go!"

The pressure stopped, and Jeric sagged forward on his hands, sucking down air.

And Azir smiled cruelly. "I see that we understand each other."

Imari ground her teeth together, trembling in her captor's grip. Furious and...defeated.

Azir gave her one last pitying glance, then turned to Bahdra. Their gazes locked, the silence stretched. Imari knew they were speaking through that mental connection, and then Bahdra bowed his head, accepting whatever command Azir had given.

Azir turned back to Imari. "Do not disappoint me, little sulazièr." He stroked her cheek, and she jerked her head away with revulsion. The gesture only seemed to amuse him further, for his thin lips curled. "In time, you'll learn to appreciate what I have done."

Imari bit down her retort, so that Jeric wouldn't suffer for it.

Azir's eyes shone. "Ah, you see? I knew you would come around."

Imari seethed as Azir turned and strode on, his cloak billowing powerfully behind him. The new master of this broken city.

Bahdra moved before Imari, and a wave of fury burned through her. She writhed and jerked against the men holding her arms, but their grip remained firm.

"I will kill you," she snarled, spitting at him, but even that missed its mark.

Bahdra looked at her without expression, and then he bit down hard. He wiped his finger against the inside of his cheek and pulled away blood—thick and bright—then reached toward Imari.

Imari squirmed. "What are you—"

Bahdra touched her forehead.

The effect was immediate. A shock of cold stabbed Imari's skull where Bahdra touched, like a spear of ice. The sensation cascaded from that point, cold as the Kjürda river. It flooded her veins, all the way to her marrow.

Completely severing her connection to the Shah.

Imari tried to reach for that infinite well, but it was like trying to move a phantom limb. It simply was not there.

"She is ready," Bahdra said.

Lestra looked over Imari with that unblinking, inhuman white gaze. "You'll walk," she said, then she turned and strode on.

The Sol Velorians released Imari, but the tip of a scim pressed sharply between her shoulder blades. And Imari walked. She caught Jeric's gaze, and the fury in them could have set Trier on fire all over again.

Don't do anything stupid, she tried to communicate with her eyes.

She didn't know if he understood, and if he had, she didn't know if he'd obey.

Imari followed Lestra through the rubble, the bodies, the smoke. Little fires burned everywhere, eating whatever they could, and silhouettes moved through the haze, picking through the rubble, the bodies, searching for treasure and survivors.

And bodies lay everywhere, bloodied and charred. The air was thick with singed hair and skin and devastation, and Imari wondered how in the stars mankind had learned to be so cruel. With every painful step, she saw those last few moments of her papa's life. The determination in his gaze, the love. He hadn't spared a single thought for his own fate. He had charged a foe far greater than himself, not caring that his steel was nothing to Bahdra's power.

He had only thought of Imari.

How cruel that she should spend so much of her life wanting her papa, only for him to be ripped right out of it.

A tear slid down Imari's cheek. She hastily wiped it away, not wanting to grieve here for the enemy to see. Not wanting them to know that she was breaking.

Imari hardly noticed when they reached Vondar's wall. Where the gate had been, now stood a gaping hole. Brick and rock mounded on either side, while the gate lay a dozen yards away, completely torn in half.

So many saredd and city guards lay pinned beneath it, dead.

One of them was Sebharan.

Imari pressed her lips together, and focused her eyes decidedly ahead, vowing to make Azir and Bahdra and all of the Mo'Ruk pay for what they had done.

At the top of Vondar's stairs, the legion waited. Darkness frothed at Astrid's feet, but Imari was happy to see that her face had suffered new scars. Imari didn't see Rasmin anywhere; she didn't know if he'd survived.

Imari caught the legion's gaze as she strode past, and the legion smiled grotesquely as Imari followed Lestra into the atrium.

Where more death and more blood waited. Sol Velorians were already working to remove the bodies and pile them outside to burn.

Imari followed Lestra down to the dungeons, past the cell where they'd kept Astrid, though the warded skal door had been ripped clean from its hinges. Two dead bodies lay before it, eyes missing and skin stained in a web of black veins.

Lestra stopped at the cell at the end, opened the door, and waited for Imari to step inside. Imari didn't get a chance to choose, because her guard shoved her on through the door.

"Sit." Lestra pointed at the center of the small, rectangular stone room.

Imari did not sit fast enough, and the same guard knocked in her knees with the butt of his scim. Imari dropped at once. Lestra knelt before her and grabbed her hand without preamble. Her grip was much stronger than Imari had expected, and cold as ice.

And then pressure—sharp pressure that squeezed all over Imari's body, and the world spun in a blur.

Lestra was sharing her Sight, showing Imari memories.

No.

Lestra was watching *Imari's* memories. Tallyn had never done this, never even asked, and Imari had never really considered that his gift could go both ways. Of course it could go both ways. That was how Rasmin had learned so much—

The pressure squeezed hard, and Imari gasped. She felt like a cloth drenched with memories suddenly wrung out while Lestra drank those fat drops of excess. The past blurred in dizzying color, images flashing and sounds warping, tone over tone as multiple scenes superimposed.

Imari's stomach turned sour, and she thought she might vomit.

Suddenly, she saw Sorai dead on the floor. She saw all the moments after: her flight to The Wilds with her papa's saredd. She saw Tolya.

More blurs and flashes as Lestra sifted through her mind. Distantly, Imari felt her hand squirm in Lestra's grip, but that grip was a vice Imari could not break.

She saw Jeric.

She saw the first moment Jeric had walked into Tolya's house, and there the flashes slowed. As if Lestra savored these memories, lapping up the drops. She took her time over Imari's journey through The Wilds with Jeric, the shades. When they were naked together in the cave, and when they were in Gavet's cellar, where he'd kissed her. Lestra paused there too, and Imari's fury burned hot. These were *her* memories, these private moments shared between them, and she hated that Lestra had—

Lestra moved on. To Imari's practicing in Skyhold's dungeon, to Rasmin. Lestra lingered there a bit, and then they were in Skyhold's hall, where Imari wove Astrid's demon back to shadow.

More flashes.

More blurs.

Distorted sound and distant echoes.

Imari was with Taran, trying to learn how to channel her

power. Then other nights, when Imari had healed the sick in E'Centro.

More flashes.

Jeric in Gamla's chambers, while she bandaged his wound.

Jeric in *her* chambers, the two of them holding her flute between them. Kissing.

Imari felt her real self snarl, and then the images abruptly stopped. Lestra knelt before her, looking at her with those milky white eyes. And Imari vomited.

Lestra might have frowned. It was hard to tell because Lestra's lips were too thin. Still, she knelt there a moment, studying her charge with a look that was impossible to read.

At last, she stood.

"What do you *want* from me?" Imari croaked, spitting residual bile from her mouth.

Lestra stopped at the door, her long, inked fingers draped against the frame. "See that she has water," she said to the guard, then slammed the door shut.

Plunging Imari into total darkness.

TALLYN PEERED out of the alley.

After he had left Imari and the small prayer room, he had tried his very best to sleep, but sleep had evaded him. So he had gone for a walk. He'd enchanted his scars so that the sight of him would not frighten the guards at Trier's main gate, and thus had easily walked into the city.

Where his unease had intensified.

He'd sensed a pervasive surge of Shah power as he'd made his way toward E'Centro, though when he'd reached out with his Sight, he could See nothing but haze and shadows. Then Rasmin had flown over his head—west, for the Baragas—and had flown right back. Straight for Vondar.

Tallyn had known in that instant, as that rush of Shah power crashed over him in a tide: Bahdra. And Bahdra wasn't alone. Tallyn had stood deliberating, wondering which path would be most effective against the strong forces of Shah that were too much for the people of Trier to withstand.

Time.

That was all he could hope for.

And so he had sprinted for the Qazzat and rang the giant bell.

And rang.

He had looked out from his post, watching as the city came alive. As another one of Kazak's spheres of guardian fire descended, and landed right on the tower where he had stood.

There was light and heat; the world exploded.

And then there was nothing.

Tallyn did not know how much time had passed when he'd finally opened his eyes, but in that moment, he'd simply been thankful he had eyes to open. He found himself atop a heap of rubble, the bell tower having collapsed, taking out the entire Qazzat during its fall. Bodies littered the ground, some pinned beneath enormous hunks of plaster, and everything was covered in a thin layer of dust—including him. Which was probably why no one had found him.

The Maker had spared him again.

For a moment, he lay listening. Stretching out with his senses as much as he dared, because if Liagé were near, they would feel the resonant ripples of Shah power, and his unexpected presence would be his greatest weapon.

He sensed other ripples of Shah from various points throughout the city. Five of them surged with a force he had not felt in a *very* long time. He did not need his Sight to know who they were, and he silently cursed himself for not realizing it sooner: Bahdra had brought back the other Mo'Ruk.

That was why he and Rasyamin had not been able to See.

Lestra had blocked their Sight. Stars be damned, he should have put it together before.

Still, he waited, listening to the occasional shout, and when he was certain no one stood within his immediate vicinity, he peeled himself from the rubble and glanced around. Smoke stung his eyes and little patches of fire still burned upon the ground.

Tallyn crawled down the pile and wiped dust from his eye. He didn't have time to linger. Imari needed his help—somehow.

A thunder of footsteps approached, and so Tallyn ducked back into the shadows, behind the rubble. A dozen Sol Velorians marched past, dragging Istraan women and children with them, and Tallyn's chest weighed heavy. This was precisely why he had abandoned Azir's and Ventus's ways in the end—their hearts had corrupted. They'd both done whatever was right in their own eyes and used for evil what the Maker had intended for good. What they needed—what they'd always needed—was a leader who did not set themselves *above* others, but put others first.

Someone like Imari.

And she needed his help.

He waited until the guards and survivors had passed out of sight, and then he moved.

He crept into the alley, looking both ways across a street littered with bodies and plaster and rock. So many dead. Mostly Istraan. They hadn't stood a chance, not against Azir and four Mo'Ruk. Not when they'd abandoned all the artifacts that might have protected them.

Tallyn crept on, keeping to shadows and stopping whenever he heard voices. He made a hasty enchantment to veil himself—nothing too powerful that would draw attention, but just enough to make anyone nearby glance right over him.

He crossed the edge of Jadarr's wide plaza, but the temple itself had collapsed completely, leveled to rubble and flame, their manmade gods crushed beneath the will of other men. He spotted the crimson robes of kahar buried beneath, and he wondered if the Kourana had been inside too.

But he couldn't waste any more time on reflection, and so he hurried on, toward E'Centro.

He knew Taran was no longer there, but if she were anything like Tolya, she would have left something behind. Just in case.

And Tallyn needed all the help he could get.

He reached the end of the street to find E'Centro miraculously untouched. He immediately wondered how much of E'Centro had fallen prey to Bahdra's manipulations. They would have been easy to persuade, so hopeless and starved and downtrodden.

The district lay mostly quiet, though a handful of Sol Velorians carried what little belongings they possessed out of what Tallyn imagined had been their specified living quarters. Tallyn pressed on toward Taran's home. He knew where it was; he'd found it the day he'd searched Trier for signs of Shah power, but he hadn't gone inside. He reached the beaded doorway and paused.

These little chips of rock and cactus wood had immediately given Taran's residence away. Innocent to the naked eye, and even most Liagé, because Taran had taken great care hiding the essence of what they were: wards to shield, and wards to conceal, so that no one would sense the power residing behind them.

And two strands were missing.

They could have fallen from the explosions. Or someone could have taken them.

Tallyn checked behind him once, grabbed the beads so that they would not clatter as he held them back, and stepped through.

He felt another presence then. A pulse of Shah, coming from upstairs—and a strong one. He considered turning back, but a talent that strong would have sensed him the moment he'd stepped through those beads.

And he couldn't shake the familiar taste of it. Like fruit from a tree he knew very well.

So Tallyn ascended the stairs, not caring overly for stealth, and when he reached the top and peered into the open doorway, he stilled.

A young woman stood within, probably nearing twenty years of age. She wore the red cloth of Ashova's servants, though hers were torn and dirtied, and blood stained the hem.

And her hands, which were raised, preparing to throw some enchantment at whoever walked through that door.

"Niá," Tallyn said.

Niá hesitated, and her wild eyes pulled with confusion.

"I'm a friend," Tallyn continued. "I knew Tolya very well, and I knew of your oza."

At mention of her oza, Niá's expression broke. "Who are you?" Her voice trembled.

"My name is Tallyn," he replied.

"What do you want?" Niá still hadn't lowered her hands.

Tallyn considered her. "I want this to stop."

"Stop *what*, exactly? It's *done*. Trier is taken—"

"Trier is just the beginning."

"And what do I care?" she snarled. "It's nothing they don't deserve for what they've done to us."

Tallyn looked hard at her. "You don't really believe that. Your oza certainly did not."

Niá's jaw clenched. "And she's dead because of those beliefs."

"Yes, your oza is dead. But her beliefs are not, and it is for those beliefs that I have come here, looking for a way to see them through."

Niá gazed at him, shaking her head as her hands dropped and her eyes shone with emotion. "There is no way—don't you see? I loved my oza, but what she wanted—what she dreamed...*it's not possible.*"

"It *is*," Tallyn said. "And Taran believed so fully in that dream that she risked *everything* to show a lost young woman the way the Maker intended. Not the path men like Bahdra walk. That was why she and Tolya refused Azir, instead choosing to fight alongside the Provinces, and without them—without their clairvoyance, and stubborn resolve in the face of overwhelming opposition—Azir would have won that war."

He could see that Niá did not know this. That Taran had not told her.

"Oh, yes," Tallyn continued. "They were the most talented enchantresses of our age, and together, they were almost unstoppable. And I daresay their talent passed on." He looked pointedly at Niá, who shrunk back a little, in shame.

"And look how the Provinces repaid them," Niá snarled.

"The Provinces were afraid. I do not say this to excuse their actions, but men do horrible things out of fear. Your *leader* is doing nothing to quell those fears, either, but I tell you this: There is another way, Niá, and I believe I've found you for this reason."

"And what can we possibly do against Azir, four Mo'Ruk, and an army?"

Tallyn smiled slowly. "Don't you know? Those are the Maker's favorite odds, for that is where he shines most brilliantly."

34

Azir Mubarék stormed Vondar's halls. He did not notice the blood, or destruction. His stride did not break for the bodies, as Sol Velorians dragged the dead away. His gaze fixed ahead, intent on one.

"My lord." Su'Vi—his Mo'Ruk enchantress—bowed her head as he approached.

Azir stopped at the crest of the dungeon's stair while gazing into the shadows. He could feel that vile taint even from where he stood. "Take me to the creature."

"Of course," Su'Vi replied.

She turned and descended the stair. Azir followed.

Su'Vi strode past the sulaziér's short corridor, where two men stood guard, and turned a corner. Their corridor ended at a small skal door.

Azir scanned Su'Vi's work, ensuring her recent enchantments would be enough. He held his palm before the Corinthian metal, felt the power pulse in magnetic waves of energy.

Because Bahdra had defied the natural order in bringing them back, their connection to the Shah had not returned without damages. Azir felt it to his core. He could access the

Shah, but it was harder to hold. Harder to grasp. His line was frayed and unwieldy. His Mo'Ruk had not awoken unscathed, either. This enchantment had strained Su'Vi greatly, though she had done her best to hide it. Such spells had cost her very little before; they cost her everything now.

But not for much longer, now that they had the sulaziér, and then they would bring this world to its knees.

"Open it."

Su'Vi spoke a word. Shah power pushed from her lips, the fresh engravings flared with white-blue light, and the door cracked open to darkness.

Su'Vi stood back, waiting for her lord's instruction.

And Azir stepped through.

The creature within had been chained to stand, though it sagged against the restraints. Its body was naked and grossly emaciated, and its arms bent at awkward angles. Azir had seen to that first. He would not have his favorite new pet flying away.

Upon hearing Azir enter, the creature looked up from wild brows.

"Dear, *dear* Rasya," Azir said, and clucked his tongue. "You don't look so well."

Rasya only rasped in response.

Azir stopped before Rasya and struck him across the face. Rasya whirled back, held aloft by the chains bolted to the ceiling. Rasya licked bloodied lips. A blot of bright red against the pale.

"The only question is what to do with you," Azir continued. "For all you've done against our people."

"Let one without blame cast the first stone—"

Azir struck Rasya again, this time in the stomach. Rasya lurched forward, gasping for breath as Azir walked around and grabbed him by the ear.

"You betrayed me," Azir snarled, his spittle flying.

"You betray us all by what you seek," Rasya managed.

Azir paused, and smiled wickedly. "So the great Rasyamin has finally discovered the truth. Tell me, Head Inquisitor: How many of our people did you slaughter so that you could piece the past together?"

"And I would do it again if it stopped you."

Azir pulled that ear harder. "Yes, and look how effective you've been."

Rasya strained against Azir's grip. "You won't...win..."

Azir pressed his mouth right against Rasya's bloodied ear. "Your hope in the sulaziér is misplaced, my dear Rasya."

"She isn't Fyri."

Azir sank his teeth into Rasya's ear, and Rasya cried out—straining as Azir tore a chunk free and spit it on the ground. Azir released him, chains rattling as he moved to stand before the creature, and he gazed down upon Rasya's face, now dripping with fresh blood. "Do not speak her name in my presence again."

Rasya sagged, and Azir left, slamming the door behind him. He looked at Su'Vi, who waited, head bowed. "Keep him alive. I will personally dispose of him when I return."

———

"FASTER, DOG," snarled a surly Sol Velorian man with a long braided beard, who held a scim's tip firmly between Jeric's shoulders.

Jeric raised his hands. "Careful with that," Jeric replied in Common.

The man only shoved harder, so Jeric increased his pace. Slightly.

Almost immediately after the Mo'Ruk had taken Imari away, Jeric and his men—and Jenya—had been completely stripped of their weapons and paraded through Trier's flaming ruins like a war prize, by no fewer than twenty-three Sol Velorians.

Jeric knew that Imari was the only reason they'd been spared. It was his greatest advantage—and quite possibly his *only* advantage, he thought, as he took in the destruction Azir and his Mo'Ruk had wrought. They had leveled an entire city, almost entirely unopposed, in the span of two hours.

He would have been impressed, if he wasn't so godsdamned pissed off.

"Such a waste..." Jeric continued in Common, as he memorized this new map.

"Cou'za?" the man behind him spat. *What?*

"Such a beautiful city, and you *incinerated* it."

"Another word, *Corazzi*," the guard said in thickly-accented Common this time, "and I'll carve out your tongue and feed it to the dogs."

Jeric eyed the guard, but he shut his mouth and continued mapping the landscape around him.

And it was a nightmare.

Most of Trier lay in ruin, and many of the invading Sol Velorians were busy heaping the dead into piles, burning them, giving the air a strong metallic scent. He spotted others ducking into buildings, searching for survivors. He watched them drag out a family. They took the children. Beat the father. And three of them dragged the woman back inside as she screamed.

Jeric curled his hands into fists and looked furiously away.

Their escort led them into what had been Trier's infamous bazaar. Yesterday, it had been a canvas of color and life. Tonight it was a graveyard of flame and shadow. Booths had collapsed, flame licked whatever was left of textiles and collapsed awnings, and then Jeric spotted what he suspected would be their temporary prison.

Cages.

Literal cages.

He'd noticed them yesterday, when Ricón had given him a tour of the city. Those cages had held boar and a wild cat. Now, they held bloodied remains and singed fur.

Jeric eyed his guard through his periphery. And then he tripped over a broken beam.

Jeric overcorrected the fall and stumbled back into his guard, who barely moved his scim in time. But Jeric used that motion to his advantage and let his weight fall completely, knocking them both to the ground. The man cursed, and two more Sol Velorians stepped in. They grabbed Jeric's arms and yanked him back to his feet.

Jeric's guard stood, cursing obscenities at Jeric while Jeric pretended not to understand them. The man patted himself down, and his hand stopped at his waist, where he'd clipped three throwing stars.

Now there were two.

His eyes narrowed on Jeric. "You took one," he said in Sol Velorian, and Jeric gave him a dumb look. The man growled and took a step closer. "You took one," he repeated in Common.

Jeric frowned. "Took one...what."

The man's expression darkened. "Zav'im." *Check him.*

The two men, who'd pulled Jeric to his feet, stepped close and started patting Jeric down. Arms and legs and backside.

"Not going to search the goods?" Jeric eyed them, flashing his canines.

One of the guards slammed an elbow across Jeric's face. Jeric turned with the impact, absorbing the force as he licked blood from his lips, and then two men shoved him into the open cage.

Jeric nearly—genuinely—tripped, and he grabbed hold of a bar to catch himself. The metal still felt hot. He couldn't stand fully, however; the cage was only as tall as his shoulders, and he was just dropping to a crouch when they shoved Chez and Stanis in after him. The cage wasn't wide, nor very long, so all three of them were forced to cram together hunched in a line. Aksel, Braddok, and Jenya were shoved into the second cage.

Braddok looked thrilled. Jenya did not.

A middle-aged Sol Velorian woman wrapped a chain around the bars and secured it with a lock.

"How do you like your cage, dog?" the surly man sneered through the bars, in accented Common so that Jeric would understand the insult.

A few of them laughed and jeered. One threw a scrap of wood through the bars, which landed at Jeric's feet.

"Go fetch," that one said, but in Sol Velorian, and the others laughed. "Not good enough? How about a bone? I'm sure we can find one around here somewhere..."

Jeric watched them without expression as they finally turned away, arguing over who would take first watch. Four stayed behind and the rest walked on.

"You get it, Wolf?" Stanis whispered, crouched right beside him.

Jeric reached into the front of his pants and withdrew the throwing star.

In the next cage, Jenya raised both brows.

"I promise mine's more impressive," Braddok murmured to her, and then yelped a second later as she knocked him on his rear.

"Now what?" Chez asked. His left eye had swollen shut, and dust stuck to all the blood soaked into his beard.

Jeric eyed those four Sol Velorian guards, who now shared a bottle of nazzat between them. "Now, we wait."

35

Imari did not know how long she sat in darkness. Time seemed irrelevant, each breath one more reminder that she was alive and her papa was not.

Over and over again, she saw her papa's face. She saw that bolt of darkness strike his chest. She saw his eyes widen, his lips part in those last few seconds of his life before death took him, because of her.

An entire city had been brought to ruin—*because of her.*

Because she had been born with something others wanted. No matter where she went, those she loved would be in danger.

Imari curled her hands into fists and pulled against the rope binding her wrists to the wall of her small prison. Twine cut into her skin, but she welcomed the pain. That mark on her forehead persisted, severing her from the Shah. Imari had not realized how much strength she'd drawn from that well of power until it was gone. Instead, a cold sludge moved like syrup through her veins, leaving her bucket dry and empty.

Leaving her utterly alone.

Where are you? she cried in her mind.

And.

Why do you spare my life only to fill it with pain?

It was too much. All of it. To get back the life she had dreamed of for years, only to have it ripped from her feeble hands. Her grief was a crushing weight on top of her, grinding her bones, and Imari curled into a ball on her side, her hands tied behind her as she softly cried.

At some point long after she'd cried her eyes dry, the door to her prison cracked open, and light stabbed into her cell. Imari blinked aching and puffy eyes as a dark silhouette filled the door.

Azir.

"You..." Imari snarled, forcing herself up. She ran at him, but the rope jerked her right back.

"I must say, little sulaziér. I like your fervor," he said, though she could not see his face. The light glowed behind him, leaving his features in shadow. But then someone handed him a lantern. Light danced eerily upon his harsh features, making the pits of his eyes more cavernous, with chips of obsidian glimmering in their depths. He looked at her as one might study a curiosity, and then he stepped into her cell, set the lantern upon the floor, and shut the door behind him.

"What have you done with Jeric?" Imari demanded.

A beat. "Your *Wolf*"—he snapped the title, chomping his cracked and gray teeth together—"is safe and secure, as promised."

"So are corpses."

He regarded her, and then he approached slowly, boots crunching softly over the floor's grit. He stopped just out of reach, gazing down upon her, and Imari thought he looked disappointed. As if he'd expected someone else. As if he'd expected *more*.

Imari remembered Fyri, and decided she couldn't blame him. Imari wished she were more too, because Trier's outcome could have been very different.

And even with the mark upon her forehead, with the Shah

wholly cut off from her, she could feel the brush of his power, thick and suffocating and corrupting the air around him, warping it like a mirage.

"Your Wolf and his dogs are alive and well," he continued, with an edge of annoyance, "but how long they remain that way depends on you, little sulaziér."

"And what is it you expect me to do?" Imari spat.

He crouched, those cold black eyes fixed on hers, and Imari felt a strange humming in her bones. "There is something in Sol Velor that I want, and I need your help retrieving it."

That was not the answer Imari had expected.

"You mean Ziyan," she said.

"You may call it whatever you wish," he said simply. "It is still Sol Velor."

"It's a *wasteland*. No one who goes in there comes out alive."

"Tell me, sulaziér," he said smoothly, gazing at his hand while picking dried blood from his fingers. His tranquil expression seemed completely out of place. "Do you know why that is?"

Imari frowned, eyeing him warily as he picked at a particularly large fleck of dried blood upon his knuckle. "I was told the sands eat people alive."

"Oh, they do more than that, little sulaziér."

Imari stared at him. "Are you talking about the tyrcorat?"

His expression brightened as if the very word brought him inexplicable joy. Which would be pure insanity, because *tyrcorat* was the Sol Velorian word for *skin eater*.

Imari had learned about those foul creatures, and not from her kunari. From Ricón. When he'd said the sands would eat people alive, he hadn't been metaphorical. Sometimes, when people would vanish after heading into Ziyan, searching for the Sol Velor's lost treasures, sandstorms would dump their carcasses along the boundary between Ziyan and Istraa—many stripped to the bone. Ricón had seen one.

Imari had never been permitted near the boundary after that.

Azir considered her. "Ah, so you do know."

"Yes, I know they're demons *your Fyri* unleashed right before her power ripped her and all of Sol Velor apart."

For a moment, Azir crouched with impossible stillness. Madness writhed in his eyes, his left hand twitched, and the air around her felt suddenly tight—compressed. Pushing against her body, making each breath a struggle. That mark upon her forehead burned with cold, and then, suddenly, the pressure evaporated.

And Azir smiled.

"They were not unleashed, little sulaziér. Nor are they demons," Azir continued, though his words were clipped. "They are the dead. *Our* dead. They are the souls of our people left behind when their bodies were torn apart in the very same blast that destroyed Sol Velor."

Imari studied him. Oddly, she did not think he was lying about this.

She had never heard that before, and she wondered how *he* had discovered it when he'd been bound to a tree for the past one hundred years.

"Fortunately for us," he continued, "I happen to know an exceedingly talented *shiva* who specializes in dealing with the dead."

"You mean Bahdra." Imari spat the name.

Azir looked pityingly at her. "It is shameful that you have been so deceived against us, little sulaziér—"

"Deceived? All I have to do is look outside—"

Azir grabbed her chin and twisted—hard.

Imari gasped, her words cut off.

"And what of the horrible things they have done to us?" he snarled, his face mere inches from hers. His breath stunk of rot. "The things *your precious Wolf* has done?" His black eyes flashed with barely controlled rage, and Imari knew that Lestra had relayed all of her stolen memories to Azir. "You are a traitor to your own kind, a bastard child of a *weak man*—"

"My papa is twice the man—" Imari started, but Azir twisted her chin harder, and Imari cried out in pain.

"I should have your head on a pike beside Branón's," Azir hissed as his nails dug into her skin. "Let the crows feast on your flesh and pluck out your eyes, until there is nothing left but your skull. And then I would have your skull brought down, and I would crush it and grind it to dust, so that I could drink it with your blood."

He wanted her fear. He relished it.

But Imari would not give it to him. "You call my papa weak, but what are you without your power? You are *nothing*—"

Azir struck her across the face with such force, she toppled back. She fell right on her hands, jamming her thumb into the rock, and she gasped in pain.

Before she could right herself, Azir grabbed her hair and jerked her up, then leaned forward so that they were cheek to cheek.

"You disappoint me, little sulaziér," he said at her ear, in a voice that was incongruously calm compared to the vicious grip of his hand in her hair. "I had so hoped to share my new world with you."

He shoved her down before she could answer.

Imari fell on her face, the ground slammed against her forehead. She was just rolling onto her back when another figure entered the room. For a moment, Imari thought it was Lestra—they bore the same patchwork skin—but as Imari's vision cleared, she saw that this woman's face was notably rounder, and so completely covered in glyphs that the only features Imari could see clearly were her eyes, which gleamed black amidst a canvas of ink.

And in the woman's hands was a pair of Liagé bindings.

Imari tensed back against the wall. "Who are you?"

Two Sol Velorian men stepped into the room and waited just inside the door, while the woman stepped around Imari and snapped the cold metal binds over Imari's wrists. Wardlight flared, and another wave of tingling spread through her body, but this also filled her head. She found it suddenly difficult to think, and a throbbing ache took residence behind her eyes.

The woman studied Imari, watching the transformation. Making sure the binds did their work.

Imari had no idea Liagé binds felt like this. One positive was that they also numbed her anguish and grieving, and for that alone, she considered wearing these bindings forever.

"Bring her," the woman commanded in a rasping voice.

The men didn't hesitate. They cut Imari's ropes, grabbed her shoulders, and hoisted her to her feet, where Imari swayed, unsteady. That icy chill permeated her marrow, making her limbs sluggish and heavy. Everything seemed murky and slow and dull.

The men pushed her into the corridor, where the woman waited. The lantern hung upon the wall, and shadows danced wickedly. The guards shoved Imari after the woman, who did not take the lantern, and they all proceeded down the dark tunnel.

It was too dark to see properly, and between the bindings and enchantment upon her forehead, Imari's feet dragged. They dragged right over a lip in the stone floor that she hadn't noticed in the darkness, and Imari pitched forward. She would have fallen, if one of the men had not caught her. Finally, they reached the stair, and ascended into Vondar proper.

Vondar had survived, but she lay like a fatally wounded warrior. Pots had shattered, dumping earth and foliage upon the tiles, and blood stained the walls and floor, though the sources had been removed. Sol Velorian men and women moved about, picking through scraps, securing corridors. Some, it appeared, had discovered Vondar's vast stores of nazzat, but whatever they were doing, they all stopped the moment they noticed the inked woman.

And then Imari.

Eyes lit with wonder; some bent in whispers. All watched.

Imari wondered what Azir had told them, if he had told them anything. She wondered how they could stand amidst such slaughter. How they could not see that they had just become the very ones they hated.

The woman stopped at the atrium, where a handful of armed Sol Velorians waited, sharing a few bottles of nazzat between them.

"Wait here," the woman said to the guards, and the guards held Imari off to the side while the woman crossed the atrium and strode through the main door.

Imari could just see through to a setting sun. Wards, almost an entire day had passed while she'd been below in that prison. The flames had quieted, but smoke hung like a fog, and the world sat quiet in horror's aftermath.

Sol Velorians looked over at Imari, curious. One approached. "Who's the girl?" he asked one of Imari's captors.

"Not really your business," the captor replied.

The man's eyes lit, he continued forward, his steps uneven.

He'd had a lot to drink.

"You think you're all important now, Beru?" the man drawled, swinging out a bottle of nazzat, which was mostly empty. "He gets reassigned to a Mo'Ruk, and suddenly he's too good for us."

Ah. So the woman was one of Azir's four. Considering all of her glyphs, Imari thought she was probably his enchantress.

Imari's guard—Beru—held out a scim.

The drunken man smiled, but Beru was resolute. The drunk eyed Beru, then Imari, and his gaze moved all over her. Imari steeled herself as that gaze settled on her waist, at the bare strip of skin visible, though it was covered in dirt, as he held the bottle to his lips and drained the last of it.

He pulled the nazzat away. "I think maybe—"

The bottle exploded in his grip. He cried out and jumped

back, clutching his bloodied palm as glass shards rained.

The Mo'Ruk enchantress stood in the doorway, one palm extended, dark eyes fixed on the man, and the man clenched his teeth and scurried off.

The other guards turned their attention away, pretending to be exceedingly busy with their tasks.

Beru shoved Imari after the Mo'Ruk enchantress and through the main doors, to the platform at the top of Vondar's broad steps. At the bottom of those steps, right against the wall, a pile of bodies burned—city guards and saredd and citizens.

A swell of...*something* pushed against Imari's chest, but the Liagé binds made it impossible to determine what that something was, and then it was gone. Drowned in ice-cold sludge.

The scent of burnt flesh hung thickly. One of the watchtowers had collapsed, and the gate hung open like a broken jaw. And above that broken gate stood a line of heads mounted to pikes.

Imari spotted Sebharan, and the Kourana.

Her papa.

Imari felt that swell again—much stronger, this time. It pushed so hard against her lungs, the air squeezed right out of her, and she couldn't breathe. She tried sucking in a breath, but her lungs would not fill. It was as though a vice clamped around her chest, making it impossible to expand. Dots swam before her eyes, the world tilted, and she collapsed.

Beru caught her shoulders.

She thought she heard the guard say something, but his voice was distant and murky. Suddenly, her forehead tingled where Bahdra had touched it, the pressure around her chest relaxed, and Imari found she could breathe again.

The enchantress stood at the bottom of the steps, watching her with one hand extended. Seeing that Imari was breathing again, the woman lowered her hand.

Beside her, a dozen armed Sol Velorians waited, mounted upon camels. Imari spotted ten men and two women, and two more camels stood with empty saddles awaiting mounts. Beru pulled Imari forward just as Azir strode through the main gate with the other three Mo'Ruk.

The sight made Imari's breath catch.

It reminded her so much of Ventus and his silent that Imari wondered if this was precisely Ventus's inspiration for his cruel reign in The Wilds.

She recognized Bahdra and Lestra, but the third she had not seen. She assumed he was Azir's Mo'Ruk guardian. Like the others, his skin was a gruesome patchwork of humanity, but his build was significantly wider and broader, and he wore two swords crossed at his back.

Azir stopped just inside the gate, looked over the riders, over Imari, and he gave his enchantress a sharp, satisfied nod. Bahdra approached a camel and mounted one.

But Imari was no longer looking at Azir or his Mo'Ruk. She was looking past him, where a certain demon had just walked through the gate, dragging someone behind it.

Imari's heart squeezed. *Kai.*

Kai was naked and leashed like a dog, covered in filth and dried blood, his knees scraped and bleeding. An enchanted collar encircled his neck, which glowed even as he crouched there, and that collar was attached to a chained leash, which Astrid held.

Astrid's pure black eyes landed on Imari, and the demon smiled viciously with Astrid's bloodied lips.

"Ah, yes. I did forget to mention that we caught a stray," Azir said lightly, noting where Imari's attention had drifted. "My leje was just taking him for a walk around the city, weren't you, pet?"

Astrid gave Kai's chain a hard pull, and Kai fell on his face.

"*Kai...*" Imari reached for him, but Beru jerked her back.

A few Sol Velorians laughed, while Kai tried to scramble back to his feet. One walked over and kicked him in the stomach, and he fell back to the ground.

Imari closed her eyes and turned her face away.

"Oh, no, no, no," Azir said with a tsk-tsk-tsk. He grabbed her chin and turned her face, pulling one of her eyelids open with his thumb. "Watch."

Imari's chest shook as they kicked him, beat him. All the while Astrid stood smiling at her, holding his chain.

"*Please...*" Imari managed.

"Do you know where we found him?" Azir asked, as if causing her further pain was his greatest joy.

Imari did not want to hear the answer.

"Ashova's." Azir looked back at Kai, who lay on the ground, moaning and barely moving. "I understand he visited there often. Do you know what happens at Ashova's?" he asked with that mocking lightness, and then clucked his tongue. Imari's eyes burned, and it wasn't from the smoke. "Of course you do. From what I understand, Ashova's kahars grew particularly fat off of your brother's frequent tithes, but I'm sure you already knew that. Fortunate you were born to a sar, wouldn't you agree? They would have made a fortune off of you, I'm sure."

Astrid pulled the chain, forcing Kai upon all fours. He looked up, caught Imari's gaze.

Right then, Imari was thankful for the Liagé bindings dulling her senses, because she did not think she would be able to bear this.

"That one." Azir addressed Beru, and pointed to a camel saddled for two.

Beru started to shove Imari forward, but she dug her feet into the ground. "You will let me see them first," Imari demanded through her tears, looking only at Azir.

Beru hesitated. The others glanced over. Lestra's white eyes narrowed.

"Show me that you have been true to your word," Imari continued, "Or I swear...I will fight you every rutting step of the way. I will be dead before I ever step foot over Ziyan's border, Maker as my witness."

Quiet.

The Mo'Ruk glanced from Imari to Azir, who regarded Imari with mild fascination. The air around him shimmered, compressing and contracting.

"Lestra," Azir snapped at last. "Show our little sulaziér what she wishes to see."

Lestra inclined her head and stepped forward, and again without preamble, she clamped a hand around Imari's neck.

Imari startled, the pressure like a vice as the world around her vanished into a swirling chaos of color and sound. Imari thought she might be sick, and then the spinning and pressure ceased.

And she saw him.

"Jeric..." She gasped and lurched forward, but Lestra held her firmly in place.

Not that it mattered. Imari wasn't *actually* standing before Jeric. She was only seeing him through Lestra's Sight.

He appeared to be in a cage—an actual cage designed to hold animals. Stanis and Aksel sat with him, but through the bars, in another cage, she spied the rest of his men, and Jenya. They looked beaten and ragged and bloodied, but they were alive.

Jeric was sitting back against the bars, legs folded and lids half closed as he watched something behind her that she could not see. The sight of him made her heart ache, and she wanted to run to him, but knew that she would only find air.

And then his gaze landed on her. Not through her. *On* her.

He went utterly rigid.

Stars...was it possible? Could he see her?

"They're taking me into Ziyan!" Imari yelled, not knowing if he could possibly hear, but she had to try. "He wants—"

The world squeezed and blurred, and Imari gasped as she was back before the camels again.

Lestra's fingertips dug into her neck and cut off Imari's breath.

"The dog saw her," Lestra hissed.

So it hadn't been her imagination.

Azir's dark eyes narrowed. "You're certain?"

Imari gasped, struggling to breathe.

"Yes. She told him where we're going."

Azir's attention burned through Imari. "Did he hear?"

"I do not know, my lord. I severed the connection immediately."

Azir considered Imari. And then struck her across the face.

Lestra let go, and Imari fell. She landed on her shoulder and rolled to her side, trying to catch her breath while spitting out sand.

Azir put one foot on the back of her neck and shoved her down, pinning her to the ground.

"Do not test me, sulaziér," Azir snarled over her. "Or I will make you watch as I rip him apart, limb from limb."

The pressure relented, and Imari breathed in deep.

But.

Jeric was alive. If it had been an illusion, Azir would not have cared that Imari had told Jeric where they were heading. The thought gave hope to her aching heart.

Lestra grabbed Imari by her Liagé bindings and yanked her back to her feet. She shoved Imari at the camel with so much force, she nearly stumbled over it.

"All matters will pass through Lestra in my absence," Azir was saying to the others, as he climbed onto the camel with Imari. "I trust you can hold this city while Bahdra and I are away."

"Yes, my lord," the enchantress replied, while the guardian inclined his head.

Imari noticed how dark the sky had become, now that the sun had dipped behind the Baragas. Apparently, he planned to ride through the night.

Azir whistled sharply and their camel rose. Imari and Azir swayed with the motion, and then he urged their camel through the gates and out of the city, and turned south.

For Ziyan.

36

A few dozen paces ahead, Jeric's Sol Velorian guards laughed and drank and smoked their heshi. But Jeric was not looking at them, nor did he notice his pack, who had taken a sudden and very keen interest in their alpha.

Jeric sat up straight, gaze fixed on a spot immediately outside of their cage. There were no prints. No physical evidence that she had been here, and yet...

"What is it, Wolf?" Stanis whispered.

"I saw her." Jeric eyed the space in wonder, his mind working fast.

"Who?"

There had been another figure with her, but Jeric hadn't been able to make it out. Imari had been a central point of focus, and everything outside of her had blurred.

"*Wolf*," Chez prodded.

"Imari," Jeric answered, low and quiet.

Braddok watched Jeric, and then exchanged a concerned glance with Chez. But Jeric didn't notice; all of his focus was fixed upon their Sol Velorian guards.

They sat in a circle, playing cards—Fates, Jeric surmised—

and empty jugs of nazzat lay scattered about them. Jeric had watched from his cage as they'd shifted from standing to sitting, as they'd emptied those jugs, as their motions slowed and their laughter barked with belligerence.

He had watched alcohol dull their discretion. Alcohol was always reliable in that way.

The guards weren't as drunk as Jeric would have liked, but he was out of time.

Jeric crept toward the lock. "They're taking her into Ziyan."

"What? Why?" Jenya whispered from the other cage, in accented Common.

"I don't know." Jeric watched the guards as he slowly withdrew the throwing star.

"Aren't there demons in Ziyan?" Chez asked.

"Can't be any worse than the demons in here..." Aksel murmured. Aksel had a new scar along his brow that had narrowly missed his left eye.

Jeric reached through the bars and held the star so that he could use the sharp point as a lockpick, his gaze fixed on the guards while he worked.

"Wolf. How in the hells do you know this?" Braddok hissed, his gaze fixed on those guards as well.

Jeric's eyes narrowed as he searched for the lock's tension. Trying to move it just...

The lock clicked; the metal opened.

Jenya grunted and sat back, arms folded.

"I know." Braddok also grunted. "He's a godsdamned showoff."

"I'm more interested in hearing how your wolf"—Jenya said it like *volf*—"thinks we're going to get out of here alive."

"That's not a question I ask." Jeric set the star down, unhooked the lock, and set it beside the star.

Jenya frowned.

Then, very carefully and still watching the guards, he began unthreading the chain. It clattered just a little, but one of the guards laughed at the same moment, drowning the evidence.

"It's a question you *should* ask," Jenya hissed as loudly as she dared. Braddok shook his head with a silent chuckle, and Jenya glared at him. "We're no good to Imari dead."

"I have no intention of dying, Jenya," Jeric said, setting the chain beside the lock and star.

"Then what's your plan, Wolf?" Jenya asked. "Azir, four Mo'Ruk, and an entire Sol Velorian army have taken this city. I don't see how—"

"Oh, Jen," Braddok said, resting his heavy paw upon her shoulder. "We don't plan. We improvise. Also, we have a wolf."

Jenya smacked Braddok's hand off her shoulder. "Don't touch me. And don't call me Jen."

Jeric ignored them as he pushed the cage door open.

A loud, grating *creeeeeak* cut through the quiet.

Scat.

Jeric threw the star at the guard with the crossbow. That guard cried out and collapsed. The other three shouted and scrambled for their weapons, and Jeric sprinted for them while Chez and Stanis crawled out after him.

Jeric ducked as a dagger sailed right past, which Chez dove for. The man reached for another, but Jeric barreled into him and snatched the second from his hands. Jeric cut the dagger across the guard's throat as the next guard dropped, compliments of Chez's sharp aim. The third swung a scim as Jeric was climbing to his feet, and Jeric jumped back, narrowly missing its edge. He took one fast and calculated step, grabbed the man's arm, and twisted his wrist. The guard cried out, dropping the scim as Jeric slammed his forehead against his, and the guard crumpled beneath him.

"Not another move," snarled a voice behind him.

What in the hells?

Jeric tensed and glanced over his shoulder.

Another figure had stepped into their little burning courtyard. A Sol Velorian woman, with a single braid hanging from the top of her head, the sides shaved, and inked glyphs over every inch of visible skin. The woman held up her hand, as if cupping a small, invisible sphere, and Jeric spotted more inked glyphs painted all over her palm.

Liagé.

Godsdamnit.

No wonder Jeric hadn't sensed her approach.

Without warning, an invisible force struck Jeric square in the chest and sent him flying. He sailed through the air and crashed through a booth. Wood splintered, exploded. Chez and Stanis ran for the Liagé, but the Liagé raised her other hand and threw them back against the bars.

Jeric groaned, pain lancing in his ribs, and he shoved himself back to his feet.

"Yes, your not-a-plan is working out very well," Jenya said loud enough for Jeric to hear.

"Nice try, dog," the Liagé hissed. The Liagé squeezed one hand into a fist, cutting off Jeric's airway.

Definitely a guardian.

Jeric clawed and gasped, trying to get air, but the Liagé held firm, warding Chez and Stanis back with her other, inked hand. Jeric dropped to his knees, his lungs near bursting as his vision swam and hearing faded.

There was a burst of light. And air. The Liagé went flying, slammed into a wall, and bounced to the ground. Her head lolled to the side, and she did not get up.

Jeric's airway opened and he sucked down air just as a Mo'Ruk stepped out into the street.

No, not a Mo'Ruk.

Tallyn.

Gods, *again*?

"I'm starting to think you time these things on purpose," Jeric managed, breathing hard as he pushed himself back to his feet.

And Tallyn was not alone.

A Sol Velorian woman stood behind him, wearing the red silks of Ashova's. Jeric had not been inside Ashova's, but he had seen Ashova's servants standing in her courtyard, and he could not fathom what in all the hells Tallyn was doing with one.

Tallyn said something to the woman, who then ran for the other cage. Her dark, Sol Velorian gaze snagged Jeric's briefly as she ran past, and she stopped before the others, held out a palm, and spoke a spell. The lock shattered.

"See? Improv." Braddok winked at Jenya and started climbing out of the cage.

Jenya rolled her eyes. "No, that's just benefitting from another man's good planning."

"Where in the hells have you been?" Jeric snapped at the alta-Liagé.

"We have to hurry," Tallyn said instead. "I just saw Azir riding out of here with Imari, but I don't know where—"

"Ziyan."

Tallyn pulled back, looked at Jeric. "How do you know this?"

"I don't know, but I *saw* her. Somehow—"

"Shah Sight," Tallyn said, watching him. "Someone must have opened the channel so that she could see you. Probably Lestra." Jeric had the impression Tallyn wasn't just speaking just for his sake anymore, but thinking out loud. "But...how do you know where they're headed?"

"Imari said he was taking her there."

Tallyn stared at Jeric with that one eye. And stared, while Jeric's men—and Jenya—grabbed their weapons from where the guards had piled them.

"She spoke to you. And you...*heard* her."

"Yes."

And Tallyn stared.

"Should I be concerned?"

Tallyn's lips parted. Closed.

"Who's that?" Jeric asked, jerking his chin toward the woman, who stood apart from the others, watching them.

"Niá. We can trust her. She's a relative of Tolya and Taran."

Jeric could not hide his surprise. "That's—"

Something clattered nearby.

They shared a knowing glance, and then Tallyn took in the sight of their battered group. "Follow me," Tallyn said. "If we work together, we may just make it out of here unseen."

Jenya gave Braddok a look.

"Where are the Mo'Ruk?" Jeric asked as he grabbed his weapons. Chez and Stanis plucked a few additional scims off of the dead guards.

"Bahdra left with Azir," Tallyn replied. He tilted his head, his eyes unfocused briefly, as if he were listening to a frequency beyond Jeric's range of hearing. "Lestra and Su'Vi are at Vondar, and Kazak is...near the Qazzat. Or what remains of it."

Jeric processed this. "Do you know if my sister is still alive?"

"Yes. She is...also at Vondar."

Jeric felt a stab of regret. "So we need to head that way." He nodded in the direction opposite as he pulled his baldric back over his head.

"Yes. There are a couple Liagé throughout the city, but nothing Niá and I cannot handle. Still, I would like to avoid them, best we can. They'll be able to notify Lestra through the Shah."

"Noted." Jeric plucked the star he had thrown, wiped it on his pant leg, and shoved it into his belt. He exchanged a glance with Tallyn.

"I'll take the lead," Tallyn said. "Stay close."

They followed Tallyn through the smoke and shadows. Trier was a graveyard of bodies and stone, though the occasional laugh lilted on the night. The invading force had let down their guard and now enjoyed the spoils of their burning victory.

"We need horses," Jeric whispered as they ran.

"I know," Tallyn said. He stopped at the end of the alley and peered around the corner. "A camel breeder lived just at the edge of Trier's fields. There should be enough for us there."

"Assuming they didn't all turn tail and run..." Braddok commented from the back.

"They didn't," was all Tallyn said.

Jeric met Braddok's perplexed gaze, Jeric shrugged, then looked back at the street, where a small band of Sol Velorians were drinking and playing the sorts of games men only played while drinking.

Tallyn started in the opposite direction, but Jeric grabbed Tallyn's robes and jerked him back under cover of their alley. Jeric pointed to a figure in their path, standing guard at the other end of the street.

Ah, Tallyn mouthed.

Jeric held up a finger, then slunk out of their alley and prowled forward. He snuck up from behind, clamped one hand over the man's mouth, and slit his throat.

The man jerked and sagged with a muffled cry, and then Jeric dragged him just inside a dark doorway, out of immediate sight. Jeric gestured, and the others caught up. They pressed on in this fashion, moving like wraiths through the smoke and shadows, with Jeric occasionally going ahead—sometimes with Braddok's help—and clearing their path all the way to the farms.

Or what had been farms.

They were now charred rectangles, all of them still smoking, and Jeric didn't spot a single standing structure. Only broken bones. Jeric glanced sideways at Tallyn, who did not look concerned in the slightest.

"They're not far. Just in the reeds there." Tallyn pointed.

The reeds lining the canal had sustained some damage, but as Tallyn had predicted, there were about a half dozen camels who had found refuge.

The seven of them tore across the open fields, then slowed once they neared the reeds, not wanting to startle the camels. Jeric noticed a fair number of other prints too, leading away from Trier—a few had taken camels. At least some of Trier's citizens had managed to escape.

Within ten minutes, they'd each mounted a beast—Braddok required a little extra help, and Niá shared a mount with Tallyn—and followed Tallyn along the canal, under cover of the reeds.

"We should probably head into the Baragas and follow them north," Chez said.

Jeric stopped his camel. Wind tossed his hair as he gazed at a full moon that limned nearby clouds in silver. "I'm not going to Corinth."

Quiet.

Then, "You sure as hells aren't going into Ziyan," Braddok said.

Jeric didn't answer.

"*Godsdamnnit*, Wolf," Braddok hissed. "Corinth needs her king! We need to prepare *our* people."

Braddok was right, of course. This was their chance to go home—Jeric knew—and Corinth would need her king in the days ahead.

But he'd never forgive himself if he abandoned Imari.

Jeric's fingers flexed around the mass of camel hair, his decision made. "The fight won't come to Corinth without Azir, and Azir has gone into Ziyan."

"So that gives us plenty of time to—"

"Go," Jeric urged, looking fiercely at his friend. "Warn Hersir. Prepare the people, but I am *not* abandoning Imari."

Braddok's expression tightened, his lips pressed together. The rest of his pack sighed, though Jenya looked impressed. Tallyn did not appear surprised in the slightest, and Niá frowned at him.

"I will go with you," Tallyn said, and Jeric thought he was probably answering for both himself and for Niá.

Jeric inclined his head.

"As will I," Jenya replied heavily. "I can't promise that my blade will do much against the forces in Ziyan, but I will do what I can to help you."

Jeric nodded his thanks.

Chez groaned. "Well, now she's just making us look bad."

"You don't need anyone's help for that," Jenya said.

"Did you just make a joke?" Braddok asked.

Jenya gazed sideways at him, then clucked her tongue and urged her camel onward.

Braddok looked back at Jeric. "I'm gonna kill you when this is over."

"He's going to make me a jarl first," Chez said, looking pointedly at Jeric with his one good eye. "And then I'll *help* you kill him."

FROM A PERCH atop Vondar's wall, Lestra watched. Not with her eyes, but with her Sight.

"Mistress...?"

Lestra's eyes refocused. "Our Wolf and his dogs have escaped," she said to one standing beside her.

The *leje* narrowed its black eyes and gazed out into the night as if it might see their fugitives with its own eyes. Beside it, the human dog whimpered and its chains rattled softly.

"Shall we pursue them?" the leje whispered.

"No need," Lestra said. "They are heading for Ziyan. I'll notify Bahdra, and he'll make quick work of it."

But neither Lestra nor the demon could sense the two Liagé riding with the wolf and his pack. Their presence had been made invisible by the beaded work of a very talented and faithful woman. And if Lestra *had* sensed them, she never would have let the wolf go.

37

They rode through the night. Imari had watched the moon arc across the night sky, sometimes ducking behind feathery black clouds, while Azir pressed them across the open sands. He avoided the main roads, instead choosing to circumnavigate the sleeping towns and villages situated along the way.

Imari did not know why he bothered. He'd just leveled an entire city with the aid of his Mo'Ruk. What threat did a few goat farmers pose?

And then she thought, perhaps it wasn't clandestinity at all, but haste that drove him. He kept a steady pace, while Bahdra rode abreast, his black robes billowing powerfully behind him as though he were some god of death, galloping across the sands while searching for any wandering souls he might steal from the living.

Imari could not look at him without seeing her papa, without feeling a rise of pressure against her lungs, and so she kept her gaze fixed decidedly ahead, on the sands that stretched endlessly before them.

The others in their company weren't as determinably quiet as

Azir and Bahdra. Their conversation smattered, and Imari caught a few words. Sometimes, when the wind shifted, Imari caught more than a few words, and she learned that most of them had families, or did once, and that Bahdra had been assimilating Sol Velorians *for years*—and not just from Istraa and Corinth. These Sol Velorians had come from all over the Five Provinces, which explained the various accents Imari had detected. There were two in their group who had been born and raised deep in the Baragas, in a secluded encampment Bahdra had, apparently, established to house the army that had just burned her home to the ground. Those two men spoke very little Common.

Imari still didn't know what Azir expected her to do, or what he needed deep within Ziyan's sands. When she asked him again, he answered only: "You will see once we're there, little sulaziér."

The following evening, Azir stopped to let their camels drink from the last watering hole before crossing into Ziyan. He dismounted, and one of the women pulled Imari down after him before Imari even had the chance to object. Imari ambled away from the group—not far enough to cause alarm, but more to have space while they led their camels to the water's edge. Her legs were stiff and sore from riding, and it felt good to stretch them. Wind whipped sand into her face, and she closed her eyes and breathed in deep. She tried to reach her power—just to check— but her Liagé bindings kept it completely cut off. That sludge moved resolutely through her blood, making it difficult to feel, but Imari was almost thankful for that sludge.

It kept despair at bay.

"You should eat something, little sulaziér," Azir said suddenly, beside her.

Imari did not answer, did not open her eyes.

"Your resolve is impressive," Azir continued, "but it will not nourish your body."

"Are you concerned for me?" Imari gibed.

She felt him watching her. Still, she did not open her eyes, instead listening to the sounds of wind howling over the dunes. The snort of a camel. The whip of fabric. A barking laugh.

"I do not wish to be at odds with you, little sulaziér."

Imari opened her eyes and fixed them on Azir. "Maybe you should have considered that *before* you murdered my papa and slaughtered an entire city."

A few of the Sol Velorians glanced over, visibly uneasy at the tone their prisoner had just taken with this man they revered like a god.

But Azir smiled. The expression did not sit naturally upon his face. It strained his features, made them razor sharp, and a fire burned madly within those obsidian eyes. He took a step closer and bent his head so that his face was a mere handbreadth from hers. His rotten breath filled her nose, and it was all Imari could do not to flinch and turn away.

"And I will do it again," he said, relishing each word, as if delighting in the memory of what he had just done. "I will burn down *every* city in *every* Province until nothing is left but ash. And from that ash, I will build a new world—a world greater than anything you can possibly imagine."

"The world I imagine doesn't involve destroying other lives in order to build my own."

Azir regarded her, then placed a palm to her cheek. It was a dominating gesture, and Imari inhaled sharply, steeled herself. His palm felt deathly cold against her skin.

"Dear, dear, little sulaziér," he continued, looking over her face with condescension and pity. "There is so much of Voloré Tolya within you."

It was not a compliment.

But his words were unexpected, and Imari didn't have a chance to hide her surprise.

His lips curled. "Oh, yes, I knew Tolya. Quite well, in fact, and what a good little disciple you've become. How proud she must be," he sneered. His gaze sharpened then, his features twisted harshly. "What a waste. The both of you driven by some futile hope that there is good. That some magnanimous god watches over us all. But I tell you: *There is no god.* And if there is, he certainly does not care for you or me. *Where was he,* when they took our children and raped our women? *Where was he* when they slaughtered us and burned our cities to the ground?"

He wasn't referring to the present; he was talking about the war.

Imari didn't know much about the war of Azir's time, other than fragments—all of which had been processed through an Istraan perspective. And after coming to know Jeric, she understood more than ever that there were always two sides to war.

"Tolya's *religion* only contains and controls us," Azir continued through his teeth. "It left us weak and vulnerable, and it nearly destroyed us. I am done with her god. It is up to *us,* and only us. To protect our people. To build our own world, to write our own rules. To become gods worthy of praise."

Imari looked straight back into those stone-cold eyes. "And what a magnanimous god you've turned out to be," she snarled. "Slaughtering and raping and burning an entire city, just like the ones you hate. Piss on your new world. You're no different than they are, you rutting monster, and I hope you burn in hell."

He looked at her.

And looked at her.

The others had fallen silent.

And then Azir struck her across the face, knocking her to the sand. She landed on her shoulder with a wince, and she was just pushing herself back up when hands grabbed her arms, hoisting her to her feet, holding her before Azir, who looked down his long nose at her.

Azir grabbed her ear and twisted hard, a crazed light in his eye. "All it takes is one little word from me, little sulaziér, and your dog suffers," he said silkily. "Fortunately for you, I have just enough Sight so that you can hear him scream."

Imari ground her teeth together, wincing and straining against his pull, and then Azir let go with a shove.

"We're done here," he snarled at the group, then strode back to their shared camel.

The two Sol Velorians holding her arms shoved her after him.

By the second evening, they reached Ziyan's infamous border. It stretched like a crack in the world, this great canyon of jagged red rock, as if a god had tried—and failed—to rip Sol Velor from the face of this earth, this fissure the only thread left holding it in place.

Beyond, the magnificent storm churned like a simmering cauldron, the sands beneath dim and gray. For light could not reach this place, and so the land had been given over to shadow. It was a storm that had never left, so long as Imari could remember, and she had also never stood any closer than this. She'd been brought here as a child once, to understand what the Sol Velorians had done through their Liagé. How their pride had been their ruin, how they had finally wielded a power too great to sustain, and it had ripped their beautiful nation apart.

Imari remembered the vision Tallyn had shown her. The mesmerizing city, the people. It was painful looking at this empty wasteland of ruin, knowing what it *had been*.

Knowing what they'd lost.

And even from the boundary, across the great divide and through her Liagé binds, Imari could not shake the ill portent carried on the wind.

"My lord," Bahdra said suddenly.

Azir stopped their camel. Bahdra brought his beside theirs, but rather than speak, Bahdra inclined his head. Not another word passed between them, and yet they looked at one another as though they were conversing. Imari surmised that Bahdra again spoke into Azir's mind, and then Azir stiffened, his arm tensed at Imari's waist, and his gaze narrowed behind them.

And Imari knew: someone was following them.

But who? Imari's mind whirled. It couldn't be Jeric, could it? Ricón, maybe? He'd left the day of the attack to investigate what'd happened at Bal Duhr. Had he seen Azir gallop off with Imari and then changed course?

Wards, she hoped not, because Ricón's scims were nothing to Azir and Bahdra's combined power, never mind the dozen armed Sol Velorians surrounding her.

Imari shut her eyes tight. *Maker, if you're there...keep him safe— please. I cannot lose him too.*

And then she silently added, *Show me the way forward. I have no idea what to do with this power you've given me. If there's a way to stop Azir—show me.*

There was no answer, not that she'd expected one. But now her prayers were in the stars; let the Maker deal with the outcome.

Bahdra and Azir must have finished their silent conversation, because Imari felt Azir's attention land swiftly upon her as she gazed across the canyon to the sands beyond.

Imari kept her expression neutral, not wanting to give him any indication that she knew they were being tracked.

At last, Azir turned his attention back to the others. "Keep close," he said. "Only the dead dwell here."

And their caravan pushed on.

They started down a narrow and rocky switchback that dipped steeply into the canyon, where the wind gained both speed and force. To Imari, that rabid gust felt like warning: *Go*, it said. *Run from this place.*

Still, Azir pushed them on. Out of the sun and into shadow, where the air bit with cold, and howled a lonely sound.

And yet...

Imari felt as though a hundred pairs of eyes watched them with every step they took. Even the camels seemed uneasy, shifting and snorting, tugging against reins. One in their caravan would not be moved from the ledge, despite his rider's efforts and cursing, but then Azir spoke a word, air pulsed, and all of the camels stopped fighting.

They reached the canyon floor, where bloodred rock rose on either side, and the wind pushed little rocks from high perches, showering their path. Imari wanted to look behind, to see if their pursuers were gaining ground, but she also didn't want Azir to know what she suspected, so she forced her eyes forward.

"This was not always here," Azir mused, interrupting her thoughts.

Imari did not reply.

"This canyon used to be a beautiful valley full of palms and high grasses, with a lake at its heart. I swam in that lake as a boy."

Imari could not picture Azir as a child, bearing a child's innocence. But she *could* picture this land before, because of Tallyn. Of course, she did not share this with Azir. It would only serve as more ammunition for him to later use against her.

But thinking on Tallyn made her wonder if he were the one following them now. It was possible. *Very* possible, and the more she thought it over, the likelier it seemed. She hadn't seen him during the battle, but the old alta-liagé seemed to have an affinity for surviving unlikely circumstances. And who else would brave the monsters of Ziyan but someone who thought they might have the power to stand against them?

"Sol Velor was a wonder to behold," Azir continued, now guiding their camel up the opposite path. The one that led out of the canyon and into Ziyan. "You want to think I'm the monster, and I do understand you. It's how we absolve ourselves of responsibility. We take all of the things we hate, the things we can't possibly comprehend, and we pin them on a figurehead so that we can still stand to look ourselves. So that we can convince ourselves that we would do better because we *are* better."

Imari swayed with the motion of the camel as they rounded a particularly sharp turn.

"That is the problem with people like your Tolya," he continued. "She sees the world in terms of what could be, and I see what *is*. Tolya's dream of peace presupposes that mankind will deny himself for another, but I tell you that is never true. Self-preservation is always our first response. Take or be taken. So it has always been, since the dawn of man."

"And so it will continue, as long as men like you keep thinking they're better than everyone else."

Azir chuckled darkly. "If not me, it would be another. People do not change, little sulaziér. The only thing we grow better at is hiding who we are. In this life of 'take or be taken,' I will take. I will always take to preserve our people, so that we may live our lives without fear. Certainly, *you* cannot fault me for that."

Imari pressed her lips together, eyes fixed decidedly ahead. She shouldn't have engaged him in conversation when she never liked what he had to say.

Thankfully, Azir stopped talking as they ascended that rocky path, higher and higher, until they were out of the canyon and standing along the last vestiges of the known world.

And passing into another.

Imari's heart beat faster, her gaze fixed on the sands. She had the strange impression that they were walking upon a great and sleeping beast, the sand its flesh, the cold wind its breath, the distant rolling thunder its constant snoring. The others fell quiet as they continued at a walking pace, the only voice that savage wind.

Run, it persisted. *Go.*

Imari gazed down at her bindings, at the etchings pulsing steadily with wardlight. She wondered what she would sense if Azir took them off, because even with them on and actively blocking her power, she felt the strange energy of this place.

No, *sickness*.

It leaked from the sand, permeated the air like a poison, and with every breath, Imari tasted an edge of metallic burning. Like cauterized flesh.

What was the source? Imari wondered. Every illness had one. Was that where Azir was taking her? Did he mean to remove whatever poison leaked into Ziyan's soil so that the Sol Velor could return home?

But if his motives had been that innocent, certainly he would have told her.

The sky turned from dark to darker as they reached an outcropping of enormous red rock. It sat like some natural outpost at sea, with rock spires—some vertical, others tilted like fins—and sand lapping at its feet.

Azir halted their shared mount between two massive spires. "We'll stop here for the night," he said, then dismounted and pulled Imari down after him.

"No fire," he said to one of the men, named Vishtal, who had withdrawn flint and kindling. "It'll draw them."

No one questioned, the silence grew heavier, and Bahdra began moving around their group, drawing wards into the sand, in blood. Here, tucked between the rocks, the sand did not blow or scatter, and Bahdra's symbols held.

Vishtal put his flint away while the others made camp. The woman with the pleated hair—Mashi, Imari had learned—and two others secured the camels.

Azir withdrew a small sash from his robes and reached for Imari.

Imari took an involuntary step back.

Azir looked amused. "We need to hide *your* light, little sulaziér."

He meant her Liagé bindings.

"You could always take them off," Imari suggested.

He smiled. "I could. And I will. But not tonight."

He grabbed the chain between her binds, jerked her forward, and began wrapping and stuffing the cloth around the cuffs. His fingers were ice-cold, his long nails sharp, and when he finished, he held out more tack for her to eat.

Imari meant to refuse, but her stomach clenched. She took the tack.

Azir tipped his head, pleased, and then joined Bahdra at the perimeter, while Imari gazed down at her wrapped binds, praying that whoever followed them would be all right.

———

"THEY'VE STOPPED," Jeric said, halting his camel at the crest of a dune.

Tallyn brought his camel beside Jeric's. His gaze skirted the sands, the clouds. "We should too. It's getting dark."

"No, we keep moving. This is the perfect opportunity to—"

"No, no. You misunderstand me," Tallyn interrupted. "It is not that we need rest, but because the things that have been resting will soon wake."

"Lovely..." Chez murmured.

Tallyn's gaze skirted the horizon, his expression distant. "We need to find shelter for the night. Preferably...something out of the wind."

Jeric's fingers flexed around his camel's hair, and the camel shifted beneath him. Gods, Imari was *right there,* between those red rocks.

"Can you See Imari?" Jeric asked.

"If I attempt to See them now, this close, Azir will know."

"But your beads—"

"Have veiled me thus far." Tallyn touched the enchanted string of rock and cactus wood he'd tied around his neck, which rested just beneath his cloak. Niá wore one too. "But out here, I cannot benefit from dilution. Azir will feel my Touch, especially if I use it in such close proximity."

"He already knows we're following them," Jeric said through his teeth.

"They do?" Jenya asked with a frown.

"While that may be," Tallyn continued, giving her a look of confirmation, "they still do not know that Niá and I are with you, and that is our greatest advantage right now."

"How long have they known we've been following them?" Jenya now had her hands on her hips.

"Since the watering hole," Jeric replied, gaze fixed on those rocks.

Jenya stared at him. "You didn't think to mention it?"

Braddok chuckled. Aksel too, as he shook his head.

But Jeric only stared in the direction of those rocks, clenching and unclenching his hands.

"*Jeric*," Tallyn continued. "Imari will be all right. Azir has need of her, and while he has need of her, he will not let any harm come to her. If it's Ziyan you're concerned about, you needn't be. If anyone can hide from death, it's a necromancer. It's why Bahdra has come along in the first place. The best thing we can do for her right now is stay alive."

Jeric ground his teeth and swallowed Tallyn's words.

Godsdamnit, the alta-Liagé was right.

"Are *we* able to hide from death?" Stanis asked cautiously.

Tallyn considered their surroundings, their group. "Niá is very talented. So long as we're able to find a place where wind and sand won't bury her wards, we should be all right."

"There's a wash back there." Jeric pointed behind them. "I thought I saw a few larger rocks that should cut down the wind."

"Perfect."

They backtracked a little, and the wind picked up, spraying sand everywhere. Braddok's beard was full of it, and Stanis, Chez, and Aksel had taken to breathing through their tunics. Jenya looked impressively unaffected, while Niá had wrapped her shawl so that it shielded all but her dark, Sol Velorian eyes.

They reached the wash within ten minutes.

Most of the dried riverbed had flooded with sand, though a few larger boulders lined what Jeric imagined had once been a river bank. Dead cacti stood like rotting corpses, arms broken off, their flesh peeled back, revealing decayed wooden bones beneath.

The wash itself abutted a large dune, which naturally blocked the wind, and if Jeric stood beside the rocks, he could hardly feel the wind at all.

"Niá, would you make a perimeter?" Tallyn asked.

Niá nodded and approached Jeric, who had been securing his camel to one of the dead cacti.

"May I borrow your dagger?" she asked. It was the first time she had spoken to him directly, and he could tell that she only did it now out of necessity.

Jeric held out a dagger, hilt first.

She reached for it, but he pulled it back.

Her dark eyes flashed.

"I wanted to thank you," Jeric said quietly. "For all you're doing."

Her gaze hardened. "I don't do it for you."

"I know."

A beat.

Jeric held the dagger out again. In his periphery, he noticed Jenya watching them.

Niá took the blade and stared at him one long moment, and then she turned away and carved the tip of his dagger right into her palm, drawing blood.

"The hells...?" Chez said. He'd been sitting down, but Niá's action made him pop back up.

Niá ignored him as she wiped the bloodied tip on her clothing then handed the dagger back to Jeric, hilt first. He took it, and she strode past him and a startled Chez, then began drawing symbols on a rock—in blood.

"What is she doing?" Stanis asked, wary.

In fact, all of his men looked a little wary. Even Jenya.

"Hopefully, saving our lives," Niá answered tightly.

"I think I'd like that statement better without the hopefully," Braddok said.

"Niá is concealing us," Tallyn explained as Niá moved on to a cactus.

"From what, exactly?" Chez asked.

"The *tyrcorat*."

It was Jenya who had answered.

Everyone looked to Jenya, except for Niá, who focused only on her enchantments.

"The...what-rat?" Chez asked.

"Skin eaters," Jenya replied, sitting and taking a bite from a fig as if she were completely enjoying Chez's discomfiture. And his swollen eye.

"Is she serious?" Aksel asked. He looked a little pale.

"Yes, and no." Tallyn gave Jenya a pointed look, then sat down upon the sand. "When Fyri's power ripped Sol Velor apart, thousands died. Their bodies were ripped right from their souls, leaving those souls trapped between worlds. They say that at night, when darkness is strongest, they roam this land, screaming and hungry for bodies so that they may pass into the afterlife to find rest."

"Nothing like a little bedtime story to put you right to sleep..." Braddok drawled.

Aksel chuckled.

"And what if the wards don't work?" Stanis asked, eyeing those wards less warily than before.

"Then best hope your gods hear your prayers," Niá answered, "because my god certainly doesn't hear mine."

Stanis frowned.

"We'll be fine," Tallyn said. "Niá comes from talented stock."

Niá did not answer.

"You mentioned she's a relative of Tolya?" Jeric asked, while rubbing his camel's neck and feeding him one of the apples they'd pilfered. Right before entering Ziyan, they'd made a quick detour to a small outlying village, where they'd watered their camels and themselves, sent a quick word to Hersir, and *borrowed* some produce from a store shed—all of it completely undetected. Jeric was beginning to see the benefit of having a Seer for an ally.

"Tolya was my great aunt," Niá said suddenly, stepping over a chunk of cactus wood to paint the larger pebbles that littered the ground. "Taran is...was Tolya's sister. And my oza."

Oza. Grandmother.

"Hey, you got those figs?" Chez asked Aksel. "I'm starving."

Aksel rifled in his satchel and passed out figs as Niá took a seat at the edge of their camp, as far from them as possible but still within her warded circle.

"You hungry, Niá?" Aksel asked.

Niá gave a subtle shake of her head, but Aksel tossed her a fig anyway.

"Wolf?" Aksel looked at Jeric, but Jeric shook his head. "You sure?"

"I'm not hungry."

"He's still full from his memory of the surina's bedchambers," Braddok teased.

Jeric glanced sideways at his enormous friend, who cracked a big-toothed smile. Braddok had known Jeric had snuck out, because they'd been sharing a room, and he'd immediately guessed where Jeric had been headed.

And then, when Jeric didn't deny it, Chez guffawed. "You were in the surina's bedchambers?"

All eyes fixed on Jeric. Even Niá's. Jenya folded her arms and glared at him, clearly still irritated by this event.

"Good gods, you were!" Chez exclaimed before Jeric could properly respond. "And in Sar Branón's own home!"

"You've got some steel balls, Wolf," Aksel said.

"Or a rutting death wish," Chez said. "Can you imagine if someone had walked in and seen you on top of—"

"It wasn't like that," Jeric said firmly, putting an end to the discussion, and to their wandering imaginations. "I'm not an idiot."

Jenya looked like she wanted to contest that last point in particular. She had, after all, caught him with his shirt off and tossed haphazardly on Imari's bedroom floor.

Chez eyed him. "Then what in the hells were you doing *in her bedchamber* in the middle of the night?"

Jeric flashed his teeth. "None of your godsdamned business."

Chez chuckled. Aksel too, as he shook his head.

"Speaking of death wishes," Braddok piped in, chewing on a fig. "Hersir's gonna kick your royal ass once he finds out where you've gone."

Jeric leaned back on his hands and stretched his long legs. "I know."

"I hope I'm there to see it."

Jeric eyed the darkening sky. "I hope so too, Brad. Gods, I hope so."

38

I *see you, sulaziér.*

Imari's eyes snapped open. Wards, she hadn't realized she'd dozed off. There was no light to see by, no moon visible beneath Ziyan's thick blanket of clouds, though she could hear the heavy breathing of those around her, deep in sleep. But not everyone slept. She caught soft whispers near the camels.

Imari rolled onto her back in the soft sand, closed her eyes and breathed in deep. That bass voice echoed in her mind, and Imari felt a prickle of unease.

Those words had felt...closer, somehow. Which was utterly ridiculous, because it was a dream.

And yet...

Wind stirred, throwing grains of sand across her face, and Imari opened her eyes again. A few of the camels snorted nearby, though she could not see them in the dark. Her bindings made her thoughts sluggish, but even through their haze, she sensed that something was...off.

After surviving all those years in The Wilds, she'd learned to trust that sense.

Suddenly, light bloomed, shattering the black of night—a pulsing white-blue glow.

A ward.

Imari stilled, her gaze whirling and settling on Bahdra's little offender. Just one ward shone, like a piece of moonlight upon the sand. The rest of Bahdra's blood-ward perimeter lay dark, though the glow from that one ward cast enough light for her to see the shapes of those around her, most of them sleeping upon the sand. Two sat near the camels—the cause of the whispers she'd heard. They were not whispering now, instead eyeing the ward that had awoken. Bahdra and Azir sat together, their faces leeched of color in the wardlight. Their black eyes reflected that pale light as they gazed into the dark sands.

Quiet.

Watchful.

They did not appear particularly alarmed, but Imari—who had spent half of her life behind wards—had never felt more vulnerable, being out here at night without a physical barrier standing between herself and whatever roamed these sands.

Wind whispered; silence returned.

Imari took a deep breath and was just settling back upon the sand when a second ward sprung to life. The camels snorted, and the two figures seated beside them rose their feet. Imari began pushing herself up to a seated position as another ward sprung to life.

And another.

And another.

Those who'd been sleeping stirred awake, and Azir spoke quietly to a few of them as Bahdra stood, black eyes narrowed on the dark.

Until their entire circle burned. Each and every ward shone with moonlight, pulsing.

Warning.

The wind picked up suddenly, throwing sand, and Imari's

heart beat faster. The camels pulled against their ties, and one growled while the figures nearest tried soothing them.

"Do you see anything?" someone asked.

"No, but stay in the circle," Azir said quietly, evenly, his black gaze fixed on the night as wind tugged at his robes.

Everyone sidled toward the circle's center, gazing all around. No one spoke. And for once, Imari hoped Bahdra was as powerful as Azir claimed he was.

Because even through her mental haze, through the sludge of her bindings, Imari felt a shift in the air. A taint, a poison. It grew stronger with every passing second, leaving the residual taste of acid upon her tongue. Wind howled and ripped between the rocks, throwing sand and pebbles, but Bahdra's wards held true. Like permanent fixtures in their shifting world. Individual specks of sand glittered in the halo of wardlight, which was growing brighter.

More insistent.

Imari thought she heard a shriek in the distance.

"Maybe it's just a sandstorm," said one of the men. He didn't believe it though.

No one did.

The wind pushed and twisted, kicking up more sand and making it difficult to see. Imari blinked, ducking her face under her arms to block the sand from her eyes. The sound crescendoed to a roar and then, in a forceful vortex of air, each and every one of Bahdra's wards blinked out.

Plunging them into total darkness.

The wind stopped; the world fell silent. Too silent.

"The hell?" someone cursed.

Imari's heart pounded as she scoured the darkness—for what, she did not know. And that acrid taste grew suddenly stronger.

"What just happened?" whispered one of the guards.

"Stay close," Azir snapped.

But Imari heard the fear in his voice.

"Are the wards still—" someone started, when a rush of wind and shrieks and light flared along one edge of their circle.

"Dashá!" Someone flinched back, and Imari's blood turned to ice.

In that wall of wardlight, floating in midair, was a wraith. It was bone and rotten flesh, spectral and horrifying, with tattered cloth still clinging to its skeletal body, and strings of hair floated around its face as though it were underwater. As though it had swam at them and struck a barrier of light. It arched back, away from that light as its jaw unhinged wider than humanly possible and let out a bloodcurdling scream—like a hundred dissonant stringed instruments all playing at once—and then it soared off, swallowed by darkness.

But the sound it had made still rattled Imari's head, and the acrid stench of burning filled the air.

The *tyrcorat*.

Imari's breath came hard and fast, her lungs pinched tight. They were so much more horrifying than Imari could ever have imagined.

Everyone crowded at the center of Bahdra's circle. No one said a word, their panicked gazed fixed on the night.

Another tyrcorat rushed them, just as gruesome as the first, with arms of bone and sagging flesh. It reached for them, but a wall of wardlight flared again, throwing the creature back.

But another was there immediately to take its place.

And another, while the night filled with shrieking.

The tyrcorat threw themselves at Bahdra's barrier, faster and faster, one right after another. Each hurling themselves against a different place along Bahdra's circle.

Checking for weaknesses.

Or...

Trying to weaken it.

Everyone in Imari's company watched in horror, while their camels kicked and pulled against restraints. Azir must have said something in Bahdra's mind, because Bahdra nodded and crouched, stabbed a blade into his palm, and began drawing more wards. A circle within a circle.

To reinforce his slowly failing wards.

Maker have mercy.

"Vizeer," Azir said, tone clipped. "Help him."

The man called Vizeer did not hesitate. He cut open his palm too, and began drawing wards into the sand.

Imari feared for the person following after them, whoever it was.

But despite Bahdra and Vizeer's added wards, Imari could not help but notice that the outer circle of light was growing steadily dimmer against the unceasing tyrcorat.

"It's getting weaker," Mashi said, her voice uneven.

A muscle ticked in Azir's jaw, and then he crouched, dug his fingers into the sand, and began to chant.

Imari felt something give. A shift of pressure, a crack from strain. In the next instant, every single one of Bahdra's wards flared a blinding white, and the air smelled of burning as Bahdra's wards burned up—overwhelmed.

Someone cursed. Imari realized it was her.

But just before Bahdra's and Vizeer's wards faded completely, Azir spoke a single word. A command. Air pulsed, exploding out of him in one concussive blast, and a dome of silvery light winked into existence, shielding them.

And the dead came.

And came.

They flooded the night, swimming through darkness and sweeping at Azir's shield of light, diving and clawing and screeching as it burned them. And with every flash of light, Imari saw the cloud of swarming wraiths above.

Wards, there were so many! Imari knew that she would have felt far more fear than she did, if it weren't for her bindings. Even so, all she could do was stare in wonder and horror.

Azir's features strained as he held that shield firmly in place, physically holding back the dead, while Bahdra and Vizeer drew symbols in the sand. But each symbol flared and burned up mere seconds after it was drawn, overwhelmed by the sheer numbers of dead.

Just then, one of the dead reached through Azir's dome and plucked Vizeer off the sand. Vizeer screamed and screamed as he was dragged into the swarming darkness, where no less than a dozen dead tore him apart, showering Imari and the others in his blood.

A few of them cursed, but Bahdra kept drawing, and Azir kept chanting furiously, and this time Mashi joined him. She carved a scim into her palm, dug her fingers into the sand, and a hazy stream of light rose from her fingers to join Azir's. To reinforce his dome, which was now flickering beneath the strain of so many dead.

Another skeletal hand clawed into their sphere and dragged a man out. Wraiths converged like flies on feces, and ripped him apart like the first.

And Azir's dome grew dimmer.

Smaller.

Azir snarled. "Give the sulaziér her talla!"

One of the guards, who stood near the stammering camels, dug Imari's flute from the bags and ran over to her. He held it out, but Imari showed him her bindings.

He cursed. Glanced around, probably trying to see which of them still lived who had the power to unlock them. "Bizret!" he shouted through the shrieking and wailing.

Bizret looked over, spotted the dilemma, then closed his eyes and spoke a word. Air pulsed, and Imari's bindings clicked open and dropped to the sand.

A rush of fire and tingling flooded Imari's blood—so sudden, and so overwhelming, Imari dropped to her knees. Her world tilted, her temples wrenching painfully, and Imari's stomach clenched tight.

Stars, she was going to be sick.

The man who'd brought her the flute screamed as one of the dead grabbed hold of his hair and pulled him through the dome, but his scream was cut short as the tyrcorat ripped him apart.

Imari struggled to focus—breathe—as she drowned in that well of Shah power now accessible to her.

Someone yelled her name.

Right.

She blinked, winced.

Azir wanted her help. Needed it.

But what could she do to stop *this*? And even if she *could* help, should she do it? She could do nothing and let the dead come. Let them put an end to Azir and Bahdra, and herself, so that no one would ever suffer for her again.

Except.

What would happen to Jeric and the others once the other Mo'Ruk learned that Azir and Bahdra were dead? What would the demon do to Kai? What mess was she leaving for Ricón?

Imari shut her eyes tight, feeling the wind and sand claw at her, while screaming and shrieking filled the night.

No, she did not want to die like this, ripped to shreds by monsters. She didn't know what she was going to do, but Azir believed she had the power to make a difference. He'd burned down a city for that power.

And according to Rasmin, sulaziérs had power over living *and* dead.

So Imari raised her flute to her lips, and played.

Melody poured from the little flute, though the wind and shrill shrieking drowned out her music. But she did not stop, did not lose hope.

And then.

Stars.

They were *everywhere*. Thousands of them, zipping back and forth like burning meteors, and they emitted a soft hum. Strangely, she couldn't quite place the tone. It was all sound at once, fluid and changing, but she could see them in that Shah plane the way she'd seen them in E'Centro and again when Azir had attacked the city. At first, Imari was confused. She didn't know what she'd expected to see, but it wasn't this. It wasn't *light*. If anything, she would have thought there'd be darkness within those wraiths, like she'd seen with Astrid. But then she remembered what Azir had said, how their bodies had been ripped from this world, leaving their souls trapped somewhere between.

And their souls were still very much alive.

One such point of light shot by, and Imari chased it with her trill, trying to find its particular resonance as she'd done before, but it moved too fast. Too...slippery, and she could not pin its tone. She could see that it was vibrating, but its note layered with dissonance.

Wait...

The light was *eclipsed*. And as she stared at this universe of shooting stars, she realized *all* of the tyrcorats' stars were eclipsed. They weren't full points of light, but rings with darkness at their core.

Imari recalled the poison she'd sensed when they'd passed into the land. The sickness.

There are many weeds in the Maker's good garden, Tallyn had told her. *The shoots will not stop until the root dies.*

And every sickness had a root. She needed to find that root, just as she'd done with Bahdra and his animated dead in Trier. She needed to find the source.

Another man's screams cut through her mind, and in her Shah vision, she saw his brilliant star being plucked from the sands and pulled into the eclipsed horde, where it sputtered out.

Imari played on, sifting and searching deeper into the

churning madness. For what, exactly, she couldn't say, only that her heart felt pulled.

Deeper and deeper.

A woman screamed.

There.

The massive cloud of eclipsed stars shifted just so, and Imari caught sight of a light shining deeper in the horde, much brighter than all the rest.

What in the world...

Imari's lungs burned as she held her tone against the wind and sand and screaming, and slowly that light began to take shape, forming edges as it stretched.

Into a person.

Imari was so surprised, she almost lost her note, gazing in wonder at the figure in the distance. A woman.

Fyri.

Something twisted deep in Imari's gut, and every string inside Imari rang out, as though the woman's very soul called to her own.

You, a woman's voice said in Imari's mind.

Even as Imari watched, the woman's features grew steadily clearer, stronger. Nearer. Like a mirage drawing into focus. And she was just as stunning as the woman in Tallyn's memories.

I know you, Imari thought, wondering if the woman could hear her thoughts as well. *You're Fyri. You're the one who—*

Get out of here. Fyri's features turned severe. *Stop your song and leave this place.*

That was...not what Imari had expected.

No, Imari replied sharply.

You must. You do not know what you are doing. I can hold off the tyrcorat to give you time, but you must promise you'll leave and never come back to this place.

And why would I trust the word's of Azir's lover?

Fyri's face twisted. *Do not speak his name to me.*

Fyri's vehemence surprised Imari.

There is no time, Fyri persisted. *Leave now, and I can spare you.*

Imari was tempted. This could be her opportunity to rid the world of Azir and Bahdra, assuming Fyri was good to her word. But it still left her with three Mo'Ruk holding Jeric prisoner. Imari could not take them on alone, and once those three Mo'Ruk learned what she'd done, they would not let Jeric live.

If I go, the man I love will die, Imari said.

Better him than the world.

No. There has to be another way, Imari said.

Go, little sulaziér. I do not want to hurt you.

Fyri's light was almost upon her.

I warned you, Fyri said.

Without thinking, her soul guided by a power beyond herself, Imari switched tones.

And then...

Sound.

Everywhere.

They were a clash of two melodies—two timpani ringing, creating a diminished interval. The sound split Imari's ears, as if someone had struck her over the head and her skull vibrated with the tone. It rolled down her body, wave after crushing wave. Imari's bones strained from the pressure, but she forced out another note, still guided by that other power. The fire in her gut seared through her body, and then there was light.

Heat—so hot, she thought her bones were melting.

An agonizing scream mixed with her own.

There was a burst of air followed by a deep bass tone, as if the core of the world groaned.

And then silence.

Total, absolute silence.

Light and heat vanished, and Imari opened her eyes. For a second, Imari thought she was dreaming. All around her, infinitesimal grains of sand hovered, suspended in midair as if frozen in time.

All at once they dropped. Just like in her dream.

The storm was gone. As were the dead, the horror.

Fyri.

Leaving only rippling waves of sand, made gold in a sun just peering over the horizon.

And Imari collapsed.

"Pride is the most dangerous of all, for it blinds us to our weakness. It whispers that we are enough, that we are better. That we can do all things, and have no need for our Maker, for we are gods ourselves.

And so we move our temples from the rock of his foundation and build them upon sand, believing our sheer will can support it. We do not see how the sand gives with time, how our precious temple begins to sink. We do not see the cracks in a structure that strains from pressure, and so we persist in our delusion of godhood until those cracks finally give and the sand pours in, and our temple collapses all around us."

Excerpt from Il Tonté,
As recorded in the First Verses by
Juvia, Liagé First High Sceptor.

39

I mari's body bounced, and her eyes opened.

Someone had draped her over the camel on her belly, between its humps, leaving her arms and legs to bounce freely on either side, though someone *had* taken the time to bind rope around her wrists. Her entire body ached—even her bones felt bruised—and a wicked pounding throbbed at the back of her skull. Sand stretched beneath the camel's thick hooves, and a sharp wind kicked bits of it into her eyes.

It was no longer night.

She blinked and lifted her head, wincing a little as she did.

The jagged red rocks where they had camped were gone, and now...

Imari had no idea where they were.

"Ah, you're awake," Azir said cheerfully. He walked beside her, guiding the camel forward, and Bahdra rode at his other side, gazing ahead with those black and empty eyes. Every time she looked at the necromancer, she saw her papa. She saw the spear of darkness cut through his heart, and anger pumped fire through her veins.

Anger...she hadn't been able to feel since Azir had first bound her in Liagé binds.

"You're wondering why I did not replace your bindings," Azir said, glancing sideways at her. "If I had severed your tie to the Shah, you would not have survived. You channeled too much, and your body needed it in order to heal."

Imari pushed herself up and maneuvered herself so that she was sitting. Her world spun. She grasped the saddle and closed her eyes until the spinning stopped.

But it did not stop; her stomach lurched and she dry heaved, for there wasn't any food left in her belly to throw up.

Maker have mercy.

Her body ached everywhere, her skin felt like fire, and nausea churned in her belly. Imari closed her eyes and breathed deep, hoping the feeling would fade. But then she remembered someone had been following them, and she cracked her eyes back open and stole a glance over her shoulder.

Their Sol Velorian escort trailed behind them, but they were *half* of what they'd been. Stars, the tyrcorat had taken so many. Mashi was still there, and Vishtal. They both looked...shaken. All of them did.

"Are the tyrcorat gone?" Imari asked Azir, though her parched throat rasped.

"Yes," he replied, then, "How did you do it?"

She met his gaze.

His cold eyes pierced, cutting deep. Searching, and...suspicious.

Imari remembered the look on Fyri's face when she'd spoken Azir's name. The vehemence in her voice. Imari did not know their history, and looking at Azir just then, as those eyes probed and intruded into her mind, Imari decided she didn't want to tell him what'd happened.

She didn't want to tell him anything.

Thankfully, she was spared a response as another heave

clenched her belly, and Imari gagged on bile. It burned, coating her mouth with acid, and Imari spit on the sand. Her saliva was tinged pink with blood.

"I don't know," Imari managed. Whatever uncertainty might have leaked into her voice was masked by sickness and fatigue.

Azir watched her a moment longer, though she did not meet his gaze. Finally, he turned his attention ahead.

"But the tyrcorat *are* gone, are they not?" Imari asked. "The land is healed. What more could you possibly need from me?"

Azir's gaze fixed on a distant outcropping of rocks, and his black eyes glittered. "You will see, little sulaziér."

They continued on, deeper into Ziyan, and Imari saw that what she had initially dismissed as rocks were ruins. Pillars jabbed up from the sand like broken ribs, domes lay half-buried, and buildings had been stripped to their supports—magnificent buildings, judging by the scale of their remains. It was a city of skeletons, its flesh rotted away with time and neglect. A massive aqueduct lay in shattered fragments upon the sand, its giant pillars cracked and bent as if stubbornly trying to lift a bridge that would no longer stand.

"Assi Andai..." Imari whispered.

Azir said simply, "Yes."

The old Sol Velorian capital.

Now that she realized what it was, she could not look at this place without superimposing the vision Tallyn had shown her. The opulence, the sun, the heady scent of jasmine—a glory to the Maker himself—and now it lay in ruin, those prized Sol Velorian temples flooded with sand. It poured from their gaping windows and doors, as if the sand were slowly dragging this city down into its depths, drowning it.

Azir gazed upon the ruins, and his eyes lit with old anger, while madness writhed in the depths. "You should have seen this in its prime. We were resplendent."

Imari did not tell him that she already had. "What are we doing here?" she asked instead.

Azir did not answer immediately, so caught in his memories of the past. "It is just this way."

At last, they reached a courtyard Imari recognized—or, at least, what remained of the courtyard. It, too, had sunk into this lake of sand, the fountain at its center broken down the middle with one side completely buried. And directly across from them stood the Mazarat.

The place where the Liagé had lived and trained and studied. Imari remembered the mural in the catacombs, the one that told the story of the Five Divines and Zussa's fall.

Where the power of the remaining Four Divines had rained upon the earth, and from it, a tree had grown.

Imari looked at Azir, who gazed greedily upon the Mazarat, and a chill swept over her body.

Suddenly, she understood.

"The tree," she whispered with growing horror.

Azir's head turned sharply toward her.

"You're here...for the Divine tree. You want...the power in it."

Azir studied her, those dark eyes probing, and then he seemed to make up his mind about something. "It was Tallyn, wasn't it? Who showed you this place." And Azir smiled. It was a strangled smile, twisted and unnatural. "You are correct, little sulaziér. I have come for the tree. And you are going to help me pull it out by the roots."

Imari stared at him. She remembered her nightmare.

Go, Fyri had said. *You do not know what you are doing.*

Azir took a step closer, holding that strangled smile. He raised a hand, madness writhed in the depths of those black pools, and Imari felt the hum of his power, cradled just there in his inked palm. It was so much stronger now, without her Liagé binds. Suffocating, almost. "All it takes is one word from me, little sulaziér."

Jeric.

Imari ground her teeth together and glared at him. "I hate you."

His eyes flashed, those thin lips curled, and then he thrust his palm at her. A blast of air knocked her from the saddle. She flew a few yards and landed hard on the sand, on her back. The force knocked the breath from her lungs, and pain shot through her spine, but even as Imari struggled to suck down a breath, Mashi and another guard gripped her arms and yanked her back to her feet.

Azir stood before her, his cold eyes fixed on her face as he grabbed her chin and squeezed, nails digging into her skin. "When are you ever going to learn when you've been beaten?"

Imari couldn't answer; she couldn't breathe.

Azir gave her cheek a good hard pat that might've been a gesture of affection had it not stung so sharply.

"Bring her," he said to Mashi and the other guard. He glanced at Bahdra, and Bahdra took position off to the side, gazing out in the direction they had come.

And Imari wondered...was it possible? Had the person who'd been following them survived the night? Imari didn't dare ask, didn't dare draw attention. But Azir had started forward, and her escort dragged her after him.

Imari's shoes sank in the sand with each step, and she wondered what she was going to do. Because whatever Azir wanted with the power in this tree, Imari wanted no part in giving it to him.

Wind pushed hollow tones through Assi Andai's remains, like breath through a piccolo. Her escort pulled her after Azir, through the Mazarat's open archway and over the mound of sand that poured from its mouth like a tongue.

Into what had been the main atrium.

Imari's heart nearly stopped.

It was the room Tallyn had shown her, though sand filled it

now, partially burying the four Liagé arches. At its center, totally untouched by destruction, stood the tree.

Imari had no idea how it'd survived when the world around it had been destroyed, but then she remembered Tallyn's story. How it had survived generations, contained by different structures.

Because it was a thing not of this world.

It stood impossibly tall and proud, its golden leaves shimmering and chiming in the wind.

A flash.

Imari saw the tree not as it was, but as the twist of spindly, oozing black in her nightmare. It was only a flash—so fast, Imari wondered if she'd imagined it—except for the splitting ache between her eyes. She looked at the tree, at those innocent, shimmering leaves chiming like bells. Still, she couldn't shake this sense of *wrongness*. Like a major melody tinkling over a steady minor root.

Imari had felt a sickness permeating the air ever since they'd set foot in this land, and after their encounter with the tyrcorat, she'd thought the root cause had been Fyri.

She'd been wrong.

It was *this*. She didn't understand how—or why—but she felt that revulsion to her core. The poison. Azir, however, gazed upon that tree, and his expression filled only with awe.

"This tree is our freedom, little sulaziér," Azir said, that golden sheen reflecting in his black eyes. "It is power manifest, and life to those who eat of its fruit."

Imari did not know what this tree truly was, but it was not life.

"It's sick," Imari said, and Mashi gave her arm a good jerk.

"Yes," Azir replied without hesitation, slowly approaching his prize. "It was never meant to be confined like this, planted here, in this soil. Of all people, you understand what happens to misplanted seeds." He looked back at her. "You see, they never told us the truth. This tree is so much more than a symbol of our people, and it wasn't until it survived the destruction that I truly understood what it was. Had I realized it sooner, the war against the Provinces would have had a very...different outcome." Fury flashed in his black eyes, his expression seething as he gazed back at the tree.

"This tree was the Four Divines' greatest secret, little sulaziér. Buried with time, and seemingly for our own good. And look how that's benefited us." He snarled those last words as he gestured wildly at the ruins. "Their religion is a *prison*. It holds us and confines us. Keeps us slaves to their will. It keeps us subservient, so that we do not take for ourselves. Because they know that if we take from this tree, *we* become gods."

Imari tried following his words, but that minor root persisted, growing louder with each passing second. It crept through her thoughts—insidious—and her vision flashed again.

A hiss.

That gnarled tree. Branches whipped like tentacles.

And the tree returned to normal again.

A gust of wind ripped through this place, like a portent, and the golden leaves shimmered, tingling like chimes. Still, that melody rang an incongruous major against the minor bass blaring through Imari's soul.

"Give the sulaziér her flute," Azir said.

Mashi produced the flute, just as the other guard leveled a crossbow at Imari. His motives were clear: Try anything, and he would shoot.

"What is it you expect me to do, exactly?" Imari asked.

"You are the sulaziér, singer of souls, weaver of stars, and shadow binder." He looked at her, his black eyes glittering. "Find its song, sulaziér, for it is buried deep in the ground by the very flute you now hold in your hands. Find it, pull it out of the ground, and set it free."

Imari looked at the tree, her flute—its glyphs lay dark, though she felt the hum of its power. "And just how do I do that?"

"The same way you ripped the tyrcorat from this world. The same way you bound my leje. Find its light, fight its song, and bend it to your will."

Imari wondered how Azir knew so much about her particular power, but she didn't wonder for very long. He had, after all, been very close to Fyri, regardless of the terms they'd parted on.

Azir's brow hardened, his gaze burned and that madness writhed. His patience waned. "Take the flute, sulaziér."

The guard aimed the bolt at her heart.

Imari considered letting him shoot her so that Azir could not use her to do whatever it was he had planned. But then she thought of Jeric.

If she died, he would suffer.

So, she swallowed and took the flute. The contact sent an electric jolt through her body. It cleared the haze, dulled the pain, and her world suddenly became razor sharp. She could hear each inhale and exhale, each steady beat of their hearts. The leaves' chiming rang clearer, louder, as the wind whispered secrets through the ruined Mazarat. Her world was sound, and the quiet spaces in between.

Azir, Mashi, and the guard all watched her, waiting for her to try something. Mashi's fingers curled, cupping energy into her palm, while the guard kept that bolt fixed on Imari's heart.

Azir waited, a mark of intrigue in the madness. *What will you do, little sulaziér?* his eyes seemed to say, as if a part of him wanted her to try to fight, just so that he could dominate, make her suffer.

But then his gaze shot past her, narrowing on the archway they'd walked through, and a figure ran into the room.

40

Jeric hadn't stopped riding since the storm. Since the dead had come in a rush—but not for Jeric and the others. Instead, they'd watched from within Niá's glowing circle of wards, gazing in horror as light flashed in the distance, as nightmarish shrieking had filled the dark.

As members of Azir's party had been pulled out of their circle and into the writhing horde of demons, where they were ripped to shreds.

Jeric had almost lost his resolve then. In fact, he would have run right past Niá's wards, if Braddok and Stanis and Aksel had not held him firmly back. He'd known he was powerless against the evil attacking Imari's entourage, but that hadn't mattered to him then. All that had mattered was her.

And then the air had convulsed. Jeric didn't know how else to describe it. It pulsed out from a point, like some kind of invisible explosion. It'd knocked them all down—even two of their camels —and then the world had gone quiet.

It was then they realized the sun was beginning to peek over the horizon, and Azir's party was on the move again.

Jeric and the others had promptly packed up and followed.

They crossed the open sands and dunes, trying to gain ground, but there were no shortcuts, and sand made speed a challenge. So they trudged on at a pace too godsdamned slow for Jeric's liking. Wind pushed across the dunes, spraying them with sand. Jeric was covered in it, and every time he swallowed, his teeth ground on bits of sand.

Jeric decided he hated the desert.

"They're headed for those rocks," Jeric said as they crested another dune. He wiped the back of his hand across his brows, but his hand was also covered in a thin layer of sand, and so the gestures only served to get more sand in his eyes.

Tallyn stopped his mount beside Jeric's, his one eye fixed on the rocks. "Those aren't rocks."

Jeric eyed the alta-Liagé.

"That's Assi Andai," Tallyn continued quietly. "Or what remains of it."

"The old Sol Velorian capital?" Chez asked from behind them. His left eye was still swollen shut, and his right looked like it might follow soon, red-rimmed and swollen from all the sand.

Tallyn nodded.

"Why bring her here?" Jeric asked with a frown.

Tallyn's thin lips pressed together. "I have no idea."

Jeric clucked his tongue and nudged his camel's side with his boot.

"Wait," Tallyn said.

Jeric stopped and looked at Tallyn, but Tallyn had turned toward Nia.

"We need to shield them," Tallyn said, and the two of them exchanged a long look.

"Shield us?" Aksel asked as Niá dismounted. "What does he mean?"

"It's an enchantment that will protect you against Shah," Niá said, striding toward Jeric.

He anticipated what she was going to ask before she said a

word, and he'd plucked a dagger from his boot and held it out to her, hilt first, even before she reached him.

She eyed him, then took the dagger and—predictably—stabbed her arm.

"Good gods..." Chez said, turning away.

"Didn't realize you were so squeamish," Aksel teased.

"I'm not really in the habit of watching someone cut themselves..."

"I thought you didn't want Azir to sense your power," Stanis said, looking mistrustfully at the alta-Liagé.

"I don't," Tallyn replied. "But right now, I'm more concerned about your survival."

Stanis frowned, and Niá moved to him first. Blood coated her fingers. "The shielding is stronger if I mix some of your blood with it."

Stanis looked down at her, his features hard.

Niá waited. "It's your life." She shrugged and started to walk on.

"Wait," Stanis said begrudgingly.

Niá stopped as Stanis pulled the pilfered scim from his belt.

"How much blood do you need?" he asked.

"Just a few drops."

Stanis used the tip of the scim to puncture his finger—Chez flinched immediately and Aksel chuckled. Stanis looked at Niá, blood welling upon his finger, as Niá stepped back to him and raised her bloodied fingers. And then she touched her bloodied finger to his.

Stanis stilled as the others watched.

"Pull open your tunic," Niá said. "It must be drawn over your heart."

A beat. And then Stanis lifted his tunic.

Jeric saw Niá hesitate as her eyes took in Stanis's scars, and then she set to task, standing up on her toes to draw a symbol over Stanis's heart. When she finished, she spoke a word. Air pulsed, the symbol flared with white light, and then...it dissolved into Stanis's skin.

Invisible.

"So, how's this work?" Braddok asked.

"We call it *jevia*. Shielding. It absorbs any Shah energy thrown at you." She made her way to Aksel next, who had stabbed his finger and was chuckling at Chez as he did so.

"How much Shah energy?" Jeric asked, thinking of Azir and Bahdra.

"Depends on the strength and manner of the one wielding it," Niá said, now moving on to Chez.

"Give me an estimation," Jeric said.

"One strong spell or five mediocre."

Jeric glanced sideways at Tallyn. "You said you believed Azir and Bahdra aren't the only two Liagé in their group?"

Tallyn nodded. "I know for certain that there are at least two others. I saw their spells last night."

Niá had finished with Chez, Jenya, and Braddok—who'd waggled his brows at Jenya when he'd lifted his shirt—and then approached Jeric.

Jeric pricked his finger, touched his blood to hers, then lifted his shirt.

Niá froze, her eyes fixed on the three black lines of shade poison. Her gaze met his. "Who healed you?"

"The same incredible woman I'm trying to save."

A crease formed between Niá's brows, her gaze dropped, and she drew a blood symbol over Jeric's heart. It flared white, just like the others, then vanished.

Niá climbed back onto the camel she shared with Tallyn, and they kept going.

Within the hour, they reached the edge of Assi Andai. Gods, Jeric had never expected to see this place, and gazing at its massive ruins, he couldn't help but wonder how it had looked in its prime. How it had been *possible*. The broken structures were still larger than anything Jeric had ever seen, and they were made of...sand. Yes, as he looked more closely, it was definitely sand, but compressed somehow.

Tallyn and Niá kept pace beside him while the others trailed behind, gazing in solemn reverence at the enormity of it all. A sharp wind ripped through the remains, singing a hollow, lamenting tone.

Jeric stopped beside a fractured wall as he studied the soft impressions in the sand.

Tallyn followed Jeric's gaze, and said, "He's taken her to the Mazarat."

The Mazarat. The temple where Liagé had studied and trained in their respective schools of Shah power.

Jeric frowned. "Any idea why?"

Tallyn sat quiet, considering.

"The Divine Tree is there."

It was Niá who had spoken.

"What's this about a Divine Tree?" Chez asked from behind Jeric.

"It's the place where the power of the Four Divines rained back to earth," Niá explained.

"Four Divines...those are the ones you Liagé worship, right?" Aksel asked.

"No," Niá said, with an edge of irritation. "They were the very first Liagé."

"What does Imari have to do with the tree?" Jeric asked her.

Niá's dark gaze met Tallyn's briefly before she looked on. "I don't know."

Jeric dismounted.

"Wolf...?" Braddok asked warily.

Jeric patted his camel's neck, checked his weapons, and continued forward on foot. Someone murmured behind him— probably Chez—but soon the others dismounted and followed after.

Wind howled as he followed the soft imprints around massive pillars and sunken domes. They reached the edge of a broken wall, and Jeric held up a hand and peered around the corner.

Five Sol Velorians stood watch in a courtyard beyond, and Bahdra made six. Behind them was the scarred face of what could only be the Mazarat. Imari was just inside, with Azir Mubarék and whoever else had gone with them.

Jeric pulled back and looked to the others. Niá clutched her clothing, wringing it in her hands.

Nervous.

"You said one strong hit or five mediocre?" Jeric asked at a whisper.

Niá nodded.

"There are two Liagé in that group," Tallyn whispered.

"Including Bahdra?" Jeric asked.

Tallyn shook his head.

Jeric flexed his hand over Lorath's hilt. "How strong are the two?"

"Mediocre."

"So...who's got Bahdra?" Chez whispered.

Tallyn looked at Niá.

Yes, she was definitely nervous.

"Together, we might be able to hold him," Tallyn answered carefully. "But you're on your own with the other two."

"What are they?" Jeric asked.

"Guardians."

"I'll handle one," Jenya said, to which Braddok puffed up his chest and looked at Jenya as he said, "I'll handle the other."

"I'll help with the guardians too," Stanis said.

"Squeamish and I can handle the rest," Aksel said, and Chez whacked him on the back of the head.

Jeric nodded, gave their group a once-over, and turned back around. He kissed Lorath's hilt, threw up a quick prayer to whoever would listen, and then stepped around the corner.

Bahdra and the Sol Velorians glanced over. The Sol Velorians looked startled, then exceedingly confused. The first, because they hadn't expected to see anyone. The second, because Jeric was supposed to be locked in a cage, in Trier.

"Isn't that...the *Corazzi*?" one of them asked, in Sol Velorian, as three of them drew weapons.

Which meant the other two were Liagé.

Jeric's men—and Jenya—fanned out behind him, and Jeric made a quick gesture to Braddok, letting him know which two were the Liagé.

And Bahdra...

Bahdra was staring only at Tallyn and Niá, who had also stepped out from behind the broken wall. Niá looked very pale.

Jeric understood her nervousness then. Niá knew Bahdra. Quite well, by the look of it.

"I don't know how you got out of your cage, dog," one of the Sol Velorians—not Liagé—was saying in thickly accented Common as he brandished two scims, "But you should have—"

Bahdra raised a single, inked fist, and the man stopped talking. They all looked curiously from Bahdra, to where Bahdra's gaze rest.

"My little Ni," Bahdra said, in Sol Velorian. He had a reedy voice that hissed more than it produced tone.

Tallyn took a defensive step before Niá, and Bahdra's black and fathomless eyes glittered.

"I knew I felt you," Bahdra continued, taking a step. "I said as much to Lestra, but she could not See you." His black gaze settled on the beads—now visible—at Tallyn's neck. "I should have known. You always had a weakness for the sisters."

"You *used* me."

The words had come from Niá, trembling and pained. She stepped around Tallyn, and faced Bahdra square. There was color to her face now.

"I did not use anything you did not wish to give," Bahdra said in that reedy voice.

"You knew what I was—because of my oza—and you used it against me. Against *her*. And you killed her!"

A streak of silver shot straight for Bahdra, from Niá's inked hands.

It was Jeric's dagger—the one he had given to her before she'd shielded them. And it hovered there, glowing with the enchantments she had drawn upon the blade, wobbling in midair, inches from Bahdra's face.

Niá had acted surprisingly fast, but not fast enough.

One of the Liagé guardians was holding up a hand, eyes fixed on that enchanted dagger.

Which Bahdra plucked from the air.

He gazed down at Niá's enchantments, then Niá herself. "Keep the dog and the voloré alive," Bahdra said, and then his gaze fixed on Tallyn. "Kill the rest, but the traitor is mine."

And Bahdra's forces converged.

Or, more accurately, three of his five converged. One guardian threw a shimmering burst of air at Jeric. The burst struck before Jeric could react, but rather than knock him back a dozen paces, it slid over him like cool water, and Niá's little symbol at his chest warmed.

It had worked.

And godsdamnit, now he only had four hits left.

All around Jeric, Jenya and his men fought. In the corner of his eye, he saw Niá and Tallyn throwing more spells at Bahdra, while Bahdra deflected and threw spells of his own.

"Go on, Wolf!" Braddok yelled as a guardian threw a spell that knocked him on his rear, but then, in the guardian's distraction, Jenya threw a scim, skewering him through the gut.

Imari.

Jeric snarled, and ran into the Mazarat.

41

I mari gasped as Jeric ran into the atrium, covered in sand and blood, with murder in his eyes.

By the wards, he had come into Ziyan—for her.

She did not know how it was possible, but right then, any joy she felt at the sight of him was quickly smothered by fear.

Azir would kill him.

Time seemed to stand still as fate teetered on a scim's edge. And then three things happened at once.

Jeric threw a dagger.

The Sol Velorian man fired the crossbow.

And Imari charged Azir.

The Sol Velorian man dropped with Jeric's dagger between his eyes—sunk to the hilt—as the bolt went wide, striking a column. Mashi threw her spell, but not fast enough, and Jeric was barreling into her just as Imari and Azir hit the ground in a tangle.

Imari grappled to wrap her arms around Azir's neck, but Azir snarled a word, and a burst of air threw her back. She sailed through the air, struck a column, and bounced to the ground.

The flute slipped from her hands and rolled in the sand as Imari cursed.

On the other side of the atrium, Jeric was caught in a fight with Mashi. Azir set his dark gaze on Jeric, who dodged another one of Mashi's blasts.

Imari shoved herself to her feet and ran at Azir again. She jumped onto his back from behind and held on like a barnacle. Azir grunted, stumbling in the sand as he tried to regain his balance. He grabbed her arms, spoke a word, and an electric shock sizzled through her body.

Imari cried out and let go, just in time to see Jeric snatch the crossbow the guard had dropped and fire. The bolt landed right in Mashi's open mouth, her eyes flinched wide, and she collapsed.

Azir snarled, and a blast of air shot from his hands and hit Jeric square.

Jeric went flying, arcing through the air about ten yards before hitting the ground on his back. He winced, hand at his chest as he tried to catch his breath, but then Azir spoke another word with a twist of his fist, pulling Jeric up, so that Jeric was hovering in midair, his boots inches above the ground.

"Stop, or Tommad's bloodthirsty little pup dies," Azir snarled at Imari, who had just picked up the crossbow that had launched from Jeric's hands when Azir's blast had struck him.

Imari froze with indecision as fear squeezed her heart.

"Drop it, sulaziér," Azir's voice almost lulled.

Jeric strained, the muscles in his neck corded. "Imari, don't—" His words cut short as Azir squeezed him tighter.

"Pick up your flute," Azir said—too calm, as he held Jeric suspended and choking. "And play."

Jeric tried to speak, but only a gasp of air came out, and his lips were turning blue.

"Wait." Imari dropped the crossbow.

"No..." Jeric managed.

Azir's lips twisted. "Your flute, little sulaziér."

Imari ground her teeth together and strode to her flute. As she picked it up, she looked back at the tree. Those leaves shimmered like jewels, so beautiful and almost mocking as Jeric gasped for his life behind her.

"I will not ask you again," Azir warned.

Imari shut her eyes, hands trembling as she drew in a breath. And played.

Her vision shifted to that Shah plane of light and dark, but to her surprise, there were no stars in this place—*none*, except for the sun over Jeric and the one within herself. Where Azir stood was only darkness, just like Bahdra. But it paled in comparison to the mass of darkness writhing over the tree.

It blotted out the world like some black hole, sucking all light into its depths, and a deep, discordant bass rattled through Imari's body. It completely swallowed her notes, drowning them in dissonance.

What in the stars...?

You do not know what you are you doing! Fyri's warning came rushing back to her, and everything became crystal clear in that instant.

Fyri had come to this place to draw the power from the tree, and she had discovered—as Imari was quickly discovering for herself—that the four Divines had never actually destroyed the fifth Divine. Instead, they'd bound Zussa here, to this tree. Imari could feel each line of their power tethered to the darkness writhing between worlds—each tether a note, binding it, and their power had rained back to the soil to keep it bound. Feeding it, so that the enchantments would never sputter out.

Imari could see it all, for the past was here, in this tree, and yet the truth of the tree had been twisted over the years. People had forgotten what really lay within its roots. It wasn't just power, nor was it wisdom.

It was the Great Deceiver herself.

But Fyri...

Fyri had figured it out. Yes, when Fyri had loosened one of the tethers—Imari could feel it now. How that particular note bent just so, having lost its full tension. Fyri had realized it too, what truly lay bound to those tethers, and she had then tried to stop it, to tighten it back, but in doing so, she'd destroyed herself and all of Sol Velor. But her spirit had remained in the sand, ruling the tyrcorat, to ward against Azir—or anyone else—returning to this place. So that no one could finish what Azir had tried to do over one hundred years ago.

Imari cut her note short, and her vision returned to normal. Jeric still hung suspended in the air, as Azir held him tight.

"It's the Deceiver," Imari said.

Azir looked unsurprised.

"That's why you brought me here. It's not just power you seek. It's *Zussa*. You want me to free Zussa."

"Of course," he said simply. "It is the only way."

But Imari was shaking her head, because she had tasted that power—that poison. Felt the taint in the strain of those tethers. "No. I will not help you do this."

Azir looked at her, and then he smiled cruelly.

He thrust his other palm at Jeric. A sheet of sand lifted off the ground, gathering and clustering into a spear. It sharpened to a point as it pierced right through Jeric's heart.

Jeric gasped; his eyes flew wide open.

Imari's heart stopped.

Azir released his hold, and Jeric collapsed. The spear disintegrated, raining grains of sand all around him, as blood blossomed over his chest.

As his blue eyes stared vacantly at a sky he could no longer see.

"*NOOOOO!*" Imari screamed.

She snarled and started for Azir, but he turned his invisible binding on her. Wrapped her up, squeezed her tight, as hot tears poured down her face.

"You can still save him, little sulaziér," Azir said in that too-calm voice. "Zussa's wisdom lies in that tree. Pull it free, and you can bring him back."

The pressure released and Imari collapsed to the ground, heaving and choking on sobs. She couldn't seem to get enough air as Jeric's still form blurred through her tears.

"But you must hurry, little sulaziér," Azir said. "Even with the power of a god, there is a natural order to this world. Once his soul crosses the threshold, there is no bringing him back. He is not Liagé. His soul does not linger with his power. Once he is gone, he is gone forever."

Imari trembled as she gazed upon Jeric, bleeding and lifeless on the sand. Jeric, who had faced Ziyan for her.

And now he was dead—because of her.

Just like her papa, and Sorai, and Taran and Tolya and Saza.

Imari closed her eyes, her tears running freely.

"Not much longer now, little sulaziér." Azir's voice wormed into her mind.

Imari fury steeled with resolve, her hands curled into fists. If this was a power Azir wanted, a wisdom, she could take it for herself. Better her hands than Azir's. She *would* take it, and she would use it to bring Jeric back.

And then she would destroy Azir for all the pain he'd caused.

Imari opened her eyes, snatched up her flute, and played.

Again, her world became light and dark. Where Jeric laid, there were no longer stars, but the imprints of them. Like when one looks at the sun for too long and looks away, but the image of that sun is still seared into your vision. It was that imprint Imari could see over Jeric's heart. So long as that imprint remained, Imari could bring him back.

Hold on, Jeric, she said in her mind, and she kept playing.

Azir told her to find the tree's song, but she could see nothing through that mass of writhing darkness. She searched and she searched, letting her heart guide her fingers. But the deeper she searched, the more her lungs strained. Like swimming too deep underwater. Pressure squeezed all around her, pushing against her lungs and her ears—which had started ringing and popping. Her head pounded, particularly at a point between her eyes.

She needed air.

But she didn't dare stop.

I'm coming, Jeric...

She played through the sludge of darkness, against the pressure mounting in her chest and head. The tingling filled her veins with fire—a fire that was growing hotter with each passing moment.

Still, there was no light, no sound.

Nothing.

Just a vast expanse of nothing.

And right when she thought she couldn't hold her breath any longer, swim any deeper, she caught a glimmer of sound.

It rang at the very edge of her consciousness, like a distant echo through a fathomless canyon. The tone brushed her ears, and her power surged in response.

And yet...

The tone felt *wrong*.

It was a pitch just out of tune, bent to the edge of itself, brittle as it strained for volume and strength.

Find the tension, that voice had told her before.

Imari focused on that warped pitch, trying to match it with her own tones as her lungs burned and her head split.

But *wards*. It was like trying to hold sand. The tone kept slipping away, deeper and deeper.

Falling.

No, Imari snarled in her mind. She pushed her breath harder, desperate. Pushing and straining until...

There.

She caught hold by a thread. And then...

Sound *exploded*.

It blared through her body, rattling her bones. Engulfing her with heat and...

Rage. Infinite and crushing rage, just like that in her nightmare. It consumed her with hate, with fury and hunger.

Somewhere, in her mind, in the real world, she felt the ground shake beneath her feet. She heard it groan. Grains of sand nicked at her face.

Yesssssssssssssssss.

It was a voice outside of time and space, all vibration, and suddenly, Imari knew that she had just made a very big mistake.

She would never be able to contain *this*.

Her world flared suddenly white—blinding—and then Imari saw...*everything*. Spells as incantations and images poured into her mind, searing through her body too many and too fast. Like drinking from a geyser. A geyser of flame. Imari was drowning in it, burning right up, and she felt her knees give as the flute slipped from her hands.

And then, as fast as it'd come, it was gone. Snatched right out of her grasp.

Her vision returned to normal, and the world around her trembled violently. Bits of rock and stone broke off from a now fractured ceiling, and behind her, Azir stood tall, his arms spread wide as wind and blinding white light spun all around him. As if he were calamity itself.

Oh, no.

Imari staggered forward, tripping on rock and the vibrations of the ground as she stumbled for Jeric. A chunk of the domed ceiling collapsed, and Imari hardly managed to dodge in time.

"YESSSS!" Azir said in that same voice. Not his own, but the one that had blared in her mind. The one that tore across both planes—Shah and physical—yawning wide open in this slowly collapsing chamber. "*YESSSSSSSS!*"

A violent temor shook the ground, and the tree exploded.

Imari dove over Jeric, shielding him from falling rock and plaster.

"You should have listened to Fyri," Azir's voice rumbled—though it was no longer his voice. And in a whirl of blinding light, he was gone.

But the earth did not stop groaning, straining painfully from the wound now gaping in its shell. Imari hardly noticed, hardly cared. She clutched Jeric's face in her hands while hot tears burned down her cheeks.

She had failed. She had failed and she had given Azir exactly what he'd wanted, and Jeric...

"Jeric..." she sobbed, pushing the hair back from his face. "I love you. I'm so sorry." But he did not hear her.

His life was gone.

A scream tore from her lips as massive chunks of the Mazarat rained all around them, as fractures split the earth where the tree had been. Where a gaping hole now existed, that sand was pouring into like some massive sinkhole. They'd be sucked right into it, assuming the chamber didn't collapse on top of them first.

She could run. She might make it, but she could not bring herself to leave him. Not like this.

Suddenly, the answer was there—a piece of information, an imprint on her heart left after that geyser of flame and heat.

Knowledge, of a way to get them out of here.

A way to bring him back.

It was all suddenly so clear.

Imari sat on her knees beside him, placed her palms to the ground, then closed her eyes and hummed.

One single note—a low tone that matched the rumbling bass of the world around her—and her vision turned to stars. They were all visible now that Zussa's writhing darkness was gone. Imari saw the walls around her like strings of light, designed to sing a specific tone, and the gaping black hole at their feet. It was to the walls that Imari hummed now.

The chamber picked up the sound, and the tone amplified it through the shattering and splitting and groaning, and Imari hummed louder. She poured everything she had into that one tone. Fire seared through her body, those vibrations crescendoed, but she didn't stop. She kept her hands pressed firmly to the ground, pouring her tone and power into the sand as though *she* were the flute.

The vector.

She pushed that energy into the sand, the walls, until those strings of light vibrated to the point of breaking. And then, in a concussive burst of air and power, stars scattered as the walls shattered. Air and rock exploded into dust, falling like ash all around, disintegrating the Mazarat completely.

And the trembling stopped.

Imari was distantly aware of figures nearby, but she had no time to spare them a thought. Not if this was going to work. Already, she felt her consciousness fading from the amount of Shah she had just channeled through her body.

Imari placed her hands over Jeric's blood-soaked heart, and closed her eyes. Hot tears streamed down her face.

And she sang.

Words and notes poured from her soul as she sang to the only one who could help her—the only one who could save him.

Hear me, she prayed in song.

Save him...

Give my life to him...

She saw the stars. A million tiny points of light infused in the world all around her. The Maker's power and word—his song, woven into everything.

Imari focused on herself, but not in the physical. She saw herself through the Shah plane, as a cluster of brilliant stars, and she focused specifically on the sun positioned just over her heart.

It was to that sun she sang now, directing her power to that brilliant pulse of her heart. She did not stop singing, not even as that sun burned brighter—blinding. Heat seared through her veins, but she kept singing, grinding her teeth as the notes pulled and snapped every string in her body. As she broke the tether and pushed her light from her chest, down her arms. And with one final tone, she shoved her light into Jeric's body.

TALLYN WATCHED Imari sob over the Wolf King. A small crowd of figures gathered near, at the opposite edge of the courtyard, watching the scene in silence. For there was no better testament to love's power than watching this child of Sol Velor grieve over the death of the Wolf King, and her lamentations brought tears to those who looked on.

Blood stained the Wolf's chest; his blue eyes stared at nothing. The tree was gone, the Mazarat totally obliterated.

Imari had done it. And Tallyn stared at her in wonder.

And then...

Imari stopped crying. She sat up straight, wiped her eyes, and shut them tight.

Resolved.

She sat back on her heels, poised before Jeric with her hands over his heart. Her face was set with concentration, though grief and blood smeared her features.

And she sang.

If grief had voice, it was this. Notes poured from her mouth, beautiful and tragic, bringing even more tears to the gathering crowd. Even Tallyn himself began to cry.

And then Tallyn realized what she was doing.

He should stop her—he should. They would need her in the war to come.

But he would not take this choice from her.

The song wrenched from her broken heart. Building and

building until Tallyn felt the softest push. A brush of air, a rumble of sound.

And Imari collapsed.

Her life...for his.

Jeric's back arched with a wheezing inhale. His body relaxed, and Tallyn already dreaded the moment the Wolf would open his eyes.

Those eyes snapped open and settled on Imari, who lay perfectly still on the ground beside him, staring at nothing.

In all Tallyn's years on this earth, he had never seen greater agony.

"No..." The Wolf King was on his knees, rolling her limp body onto her back. Checking for breath, for pulse, but there was none. "Godsdamnit, Imari, *no*."

But Tallyn knew she was gone.

He saw the moment the Wolf realized it too.

Jeric gathered her up in his arms, against his bloodied chest, and he screamed. The sound filled the ruins, echoing across time and space with unbearable pain.

The Wolf's pack looked away. The crowd bowed their heads.

And then the Wolf bent over her and cried.

42

"Jeric."

Jeric held her to his chest, feeling the warmth leave her body.

"Jeric."

Someone crouched beside him, but he didn't turn.

Didn't care.

He would kill Azir—kill him with his bare hands...

A big hand rested on his shoulder. "Someone's here to talk to you."

Jeric glanced up and focused on Braddok's square face a second later. Braddok gestured to a figure standing over them—an older woman Jeric had never seen before. She wore a long white robe and her dark, Sol Velorian gaze slid from Jeric to the woman in his arms.

And Jeric drew Imari closer, protectively, as he turned away from the woman.

"I am not your enemy," the woman said in thick Sol Velorian.

Jeric noticed others then. A small crowd of Sol Velorians had gathered, and a few more figures robed in white. Jeric had no idea where they'd come from.

Nor did he care.

He looked down at Imari, over this beautiful face that was already losing color, and his chest felt like it was caving in.

Gods, if he'd been faster...

"If we're to save her, you must bring her to the temple," the woman said.

Jeric's gaze snapped to the woman, and narrowed. "*Save her?*" he nearly yelled. He was a bow strung too tight, ready to snap at any second. "You can't save her. She's *dead*."

Braddok flinched. Jenya too.

Tallyn knelt beside Jeric, staring at him as if he could will him to calm. "Wolf. *Listen to me.* These people can help her, but only if we hurry. Her soul hovers between life and death, but death's pull is strong and swift."

Jeric stared at him, trembling with fury.

Fearing hope.

Tallyn placed a hand on Jeric's shoulder. "Will you carry her?"

Jeric looked down at Imari.

"*Wolf.*"

Hurry, that one command said. *Pull yourself together*, it demanded.

Jeric ground his teeth furiously together and held Imari close as he stood. He cradled her against him, her legs dangling over his arm. Blood still stained his chest where the sand spear had sunk.

Where it should have killed him.

In fact, the spear had hurt less than the pain coursing through him now.

"This way." The woman in white motioned for Jeric to follow.

He exchanged a hard glance with Tallyn, but he followed.

Jeric took in their surroundings at a glance. The great fissures in the ground, where that tree had been. The complete annihilation of the Mazarat, which now coated the sand like ash. Azir's

Sol Velorian guards were dead. Bahdra was nowhere to be seen, but Niá, Jenya, and all of Jeric's pack had survived.

It was hard for Jeric to feel very grateful just then.

A crowd of Sol Velorians had gathered within the ruins, and Jeric had no idea where they'd come from. Jeric easily counted near a hundred men and women, a few children, and they all parted for the robed figures and Jeric, watching the procession in wonder. Some whispered, some strained to see. Once Jeric and the others had completely passed through, the crowd followed.

Meanwhile, Imari's face grew ashen.

For Jeric, it felt as though the world had just lost its sun.

They had walked about a mile before the ruins ended at the slope of the foothills. Their path morphed into a small trail, indented with countless footsteps that followed a line to a rocky wall and a cave. More people gathered outside of that cave, lining the trail and parting to make room for them.

"Who are they?" Braddok asked Tallyn, who walked beside him.

Tallyn did not answer immediately. "It appears that a small vestige of Sol Velor survived, and has been hiding here all this time."

Jeric did not know how it was possible. There was nothing in this place—nothing but sand and rock and ghosts. But here they were, more numerous than he could've imagined. Healthy and strong and hopeful.

Jeric carried Imari into the cavern, which turned out to be a tunnel lined with burning torches. The tunnel emptied abruptly into a massive dome, and Jeric stopped in wonder.

It was a city—underground.

Great shafts of natural light pierced the stone canopy above, dusting the floor and buildings below in light and gold. Jeric carried Imari on, following the robed figures down the sloping path where more people gathered, watching as they passed by.

Finally, the robed figures turned a corner and the structures gave way to a courtyard.

And a tree.

It was a giant, reaching oak with shimmering leaves of crimson contrasting its rich brown bark, and a great shaft of light fell upon it, throwing glittering red prisms over everything.

Jeric might have been awed had it not been for the woman lying dead in his arms.

"Bring her here," said the robed woman, gesturing to a place between two massive roots.

Jeric laid Imari down, taking care with her head as though he were putting her to bed.

"Stand back," the woman whispered.

"No."

The woman eyed him. A second robed figure approached the woman and whispered into her ear.

The woman looked at Jeric, then inclined her head. "As you wish."

She stepped away and joined more robed figures—six, in total —who formed a circle around the tree. The figures joined hands and began to chant in low voices. Jeric didn't know what they were saying, but he felt the power in their words. A force he could not explain, only feel.

He grabbed Imari's hand and squeezed it tight, his head bowed over her as that power rolled through him. And then a wave of it came all at once, striking him like a bolt of lightning.

My son, said a deep, thunderous voice.

It was not a sound Jeric heard with his ears. No, this voice called to his soul, maker to creation. And suddenly, without warning, Jeric saw all that he had done. All that he had been, all that he was, and all that he was not. It flashed in his mind in a blink, completely exposed to the one who had spoken.

And in that moment, Jeric knew the Maker was real. He felt it with a certainty he had never felt before.

Jeric expected condemnation. He waited for that swift hammer of judgment to fall. He deserved it—he knew. He had committed too many unspeakable atrocities, thinking he had done right, when it had all been so very, very wrong.

But that hammer did not fall.

Instead, Jeric felt an overwhelming wash of love.

You are my son, the voice repeated—proudly, as though claiming Jeric as his own.

It nearly broke Jeric in two. His own father had never spoken to him like this, and it was too much to bear.

Take my life for hers, Jeric pleaded in his mind, as his eyes burned. *Take it. Give it to her. I deserve death for all I've done. Spare her—please. She has suffered enough.*

Not today, my son, said the voice. *She has need of you. Serve her well.*

There was light.

There was fire.

And then nothing.

The chanting ceased.

Jeric opened his eyes. His hand still clutched Imari's, though Imari lay stone still. And then her back arched as she sucked her soul back into her body.

43

There was nothing.

And then there was.

Imari's world was dark. And cold.

So bitterly cold and empty. As if she alone existed in this infinite abyss of nothing, floating endlessly through the expanse of space and time.

Suddenly, a brilliant beam of light cut through the dark, pure and unfiltered. It chased away all shadow, all cold, and Imari was overwhelmed with heat, and pain. Maker's mercy, the pain! It felt as though her soul were being welded back to its shell.

The pain dimmed and faded, until nothing remained but a slight tingling. That tingling concentrated in her belly, and then she grew aware of her body. The soft ground beneath her, the scent of earth and dust in the air, with a faint edge of something sweet. She became aware of her breathing, and her steadily beating heart. Of the large, strong hand clutching hers so tightly.

She knew that hand. She knew the very shape of it, the way it gripped hers, and it was warm and firm and *alive*.

Imari's eyelids snapped open and landed on Jeric's storming blues.

Imari gasped, hardly able to believe her eyes as she bolted upright, and Jeric wrapped her up in his arms, crushing her to him.

"You're alive..." she gasped, wrapping her arms around him and squeezing him tight.

Thank you, she prayed silently. *Thank you for saving him. Thankyouthankyouthankyou.*

"I thought I lost you," she managed.

Jeric pulled back, looked at her. His eyes were so blue, and clearer than Imari had ever seen them. "You should have," he said, wiping her tears with his thumbs. "But you just won't let me die for you, you stubborn, beautiful woman."

Imari smiled, and Jeric kissed her. Through all of her tears, her hair, and when he pulled back, he grabbed her face firmly between his hands.

"I love you," he said, and Imari felt her eyes burning all over again. "I've loved you from the moment you dragged my ass from that river, and if you *ever* try to sacrifice your life for mine again, I will kill you."

Imari laughed, and he kissed her again. Once, softly, then pulled back. Imari tried to hold on to that kiss, but he pressed two fingers to her lips. "Later," he said like a promise. "We have an audience."

And Imari realized they *did* have an audience. She went utterly rigid, her hand in his as her eyes widened, taking in the crowd standing all around. There had to be at least two hundred people, men, women, and children—all Sol Velorian, though she did not see Azir's guard or Bahdra in their midst. And then she noticed the strange tree with crimson leaves she and Jeric sat beneath, similar to the one she had just destroyed, but also different. There was no off key here, no poison in the air. This tree stood like an antithesis to the one that'd been inside the Mazarat. And beyond the dark sky was—no, it wasn't a sky at all. They were *inside*.

What she'd initially taken for a night sky was, in fact, a high cavern, and shafts of light pierced through. Tallyn and Jenya and Braddok, and the rest of Jeric's pack, waited nearby, but she also spotted a young woman standing with them, watching her with strangely familiar eyes.

"They saved your life," Jeric said, gesturing at a handful of robed figures standing close by.

"Where...are we?" Imari asked.

"An underground city in the foothills outside of Assi Andai."

A woman in white robes stepped forward. Long, dark hair framed her face, though it was more silver than black. Her features were sharp, almost severely so, but her kind eyes softened the effect.

She steadily approached and held something out to Imari.

Her flute.

Without even touching the little object, Imari knew that it was broken. Imari released Jeric's hand and got—unsteadily—to her feet. Jeric stood with her, one arm around her waist for support, and Imari took the flute.

The glyphs didn't shine at her touch, and the flute felt cold— its power gone, due to the long crack along its length. Its song gone forever.

"I'm afraid you'll need a new *talla*," the woman said in thick Sol Velorian. She had a friendly voice.

Imari's brow creased as she gazed upon the little object that had shaped so much of her life. She wrapped her fingers around it tight, remembering the last song it had played.

One that had set the Great Deceiver free.

And these people needed to know—everyone needed to know what she had done.

Imari looked at the woman. Jeric's arm was a steady anchor around her waist. "I...set something free that I should not have."

The woman studied her, her expression inscrutable, and then at last, she said, "Yes, you did. However, the verses tell us this has always been the Deceiver's ultimate design, which is why the Maker also gave us *this* tree." The woman gestured at the earth and crimson oak. "A way to defeat her, through the Maker's tree of life."

Imari thought back to the verses: *Though the binding of the Great Deceiver overwhelmed the Four Divines, their power rained back to our soil—untouched. From this, we received the tree of wisdom, the tree of life.*

Imari had always assumed that they were one and the same.

"It is the power of Asorai's tree that saved you," the woman continued.

"I don't understand," Imari said, glancing at the flute, then the woman. "I just helped Azir unleash the Great Deceiver, and you're not angry?"

"Did you do it on purpose?"

Imari blinked. "No, but—"

"Zussa was never defeated, child. The Four Divines bound her in the space between worlds, but it was always our weakness. Always a tear in the Maker's perfect creation, bleeding evil and corruption into our world. In order to make it right, the Deceiver needed to be freed. So that she can be defeated once and for all."

Imari tried to wrap her mind around the woman's words, to understand them.

"And we have been waiting here all this time," the woman continued. "The Maker has spared this place, knowing this world would need you."

Those words brought Imari up short.

"*Me?*"

The old woman glanced briefly at Jeric before answering. "Zussa was the first sulaziér, and only a sulaziér can stop her. The greatest of all sulaziérs—*you.* You are Asorai's chosen. And that is why they have all gathered here." The woman gestured at the crowd. "We have been waiting a very long time for you."

Imari felt completely and utterly overwhelmed, and also dizzy.

The woman extended her hand. "I am Hiatt."

Imari looked at that old, wrinkled and inked hand. Which she took, returning the gesture. "Imari."

The old woman—Hiatt—smiled and looked to Jeric. There, her gaze focused, narrowed, and the smile disappeared. "You must be the Wolf of Corinth."

That one statement was a package of emotion—all of it charged, and none of it approving—and a silence fell over the crowd.

"I am," Jeric replied, his cello unwavering.

Hiatt appraised him, keeping her thoughts close. Her gaze flitted to Imari only briefly, before settling back on Jeric. And then she extended her hand again.

Jeric looked at that inked hand, and he clasped it in his.

The crowd looked on in silence.

"Welcome to Assi Andai." Hiatt released Jeric's hand, and added, "Let's get you all washed up and fed, shall we?"

THEY FOLLOWED Hiatt through the crowd.

Jeric kept pace with Imari, constantly watching their surroundings, while his men and the others followed close behind. The crowd parted for them, everyone staring. Children ducked out from behind legs, trying to sneak a view of the Provincial strangers.

Mostly Imari.

It had been a very long time since they'd seen anyone from the wider world, Hiatt explained. One hundred and thirteen years for some of them.

Imari still could not believe that this had been here all this time. An entire city, hidden beneath sand and rock. Shafts of light pierced the great rocky dome like that canopy of a forest, dusting the floor in gold. There were dozens of buildings, though none of them were very tall or wide, and dirt paths wove in between.

And at the center of it all stood Asorai's tree.

Hiatt explained, as they walked, that this place had started with one temple, in a time well before Azir. Through the years, people forgot it was here. Even Azir had not known, and when Sol Velor fell, and survivors found themselves without homes and at the mercy of Fyri's tyrcorat, Hiatt and her temple brothers and sisters gave refuge. Of course, they quickly ran out of space, and so with Shah and absolute care, they were able to expand this cavern, carving out more rooms deeper into the rock. They built gardens beneath those natural shafts of light, constructed a system of water collection from the holes high above, and even uncovered hot springs down below, where people bathed.

It was nothing short of a miracle, and twice Imari nearly bumped into Hiatt because she'd been looking up when she should have been looking ahead.

Tallyn also explained what'd happened while Imari had been in the Mazarat with Azir. How they'd killed the rest of Azir's guard, but Bahdra had vanished into Azir's whirling vortex of light and power. He did not know where they'd gone, but Imari suspected they'd returned to Trier.

Hiatt led them first to the hot springs, situated along a little winding path. The path split at a rock wall, and at each end of that split stood an arched opening.

"I'm sure you're all starved, but you're going to frighten the children looking like that, so best clean up first. Women to the right," Hiatt said, pointing to the archway on the right. "Men over there." She pointed to the left. "Leave your clothing by the door, and I'll have new garments brought for you."

Jeric's men started down the path on the left, but Jeric did not move.

"She'll be fine, Wolf King," Hiatt said. A mark of curiosity reflected in her eyes as she studied him. "I will ensure that no one wanders down to the springs while you're in them."

Jeric did not look satisfied.

Imari placed her hand on Jeric's arm, and that sharp gaze landed on her. "Jeric, I'll be fine. I've got Jenya too, you know."

A muscle worked in his jaw. His gaze darted to Hiatt, and then —reluctantly—he strode on after his men, with Tallyn following after.

Imari watched him duck through the opening, but just before he turned out of sight, he glanced back, met her gaze. And then he was gone.

Imari looked back to find Hiatt watching her.

"I'll return to escort you to where you'll be staying," Hiatt said. "But please take your time."

"Thank you," Imari said.

"You're most welcome." Her gaze flickered briefly in the direction the men had gone, and then she left.

Imari, Jenya, and the woman with the strangely familiar eyes walked through their designated opening. As soon as Imari passed through the archway, warm, damp air engulfed her, and she found herself very grateful that Hiatt had suggested a bath first. Imari was still covered in blood from the battle in Trier, now mixed with dirt and sand and Jeric's blood, and she was eager to scrub it all from her skin.

The spring was a hole in the ground, and much larger than Imari had expected, with steaming water and little braziers burning all around. A small shelf of soaps and fringed towels stood off to one side, and Imari was admiring that shelf when she heard a small splash.

Imari glanced back to find the woman already naked and in the water.

Jenya remained near the door.

"Won't you get in?" Imari asked.

"I will later. Right now, I'd rather not find myself at the end of your Wolf's sword." Jenya said it with a knowing grin, which Imari returned.

So, Imari undressed, feeling slightly awkward. Communal baths were not uncommon in Trier, but Imari was out of practice for them. Imari also had a bit of a time peeling her clothes from her body, since they were caked in dried blood. She had the sudden thought that she was molting, and she left that ruined skin by the door and climbed in the hot spring.

The water felt hot and steaming and glorious.

Imari caught the young woman's gaze, and the woman looked away. The woman sat very low in the water, up to her chin, but this close, in the water and without everyone else around, Imari felt the slightest ripple of power radiating from her.

"You're Liagé."

The woman looked at her, those dark eyes sharp. Imari didn't miss that the woman had reached for the beads at her neck, and though Imari couldn't see them beneath the water, she knew they must have held some kind of suppression enchantment.

"You seem familiar," Imari continued.

The woman looked to the side, but did not answer.

"Did you travel with them all the way from Trier?" Imari asked. The woman was obviously Sol Velorian, and Imari couldn't figure out what she was doing with Jeric and the rest of them. Why this stranger had risked her life to help them find Imari.

"I did."

Something in the woman's voice struck a familiar chord as well.

"So you lived in Trier?" Imari asked, trying not to intrude, but this woman had been a Liagé in hiding, directly in the city. All this time.

The woman looked at her, though Imari couldn't read the look there. "Yes."

Imari pressed her lips together, then said, "Thank you."

"For what?"

That familiar chord struck again.

"You're Liagé. I know they could not have reached me without your help. So thank you."

A crease formed between the woman's brows.

Imari tipped her head back and closed her eyes, listening to the sounds of water lapping against the sides of the natural spring.

"Did Saza suffer?" the woman asked, so quietly.

Imari's eyes snapped open.

The woman's dark eyes were glassy, though she steeled her expression as if fearing it might shatter at any moment. And all of the pieces suddenly clicked into place.

This was Saza's sister. The one who had gone to work at Ashova's, to serve Istraa's pleasures.

Imari's heart broke for her, for Taran and for Saza. "He didn't suffer long, Niá."

Niá nodded once, and closed her eyes. Then, "She warned me." Her voice was barely a whisper. "About Bahdra. But I didn't listen."

It was a confession, and Imari wondered as to the extent of Niá's. If, perhaps, Niá had known the one the Kourana had apprehended, the one connected to Kai.

Or...perhaps they were one and the same.

But Niá did not elaborate, sitting there as if awaiting Imari's judgment.

"Tolya used to warn me too," Imari said, and Niá's eyes cracked open. "Every time I snuck out to steal from a man I hated."

A beat. Then, "He probably deserved it."

"He definitely did."

"Tolya probably knew it too."

"I think so. Though I did get whacked on the hand pretty good a few times."

Niá chuckled. Her laughter reminded Imari so much of Saza's that her heart ached. "I never met her. But...Oza Taran used to talk about her often."

"You inherited their gift?" Imari asked.

Niá hesitated, then pulled the beaded necklace over her head and tossed it at Imari. Imari snatched it from the air, looked down at the beads, and her eyes opened wide. "Are these...from Taran's?"

Niá nodded.

Imari noted all the little glyphs, feeling the power radiating through her fingers like an electric current.

"They're wards of concealment and suppression. It's how she evaded being found for so long."

"And you used them to get out of Trier," Imari said, understanding.

"Yes."

Imari slipped the beads through her fingers.

"I've been studying them since we left," Niá said quietly. "I think I can make more. For when you're ready to return."

Imari met Niá's gaze.

"I want to help...if you trust me," Niá said.

Imari tossed the beads back, and Niá caught them. "If you trust *me*, I'd be honored."

44

I mari climbed out of the hot spring, toweled off, and changed into the dress Hiatt had left. It was a long and flowing caftan with winged sleeves and a low neckline, and a hem that pinched loosely above the knees, creating a cascading effect on the skirt. The fabric was soft and thin, and dyed a rich lapis. Imari wondered at the skill that'd made such a beautiful garment in this place, and why, but then she recalled Tallyn's memories of Sol Velor. Of the shame they had not worn.

Though they had lost their home, though they had been trapped underground for the past one hundred years, they had not lost their hope or their purpose.

Niá had donned the long dress Hiatt had left—Niá's was simpler, a bit boxier in shape, and shaded cream. Together they joined Jenya in the hall.

Imari immediately looked in Jeric's direction.

"They were already escorted away," Jenya said before Imari could ask. "Your Wolf was...not thrilled. I had to swear my life away."

Imari chuckled, though truthfully, she loved hearing how protective Jeric was over her.

"He's dining with the village elders," Jenya continued. "They all are. Hiatt asked that you join them as soon as you're ready. She also has a place for us to stay."

Imari glanced at Niá, who nodded.

"We're ready," Imari answered.

Jenya inclined her head, and then led them back down the winding path and into the village proper. Children giggled and ran past, chasing a squawking chicken. A goat bleated somewhere, and Imari marveled at how there could be so much life buried in this dark place.

So much hope.

Jenya led them to a squat mud-and-wattle-style building. Holes had been carved out for windows, and golden light flickered within. Imari could just hear voices and smell the sweet char of burning meat, and her stomach clenched with hunger.

Wards, how long had it been since she'd eaten a full meal?

Another robed figure stood at the door. A young man, with a single inked glyph upon his forehead. He nodded at Imari, and pushed the door in.

Warmth and chatter engulfed her, but the chatter ceased as soon as she stepped through the door.

"Welcome, Imari. Niá," Hiatt called out—in Sol Velorian—from the head of a long and very full table, where Tallyn and Jeric sat amongst other faces Imari didn't recognize, plates of food before them. The rest of Jeric's men crowded about the room—someone had bandaged Chez's swollen eye—alongside a few more strangers, all of them holding their plates. "Please have a seat."

Imari didn't know how there could be room for her at the table, but Jeric stood and gestured for her to take his seat.

He looked revived after his bath, dressed in fresh and fitted tan breeches and a long cream tunic, which he'd left untied at the neck. She didn't see his sword, but he'd strapped a dagger to his waist. He'd combed his hair back, and his blue eyes pierced as he looked at her.

For a moment, Imari forgot to breathe.

His lips curled, and she realized *everyone* was looking between them, waiting for her to sit.

She started forward, aware of Jeric's eyes on her with every step, and then she climbed over the bench and sat in his place. His fingertips brushed her shoulder, sending a shiver through her body.

"We were just discussing sleeping arrangements," Hiatt said, still in Sol Velorian. Behind her, someone translated for Jeric's men. "Multiple families have offered their residences, and so it's not really an issue of room, but how you want to be divided."

A young boy reached over her and set a plate of steaming hot food upon the table before Imari.

"So far, we've decided to split the Wolf's pack in half," Tallyn said, from his place beside Hiatt. "Braddok and Stanis will go with Jenya and Niá to Gezze's." Tallyn gestured at a middle-aged man with a long beard, who nodded. "Aksel and Chez will go with myself to Urri's." A stoutly built woman with silver hair lifted her hand. "And you and the Wolf will stay with Hiatt."

Imari stilled at those last words.

Jeric's fingertips brushed her spine. Letting her know that he was there, that he had heard. That they could discuss it later.

But for Imari, there was nothing to discuss.

"Well, as long as you three don't mind," Imari said at last in Sol Velorian, resisting the overwhelming urge to look back at Jeric, "I see no problems. And we'll do whatever we can to earn our stay."

The man continued translating a few words for Jeric's men.

"Good," Hiatt said, clasping her hands. "It's done then. Mazz..." She looked to an older man with long, silver hair and a bush of a beard. Imari recognized him as one of the few robed figures who had stood around the tree. "Could we see about fashioning a new talla for Imari?" Hiatt asked.

Ah, so he was an enchanter.

The old man—Mazz—bowed his head, and then looked to Imari. "Find me tomorrow," he said. "I'll need to ask you a few questions before I get started."

"Of course. Thank you," Imari replied.

"Back to the subject of Azir..." Gezze interjected. He gave Hiatt a look that suggested they did not agree on whatever it was they had already discussed. "The people are not ready for this, Hiatt."

"They'll have to be," Hiatt responded. "Azir saw us before he fled. And with the tyrcorat gone, it's only a matter of time before he turns his eye back to us. I'd rather force his hand before he uses Zussa's power to conquer all the Provinces."

"How many did you say were in your number?" Gezze looked to Jeric.

"Five thousand," Jeric replied, in Sol Velorian. "But we have no contraception against Shah power."

The room fell quiet.

A few snickered, and Hiatt raised a brow.

Imari looked at Jeric over her shoulder and grinned.

His eyes narrowed, wary.

"You mean *fezia*," Imari said, placing her hand over his. "Protection."

"What did I say?"

"*Fazi*." She ducked closer. "Which means: contraception."

Braddok snorted into his cup.

Ah, Jeric mouthed, giving her a wicked smile. "Apologies," he addressed the room, in their native tongue. "I definitely meant *fezia*."

Hiatt looked as though she were fighting a smile.

"Well, in that case, we can help," Mazz offered. He threaded his fingers before him. "We have a dozen enchanters."

That surprised Imari. It surprised Jeric's men too, once their translator finished.

"I can help too," Niá said quietly, and all eyes looked to her.

Imari caught her gaze across the room and smiled.

"Voloré Taran was my oza," Niá continued.

Her words were met by a stunned silence.

"Taran of Bassi?" Mazz stared at her.

"Yes," Tallyn replied for Niá, who did not appear to know anything about Bassi. "*That* Taran."

Mazz exhaled through tight lips and leaned back, the bench creaking.

They spoke well into the evening, figuring out the best way to equip the Provinces against the Great Deceiver—who was now operating through Azir—while also trying to determine where he would strike next. They talked until their plates and chalices were empty, until Chez yawned and two of Hiatt's guests left, and they finally decided to leave all the other uncertainties for tomorrow.

"Gods, I need a drink..." Braddok said by the end of it.

"What else is new," Aksel commented.

"We have a tavern," Urri said—in heavily accented Common—as she stopped by the door. "It's probably not as nice as what you're used to, but we like it."

Braddok lit right up. "It's not too late?"

Urri shook her head. "I'll take you there, if you want."

Braddok was already walking to the door. Stanis exchanged a long look with Jeric, and then followed, as if he more intended to watch out for their large friend than indulge in local custom.

"You comin', Wolf—ow!" Aksel glared at Chez, who gave him a look and shoved him out the door.

Jenya looked at Jeric, at Imari, then bowed her head. "Good night, surina. Wolf." She left, and Niá slipped out behind her with the rest.

Leaving only Hiatt.

"Your room is just through there." Hiatt gestured to a small door between two shelves of books. And then, "I'm going to bed. I'll see you in the morning."

She turned down a tight corridor and through a back door. Quiet.

"Well, that's not obvious at all, is it?" Imari said, standing.

Jeric chuckled behind her, and she turned around to face him. Suddenly, the room felt very small, very close.

"Did you want to join them?" she whispered. Her voice trembled despite herself.

"No," he said, his voice edged with amusement, his blue eyes fixed on hers. He took a small step closer, so that his boots rested beside her feet and their hips *almost* touched, but Imari felt him everywhere. "No, I'd much rather be with you."

Imari arched a brow at him, though she felt a flood of excitement and nervousness all at once. "What did you have in mind?"

His lips curled, and he placed his hands on either side of her, upon the table, so that he boxed her in with his long arms. "I might have a few ideas." His head bent close, and Imari smelled the soap in his hair as his lips brushed her ear, sending a shiver through her body again. "Though I should warn you. They all revolve around a certain request you made of me in your bedchamber."

Imari's pulse fluttered, and she was very aware of every inch of space between them. The sound of her own breathing.

"I need you to be more specific, Wolf," she said, throwing his words back at him.

He chuckled, more breath than sound, and pulled back, but not very far. Just enough to look at her, and his expression turned serious. "I meant what I said, Imari." His gaze bored into hers. "*I love you.* More than I have ever loved anyone. More than my own life. I need you to know that."

Wards, she would never tire of hearing those words, from him.

"And I made a promise to your father," he continued, placing one palm against her cheek. It covered the entire half of her face. "Maker as my witness, I promised to lay down my life for yours for the rest of my days, and by your mercy, I intend to keep that promise. Not that you need my protection, but *I need you*. I have always needed you."

His words rendered her speechless, completely and utterly.

Jeric brushed his thumb along her cheekbone, and wiped a stray tear. She hadn't even realized she was crying.

The edge of his lips curled upward. "Not really the response I was going for..."

Imari choked on her laugh, her tears, and then stood on her toes. "I love you, Jeric," she said on his lips, and then she kissed him—firmly.

Jeric moaned and kissed her back, long and hard and deep. Right up against the table, but Imari hardly noticed, or cared. Not until a chalice toppled and fell, spilling water everywhere.

They both stopped to look at the chalice and spilt water, then at each other. Imari laughed. Jeric's eyes flashed with mischief and something deeper, and then he grabbed her hand and pulled her from the table, and led her straight to the bedroom door.

Imari's excitement and nervousness increased tenfold.

Jeric pushed the door in.

The room beyond was small and dark, though in the shadows, Imari spotted a bed just large enough for two. Jeric released her hand and strode toward the bed, then knelt before the little table Imari had just realized was there. Within ten seconds, he had a lantern lit, then stood and turned around to face her.

Maker have mercy, he was beautiful, and looking at him then, knowing that they were alone, that there would be no interruptions this time, made her heart skip two beats.

She was thrilled. And terrified. But mostly thrilled. She didn't really know where to start, or *how* to start. This was all entirely new for her, but she *did* know that she wanted this. Him, completely.

Jeric approached, never taking his eyes off of her—not for a second. But then he walked right past, brushing her arm as he did so, and shut the door with a soft click. A board creaked beneath his weight, and she felt him stop behind her.

Before she could turn, his hand was in her hair, and his fingertips brushed her skin as he pushed her hair aside, exposing her neck. His lips followed, velvety soft as they pressed in the space his fingertips had grazed. Imari gasped, closing her eyes as she gave in to the sensations of him. The heat of his mouth brushing fire against her skin, the soft press of his lips, and the feel of his fingers as they slid through her hair.

Imari's heart was a rolling drum in her chest.

"You have such gorgeous hair," he whispered on her neck, sending a shiver down her spine again, and then his fingertips trailed from her hair and tickled along her clavicle.

Imari's next breath shuddered. She couldn't move; she couldn't seem to stand still.

Jeric's fingers traced the edge of her sleeve, teasing just under the fabric's edge, and there he paused. His mouth moved to her ear, sending shivers all over again. "Is this all right?" he said at her ear. "I want you, but I can wait. As long as you need."

Imari had no intention of waiting. Not when every day could be their last, and she'd been so close to losing him forever.

She wanted no more barriers between them.

"I need *you*," she whispered, heart pounding, as she draped her hand over his and helped him push her sleeve over the bend of her shoulder. The sleeve wouldn't push down completely, because her other sleeve still held her dress in place, but it was enough to drag the neckline lower and expose one of her breasts.

Jeric's lips returned to her shoulder, where he planted hot kisses against her skin, and his hand slid around to her now-gaping neckline, touching her. Imari gasped again as desire flared through her body, swift and ravenous. But Jeric took his time, delighting in the discovery of her body. Memorizing every turn, each supple rise and curve, while his warm palms slid deliciously over her bare skin.

By the wards.

Imari moaned softly, and arched into him. She couldn't help it, couldn't hold still. Unable to take it any longer, Imari turned around in his arms. Jeric towered over her, and when he looked down at her, and at her gaping neckline, the look in his eyes made Imari's heart drum so hard and fast, she was certain he could hear it.

And then they were kissing. She didn't know who moved first —probably both at the same time. They wrapped arms around each other, the both of them grasping and clawing desperately as their kisses turned feverish. Imari pressed her hips to his, and she felt his desire through both of their clothes. The feel of it sent a thrill through her, and so she shoved her hips more firmly against him.

Jeric growled, his tongue consumed hers, and he moved one hand to the other sleeve of her dress, hooked his thumb beneath the fabric, and slid it down.

And down.

Imari moved just a little, so that the dress could slide free from her arms and over her hips, until it pooled on the floor at her feet.

Jeric pulled back and stared at her.

No, he *devoured* her.

Imari had always wondered if she would ever feel comfortable being naked with someone like this, but right then, with the way he was looking at her, she had never felt more beautiful or desired. All of her nervousness fled in that instant.

She grabbed the hem of his tunic. Together, they pulled it up while he ducked out of it, and then she tossed it aside. Amber light danced over his skin, his scars. He had so many of them. Imari trailed her fingers lightly over the new one just over his chest—the one he had taken for her—and then slowly traced her fingertips down, all the way to his belt. He watched her unfasten the clasp and pull the belt free of its loops, and he kicked off his boots as she set both belt and dagger aside. She unbuttoned his pants, and then he helped her pull them all the way to the floor.

Imari had seen him naked before, in the cave in The Wilds, when they had been hiding from shades and trying not to freeze to death, but she had not seen him like...*this*. And the sight of him so hard with desire—for her—made her pulse speed out of control. Her gaze lifted to his.

He was the Wolf, but she had not felt herself in the presence of one until that moment.

And the hunger in his eyes set her on fire.

Imari walked to the bed, then lay down on her side and gazed expectantly back at him.

"Gods, you are so beautiful..." he said as his gaze slid all over her body. "Did I mention that?"

Imari arched a brow. "You might have mentioned it. But I'll never tire of hearing it."

Jeric's gaze burned, and he stalked forward, almost predatory, as he climbed onto the bed. The mattress shifted beneath his weight and he prowled over her body. He placed his elbows on either side of her, rested his long legs against hers, but he held the rest of himself over her. Witholding the full weight of his body, letting his heat touch her instead.

"You're exquisite," he said, dipping his mouth, and only his mouth, to plant a kiss upon her jaw. "Magnificent." He planted another kiss on her neck. "Shall I go on?"

"I'm not really interested in conversation right now," Imari managed, impatient to feel that full weight.

Jeric chuckled lowly, and then he lowered his body on top of hers—every solid inch of him—and kissed her deep into the pillows.

Imari moaned. His skin blazed like the desert sun as the weight of his body rested gloriously upon her, and Imari slid her hands all over him, following the hard lines. Feeling his back flex as he devoured her, touched her. His hands moved everywhere, greedy but also tender—reverent, as if he worshipped her very shape. His mouth pressed down her neck, her collarbone, and when his lips reached her breasts, Imari's breath hitched.

And she'd thought his *hands* had felt wonderful.

Jeric's lips lingered there, tasting and delighting, drawing her into his hot mouth.

Driving her crazy.

Imari reached for him, but he caught her hand, and when he looked up at her, his pupils were huge. "I will not be rushed, darling."

The endearment sent a thrill through her, and Imari was about to argue, but then his other hand slid to her upper thigh, his thumb traced the crease, and she reconsidered rushing him.

Jeric smiled viciously and resumed kissing her breasts as his hand slid between her legs.

Oh.

Oh.

Imari's entire body seized as his hands moved, bringing forth sensations she'd never felt before—hadn't even known her body was capable of feeling. A tingling spread through her body, followed by a mounting pressure that built in her very core, pulsing and overwhelming and consuming her with need.

"Jeric..." She craved him with an unquenchable fire, and she reached for him again, but he moved out of the way with a low chuckle.

"Patience," he whispered on her belly, and kissed her naval softly.

The pressure built.

And built.

"Jeric, *please*," she gasped, unable to bear it any longer, the pressure near bursting inside of her. And then she cried out, gasping and breathless, and Jeric looked at her with a mischievous smirk on his face.

Imari glared at him, grabbed his arms and rolled him onto his back—so fast, he chuckled—and then she straddled his legs and sat on top of him, burying him inside.

His laughter turned into a groan, his features tensed almost painfully as he sank deeper, filling her completely. Imari hadn't expected the fullness of him, or the pain. It shocked her, and she clenched her teeth so he wouldn't notice.

But he did. He noticed everything, with her.

"Imari, I don't want to hurt—"

Imari grabbed his broad shoulders and rocked her hips forward. Firmly. Again and again, kissing him through the pain until he melted beneath her. His fingers dug into her hips, steadying her so that he wouldn't hurt her further, but Imari only kissed him harder, sliding her hands over him as they found rhythm together. Like two distinct harmonies weaving together, matching in tempo and climbing in crescendo until Imari cried out and Jeric groaned, shuddering against her with one final, resolving chord.

Complete.

Imari sagged forward, breathless, as Jeric brushed her hair back with his fingertips.

"Are you all right?" he whispered. The wolf was gone. Jeric's features were completely relaxed. More so than she had ever seen them.

She loved that she had done that. That she could bring this side out in him.

She kissed his mouth. "I'm perfect."

He looked up at her. "You are." And then he slipped his hand into her hair, and brought her swollen lips back to his again.

Wards, she would never have enough of him.

Finally, Imari slid off of him, guided by his strong hands, and she curled into his side with her head on his chest and one leg draped over both of his. He wrapped his arm around her, holding her close, while his fingertips traced invisible patterns along her leg. They lay like that for some time, with Imari lulled in and out of consciousness by the deep and steady rhythm of Jeric's breathing. Never, not once in all her life, had Imari known such peace or contentment.

But she knew it could not last. Astrid and the Mo'Ruk held Kai prisoner, Ricón was still out there somewhere, and now Azir possessed Zussa's power. The safety of the entire Five Provinces was in jeopardy.

"By the way, I like this much better than the last time we were naked together," Jeric said, interrupting the quiet and her thoughts. He cupped her bottom and pulled her closer.

"Really?" Imari smirked. "I'm astonished you prefer this to shades and hypothermia."

"I'll have you know that it took every ounce of willpower not to touch you in that cave."

Imari snorted and gazed up at him. "Jeric. You hated me."

"Hate is a very strong word."

Imari eyed him. "Also, you weren't supposed to be looking at me in that cave."

He flashed his canines and pinched her bottom. "I'm sorry, but I have eyes, darling, and if you'll recall, I'm not perfect. *Impressive* is the word you're looking for."

Imari chuckled softly and nuzzled closer to him, and the two of them fell quiet.

Jeric rested one heavy hand upon her thigh. "You're worried."

Imari sighed and absently trailed her fingers along one of his black-rimmed scars. "Kai is still out there. And Ricón," she said at last. "I have to help them." *Somehow.*

She thought of Roi Naleed, and the betrothal which would secure the arms they needed now more than ever. She hated even thinking it, especially right then, but also she couldn't *not* think about it. She was Istraa's surina, and Azir was a very immediate threat to her people. Istraa would need strength in numbers if they meant to have a fighting chance against him and his Mo'Ruk.

And now...now that her papa was gone, Ricón would need her help procuring Roi Naleed's fealty. What else would stop the roi from seizing this very opportunity to take Istraa's throne for himself? But if she promised to—

"*Don't.*"

Imari's fingertips stilled on Jeric's skin. She craned her neck and met his piercing blue-eyed gaze.

Jeric raised a brow. "You're not marrying Fez."

Imari stared at him, baffled yet again by how he could read her so precisely. "*How* do you do that?"

Jeric smirked and his fingertips traced patterns alone her hipbone. "And honestly, I'm a little concerned that you're thinking about another man after what just happened in this bed."

Imari rolled her eyes with a chuckle. She turned around in Jeric's arms so that she lay beside him, on her stomach, propped upon her elbows to face him directly. "Jeric, it's not like I *want* to think about that—stars—it's just...we don't have the ability to fight Azir, especially now that he has Zussa's power—"

"So optimistic..." Jeric drawled, now tracing patterns along her lower back.

"I'm serious," Imari persisted. "I wish I had a fraction of Fyri's strength, and I know you're all expecting me to find it, but we can't rely on my power. I don't know if I'm enough."

His fingertips stopped; his gaze landed on hers.

"Our best hope is to overwhelm him with numbers," Imari continued, "and Naleed has two thousand able men—"

"I don't rutting care if he has ten thousand. You're *not* marrying his son." Jeric tilted his head and mischief danced in his eyes. "Unless I've completely misunderstood how you feel, in which case, you should know that you're really giving mixed signals."

Imari grinned and nudged him playfully. "All I'm saying is that Naleed won't sacrifice his forces out of the goodness of his heart. Neither will the other rois and roiesses. They'd just as soon overthrow Ricón and fight that war for themselves, may the last man or woman standing take Istraa's throne. And *you* have to make an alliance of your own," Imari reminded him as she poked his chest. "I remember Corinth when I left. I know you need to secure your jarls' support, and that won't happen with me."

At this, Jeric grabbed her hips and slid her directly on top of him, hip to hip, all of his former levity gone. His gaze seared into hers, his features sharp as steel. "To hells with them, Imari. I am not letting you go."

Imari opened her mouth to argue, but Jeric pressed two fingers to her lips, silencing her.

"Whatever comes, we face *together*." Here he paused, letting those words sink deep, fill every crack and solidify. "*I love you.* There is no one else, and there never will be. You are like a sun in my cold, dark world. By you, I see everything so clearly, and when this is all over, I am going to marry you, and the whole world is going to watch."

Imari stared into his eyes, so deep and clear and blue. She didn't know how he could be so certain with the laws written as they were, and with generations of enmity standing between their people, but his resolution gave her hope.

"Are you?" Imari teased, though her heart swelled. "I'm not sure if you're aware, *Your Majesty*, but normally a person *asks* first."

Jeric chuckled softly and slipped his hand into her hair. "You should know by now that I never ask for permission when refusal is out of the question."

Imari smiled. "I love you, Jeric Oberyn Sal Angevin. *Jos*." His gaze deepened at that. "I will fight this war beside you. And when it's over, I might just let you marry me."

His lips curled. "There. I knew you'd see reason." And then he pulled her mouth down to his, and it was a long time before either of them came up for air again.

EPILOGUE

"What is it, mi sur?" Hoss asked.

"I'm not sure yet..." Ricón stood at the crest of the hill, scanning the Baragas' broad backs, and the valleys that dipped between them. For a fleeting moment, with that last gust of wind, he'd caught a whiff of decay. The stink of rot and blood.

But it was gone so fast, Ricón wondered if he'd imagined it. He might have moved on, but after what they'd found in Bal Duhr, and the shocking news of what'd transpired in Trier, Ricón was not taking chances.

An army had passed through these hills. A force near one thousand, he surmised, judging by the tracks they'd found. Not a force he could face with two dozen men.

And so he'd pressed northwest, in the direction of Roi Naleed, who had the reinforcements they would need, but he didn't dare travel out in the open. So they kept to the Baragas. It'd slowed them down, but better to be slow than dead.

There.

He caught that whiff again.

Ricón picked up a handful of sand and tossed it in the air. He watched the wind snatch it up and carry it south. Which meant the stench originated due north of where they now stood.

Ricón gestured at Hoss.

"Wait here," he said to the others.

Ricón and Hoss half walked, half slid down the dusty slope, kicking up sand and dirt on their descent. Beetles skittered. He thought he heard a rattler nearby. There were many in these hills, which was why he avoided the larger clusters of rock. He crested the next rise and stopped in his tracks.

A pile of carcasses lay ahead, the blood long dried, the flesh almost gone completely. Flies still buzzed and a few vultures picked at the remains.

"Saints..." Hoss said. "Those pigs?"

"Looks like it." Ricón scanned the area, though he didn't spy any signs of recent life. "Careful." He started into the ravine.

Hoss followed.

The vultures did not startle. They ripped and tore and dug, glaring viciously at Ricón as he passed.

"I'm not interested in you," Ricón murmured, hand on the hilt of his scim.

And then he spotted an old trail leading into a crack in the face of a cliff. His eyes narrowed, he pulled his scim free and gestured at Hoss.

Hoss had spotted it too.

Together, they crept forward, boots crunching softly upon the sand and dirt. Ricón paused at the crack and listened, but all lay quiet within.

He ducked inside.

The smell was much worse in here. Hoss coughed.

Someone moaned from deeper in the shadows.

Ricón froze. "Who's there?" he called out.

Another, longer moan.

"I need light," Ricón hissed behind him.

Hoss fumbled in his waist pouch. Two clicks, a flame caught, and Hoss held a small torch. It took Ricón a moment to make sense of his surroundings. They were in a large cave. Blood stained the floor and walls, Liagé symbols had been painted everywhere, in blood, and rotting corpses littered the floor. Rats scurried away from the light, and then the air exploded in wind and shrieks.

Bats.

Ricón and Hoss ducked, air beat overhead, and within minutes, the cloud of bats swarmed out of the cave.

Quiet.

And then Ricón spotted the cage, where a figure hunched against the old bars, barely alive.

Ricón gasped. "*Uki Gamla...?*"

TO BE CONTINUED...

ALSO BY BARBARA KLOSS

THE GODS OF MEN SERIES

The Gods of Men

THE PANDORAN NOVELS

Gaia's Secret

The Keeper's Flame

Breath of Dragons

Heir of Pendel

ACKNOWLEDGMENTS

As always, there are sooooo many people I need to thank for helping this book come alive. It takes a village, and I could not do this without mine!

To Briana, Carly, Daniella, and Jenny. Could not do this without these ladies! These four read the earliest versions of SANDS, and all the versions thereafter, and saw what COULD BE through the mess of what WAS. Briana, you always find the weak supports and consistently protect the integrity of my characters (well, one... specifically. Ha!). To Carly and Daniella, for your strong opinions about love, for reading a million versions, and for your constant enthusiasm about... everything. To Jenny, for pointing out all the logistical issues and contradictions IN LINE EDITS, for your honesty and support (for YEARS), for sharing your expertise about the human body, and also for calming me down —all while juggling three very small children. My superheroes, each and every one of you!!

To JA Andrews and Sarah K. L. Wilson and Melissa Wright: I will forever be grateful to the writing community for bringing us together. I'm so thankful for the many conversations about life and humanity, and how to untangle my own mess (and for providing fantastic distractions in the forms of your own amazing fictional worlds. Jerks.) Also, I'm grateful for our WIP Wednesdays, and Melissa's Henry channel. And to the rest of my Noble Turtles: Thanks for making the vast world of writing feel so much smaller. #turtlepower

To Fritz, for advice on war and the aftermath.

To my editor, Melissa Frain, for wanting more and finding all the stray threads (and there were a lot!), and also for all of her comments in the margins. The best! I'm really gonna try to work in a howling drunkard wandering in the sands.

To my mom, for watching my little lady so that I could have uninterrupted mornings to work as that deadline stalked nearer.

To my gorgeous husband for *always* listening to me talk about writing and story and craft, for enduring my obsessions, for correcting my male perspectives, for being my largest support (he's 6'6", so I mean this quite literally too), and for pulling so much weight with the kids when I'm drowning in edits. Love you, babe! You finally get your wife back!... kinda sorta.

To all of my wonderful readers for loving these characters and this world, for your emails and comments, and for being so enthusiastic for the next part of the journey!

And to my own Maker, for always being my light in the darkness.

ABOUT THE AUTHOR

Barbara studied biochemistry at Cal Poly, San Luis Obispo, CA, and worked for years as a clinical laboratory scientist. She was lured there by mental images of colorful bubbling liquids in glass beakers. She was deceived. Always an avid reader, especially of fantasy, she began drafting her own stories, writing worlds and characters that were never beyond saving.

She currently lives in northern California with her gorgeous husband, three kids, and pup. When she's not writing, she's usually reading, trekking through the wilderness, playing the piano, or gaming—though she doesn't consider herself a gamer. She just happens to like video games. RPGs, specifically. Though now that her kids are getting older, she's finding she has to share her PS4 more than she would like.

www.barbarakloss.com
contact@barbarakloss.com

Be sure to sign up for Barbara's email newsletter:
https://www.subscribepage.com/barbarakloss

f facebook.com/GaiasSecret
instagram.com/barbaraklossbooks
g goodreads.com/barbarakloss